CIRCUS HOME

A Novel of Life, Love and New Jersey

Jason Ollander-Krane

ISBN 979-8-9868308-1-0
eISBN 979-8-9868308-0-3
Library of Congress Catalog Card Number: 0000-0000

Published October 2022

My gratitude to…

Rob, my great love, my first reader, my harshest critic,
and my best friend.

My father-in-law Joel Ollander, who read as I wrote
and energized this project at every stage.

My Mom and Dad who taught me that I can do anything.
All I need to do is imagine.

PROLOGUE

The Barker

Brendan Hardy

NOW

*W*e call it pretend, yet there is no pretense about it. Those of us who make a living with rouged cheeks, enveloped by canvas, draped in velvet, lit by Surprise-Pink-gelled Fresnels—working the carnival, the circus, the stage, magic—are the most genuine people on earth. So, when the daughter decided I needed assisted living, naturally my choice was to live with guys who can juggle. On the way to my final curtain, I wanted to be alongside people who know how to walk a tightrope. Tame a lion. Balance a dog on their nose.

This is my story. And theirs.

Tonight! Cast party in Heaven's Dressing Room!

Places, Mr. Hardy...

Maestro, the Overture please!

OVERTURE

Today, if you look off towards the western horizon at sunset, all you see is a jumble of post-war industrial skeletons against the summer sky—what remains of the Elizabeth gas fields. The delicate steel spine of late 19th-century industry looks quaint, like cut black-paper silhouettes against the sky as traffic races from New York to Trenton down the New Jersey Turnpike. Today, the view can be missed completely as minivans zip from Elizabeth to Princeton with driver's eyes on the road, passenger eyes down on Instagram or the marsh grass (Jimmy Hoffa buried here?) bending in the tailwind of passing Teslas.

This road, from (Dutch) Nieuwe Amsterdam to (Quaker) Trent-towne was built for speed. Well, technically it runs from Secaucus to Trenton. And yes, speed. The modern road, built in 1938, was intended to solve the problem of New Jersey. The New Jersey problem. The Joisey Pro'lem. What, you ask, is the Joisey Pro'lem ? That Jersey exists! New Jersey—the barrier that lies (and always laid) in the way between Philadelphia (a place you want to be) and New York (a place you want to be more). Even the old roads, the ones that came before, were built on the idea that any place was a better place to be than New Jersey.

Then. Original Route Something, the wheel-rutted dirt road that lay between New York and Perth, the Turnpike was rutted to speed travel. Guide your carriage's, or wagon's, wheels into those ruts in Secaucus and speed along in the same ruts until the Shun Pike Road in Amboy. A neat (if hot in summer, slippery and cold in snowy winter) eight hours with driver's eyes off the road, passengers sleeping, blithely passing dewy deer in frosty January or mosquitos languidly circling in fetid July. Then, from Amboy to Brunswick, another day's ride. Then, New Brunswick (the Raritan Canal carried more coal than the Erie in 1929!) through Cinnaminson in a haze of chicken shit to the Pine Barrens of Smithville for the last day, and WHAM—Philly...as blousy and suggestive as a whore trying to fill her dance card. As prim and proper and starched as a Puritan's collar. Plus...the first Continental Congress!

Now. Today, you'd pass through the Brunswicks and Cinnaminson in a rage of maple leaves and a humus-y fecund topsoil to race to Philadelphia without noticing the increasing number of double-wide trailers and abandoned horse troughs spreading out around you. You'd easily miss the teeny farms, subsistence tomato patches, abandoned cotton fleecing shacks. Driving through in the late twenties (or early thirties) you'd have barreled past stills pumping out Jersey Shine, the prohibited tipple made from potatoes and pine needles responsible for a prodigious number of cases of temporary blindness, taking leave of the senses and taking up with Jesus. The savior having been accepted by more than one lady of the evening or drug dealer who, assisted by the Shine, saw the error in their ways and ended up on their knees begging for forgiveness, salvation, or sometimes both. Other times the begging came from the closed trunk of a Nash with the headlights blacked out, said vehicle having peregrinated through the Pine Barrens hoping to make a straight deal on crooked hooch but things came down wrong. Find that kind of action and you'd likely come face-to-face with a desperate soul who fell victim to a slow, underfunded game of craps, or a lost a marked hand of 21, or simply an unrepentant sinner hankering for a bender. At any cost.

This was the back woods of Jersey. Chicken-farm land then, chicken farm land now. At least where the land is being farmed. What is much more common is that it isn't being farmed, since no one really farms in this age of Whole Foods. Likely what you see (and mistake for farm land as you pass through) is a scrabble patch of friable land that is empty and neglected—visited occasionally by a late-model pick-up truck with a hoe and rake in the back (along with a rolling container of Lysol wipes), which stops to gather up the newspapers blown against the aluminum legs of what would have, then—in the old days—been the legs of a water-pumping windmill and now—in these days—are the legs of a cell phone tower.

Zoom out: South Jersey. Zoom in: Portage, NJ. 08008.

The Silverson family owned a 700-acre parcel of Atlantic County in 1756, which stayed owned until the Civil War when Edwin Forsythe brought a suit claiming the Silverson's eastern-most 176 acres had originally belonged to his father, Colby Forsythe. If Silverson could not produce a bill of sale, claimed Forsythe, the land was rightly his. The Silverson family suspected this to be a con intended to bring Forsythe his only tract of arable land, seeing that the disputed 176 acres lay inland of the marshes that comprised all of the Forstythe tract. Protest though they did, Silverson's 700 acres became 524 and a sizable farm became the state's tiniest incorporated town. Gavanroe Silverson (his headstone reads "At Least We Kept 'em Out!") filed the incorporation of Portage, NJ in 1865 and was successful (not only because his brother-in-law Emanuel Porter was county assessor!) at turning his entire farm into his .83-square-mile hometown.

Portage thrived with an entire, if somewhat inbred, population comprised of Silversons and Porters, two barns, seven homes of various sizes, a smokehouse, a larger-than-average hen house, and a small, muddy pond stocked with bluegills. This tan-earthed Eden kept steady-state until the mid-1960s by which time Gavanroe's Curse (the curse of congenitally low sperm count among Silverson men) had, decade by decade, pruned the Silverson family tree so severely that it petered out completely in 1963, leaving the family without a scion and Portage, NJ without a population.

The land bounced around for a few years between Silversons and Porters, Porters and Silversons, until Nana Greta Silverson was the last remaining Silverson with a working liver and enough brain function to realize she had bet ter do something, and had better do it quick. The something she did was to put Portage up for sale—all 524 acres—and move closer to Trenton where there was a nice Del Webb complex with two pools and competitive BINGO every Thursday night.

To save money, the "Welcome to Portage (A Great Place to Come Across) Population: 001" sign was whitewashed and repainted "For Sale - 524 Acres. Cash ONLY." It faced White Horse Pike for so long that it became pocked by bullet holes, veiled by the splat-splat of overripe tomatoes, punctuated by several raspberry-blue Rorschachs inked in 7-11 Slushies tossed by joy-riding teenagers. It blared its simple message in South Jersey sunlight by day and light from a tinny pale bulb by night.

What it did not do was attract a buyer.

Greta Silverson reduced the price every time she sent someone over to mend the barbed-wire fence, pick up the beer cans, and rake in the condoms until it was, in her words, "a fucking fine deal."

No action.

Then, "a fucking steal."

Still no action.

Then, "my last fucking offer."

Magic!

For less than she could have sold her Del Webb "The Retreat" model home, Greta sold Portage, NJ and 210 years of family history to the only cash buyer she could find. It felt bad to sell so short. Yet it also felt good.

"I am selling my land," Greta told her BINGO pals. "To a charity. A fine charity, which does good work for needy people."

It was possible to reuse the signposts from the for-sale sign one more time. The Monday following the signing of the deal, a new sign went up on the old posts:

**FUTURE SITE OF THE
NEW JERSEY
HOME FOR
RETIRED
CIRCUS and CARNIVAL
PERFORMERS
(NJHRCCP)**

ACT ONE

The Barker

Brendan Hardy

THEN

As the puller raised the curtain on the stage of the Belasco, Siobhan O'Connell felt a wave of nausea cross her throat and midsection.

"Could this be it?" she asked herself out loud with a sigh.

The hoarse squeak of four-strand hemp, as the rope caught the capstan and the puller applied more force, covered the sound of her voice.

The curtain was new, hung two days ago—a job that took twenty-three men, first loading its hundreds of pounds of red velvet and gold braid into a lorry parked with three wheels on the sidewalk in front of 490 West 33rd Street. This loading alone took the work of fourteen stevedores (their afternoon booked for this land-locked project) in addition to the eight movers and one errand boy already employed by Murawski Stage Curtain and Batten, Inc., supplier of curtains to almost every theater on Broadway. It required a blend of pure balance and brute strength to carry the pool of deep Chinese-red Ciselé from the trimming room through the warren of corridors that led to the street. The Murawski men brought strength, along with sharp eyes trained on every hang nail, light-switch, or doorknob, to insure none of the gold Italian brocade caught up and tore. Then, all a twenty-two men (and the boy who could maneuver in the tight spaces) arrayed themselves around the folded velvet cargo like pall bearers and hiked it up the makeshift ramp mustered from twenty-four five-foot-long, six-inch-by-six inch ties of Spanish pin oak. They placed it carefully on the truck bed covered with wax cloth and folded the wax cloth over the curtain for protection. Once loaded, the truck trundled away under the weight of its cargo. The stevedores clung to the sides of the lorry like so many body guards to a king's carriage as it sputtered its over-loaded way to the Belasco, where it blocked the southernmost lane of West 44th Street for nearly three hours to finish the delivery.

Hanging the curtain took ten men alone, supporting the top hem of the fabric a yard off the stage floor while three other men passed rope through the heavy stamped grommets and tied it to the pulleys. A counterweight of sandbags was hung and a winch was set, with a capstan as emergency brake. It was the squeak of rope tightening around this capstan that masked Siobhan's sigh, covered her whispered, "Could this be it?" and brought her back to presence stage right in the wings of the Belasco.

Surely it could not be. It wasn't. It couldn't. Surely it wasn't.

Back to the task at hand: the *I Want* number (the third number after the Overture) in the score of Broadway's new musical *Shirley, You Jest*. Siobhan hiked her skirt, ready to sweep onto the stage when she heard her cue. But no. There it was again. An exquisitely clear twinge almost an infinite distance away in her lower abdomen just below her navel. *Certainly*, she thought, *I have enough time.*

Siobhan knew she was close and the baby could come any time. Yet, she had been telling herself (and Tom) she would be late and would easily clear opening night. Especially since Daria—Daria Chausable, her understudy—had herself been replaced by the under rehearsed Sylvie Montrose due to Daria's untimely case of measles. Siobhan simply couldn't imagine nor willingly countenance a world in which she did not open in *Shirley, You Jest* as planned on November 21, 1938. That was two days away.

This could simply not be final contractions.

Just a ripple. Not a wave. Pregnancy had brought so many odd feelings, strange, unexpected vibrations, and short-lived weaknesses, abrupt changes and gradual ones. How odd it had felt to be kicked from inside or to suddenly crave the smell of dryer lint and to even want to eat it! Siobhan was sure this was just another step in the process—"the twinge stage"—that every woman experienced.

Three bars of musical introduction and the Butler cried out, "Where ever is Miss Shirley? Why, it is almost dinnertime!" That's her cue. Bar one. Bar two. Eight beats. Bar thr—and the twinge became a tightening in her belly.

BUTLER: Where ever is Miss Shirley? Why it is almost dinnertime!
SHIRLEY: Here I am! I had such a time closing my closet door after I changed for dinner!
CLIVE: (crosses to Shirley, extending his arms) Hello, darling. You look magnificent!

Hiram Candy plays Clive. Candy, a stock leading man for the Shuberts, who joined the cast fresh from *Right This Way*, which flopped in late summer, leaving Candy, Joe E. Lewis, and a cast of thirty-two others at liberty to take new roles. Although she had heard of him, Siobhan noticed Candy (and his stock-leading-man moustache) for the first time during the initial read-through for *Shirley, You Jest* and moved her seat during a pee break to get closer to him. For professional reasons, of course.

"I like your necktie...," led to a bit of banter between the two, which led to Candy spilling a cup of (thankfully) cold coffee into Siobhan's lap. Reading a line and gesticulating with a grand Stock-Leading-Man-Gesture, Candy (as Clive) threw wide his arms, catching a cup of cooled coffee on the link on his left cuff. Seeing the wave of coffee billowing toward her lap, Siobhan jumped back, then up and away, spreading her legs in a most unladylike splay of tweed and stockings, the wave of coffee landing on her knees and the hem of her skirt while sending her Nutria wrap—like a flying squirrel—off her neck and squarely and hilariously onto the stage manager's head, akimbo. In the same seconds, Siobhan realized the coffee was cold and her scream of impending horror turned to a laugh of relief. An undertow wave of agitation took over the entire table and during the bubbling confusion of "oh no!" and "whew" and "thank the Lord" Siobhan found her hand being held by Candy whom, in that moment of bonhomie, became simply Hiram.

In the subsequent days this comic brush with calamity flooded the hearts of both Siobhan and Hiram (since the heart is where both love and incaution reside) and the co-stars fell childishly in love. Or lust. Siobhan felt each subsequent morning more and more like a blossoming cherry branch—new, fresh, delicate, pink—in Hiram's eyes and at the tips of his tobacco-stained fingers. And Hiram felt more and more each morning like an old, weathered valise—full of secrets and shame. He hid this (and his longstanding reliance on prostitutes for "love") from Siobhan (as she hid her marriage to Tom), and they both sailed incautiously onward in the first energetic throes of careless love.

✦

Siobhan was hiding her pregnancy from the world. As a stipulation in her contract with the Shubert Organization, she would not mention it to the press and the Shuberts would provide the shield of a talented and sympathetic costume designer and a slight rejigger of the time and setting of *Shirley, You Jest*. The play was relocated from Cleveland in 1905 to Atlanta in 1864 to provide Siobhan with an era and location supporting the wearing of hoopskirts. That allowed her baby to expand as it might while nothing was noticed by her audience. Siobhan's street clothes were redesigned by her Broadway costume designer and a closetful full of bias-cut skirts and materterally-flounced dresses was delivered to her Hasbrouck

Heights flat. Tom, Siobhan, and the costumer believed themselves to be the only ones who knew Siobhan was pregnant.

Hiram kept the fact that he had married four times (the last wife abandoned, drunk, in a corner walkup above a Palisades Park liquor store) to himself as well.

✦

Their Tuesday, Wednesday, and Thursday trysts in the Hotel Edison (on opening day in 1931, the hotel lights were turned on remotely by Thomas Edison from his home in Menlo Park) started with gin-and-tonic with lime for Siobhan and whiskey-and-water for Hiram, a lengthy series of romantic kisses, and an exchange of humorous stories of theater productions past. Over subsequent meetings, this bonding devolved into less sociable time with less and less water in Hiram's drink and less and less gin in Siobhan's. Siobhan had no need to tell Hiram she was pregnant since from the first time they had met at the Edison until now he had only expressed an interest in oral pleasure (and that only drowsily before napping, unsatisfied). The one time he had remained awake during their afternoon trysts she was able to perform the act fully clothed, keeping her secret for another day. Yet when that (or any other) day came, he would mumble "blow me" seconds before his hand fell to his chest and he dropped into a narcoleptic sleep.

Dead to the world. Snoring.

Siobhan found herself passing the time while he slept by running lines silently in her head and staring out of the room's only window through a web of crossed telephone wires onto busy 47th street.

✦

Then there was Tom. Thomas Hardy covered the entirety of the Bronx and Brooklyn selling Murray Space Shoes, handmade and molded to the wearer's foot. "The best shoe for your posture, collinear toes, and a stout breathing arch," Tom would say as he stood at your front door in his own pair of Murray's in the Pebble Gray color. "Only Murray's can boldly face the irregularity of the human foot!" He'd shift on his feet dramatically to show how stable the shoes were, sample case in this left hand and beaver-felt fedora in his right.

"I bet you scrub your floors at least once every other week, M'lady," Tom would say. "Do you concur?" Of course, this was meant to provoke the Lady of the House to protest that she—of course—washed her floors *much* more often. "If that is true...and [looking dramatically over M'lady's shoulder] I have no doubt it is, based on the way your floor simply shimmers," Tom would say in his most concerned tone. "You know how a bent toe can irritate the Plantar's fascia" —this with his most sincere smile—"and Alan E. Murray knows, too!" Then, Tom would launch into his memorized pitch:

> *Who is Alan E. Murray? Why, humanitarian and inventor of Murray's Space Shoes! You might [point down] think these shoes look like they come from space. They certainly do look that way! [Chuckle amiably] We call 'em Space Shoes for an entirely contradistinctive reason. May I show you? [gesture toward sample case; place squarely in doorway.] It will just take you a moment to see that these shoes provide ample space for the toes inside what we call [step forward into doorway and flip latch on sample case] 'our expanded digital containment feature.' It will just take me a moment to demonstrate...may I come in?*

At this point the Lady of the House would have either stepped backwards (a sure sign to Tom that she was a mark and might place an order) or held her ground in the doorway (to Tom a sign to move to Remarkable Proof Point #2: Heel Slope).

By the time he arrived at this crossroads in his speech on his first encounter with Siobhan (Tom having walked up eight flights to the door of her Hasbrouck flat) she had distractedly swept her arm toward the green and brown plaid sofa.

"Yes, please do come in." She couldn't help but let her eyes alight on the pleated front of his suit pants.

"Might I inquire, Madam," Tom continued, "how many children grace your family?"

"Oh, well...children?" Siobhan was caught off guard. "Are the shoes for children?"

"Why, no. Not yet. I mean...only for adults at the moment." Tom looked around trying to apply his Customer Characterization Training to the situation. He could not find a...er...toehold. There were no religious objects or family photos or indicative knickknacks of the sort he typically used to place a potential mark into one of the Murray's Multiple Buyer Categories (MMBCs). He'd have to use Murray's Buyer Qualifying Questions (MBQQs). "What sort of housework do you do, Madam?"

"I do no housework!" snapped Siobhan, immediately realizing she was, by saying so, inviting this handsome man with the attractive bulge in his pleated suit pants to leave.

Thinking quickly, although not quite all the way through, she rephrased her answer: "I do *know* housework! I certainly do! Why I polish the...um...silver every day with these hands!" She held up her hands, the palms towards her and the backs to Tom, and wiggled her fingers.

Tom wanted, in that moment to take her hands in his and touch his cheeks with her fingertips. Instead, he soldiered on with his Murray's script:

> Any woman, like you, who does housework, knows, as you surely do, the value of a well-lasted, well-made leather shoe. This is what Alan E. Murray knows too. We simply measure your feet using our patent pending Murray's Metrical Measurer [produce MMM from case]. We measure not one way, not two ways, but 17 ways to ensure the best fit...

Looking up from his measurer and noticing her wistful staring at the bannister lintel, Tom successfully identified Siobhan as a Passive Denier (category PD on the Murray's Multiple Buyer Categories buyer-typing tool). Once this process was complete, he became focused on making a graceful exit.

"Gin?" asked Siobhan standing awkwardly and smoothing her skirt front.

From that day to this she had slept in Tom's arms.

✦

Three bars of musical introduction and the Butler cried out: "Where ever is Miss Shirley? Why, it is almost dinnertime!"

And the tightening in her belly.

SHIRLEY: Here I am! I had such a time closing my closet door after I changed for dinner!
CLIVE: (crosses to Shirley, extending his arms) Hello, darling. You look magnificent.
SHIRLEY: Oh, this little thing? I had it made with the summer lace from Mother's old ball gown. It's delightfully—

At that moment, Siobhan's legs seemed to get sucked into her abdomen with her second contraction. She nearly fell forward into the footlights. The orchestra played through twelve bars of introduction and, just where Siobhan was to start singing her first line, "the night is warm and wafts of springtime," instead there was a third contraction and a massive sucking in of breath. She felt her velvet pumps tighten on her feet as if her they had come alive and were seeking revenge. All she saw was white shapes—the milky petals of giant magnolias spinning in the air in front of her.

Then, nothing. Back to normal. As she came back to the Belasco stage, the conductor was feeding her the lyrics in a stage whisper: "...wafts of SPRINGTIME and your ARMS call me to DANCE!"

Siobhan started to sing, her voice wavering at first, then normalizing with each note—her professionalism overtaking nature. She began exaggeratedly tapping her silk-toed foot to show the conductor where to pick up. The orchestra vamped and started the melody from the top.

Siobhan sang:

> The night is warm and wafts of springtime
> and your arms call me to dance
> My head is light and tells me big time
> this could only be rom—

The -*ance* of rom-*ance* was swallowed whole as Siobhan's water broke. She felt the warm, then cooling wet, in her costume bloomers and thanked heaven for the hoop-skirt she was wearing. The orchestra continued to play The Night is Warm while the conductor spit the lyrics over the footlights to his distracted star.

Hiram took a step toward her.

"Is the night cool and smelly like springtime, my dear?" He asked nodding toward the conductor, followed by a hoarse stage whispered aside: "Sing the goddam song!"

"Bastard!" whispered Siobhan back, cheating a few tentative steps toward stage right where she knew Kelly, her dresser, waited to help make a quick change at the end of the song. If she could make it to Kelly she could explain her missed cue and sit down. At the very moment she cheated stage right came a huge cramp that sent her tumbling indiscriminately and blindly into the stage-right wings and right into the arms of Kelly, who held her Scene Four costume over one arm and a pink tulle-trimmed hat with a six-inch pink rhinestoned hat pin in her left hand.

"What's wrong, Miss O?" asked Kelly, with a combination of professional sympathy and unprofessional judgment. "You went up on your song! That's not a bit like you. Why I—"

"Kelly! I will vomit on your shoes," shouted Siobhan, "if you don't get me a chair!!"

By this time the auditorium was buzzing with the unique sound a theater audience makes when something on the stage has gone wrong— a low, buzzing murmur of incredulity.

"Ladies and Gentlemen," the sound of Gordon Waxman, the House Manager, was muffled backstage by the fire curtain, which had been wrung down. "Ladies and..."

Hiram presented himself in front of Siobhan, his bowtie askew and his jaw puffing as the House Manager continued to try to quiet the crowd from the stage. "Ladies and...Gentlemen, as you can see a slight indisposition has presented itself..." A ripple of *ahh* and *ooh* went through the audience, Waxman bending over the footlights. "Ladies and Gentlemen, as you can see a slight indisposition has presented itself in the form of illness to Miss O'Connell...We will undertake a brief interval of fifteen minutes after which we will certainly resume."

HIRAM (STANDS IN FRONT OF SIOBHAN): "You enter late and then miss your cue! Can't you memorize a goddam script?"

Siobhan's first thought was that Hiram was drunk.

Kelly came back with a brown bentwood bar chair, nabbed from the saloon scene (Act One, Scene Five). She used the chair as an excuse to step between Siobhan and Hiram, sat Siobhan with a teetering chop to the shoulders and began to unlace the hoops under Siobhan's overskirt.

"You enter late and then miss your goddam cue!" Hiram was still going at it. "Three nights from opening and you haven't memorized the goddam script?"

Siobhan was momentarily all focus and composure. "Kelly, be so kind as to ask Mr. Candy to leave the area while I dress, won't you please?"

The dresser gestured to Hiram and lilted: "Could y' please step aside, Mr. Candy?"

Hiram stood his ground.

"I will not have you make a grandstand play," he said bending and pointing into the cleft between Siobhan's breasts. "I demand you explain—"

On the word "explain," Siobhan felt her abdomen tighten like a ball and a wave of pain rippled down her back. She winced and her feet left the floor.

Kelly: "Miss O—tell me what's wrong?"

Siobhan kicked off the hooped skirt and noticed a cauliflower of slightly yellow liquid spreading across her bloomers.

Siobhan: "Oh Kelly...I am having a baby!"

"A baby!" Oddly, it was Hiram's voice that responded. "That's impossible!"

"You cannot know. You don't know," spit Siobhan. Then "YOWWWWWWW!" As her fifth (and second major) contraction overtook her. *Fuck, that's powerful,* she thought.

Then, like a winged horseman of the apocalypse, Gordon Waxman was suddenly in front of her.

"I told them you are indisposed and we resume in fifteen minutes." He said tapping his watch crystal, "Twelve minutes now! I will call places in twelve—wait—now eleven minutes!"

"There will be no show!" barked Hiram. "O'Connell says she is having a baby!" Hiram just then noticed the crowd of stagehands and actors gathering, necks stretched to see Siobhan. "Just whose baby none of us could know!" he frizzled, looking to the crowd for support. Then, realizing he was alone in his interest, he raised his chest, and pointed a finger accusatorially. "Goddam show folk!"

"And what're you, Mr. Candy, but show folk your own self?" replied Kelly, in her most Irish indignation.

"We have a full house of paid preview ticket holders," continued Waxman, his eyebrows twitching and eyes rolling. "And the Messrs. Shubert frown mightily...I say mightily frown...upon refunds!"

"YOWWWWWWWWW!" Siobhan cried, rocked by another contraction

"Her water has broke and this baby is coming!" shouted Kelly, combining her boldest take-charge tone with resignation. She wanted to help yet, the truth was, she knew nothing about labor, babies, or waters breaking. She *had* worked on a production of *The Russian Doll*, a three-act drama where in the second act (Scene 3) a papier-mâché baby was "delivered" on stage.

"The Messrs. Shubert do frown upon refunds!" Gordon Waxman said again only, this time, no one was listening. He turned quickly, realized he stood abandoned and walked back to center stage, found the curtain part, and stepped in one, downstage of the first curtain, to address the audience, weakly:

"Ladies and Gentlemen...if there is an obstetrician, or a similarly-gifted physician in the house, would you kindly make yourself known to me?"

✦

In front of the Belasco's new red velvet curtain the audience made an orderly exit (their passions cooled and negotiations saved for the box office staff). In a few minutes, the shuffling of feet subsided and the auditorium fell silent.

The theater was restored to its rightful owners—the show folk—and the energy was all behind the curtain.

Suddenly, and thankfully, Siobhan was surrounded by purposeful people doing their job. A crew of stagehands bolstered a lying-in area with piled costumes and horsehair-stuffed leather sofa cushions, hastily brushed clean of dust and ashes, positioned into a makeshift chaise. Kelly, the dresser, undressed Siobhan in full view of everyone (which was normal for a quick change) and replaced her show costume with her dressing gown. Miss Olivia Juness, head of the costume shop, gathered clean rags and cloths in case swaddling was necessary. Jake Reilly, the show carpenter, rummaged around the wings for spare, clean one-inch-by-one-inch pine for Miss O'Connell to bite on should she need fortification. Backstage in every theater is a double burner gas stove used to boil hoof glue, its resin used to patch, starch, and stiffen scenic flats and battens. This was hastily taken over by two carpenters who placed a pot of water on each burner to bring to a boil. Johnny Centrolo, the production's electrician, rang the backstage intercom, connected with the upstairs lighting booth, had them kill the current lighting cue, and bring up the work lights. No one but Hiram seemed to question the event at hand. Instead, they all pulled together to help.

Only a few minutes passed before a doctor presented himself (actually, to Gordon Waxman's surprise, herself) at the foot of the stage. Dr. Clarice Heffernan, Obstetrician and General Practice, was ushered backstage by Gordon, who had now accepted the fact that he was going to house manage the birth of Siobhan's baby. The doctor made her way around several piles of swaddling cloths, a standing ghost lamp, and, oddly, a Victrola—two stagehands having lugged it from Siobhan's dressing room—playing the Seven Dwarves singing *Whistle While You Work* to anyone who was listening.

Businesslike introductions were made and, then:

DR. HEFFERNAN: How long since the last contraction?
KELLY: Less than two minutes
SIOBHAN: (IN UNISON WITH KELLY'S ANSWER) —five minutes at least!
DR. HEFFERNAN: Something more accurate would be helpful. A wristwatch?
GORDON WAXMAN: (STEPPING FORWARD, ARM EXTENDED, NOW EAGER TO HAVE A ROLE) My Howard Repeater went through the great war with me and I trust its accuracy implicitly!
SIOBHAN: YOWWWWWWWWWW!

"You! Howard Watch Man!" the doctor shouted against the muffling bulk of curtain. "Tell me the time it takes from now to the next contraction!" Then, to Siobhan, "I want you to tell me when your next contraction ends. How long as this been going on?"

"They started about an hour ago," admitted Siobhan, wishing she were in an entirely different place doing an entirely different thing.

The next contraction came about three minutes later (and was duly recorded by the Howard watch). It lasted about 85 seconds. With this information confirmed, Dr. Heffernan announced what most of the assembled theatre people already knew: there was not time to get to a hospital. The baby would be born on the stage of the Belasco Theatre.

✦

What followed for Siobhan was nearly an hour of pushing, hard breathing, and name calling. From the generally offered "bastard!" to the specific and refined "Jesu Christo!" (Siobhan was Catholic, after all) there came a panoply of expletives aimed at no one, everyone, her specific condition, and life itself. Then there was "YOU BASTARD," reserved for Hiram when Siobhan's gaze happened to find the leading man leaning against the casement of the Stage Manager's booth gazing at his boots and picking at his fingernails. There was also the varietal shriek of "Tom!" or "TOMMMMMMM!" or the tenderhearted "Tommy, I need you…" This last was followed by the dispatch of the stage door errand boy to a nearby public phone to fetch Tom Hardy (at number GReely-5-141), and Tom's nearly overlooked arrival at the time when two-thirds of the baby's head was visible to those gathered close enough to see.

The baby emerged blotchy, smudged, and windy with his natal cry precisely at 11 p.m. (actually at 11:04 by the Howard Watch, although the story would always be retold as "precisely at 11p.m.! He was my 11 o'clock number!"). The baby (Brendan was the name Siobhan and Tom chose and now could use) was the color of Rosalia pink marble and veiny like that, too, with more of Tom's brown hair than anyone expected, including Tom.

Tom was the first to hold the baby, since Siobhan found mothering, from its very first moment, an overwhelming prospect. Kelly was second to hold him and— oddly—Hiram was third.

Hiram held the baby looking like what he privately wished he was—a nervous uncle—and then, convinced that he had two left hands for baby-holding, baby-mollifying, or baby-anything, he quickly passed Brendan to Siobhan to hold for the first time. Hiram unsteadily put the baby in Siobhan's hands, supporting its neck as best he could without formal training. Siobhan looked into baby Brendan's pink and puffy face and saw his tiny hands for the first time. She became entranced by her child's perfect, tiny nails. She settled the baby into the crux of her arms and looked up from her improvised birth bed at the row of work lights in the dark fly space of the Belasco. As she focused her eyes in the middle distance between her and the lights, she saw a ring of concerned cast members looking lovingly at the rosy gift in her hands.

I can do this. I can, she thought, feeling herself put motherhood on like a warm woolen coat.

Hiram leaned over. He blocked her view of her co-workers— her community. He winked at Siobhan and then gave her a peppy thumbs up.

This gesture was responsible for the undisputed fact of the first two words I heard in my life being my mother saying:

"Fuck You!"

ENTR'ACTE

The Barker

Brendan Hardy

NOW

*S*o, that's where I came from. You know where I ended up—
Suite— let's say "room," shall we? Not to be taken in by the
marketing department — Room 203 of The New Jersey Home for
Retired Circus and Carnival Performers. We residents call it the
NJHRCCP for short. For short! Anyway...retired—

Shit, I am so fucking retired!

Retirement happened 12 years ago when I moved in with
Sylvia, my daughter, who put up with me until two years ago
when I moved in here. Put up with me, along with what she
euphemistically calls my "Circus Ways." What she means is, not
only that I could feel completely comfortable taking a crap behind
a trailer into a white plastic bucket, or that a square meal to me
could easily be two corndogs and a pickle (is mustard its own food
group?) my Circus Ways, to her, amount to that I couldn't give
up smoking when she wanted me to. I haven't got any idea why it
was important to her if I smoked or not. They are my lungs, after
all, and I didn't wear them out talking or thrumming or tummling
(all three are acceptable terms for what I do. Did...according to

my carnival barker brothers) so why the hell should she worry about twenty-five cigarettes, or so, a day?

Sylvia needs something to do, if you ask me.

It's not just that she visits me in Room 203 every goddam day at 11:15a.m., which is right in the middle of the day when I have things to do. Or that she calls every day just before she comes to be sure I still want her to come. Or that I never have the courage not to want her. How could I say no? It's that she comes all the way from Cherry Hill to fucking remind me not to smoke. Lately, she has even turned the staff against me from a cigarette perspective. They are accessories to her campaign. Tools in her arsenal.

A man needs his vices. I don't drink. So, cigarettes are my only weakness.

Okay, not really.

I occasionally have a slug of brandy with the Siamese twins (those fakers). But a guy should be allowed his vices. And, of course, the NJHRCCP being a place that serves oxygen along with brandy, I have made it my practice to never smoke inside.

I follow the rules.

You'd almost think I want to live here by the way I follow the rules. Do I want to be here? Well, if I am going to jones for nicotine, I guess it's a good place to go cold turkey. They've got a staff with a sense of humor.

Like when I got pissy and put a whole pack of cigarettes in my mouth at once. It was supposed to be funny. I looked like a gatling gun that had caught on fire. It was just a prank, but— wouldn't you know—something that was just me joking around turned into nicotine poisoning. My breath got fast and my eyes got all whoosh-y with sparkles inside and I started to sweat like an acrobat. Not fun. But tall Donald, a staffer, saw me walking down the hall bobbing and weaving. He took it in stride and just said, "You okay, Mr. Brendan?" Then he smiled and walked me to my room like I was a lost child at K-Mart.

"The blue light of value is flashing in the idiot department!"

I suppose you've got to have a sense of humor to work in a place that has Siamese twins. Which we kind of do and kind of don't. And clowns. There aren't that many places where you can live full-time with clowns. But here you can and hardly anyone notices. True, seeing a clown in an old-age home isn't that odd. At least not out of the ordinary. In fact, you might not even notice if you were visiting an old-age home and there was a clown on hand. Old people like clowns, you'd say to yourself, and clowns like old people. Or you'd see some balloon animals tossed in a corner, losing air. You'd simply assume a clown was entertaining the old people, who (like I say) like clowns. Or maybe you'd pass a resident clown on a no-makeup day. Clowns look like every day normal people when they're not clowned up or fitting into a teeny car. So you'd just think it's another resident. Then she or he'd suddenly break out juggling and wham! Clown-O-Rama!

Herbie Gopnik taught me to play Pinochle. He is one of our resident clowns. The kind of guy who is funny just to be around but is also a serious guy at cards.

ACT TWO

The Clown

Herbert Gopnik

THEN

O f course, there is New York, The Empire City. And Chicago, The White City. And Pittsburgh, The Iron City. There is the Horseradish Capital of the World (Collinsville, Illinois), The Earmuff Capital of the North (Lewiston, Maine), and The Masterpiece on the Mississippi (Dubuque, Iowa). In mundane circles, Hoboken, New Jersey is called the Mile Square City but in other, more rarified, circles—inhabited by members of the Professional Orators and Pranksters Association of the Northeast United States (referred to by insiders as the POP ANUS)—it is called the City of Big Red Shoes.

It remains a mystery evading reasonable explanation that, as the country listens to FDR yak about the Coal Crisis and lumbers toward the Second World War, the square mile on the west bank of the Hudson known as Hoboken should have the highest per capita population of professional clowns in America. Clown population: 99, counted in June, 1931. Impossible to explain.

Clowns of the Vaudeville variety (population: 12). Okay, that's not hard to explain, seeing as Hoboken is only an eight-minute ferry ride and a brief walk to the corner of Broadway and 42nd

Street. These clowns choose to live in Hoboken for the convenient commute.

The Benevolent Order of Elks variety (population: 22). Wait, that's also easy to explain, since those practitioners obsessively study the acts of the Vaudevillians, so they choose to live as close to them as possible.

The Shriners variety (population: 27). Makes sense, too, since these guys are the alcoholic cousins of the Elks Club clowns. They stay close because that is what family does.

The Wedding variety (population: 6). Yes, clowns work weddings (almost entirely, but not exclusively, at the reception) for an economically pragmatic group of wedding planners, when the happy couple cannot afford a reception band. Wedding clowns go where the bookings are. So, they naturally choose the nuptial-rich towns of Hoboken, Weehawken, and Jersey City.

The Kid's Birthday Party variety (population: 32). This is the farm team of the clown-talent-development system; if you plan to eventually entertain adults as a serious clown (in other words, a "professional practitioner"), you hone the basics with the wet-diaper crowd over cupcakes, candles, and card tricks. Birthday party clowns choose to live in Hoboken because of Glaser's Bake Shop.

To demonstrate the extent of this strange quirk of population, here are the top twelve jobs from the Hoboken census by occupation in 1930. The total population was 50,112:

Business Owner............................117
Cook...017
Clown..**099**
Dentist...008
Dockworker..................................172
Fishermen 021
Tailor/Seamstress 005
Taxi driver 081
Teacher...054
Photographer 001

Behold, a small batch of highly elucidating facts:

- In 1930, Hoboken had only 18 more citizens who described themselves as "business owner" than described themselves as "clown".
- There are eleven-times more clowns in Hoboken than clergy and eight-times more clowns than physicians. If you were in need, you could much more easily arrange some mischief with balloons than a hospital stay, a wedding, or a funeral.
- Hoboken is adjacent to Jersey City (which has a sizable regional dock and dry dock). Yet every other stevedore sitting on a bar stool in The Safe Harbor bar is nursing his evening high-ball next to a clown.
- If you bump into someone on a Hoboken street, you're twice as likely to have bumped a clown than a teacher.
- On a Sunday (the day of rest), you would be 12% more likely to be in church worshipping next to an off-duty clown as you would an off-duty taxi driver. Which does not take into account the number of clowns who drive a hack in their spare time to help make ends meet and pay off the medallion fee for their brother-in-law's cab. If you add in those part-time cab drivers, it is more like twice as likely that, come any Sunday, you will share a pew with someone named BoBo than someone named...well...anything else.

"Fun!" you say?

Well...what seems to the average person to be an enrichment of the population is seen as less than auspicious by the local constabulary. Try being the dispatcher who gets a call at 2:30 a.m. on a Thursday because Shilltoe and Primo (both birthday party clowns) are disturbing-the-peace by popping balloons as they practice tying balloon animals on the corner of 12th and Hudson. Or being the officer who has to enforce local ordinance CB702, which states: "the maximum number of people legally permitted in an automobile, whether moving or parked, in Hoboken City, must not exceed six, regardless of the employment of said occupants." Being a Bluecoat in the City of Big Red Shoes means enforcing the law among a lawless— and sometimes wacky—crowd. Which brings us to the Era of Unrest.

The ten years commencing with January 1931 are known as the Era of Unrest in the North Jersey clown community. It is during this time that the Golden Red Nose Award, which (since 1907) had been taken home annually by a deserving "Best Overall" clown and then dutifully passed along to another clown a year later, went un-awarded. During this tumultuous period, there were five separate incidents of near-fatal confetti-splashing and three incidents of substituting Ex-Lax for chocolate, creating a completely other sort of near-fatal splashing. Additionally, it is during this period that the Roller Coaster Nostra emerges —a mischievous and violent set of rival clown crime families headed by Paco D'Abruzzo and Donald O'Sullivan. D'Abruzzo lived in North Bergen, not Hoboken, but he was able to nonetheless leverage his influence over the Board of Directors of the Jack B. Nimble Candle Company to control the birthday candle supply in northern New Jersey. This allowed him to bring a group of otherwise-innocuous party clowns under his nefarious influence. The Coaster Nostra (as it came to be called in the tabloids) was alleged to be responsible for a series of increasingly-sadistic abduction, wig-snatching, and de-costuming incidents which left several clowns stranded—naked and afraid—in the swampy grasslands of Newark.

It was also during these tumultuous years that power struggles distracted and waylaid the clown community's efforts to come up with new gags, creating what historical scholars of the period aptly called the "Goofy Brain Drain." Experts agree that these years of power struggle wiped out the equivalent of 20 years of unfettered inventive progress on the clown stage. And while a few notable ideas did escape under the door or over the transom (the Handshake Buzzer is just one example) it has been hypothesized that the

Frustrating Parasol, the Dimwitted Life Guard, Size 8 Collar/ Size 12 Neck, and The Mexican Throat Tickle—all four routines referred to as "clown-jewels of the second half of the decade"— would have paid off in the first half of the decade had it not been for the unfortunate syphoning of creative thought caused by the Brain Drain.

Chief among the cultural insults of the latter part of this period is the theft and destruction of the design for perhaps the greatest act in all of vaudeville, bigtop, and event clowning—what has often been called the *Enchilada Granda* of clown entertainment—Feline Juggling. This act, studied by the top echelon, the inner circle, the royalty of the POP ANUS (all of whom were sworn to secrecy unto death), remains the Holy Grail of clowning to this day. Only one man (maybe two) in the world (in Hoboken or beyond) has any idea how it was done. And only one did it. "It," of course, being the juggling of eight—that is EIGHT!—live cats—that is LIVE!—for three minutes—that is, THREE MINUTES!—without wires, strings, or the use of veterinary sedatives. No one knows the true identity of the thief, although a tantalizing theory has been posited. No one has ever found the fastidious notes that must have accompanied the planning of such an entertainment. No one admits to knowing how the theft came about, was executed, or subsequently covered up. And no one knows the perverted mind that is responsible for conceiving and carrying out the crime.

No one, that is, but the man who did it!

✦

A pot of white icing boiled over on the stove.

"Heavens-to-Betsy!" yelled Irma Gopnik, reaching to turn off the gas. "I take my eyes off of the darn thing for a second and disaster strikes!"

She needed every ounce of icing for the cake, so now she would have to start it all over again. In the meantime, the three layers of yellow cake, stacked on lemon curd filling, sitting on the crystal cake stand, would have to wait. Herbie loved her Double Lemon Ermine Icing Cake more than any cake she had ever made, so she just had to make it for his special birthday. She planned blue candles to contrast with the white icing and yellow writing: "Happy Sweet 16 Herbert!" She had debated whether to put Herbie or Herb or Herbert but that was settled when Herbie saw her practicing piping the message on a plate.

"Aww, Mom," he said like she was chewing on his last nerve, "not Herbie. I'm a grown man! You can't treat me like a kid anymore."

"Yes, Herbie," she replied.

"Mommaaaaa!"

"Alright, Herbert," she conceded. "My grown man still wants to play Pin the Tail on the Donkey, though?"

"Of course I do. What does that have to do with anything?" Herbie said, licking the rubber spatula from the cake batter bowl on the counter. "The Pin the Tail game is *the bona fide* birthday party game and we are doing everything *bona fide* for my last official kid birthday. Which reminds me...Mirakolo needs that pitcher of lemonade for his act. Did you make that yet?"

"I have 'make lemonade' on my list, Herbie."

"Okay. Good."

"For a clown, this Mirakolo sure is demanding. 'Have this! Supply that! Give me more of this!' He better be worth the trouble!"

"He's not just a clown, Mama. There is no better clown-slash-magician all over metropolitan New York or New Jersey than him. He is totally, completely the best. If he asks for it, he needs it!"

"Well, he better, 'cause I spent a pretty penny on his eggs and celery, whatever those are for. Egg salad? Haha...Oh! That reminds me...I nearly forgot to boil those eggs!"

"See? You need an assistant like me to keep you on the ball. Remember, he needs the Hoover, too. Don't forget he wants a fresh bag in it."

"And why, pray tell, does he need our vacuum cleaner?"

"Only to do the greatest magic trick-slash-illusion of all time: the 'A Chicken in Every Hoover' trick! He vacuums up half-a-dozen hardboiled eggs and then he opens the vacuum, takes out the bag, rips it open and—POOF!— a live chicken!"

"A chicken in my Hoover? My goodness...it's astounding what I do for you Herbie," said Irma with a smile.

She had 90 more minutes to pull the party together. Then, Mirakolo and his assistant would arrive to take over the parlor for their act. Irma still had to finish the cake, make lemonade, finish cutting out the paper tails for Pin the Tail on the Donkey, cut the crusts off the sandwiches...and boil the eggs. Then the party would be ready.

She washed her hands and went to work.

At exactly the appointed moment for Mirakolo's arrival, the telephone rang.

"I'll get it!" shouted Herbie bounding down the stairs to the hallway table where the phone was located. "Hello. This is the Gopnik residence. Herbert Gopnik speaking. How may I—? Yes. Just a moment, please."

He put the phone receiver tight against his thigh and yelled "Maaamaaaaaaa! It's for you!"

Irma toddled breathlessly into the hallway from the kitchen, wiping her hands on a dish towel. She put the receiver to her ear. Herbie stayed to listen, since he knew the call had to be about his birthday party.

"Hello...Yes, this is Irma Gopnik...Oh, hello. Yes...yes...indeed, yes. Oh, goodness me. I am sorry to hear that. Yes. Yes...alright. Of course. We will work it out somehow...Oh, yes! Yes. Good idea. I will tell him. Thank you...Goodbye, now."

She replaced the receiver in its cradle.

"Who was it?" asked Herbie anxiously. "What did they want? Somebody's not coming to my party?"

"It was Mirakolo's wife, Diane. He will be a few minutes later than he planned."

Herbie looked pained.

"It seems," Irma continued, "his assistant ate a sour mussel last night at Domenico's of Newark so she is out sick. Mirakolo suggested you step in as his assistant for the party show. Could you?"

"Could I? Could I? Damn right I can!"

"Herbie! Language!"

Herbie reined in his enthusiasm and quieted down. "Sorry, Mama. Darn right I can! I know every joke, every gag, every trick in Mirakolo's act. Every one! I knew someday I'd get to do this. And I will! At my very own party! Whoa...will my friends be jealous!"

Ten minutes later, Mirakolo arrived. He was dressed in a black-and-blue robe spangled with gold lamé stars. He wore his costume beard but had not yet put on his ample costume wig. Instead, he wore a dark gray fedora with a burgundy bow in the back. When he doffed his hat to Irma Gopnick, Herbie could see his stringy black hair parted on the left and combed over to behind his right ear. Herbie momentarily resented Mirakolo's baldness. His humanness. Herbie recovered quickly, however, thinking *I am his assistant now, so I have the exclusive right to see what is behind the magic. It's just hair. He's got hair. Or doesn't. It's fine.* Still, Herbie wished that there was nothing to see behind the magic. He wished that Mirakolo was truly magical and not-at-all human.

"Hey, kid!" barked Mirakolo sidling up to the front window looking out onto Washington Street as if he were used to checking for assassins. "See that Hudson parked right there by the fire hydrant? In the back seat I have six valises. I need them six valises up here. Post-haste!"

Herbie stood still, trying to figure out what "post-haste" meant.

"Get your ass moving, kid—," continued Mirakolo. "— I'm already behind the eight-ball in terms of time. I need that shit up here fast so I can set up!"

"Yes, sir," said Herbie. Then, he ran down the stairs to Mirakolo's car.

In three trips Herbie lugged the clown's valises up the stairs and into the parlor. Mirakolo opened them, set up his act, and placed the last prop in place as the first party guests arrived at the doorstep and rang Herbie's doorbell.

Soon the house was pulsating with 16-year-olds (six girls and six boys). Mirakolo had locked himself in the privacy of the bathroom to glue on his wig. The guests played games, ate pimento cream cheese pinwheel sandwiches with potato chips and, when invited to by Irma, eagerly sat down for Mirakolo's show.

As Mirakolo paused before making his grand entrance, Herbie approached the clown who was now wigged in a mane of theatrically-upswept gray hair. "Mister Mirakolo, I've seen every gag and trick, every joke and illusion you do. I know them all. Inside and out. I know your assistant's role as if being your assistant was my summer job. Even more—like it was my summer job *two summers in a row!* You can rely on me!"

"The assistant in this act," replied Mirakolo absently checking his sleeves to be sure his hidden coins were still hidden, "doesn't do shit. She just stands by and looks pretty, hands me stuff, and takes stuff away. You keep the floor clean and keep crap out of my way when I tell you to, and you'll be doing everything I need."

"Yes, sir!" said Herbie, covering his disappointment with a stiff-backed left-handed salute.

"I won't need much!" said Mirakolo.

Mirakolo unwound his party act:

1. Introduction of the Great Mirakolo
2. Mime: Card and Coin Tricks
3. Mirakolo's Lurid Lemonade
4. Balloon animals (including Mirakolo's exclusive Balloon Wooly Mammoth)
5. The Celery Charmer in Calcutta
6. Five Greeks in Dallas
7. Ballerina with Size 90 shoes
8. A Chicken in Every Hoover

9. Colloquial Penguin
10. If Pigs Could Swim
11. Finale (Mirakolo's Party Parade)

As Mirakolo performed, Herbie took the props the clown used and replaced them in the valises exactly as they had been. Herbie added a small theatrical flourish or comical mug here and there (in spite of the upstage whispered admonition to "*lay off the cute*" from Mirakolo). When, during Colloquial Penguin (much to Irma's horror) Mirakolo clumsily tipped over a large bowl of ice- water onto the parlor rug, Herbie danced in to comically mop the floor and replace the ice without causing the clown to miss a beat.

After the party, as they were working together to re-pack Mirakolo's car, Mirakolo took Herbie aside and, in hushed tones, said:

MIRAKOLO: Kid, you weren't half-bad up there. You have a gift for clowning. And you really came through for me cleaning up that ice!

HERBIE: A clown. That's what I want to be!

MIRAKOLO: Lots of people do. Being a clown looks like fun but it's really a lot of hard work. Hard as fuck.

HERBIE: I know I can be as good as you someday if I just work and work and work!

MIRAKOLO: Yep. It does require work. You know...I've been looking for an ambitious kid like you to do some work for me. Kind of get your start in clowning. Pay your dues, so to speak.

HERBIE: I'll assistant you any time you need me, Mr. Mirakolo!

MIRAKOLO: This is to help me with my other job. I am also Chairman of Local 64 of the Clown's and Acrobat's Union.

HERBIE: Oh?

MIRAKOLO: Local 64 takes on some of the tougher issues facing clowns today and solves them. We are activists for clown independence. Sometimes we go through channels and— sometimes—well...we need special people like you to help us get things done.

HERBIE: What does that mean, Mr. Mirakolo?

MIRAKOLO: Sometimes life is clowning around and other times people need, I'd say... *encouraging...* to do the right thing.

HERBIE: Yes, sir. I can see how that might be.

MIRAKOLO: Local 64 always plays by the rules. But sometimes we are forced to... make our own rules. Get it, kid?

HERBIE: I guess I do. And I can help?

MIRAKOLO: If you do what you're told—and just what you're told—I think you could help. You might occasionally have to clean up a mess like you did with the ice today. Without being asked. Just like you did today. Smooth. Quiet-like. No fanfare. That's the kind of help I need.

HERBIE: I can do that!

MIRAKOLO: Well good. [GESTURING COME HERE WITH HIS FOREFINGER AND HUSHING HIS VOICE] Now sometimes Local 64 needs to keep what it does to help members sort of in the background. Get what I mean? Behind the magic curtain so to speak. [WHISPERED] Out of sight. So, I need a kid I can trust to keep certain things just between us. Or maybe just between us and some of our union brothers. Could you do that, Herbie?

HERBIE: I can keep a secret, Mr. Mirakolo!

MIRAKOLO: Good, Herbie. Why don't you call me Don?

HERBIE: Okay, Don.

MIRAKOLO: Good boy. When do you think you can you start helping me?

HERBIE: As soon as now, Mr. Mir—I mean...Don.

MIRAKOLO: Well good. Herbie, I have an envelope I need delivered. Could you help me with that? [TAKES AN ENVELOPE FROM A BOX IN HIS CAR TRUNK]

HERBIE: Just deliver an envelope? Sure!

MIRAKOLO: You deliver this envelope to Maximus Rabbit—

HERBIE: Maximus Rabbit? The clown Maximus Rabbit? *The* Maximus Rabbit?

MIRAKOLO: You know him?

HERBIE: Of course I do. I saw him headline at the Orpheum last New Year's Day. Early show.

MIRAKOLO: So you know him. Good. Just bring him this envelope—1262 Willow Street. His address is written right on here [HANDS HERBIE THE ENVELOPE]. Then, get an envelope from Maximus and bring it back to me. On time. I need my envelope back tomorrow by post time...umm...4PM.

HERBIE: What's in the envelope?

MIRAKOLO: See? This is where I just need you to trust me. It's official Local 64 Clown's and Acrobat's Union business. That's all you need to know. Our secret. Yours and mine.

HERBIE: And Maximus Rabbit's, too, of course. 1262 Willow Street. You got it, Don!

✦

Glaser's Bake Shop of Yorkville opened its Hoboken branch (on the southeast corner of Willow Avenue and Fifth Street) in 1927 and, aside from its famous Black & White cookies, quickly became known as the most desired bakery for uniquely-decorated birthday cakes for youngsters. Everyone who was anyone (along with quite a few who weren't anyone, but had ready money) bought their birthday cakes at Glaser's. As a public service, Glaser's maintained a bulletin board listing "the finest birthday party resources," and professional clowns knew that serious hostesses looked to the coveted Endorsed Party Clown spot on the Glaser's bulletin board as the tip-top source for the best birthday party entertainment. Getting Glaser's endorsement was both coveted and highly lucrative. Schatzi, Endorsed Clown of both 1929 and 1930, booked the headliner spot at thirteen birthday parties in the five weeks after his poster was tacked to the bulletin board at Glaser's. Upon winning Endorsed Party Clown, however, he booked a solid year of 152 parties in eleven minutes. Some of the best-known clowns in Northern Jersey got their start on Glaser's bulletin board. Emmet O. Kelly (third cousin to the well-known Emmett Kelly of Weary Willie fame) catapulted to prominence on the prestige of winning 1926 Glaser's Endorsed Party Clown. Platzo the Clown, Schmendrick, and Schatzi scored the coveted title in '27, '28, '29, and '30 respectively.

"Win Glaser's Endorsed Clown," said Manfred Schatzinger (who performed as Schatzi), "and say *auf wiedersehen* to parties in dank, pine-paneled basement rec-rooms and *guten morgen* to parties in the sparkling Elks Lodge party room!"

It was not easy to apply for the sought-after Endorsed Party Clown designation. Candidates were required to:

1. Apply in person at Glaser's on April 7th (the anniversary of P.T. Barnum's death) with a resumé and 8" x 10" headshot photo
2. Write a 1400-word essay (required topic: "The Clown as Embodied Critical Pedagogy")
3. Supply a list of new birthday party gags, bits, stage business, and/or stunts they would add to their act if named Endorsed Party Clown.

From over 100 applicants, five finalists were chosen. These selected clowns received a live audition in front of a group of precocious eight-year-olds attending a simulated birthday party. Using these highly-competitive auditions, plus the essay (read and judged by Dr. Candace P. Elfman, Professor Emeritus of English Literature at Rutgers College) and the list of new gags and bits, a field of five clowns was winnowed to four. Four winning clowns were chosen to comprise the Comical Court—the chosen Endorsed Party Clown plus a court of three: Second Banana, who automatically substituted for the Endorsed Party Clown in case of illness or hangover, Next Clown Down (first runner-up) and Just Kidding (second runner-up). The runners-up carried the top clown's gear and served in the coveted role of apprentice for the duration of the Endorsed Party Clown's year-long reign. The fifth, losing clown received professional ridicule, mockery, and the opportunity to apply again in the succeeding year without having to submit an essay.

The Saturday line at Glaser's was always long as housewives waited to pick up dozens of Black & White Cookies to serve at their evening Bridge or Mah Jongg games. This particular Saturday, the length of Glaser's line was increased a hundred-fold by interest in Glaser's Annual Live Endorsed Party Clown Auditions and the in-person presence of the five finalist clowns who were vying for that year's Endorsed Party Clown spots. Hundreds of mothers showed up to catch sight of the five finalists, in costume, waiting for their simulated party audition and offering snippets of their acts while they waited. The Hoboken block rimmed by Fifth Street, Willow Avenue, Park Avenue, and Sixth Street became its own small-town circus as, about every 150 feet, a different clown performed.

"I get to see these jokers in action," said customer Marjorie Goebbels, "so I can pick the best clown to have at my Gerald's, party this year. It's savagely competitive, yet with pink and yellow balloons!"

This year, in 1931, the finalists are:

SCHMENDRICK: A sad-faced clown, Schmendrick (Endorsed Party Clown of 1928) walks a trained rat on a leash and carries an umbrella that produces rain on cue. To appeal to children, he has taught the rat to turn on its back and play dead. In the finale of his act, the rat disappears by climbing up inside the clown's pants leg, creating a huge and comically-active bulge between his legs.

CHAUNCEY OF WEEHAWKEN: An Upper-Crust clown who performs wearing tails and a top hat with a daisy sprouting out of it. Second Banana in 1930, this year he has added a six-foot-tall unicycle to his act. He makes a full bowl of salad while riding the unicycle by alternately juggling knives, a head of lettuce, fresh tomatoes, bell peppers, and carrots.

GOP-NICKEL: A Buffoon-style clown wearing a greasepaint smile and a suit covered head-to-toe with pockets, Gop-Nickel is a walking Five & Dime. He spends a few minutes with each party-guest child, talking about their life, their interests, and what they are amused by. Then, through sleight-of-hand, he produces a nickel from their ear, or nose, or mouth. The child returns their nickel for chance to pick a prize from one of Gop-Nickel's many pockets.

SINBAD THE SPACEMAN: Proven to amuse the typically un-amusable 13- to 15-year-old audience, Sinbad is a midget who wears a silver-sequined space suit, topped by an oversized globular plastic helmet. He is a gifted acrobat whose act consists of expressing the erratic vagaries of being weighed down by his helmet, which is too large and too heavy for his diminutive body. The act ends with firework sparklers shooting from what appears to be his rear-end—targeted to enchant early adolescents.

WILLOWFANT: Speaking only German to the audience, Willowfant specializes in close-hand magic with rubber sausages. "Whether single sausages or in strings," says Willowfant's press kit, "you'll be enchanted as Willowfant makes them appear from and disappear into various orifices." His P.R. man adds: "you'll be positively floored by the possibilities created by the most innovative rubber sausage play on any stage!"

The Tuesday after the Saturday when the auditions took place, Glaser's hosted a carnival food social in Hoboken's Washington Park to announce the winner of Endorsed Party Clown. Foot-long hot dogs, potatoes-on-a-stick, Amish funnel cakes, caramel corn, beer from a keg, and Black & White Cookies (of course) were served using paper plates and cups at tables with red-and-white checkered tablecloths. Nearly the entire clown population of New York/New Jersey attended. Entertainment was supplied by Erango Flotidisse and his Gypsy Accordion.

Marty Glaser, doyen of the bakery family, announced the results:

1. Chauncey of Weehawken won Glaser's Endorsed Party Clown

2. Sinbad the Spaceman placed as Second Banana
3. Schmendrick was Next Clown Down and
4. Willowfant placed fourth in the Just Kidding spot.

Gop-Nickel came in for ridicule and mockery by finishing in last place.

Losing to a German-speaking competitor was particularly degrading since, at the time, anti-German sentiment was already emerging in the United States.

"Well, since'a yous'a ask'a me," said Gargantuo, the well-known acrobat clown in heavily Italian-accented English. "I wouldda t'ought a kike shoulda beat a member a' da Socialist German Worker's Party down'a hands. In odda word, peasy easy. Gop-Nickel ess 'umiliate iff'a yous'a ask'a me. I t'ink."

Gargantuo was right. Herbie was disgraced. He endured weeks of ridicule from both Teutophile and anti-Semite flanks. He saw his twenty-or-so pre-booked parties for the 1931-1932 season evaporate overnight and move over to Willowfant's date book. Desperate for an explanation, Herbie asked Adele Glaser how (*"in heaven's name"*) he could have come in fifth. Miss Glaser responded matter-of-factly that his essay was found to be lacking "in argument validity" by Dr. Elfman. He wrote a letter to the Rutgers professor asking for a more articulate critique. She returned the following:

From the Desk of
Dr. Candace P. Elfman

May 17, 1931

Dear Mr. Gopnik,

You demonstrated a complete lack of talent for research and a highly refined talent for making things up, neither of which benefited your essay in the slightest.

Yours sincerely,

Candace P. Elfman

Dr. Candace P. Elfman
Professor Emeritus
Department of English Literature
Rutgers College at New Brunswick

CPE:dk

Humiliating.
As he had done several times in the past few years, Herbie landed on the soft eiderdown of Local 64 to heal his bruises.

✦

While a working clown needed to have a minimum of seventy-five bookings in a year, two years in a row, to qualify for membership in Local 64, Herbert Gopnik (the clown Gop-Nickel) was awarded his union membership in exchange for carrying secret envelopes for Don O'Sullivan (the clown Mirakolo). Of course, envelopes were only the start—a sort of qualifying round. A training lap. By the time Herbie turned twenty-one, he was what was called (in Coaster Nostra terms) "a made clown." He was regularly involved in what the Investigations Unit of the Hoboken Police called the "underworld activities" of Local 64. Herbie had abetted several initiations of other clowns into the "work" of the Union. He had hardened to the realities of clowning. He knew it was clown-eat-clown in Hoboken, North Jersey, and New York. He understood only too well that the beast called clowning ate its young. He knew it would not be easy to extricate himself from the creature's enveloping tentacles. He pushed that aside, telling himself union involvement was good for his career.

Don and his union minions determined that the time had come for Herbie to move to the next level of "involvement" in Local 64. Don was ready to test Herbie's moxie and see how strong a stomach he had for some of the more—as Don would say—"indelicate aspects" of the enterprise. One night after they attended a wig-making demonstration offered by Max Factor in the Union Hall, Don told Herbie to walk with him to his walnut-paneled office. Once in the office, Don noisily dropped a yellow-and-silver Naugahyde-upholstered kitchen chair in in front of Herbie and gave him a frustrated look.

"Sit."

He indicated the chair dismissively with his right hand.

Herbie did as he was told.

Don walked around to the business side of his massive glass-topped desk and sat in a large mahogany swivel chair directly across from Herbie. Herbie, determined to make the conversation a brief one, balanced one buttock on the edge of his kitchen chair and picked at the fibers sticking out of a hole in the yellow vinyl.

Don cast his line and let his fish run with it:

DON: Herbie, I have always treated you like a son. Always have. Always will.

HERBIE: [LOOKING DOWN AT THE FIBERS] Yes, you have, Boss.

DON: You know why I treat you like a son, Herbie?

HERBIE:[STILL LOOKING DOWN] 'Cus you like me?

DON: Not really. [LAUGHS]

HERBIE: [LOOKING UP AND STRAIGHT AT DON] No?

DON: No. Well...I do like you. But that's not the reason I have treated you like a son. There is more to it than that.

HERBIE: What more?

DON: I took a solemn oath to the Union to "lift up clowns and protect them from all threats to comedy." So, I have an obligation to you and our Local 64 brothers to do just that. No matter what it takes.

Herbie took the bait:

HERBIE: I understand, Don.

DON: I'm not sure you do. I pour my soul into this job—being the guardian of young clowns like you, making sure you come up in an environment that is conducive—,
HERBIE: You have always created a good environment, Boss.
DON: —conducive, but also safe for the profession.
HERBIE: You do that, Boss.

Don set the hook in Herbie's cheek:

DON: We are a big, party-balloon-colored family. I could have let you go the way you wanted. The way you thought was right. Among these sneaky, grasping, obnoxious men you wouldn't have lasted a split-second. Remember Atlantic City? You would have been mincemeat for those assholes behind that curtain if I hadn't been there with my big rubber club. And my loud-mouth. They would have snatched your wig, stolen your nose, and left you for dead. But I showed up. And just at the right moment, too.
HERBIE: I could have defended myself, really.
DON: Could have, yes. But should have? No! Union brothers take up for Union brothers. It was my job to protect you. Take the "R" out of "brother" and you have "bother." You've never been a bother to me. Maybe you don't know it, but I have always been here, in the wings, out of sight, looking after you. Protecting you.
HERBIE: I can protect myself, Don. I don't need your protection. Haven't I proven that?
DON: Cocky schmuck…you dismiss my efforts like they don't matter.
HERBIE: I can take care of myself. That's all I'm saying. Do I need to prove it?

Don reeled Herbie in:

DON: Prove it? Prove that? Yeah, Herbie. You do. Otherwise, I am going to need to watch out for you your whole fucking life.
HERBIE: No, Don! No one needs to watch out for me!

DON: Well, if you think you are ready for bigger things…go ahead. Show me you are ready and can take care of yourself. If you're ready, I have some bigger things I can throw your way. [LAUGHS] We can see how you do. How you hit a change-up pitch. What d'ya say?
HERBIE: I say give me the job, Boss. Let me show you what I can do!

The next day, back in Don's office, with Herbie once again sitting on the kitchen chair, Don presented the project: Willowfant, the German clown, had been garnering bookings at what seemed (according to his Local 64 brethren) to be an alarming rate. This year alone he had opened at the Pantages Theatre for the world-renowned tenor Sidney Frances Morrow, performed solo at the rooftop club of the Hudson Hotel on New Year's Eve, provided intermission entertainment at the Annual Tiny Awards ("for excellence in puppeteering"), and was a finalist for the seventh time in Glaser's Endorsed Party Clown competition. Members of Local 64 who witnessed Willowfant's steady rise were suspicious (or concocted suspicions) of his political sympathies. A complaint had been lodged with the Union membership committee implicating that Willowfant favored the political party rising at the moment to power in Germany. Of course, the committee could not ban Willowfant from clowning outright just for being sympathetic. A more subtle (and subtly injurious) solution was needed.

When the Local faced a similar issue in 1911 with the Czech clown Mystro, they were forced to deploy "Opening Night Walkout," an action comparable to clown assassination. To execute an "Opening Night Walkout" the Union quietly purchases every seat in the theater for an important opening night of the clown who is to be "assassinated." The purchased tickets are then distributed to union members, their wives, and children. On opening night, the all-Local 64 audience shows up in disguise to fill every seat in the house, except the house seats occupied by the press and the critics. At key moments during the first half-hour or 45-minutes of the show, the disguised clown families, demonstrating fabricated dissatisfaction or feigned disgust, stand up and remark loudly about the poor quality or low value of the entertainment. Then they clamorously walk out. This continues until the theatre is empty of an audience and the press and critics are the only people left to report on how alienating the performance was and to detail how it ended in complete audience abandonment.

After the press reported on his "Opening Night Walkout," Mystro never worked again.

Arranging and leading Willowfant's "Opening Night Walkout" was Herbie's initiation into placing a successful "hit" on— assassinating—a fellow clown. As with all of his Union activities, Herbie did a superb job, pleased Don, and advanced his reputation in the Coaster Nostra.

Herbie also worked hard during these years on his clowning. At first, he honed his craft in small venues, paying his dues like any clown. He took gigs anywhere and, through on-stage trial and error, he learned which parts of his act worked and which to drop. He took his refined act to Vaudeville where—although the Vaudeville audience was dwindling quickly—night-after-night, he developed new material in front of real audiences. The crowd started out hostile and demanding but, over time, became supportive and adoring. Based on his Vaudeville success, he was offered a three-month run at Coney Island's Fortnight Showtime Theatre CLOWN-O-RAMA in 1938. At the Showtime Theatre, he worked nightly with the celebrated headliner Otto Griebling (performing as Grumbles the Clown). Through Herbie's observations of Griebling from the wings and nightly post-curtain notes from Griebling on Herbie's performance, Gop-Nickel was carved and sanded into a plausible character and Herbie was molded and gilded into a charismatic performer. From CLOWN-O-RAMA, Herbie graduated to a Broadway run, opening for Don O'Sullivan as Mirakolo in his show "Mirakolo of Life." He worked with his mentor each night and collaborated with four of the top clowns of the day: Fred Sherrin (performing as Ef-Red), Salvatore Minerva (as Crystal Chris), Mike Saccoloni (as the Cyclone) and Hans P. Schmerz (as Navels). The show ran 702 performances over 78 weeks, making Gop-Nickel nearly as well-known among clown fans as Weary Willie.

After 702 continuous performances without ever calling on his understudy—at the acme of both his clowning and his Local 64 career—Herbie was tired. He was giving all he could to his stage career. Ten shows per week was positively draining. Plus, he had his Local 64 responsibilities. He resolved, in late 1939, that it was time to be liberated from both the Local and the stage. He determined that there were three ways to get out:

1. He could leave clowning abruptly, be blacklisted by the union, and never work as a clown again.

2. He could clown with less energy, lower his quality, and give up bookings until he was just one of hundreds of nameless clowns, then sneak off to Iowa or Nebraska to become a haberdasher, insurance salesman, alfalfa farmer, or the like.

3. He could accelerate his performing trajectory while engaging in even more acts of clown-on-clown cruelty, becoming so intensely admired as a clown and so intensely feared in the Roller Coaster Nostra that he could do what he pleased— including retire—without serious consequences.

Herbie chose option 3, because it deviated the least from his current path: to rise as fast and far as he could on stage, with as much ruthlessness as possible behind the curtain. To accomplish this, he would need to devise a single deed so heartless—and so well-publicized—that he could retire as both a top performing clown and *the* indisputable miscreant of the clown community. He would then settle someplace safe (Reno? Boca Raton? Leningrad?) where he could remain untouchable by his fellow clowns.

He needed help to conceive and execute his plan and he knew just where to find that help.

✦

Herbie Gopnik told—didn't ask—Donald O'Sullivan to meet him on a dark-clouded, rainy Tuesday just after midnight in the alley just behind Lucky O'Brien's bar. Don stooped in a rain-soaked circle of light thrown by a streetlight at the deep end of the alley, his galoshes clipped tight, their rubber dull against the shiny, slick cobblestones. His coat and his pants cuffs were soaked through with rain. His face, smeared gray with Albolene Cream and greasepaint he had hurriedly wiped off after his 9 p.m. show at the Goodfellow Theater on West 47th Street, shined like a half-moon under his dripping fedora. The angle of the light left his eyes in darkness and his mouth highlighted, a red caterpillar inching across his fleshy, drooping chin. Don was a tall man, athletic for a theatrical. He had long arms and lanky hands that shook from age, constantly in motion, as if they had forgotten how not to be juggling. He stood in the cold drizzle waiting for Herbie.

Herbie sat in the dark in his chauffeur-driven Cadillac and watched Don waiting. Herbie was now an established Broadway star as well as the star operative in the Local 64 firmament. He was known equally for his peerless clown act and his peerless savagery with a juggling pin (among other weapons). As the boss of Local 64 in everything but title, he took this meeting as yet another opportunity to remind Don that he, Herbie, held the future of clowning in Northern New Jersey in his lithe, nimble hands—a future that Don had let run through his shaky, arthritic fingers.

When the drizzle turned hard, pelting the alley with rain, Herbie opened his car door and stepped out of the car. His black leather boot-heels clicked in the splashing water as he walked up the alley, in the light of the car's headlights, towards Don.

"Herbie!" called Don.

"Sit," said Herbie, dismissively indicating the pavement with his right hand.

"Where?" asked Don. "Sit where? I'm supposed to park my ass on wet cobblestones?"

"Why not?" He paused for a moment and when Don didn't move, he ventured again. "I said sit!"

This time, Don did as he was told. Herbie walked out of the spot of light thrown by the streetlight and stood in the dark, facing Don. Herbie gestured to his driver, who turned off the automobile lights. Herbie knew the remaining glare of light catching the sheets of rain kept Don from seeing his face.

Don, hoping the conversation would be a brief one, fidgeted with a rosary he neglected to return as he left church on Sunday and discovered in his raincoat pocket just then. He twiddled the beads in his right hand.

Herbie cast his line and let Don swim around his hook, sniffing:

HERBIE: Don, I have always treated you like you were my father.
DON: [LOOKS DOWN AT THE ROSARY BEADS] Yes...you have, Herbie.
HERBIE: Do you know why, Don?
DON:[LOOKS UP] Because you respect me?
HERBIE: Not exactly. [LAUGHS]
DON: [LOOKS STRAIGHT AT HERBIE] No?
HERBIE: No. I mean...I do respect you. But that's not the reason I have treated you like you were my father. There is more to it than that.
DON: What is there? What more?
HERBIE: You saw something in me I didn't see in myself and you nurtured it. You gave me a break, brought me up in the clown world like your son. You helped me make sense out of this amazing, frustrating world of obnoxious, sneaky, grasping men. If it wasn't for you watching out for me when I knew less...and did less...and was less...I don't know where I'd be.

Don struck at the bait:

DON: I've always put my heart into being a guardian of young clowns, making sure you knew when to take things seriously. And when not to. I mean, to be a good clown, you have to see what's serious and what's funny in a situation.

HERBIE: True. So...in this situation...what's funny in this situation, Don?

DON: No Herbie. I mean in all situations. Uh...what's funny now? Well you think you have something over me. That you are on top. That's a laugh, Herbie, right there. That's high comedy! [LAUGHS AWKWARDLY]

HERBIE: I do have something over you Don. I'm the future. You're the past. The world doesn't need you anymore. You, on the other hand, cannot live without me—

DON: Of course, Herbie. I know that. Can't you see...that is precisely why I've brought you in. Made you. Taught you what I know.

HERBIE: Like a father.

DON: Yeah. To make a smooth transition to your generation. [PAUSE] So if I am like a father...why not let me stand up, Herbie?

HERBIE: In a minute. Being down there focuses you, doesn't it?

DON: Focuses me? Focus? Why you—

HERBIE: It's nothing personal; it's just business. All business.

DON: Why you ungrateful son-of-a—

HERBIE: Now Don...you're being petty. I am not ungrateful. I just need your attention.

DON: You're an—

HERBIE: [TICK-TOCKING WITH HIS FINGER] Uh...uh...Now, Don...no name calling. If I'm an—just remember...you made me what I am!

Herbie set the hook in Don's cheek:

DON: I did make you. You can't say where you ended up is bad. Can you, Herbie? You're lucky. Would you say that, Herbie? You own all these assholes now, Herbie. They eat like squirrels—baby squirrels—right out of your fucking palm.

HERBIE: You're right. I am a lucky man.

DON: Damned lucky!

HERBIE: You helped me.

DON: I did, Herbie. I brought you along.

HERBIE: You did.

DON: And I never say you owe me. I give it to you like a gift. Like you Hebes say—a bar-mitzvah gift! [LAUGHS]

HERBIE: *Hebes*? Don, don't carry me too fast. You're lucky I owe you, Don. I owe you big. Or I'd knock your jaw out of your fucking head—.

DON: —no, Herbie. You don't owe me. It's what I wanted for you. I wanted you on top from the start. You earned it. Yourself. [PAUSE.] Hey Herbie...my back hurts. Can I get up? Lemme up...will ya? Like a father. Remember? Help me here, will ya?

HERBIE: [HIS BOOT HOLDS DOWN THE MUDDY HEM OF DON'S RAINCOAT] Before I let you up...

DON: [TRYING TO STAND] Thank you! Thanks Herb—

HERBIE: [STILL HOLDS THE COAT DOWN] I said...before...I let you up...I need something. Give me what I want and I will give you what you want. Okay?

DON: What I want? I want to get up! Lemme up, will ya?

HERBIE: You want a future.

DON: Do I? Let me up and I will tell you what I want. I'm cold. I'm wet. And my ass-bone hurts.

HERBIE: You want a future. A nice retirement—Cape May maybe. With your people. The golf course *goyim*. I want to give you that. But, there is something I want even more.

DON: Of course, Herbie. Just tell me. Speak to me!

Herbie reeled Don in:

HERBIE: At first, I thought I could take care of it on my own. But this thing I can't do alone. I need your help—.

DON: Herbie, I have watched out for you since you were sixteen. Your whole fucking life almost. Why would I stop now?

HERBIE: —I need you to do one thing for me. It's big. Whopping big. I need the biggest thing you can come up with.

DON: I always said when you think you are ready for bigger things, I have bigger things I can throw your way. I will do that. So, you want a big thing. Let's talk. Just let me stand up.

HERBIE: [REACHES HIS HAND INTO THE CIRCLE OF LIGHT TO HELP DON UP] This time, Don, I need to whack the ball—broken bat—over the left field fence. So big they won't know what hit them and they won't ever recover the ball. What d'ya say?

DON: [BRUSHES THE SEAT OF HIS PANTS WITH BOTH HANDS] I like the sound of it. Why do you need something so big?

HERBIE: Because. Because, Don.

DON: Tell me, Herbie.

HERBIE: Because the time has come.

DON: The time?

HERBIE: I want out, Don.

DON: Holy shit! Herbie. Not that! Not that! You're just getting to the top—.

HERBIE: —I want a blaze-of-glory final act so big that I can end life as Gop-Nickel. And with Local 64. Retire to—I dunno—Havana, maybe. Go where I don't need to be watching behind me all the time. Something big enough that I could marry that blonde cigarette girl from the Midtown Theater and not worry people will talk behind my back. Or if they did I could say, "fuck you," and not care that she never finished high school. Know what I mean?

DON: [INTROSPECTIVELY] Do I know? I know, I know.

HERBIE: I figured you'd get it.

DON: I know, Herbie. I know. It's what I want, too. I wish I had the balls to do that myself. Truth is, I have been thinking about it for a while. I am too old for this shit anymore. Herbie...if you could blaze me up in your blaze of glory, I'd be beholden to you the rest of my life.

HERBIE: Maybe we come up with something so incendiary we'd cover both our escapes with the explosion?

DON: It's your lucky day, Herbie—.

HERBIE: Oh yeah?

DON: —I know exactly what that would be!

✦

Broadway Glitters as Vaudeville Flickers: Clown Gop-Nickel Opens Two-Week Run to Thundering Ovation

By Hermione Leigh Thorsten, Society and Arts Desk

October 15, 1941 - New York, NY - UPI - The rain in New York City held off until just after 11:30pm last night giving the star-studded crowd at Broadway's Vaudeville Palace Theater a chance to disperse before the downpour. More than a few silver chinchilla coats and a several dozen tease-and-dry hairdos were rescued by Mother Nature's good timing as a be-diamoned throng hailed taxis and limousines under the marquee while extolling the triumphant performance of the prominent clown Gop-Nickel.

In the lobby it just happened tonight that **Clark Gable** was holding court in white tie and tails accompanied by his date **Grace Chisholm**, of the South Bend Chisholms... **Shirley Temple** charmed the crowd in flounces of pink and blue lace with a rhinestoned red, white, and blue Colonel's hat jauntily perched on her eruption of curls... **Will Rogers** drawled with a comely blonde on his arm. No one seemed to know her. Will himself identified her to this humbled reporter as **Countess Kitty de Blaze**... Wondering what ever happened to **Joan Crawford**? She was right here at Gop-Nickel's opening night, blinding in a sapphire Crepe de Chine Empire frock, her dark hair topped with a 12 ct. diadem. Harry Winston? Rented? And where was **Franchot Tone**? On the rocks again?... Anything goes when **Ethel Merman** and **Vivian Vance** are in the house, as they were last night. Ethel avoided this humbled reporter (silly Ethel!), but I still admired her lovely lime-green silk Staggerhold Atelier dress with dyed-to-match heels...**Warner Baxter** fit the Broadway

Bill perfectly squiring the stunning **Myrna Loy** striking in an eggshell wool suit by Charles Napper with emerald earrings that could choke a horse... **Wallace Beery** arrived directly from dinner (at eight) at the nearby Chandelier Restaurant with none other than **Marie Dressler** on his arm. Could there be billets-doux?...I caught a glimpse of **Robert Taylor** in the queue of young act-ors and act-rices nuzzling up to the bar....**Katherine Hepburn** was among them, too, looking positively gamine in black woolen britches, a cropped, jewel-crusted Schiaparelli bell-boy jacket paired with a kitten-heeled black patent pump. There were countless dimmer stars in the bar and, sad though this moment may be for Vaudeville, last night there was no place more glittering to be seen than at the vaunted Gop-Nickel opening night.

The show opened with a comic duet by **Will Ahern** and **Gladys Reese**. He beguiled with cowboy songs and rope spinning. She played the Señora and sang. Next came newcomer **Pearl Bailey**, making her Palace debut singing gusty, lusty songs that sneer at men (as who doesn't?). The comic team of **Clark and McCullough** were in third slot and singer **Peter Lind Hayes** in fourth, just before Act One closed with a fresh face: the winner of the Apollo Amateur Contest, song stylist **Ella Fitzgerald**.

After a scintillating see-and-be-seen-intermission, Act Two opened with **Birdie Reeve Kay**, a typist who wowed the somewhat jaded crowd with his virtuosic speed typing. In second slot **Isa Kremer**, the riveting Russian soprano, sang, followed by the very amusing Dutch dialect knockabout comic duo **Clarence Kolb and Max Dill**. The second intermission was preceded by **Oliver Nambler's 22-piece orchestra** energetically playing Waltzes from Vienna (arranged by Hans P. Lempl).

After that intermission, headliner **Gop-Nickel** commenced his long-awaited and highly anticipated show with twelve sleight-of-hand tricks performed while walking in the theater aisle. He then told his highly-comical story of growing up in Hoboken. While he told his story, he intertwined simple, yet effective magic tricks, capturing and keeping the audience's attention with what seemed to be casual and unrehearsed banter. Gop-Nickel then sang four hit songs, accompanying himself on the ukulele: "It Had to Be You," "Stay as Sweet as You Are," "The Object of My Affection," and "My Old Flame." He then returned to his roots and donned his now-famous pocketed coat, chose four children from the audience (up late for the show) and spoke quietly to them. In classic style, each got a nickel from the clown and chose a prize from his myriad pockets. This was followed by one of the great Donald O'Sullivan's Mirakolo the Clown chestnuts. In loving homage to his mentor, Gop-Nickel honored the classic, well-worn Colloquial Penguin routine to loud guffaws and appreciative applause.

Then it was time for the finale of a show that no one in the audience wanted to end. Gop-Nickel introduced us to eight live house cats, each in a small, neat cage. He removed each one from its cage and held it up to the audience. This showed that they were, indeed, live cats. He told the intricate story of devising the act and working with the cats for over two years to "refine their participation." The cats did sundry tricks: walking a tightrope, bouncing a ball, pushing a lever to make a taxidermy canary fly. Gop-Nickel then, matter-of-factly, began to juggle the live animals, adding one at a time to an arc that became nearly eight feet tall. The audience was flabbergasted when he had all eight cats going. The band played as he kept the seemingly relaxed animals moving for nearly four breath-stopping minutes: cascade, shower, half-shower, fountain, over-the-back, behind-the-head, columns. The resulting ovation was deafening. As the sound of clapping died in the god's-seats of the second balcony, a short, bald man, sleeves shiny at the elbows, walked up the stage left stairs pointing and yelling, "You stole my act, you son of a b****!" Gop-Nickel ignored the intrusion, focusing only on the ovation. "I will wring your neck you thieving bastard!" the man shouted above the applause. Two beat cops entered quickly from the wings and ushered the intruder off to stage right.

Planned as part of the entertainment? Or the vindictive act of an embittered rival? This humbled reporter could not tell. You will have to judge for yourself by attending this

swell and satisfying entertainment which may provide
the perfect cap on the Vaudeville era at the Palace!

✦

Just outside, on the patio overlooking the *Malecón,* the band
Lecuona Los Tipos Cubanos percolated through "Cubanakan." The
song rumbaed through the French doors carried on a cloud of silver
cigarette smoke rising from the nostrils of a small crowd sitting in
front of a makeshift summer bandstand beneath a monumental
oak tree. The smoke caught a light sea breeze that pushed it deeper,
swirling past the bar and far into the room. Trapped there, the
wet-slate scent of tobacco mixed with the earthy funk of worn
leather sofas and chairs, the pungent scent of lemon-oil soaking
into Madera oak paneling, and the salty, fishy, sun-roasted tang
of seaweed drying on the nearby rock jetty. Plump, mahogany-
skinned, fuchsia-lipped waitresses in gauzy dresses buzzed
from table to table, wafting the smell of oak-aged Scotch and *Mi
Gardenia Blanca* perfume behind them, sharpening the bouquet.
The occupants of the bar sweated in the mid-day, pre-siesta heat
stirring a peppery top-note into the stew of smells to create an
attar tropical that was unique to the place.

The waitresses carried Slings and Rickies and Saocos and
Presidentes to tourists who gulped them in order to abandon their
tables fast, rushing off to see their next sight. Or, the waitresses
carried Something-On-The-Rockses to serious-faced men in tan
suits who nursed their ice cubes, chewed the ends off of thick
Cohiba Esplendidos, and kept their tables all afternoon. The room
gave off both the disinterested repulse of a tourist trap and the cozy
allure of a refuge. The Havana residents who came here came to
duck out of sight, since no self-respecting *Habanero* would set foot
in the *Bar del Lobby* of the *Hotel Habana Primo* unless they were
hiding something or hiding from someone. The *Americanos* who
came here came for a shallow swallow of the *verdadera experiencia
habanera*—the True Havana Experience.

Americano Donald O'Sullivan (formerly the clown Mirakolo) stood at the bar, his back to the smoke-imbued room, watching three houseflies vie for King of the Mountain on a wet terry dishrag next to the sink. Don distractedly waited for the barkeeper to mix one *El Presidente* for him and one Boodles and Tonic for the other resident *Americano*, Herbie Gopnik (formerly the clown Gop-Nickel) who sat in the farthest (and darkest) corner. After a recent incident with some clam juice in a Bloody Mary, now scared of being poisoned, Herbie would not allow any waitress to fetch him a drink. Instead, he sent Don, his major-domo, to order, then monitor the bartender making the drink and to watchfully wend his way back through the crowd of strangers to the far corner scanning for reprobates. Herbie never wanted to turn his back to a room.

While Don was at the bar, Herbie waited to meet the features editor of LIFE Magazine, who was now seventeen minutes late for their two o'clock appointment.

"Stupid bitch! Keeping me waiting," said Herbie to Don as Don put the drinks down on the table, "which is something I don't appreciate in the slightest."

"Aw, Herbie," said Don glancing around the room, "it's no big deal. They live by *mañana* here. Nothing in Havana ever happens on time. You know that."

"I am doing her a favor even giving her an interview," said Herbie. "I have better things to do with my time."

"Actually...no...you don't," said Don. "We need this article. The publicity. To feed your rep. Now...drink your gin, Boss, and enjoy the place. [PAUSE] That's the nice thing about retirement, isn't it? Nothing is pressing on you. You can take your time. I mean if we weren't here waiting for Martina, we'd be in some other crap-house bar doing nothing, right? Just staying out of the midday sun. [LAUGHS.] Or I'd be having my usual Tuesday afternoon *siesta-rooni*. Can't beat the tropical life, Herbie, can you?"

"It's easy for you, old man. You can nap. I've got a reputation to worry about. Plus my safety. You? You can go along like an anonymous clown. I have to keep up appearances...and keep up my guard."

"What appearances? And what guard you gotta keep up, Herbie? No one cares a hair about us!"

"Not true! I've got LIFE Magazine kicking down my door for a cover story. [WHISPERING] And I need to stay untouchable for a few more years until I slip off people's radar. If I avoid getting killed."

"You're crazy *loco*, Boss. No one is trying to kill you!"

"Shhhh! Quiet, you idiot! What about that tricycle? That kid was definitely trying to get me!"

"He just didn't see you when you stepped off the curb. And you didn't see him, either. You gotta look both ways, Boss."

"Without a doubt a failed hit!"

"Herbie, this is Havana. If someone wanted to kill you, you'd be dead. No one messes around here. It's fucking Havana—."

Don abruptly stopped speaking when a woman in her early thirties with black hair pulled back in a ponytail entered the bar.

"This is her, Herbie," said Don, getting up from his seat. "I'll go grab her."

She swept into the bar wearing silver-and-white striped silk harem pants, a cerise blouse tied at the waist (leaving her midriff bare to show off the rhinestone glued in her navel), deep-red lipstick, white stockings, and black patent leather pumps. A sort of Town & Country magazine meets tropical-paradise-floor-show look, which didn't work well. She carried a worn black leather briefcase that perfectly completed her ensemble (perfectly, if fashion-awkward was what you were after). It was hard to tell whether she was a Westchester matron trying to look Cuban or a Cuban trying to look like she was visiting from Larchmont. If attention was what she wanted, she got it. Her entrance was remarked upon by every occupant of every table she passed as she headed for Herbie and Don's corner table.

Don crossed the room quickly to head her off so she wouldn't say Herbie's name out loud.

"Martina!" he said extending his hand. "Good to see you. Don O'Sullivan. We met once before. In New York. I work for Mr. G. Come right this way." He ushered her through the maze of tables to their table in the corner. "What can I get you to drink?"

"I'll have an iced coffee, please."

"Right away! Sit! Sit!" Don headed back to the bar again.

This will be fun, Herbie thought. *She doesn't even drink!*

Martina Olivedo abruptly sat and immediately dumped the contents of her briefcase onto the table. She surveyed the pile of belongings, picked out a steno pad and pencil, and then shoved everything else back in the bag.

"How long have you been in *La Habana*?" asked Martina crossing her legs and propping her pad on her knee.

"About a month."

"How do you find it?" asked Martina in her lightly-accented English.

HERBIE: Find it? Why, every morning when I wake up it's just there, outside my door! [LAUGHS.]

MARTINA: [LAUGHS. Then, PAUSE. Then,] I meant how do you like it? To put a sharper point on my question.

HERBIE: It's like Passaic, New Jersey, but with charm. [PAUSE] And fewer Jews. [PAUSE] And better music.

MARTINA: Yes, we Habaneros love our music. This band, *Lecuona Los Tipos,* playing outside, is one of our best at the moment. Have you been listening?

HERBIE: Not really. I didn't pay attention. I've got better...er, other...things to do.

MARTINA: Is there anything better than listening to music?

HERBIE: Silence?

Don returned to the table with Martina's iced coffee.

DON: Here you go, Martina. [TO HERBIE] All set?

Herbie nodded.

DON: [TO MARTINA] Mr. G. is ready for his interview.

Herbie cleared his throat in an extravagant display of readiness and shifted in his chair, taking a swallow of gin.

DON: Or are you, Herbie?

HERBIE: I am ready. To go on the record? Yes. I am.

MARTINA: No 'on the record' here...this is a lifestyle story. With a cover photo. Esteban, my photographer, will join us soon. He will shoot you—.

HERBIE: [LOOKING AROUND QUICKLY] Don't ever say that, Martina! If you don't mind...say "photograph you."

DON: Mr. G. is thinking someone's got a hit out on him. Like— out to get him.

MARTINA: [LOOKING PUZZLED] Oh? And why would someone be out to get you?

HERBIE: I am...I was...the most powerful—and most feared—clown in the Tri-state Area and I—allegedly—got there by stealing another guy's act. Not only his act but the most coveted clown gag in all of clown history. Allegedly stolen. Guys in our line of work don't let that stuff go unnoticed. Or unrequited.

MARTINA: Hmmm. Maybe that is a good place for us to start. Tell me how you became the most powerful—and most feared—clown...

✦

A CLOWN IN EXILE

He broke records with 42 sold-out performances at the Broadway's Vaudeville Palace. He made history with his most-ever 702 opening appearances for headliner Mirakolo (Donald O'Sullivan) at the Forrest Theatre. He served on the executive committee of Local 64, Clowns and Acrobat's Union for just under 17 years. Yet today, Herbie Gopnik can be found sipping gin and tonic anonymously in an out-of-the-way hotel bar in Havana, Cuba. Why is this clown superstar on the lam?

Ask Philip Rothenberg, the clown Vinkledoodle, who made an unexpected appearance on opening night at the Vaudeville Palace claiming that Gop-Nickel had stolen his act—or at least part of it—when Gop-Nickel brought down the house by juggling eight also began clowning at parties. Now famous as Mirakolo the Clown, he had an almost two-year run of headliner performances at Broadway's Forrest Theatre. No less than entertainment columnist and critic Abe Marcus called O'Sullivan "a clown's clown." He noted "Mirakolo performs like a classical actor. He is as serious about clowning as a great actor is about Shakespeare." Gopnik followed O'Sullivan on and off the stage, becoming an active member of the Local 64, Clown's and Acrobat's Union (where O'Sullivan was Chairman) and an essential contributor to the professional clown community as a result.

Gopnik was the first to move the Local towards animal owner's rights, an important and seminal change the union drove allowing owners of performing animals to travel with the animals on trains (and lately even planes) tethered only with a jute rope.

live cats. Rothenberg claimed he, not Gopnik, designed and developed the training device that makes feline juggling possible and that, through a nearly three-year-long subterfuge, Gopnik was able to pry the device from Rothenberg's ownership. "I did nothing like that," said Gopnik from his corner table at Havana's *Hotel Primo*. "Rothenberg gave me his plans for the device and his entire training idea willingly. Then, as anyone would, I put it to work for my own purposes with his full knowledge and assent."

Gopnik began his career as a clown at children's birthday parties, a member of a sub-set community of clowns that centers around Hoboken, New Jersey. He honed his skills under the watchful eye of his now-close friend and valet, Donald O'Sullivan. O'Sullivan, himself, "Animals were taking over the field and the law required them to be treated like royalty," said Gopnik. "Local 64 brought attention to this issue and did what was right. Why should a trained dog have to be in a kennel or carrier? That same dog can walk a tightrope or balance a guinea pig on his nose. Why shouldn't it travel unencumbered? What we did for animals," said Gopnik. "Shows how much we care about their owners. Owner's rights simply cannot be overlooked." This important policy shift put Local 64 into the vanguard of the animal rights rollback. The Local 64 Animal Rights rule became the template for a number of similar rules in other unions, including the musician's union's limitation on program credit and pension contributions for Page-Turners in theatrical pit orchestras.

Gopnik failed numerous times to win Glaser's Bakery-Endorsed Party Clown competition, which he said simply fueled his ambition. "If you play the birthday candle circuit, there is always a hot dog or an egg salad sandwich provided gratis. Those keep the wolf from the door," said Gopnik. "As a result, you get soft. BP clowns (as we pros call them) nibble at the edges of clowning, technically speaking. I wanted to really satisfy an audience with major impact."

So Gopnik began to adapt his act for the Vaudeville stage. He went for bigger effects and more impressive analogies. "Clowning is like painting. You know? There is Monet, and Seurat. And you have Picasso, too. Different levels of realism and suggestion. I wanted to combine Picasso and Monet— what I call 'Embarrassed Realism.'" Gopnik not only coined the term (which has now become common in both the theater and art worlds), but he manifested it in his work. His now famous mime piece "Gop-Nickel's Winter in Antwerp" contemplated the "dilemma we all wrestle with," said Gopnik, "namely how to walk in a great gust of wind. When I took that on, no one was doing serious wind work on the stage. Well, maybe Marcel Marceau was...but only him. I took wind and made it *visible*!"

Just prior to his exile in Havana, Gopnik took a run at Broadway himself, obtaining a sold-out limited run at the Vaudeville Palace. In typical fashion, he both advanced his art and caused controversy. In this exclusive interview with LIFE, he tells the story for the first time: Gopnick, three years before his opening night at the Palace, opened a clown equipment store on 37th Street and Seventh Avenue in what is known as Magic Alle—where New York's performing community builds and purchases equipment for stage shows.

"I was not interested in advancing my name or reputation, just advancing the techniques clowns use. I was famous by this time so I didn't need to use my own name. I opened the store under the name Hermann Pincus. I worked in the store but didn't need to be recognized when I was there so I wore a wig, prosthetic nose and fabricated beard. What was wrong with that? I just wanted to avoid notoriety, which had no benefit to my business." Gopnik glosses over the fact that his was the only equipper in the city that built clown paraphernalia.

"The court said I 'lay in waiting' for Vinkledoodle but I did nothing of the sort. I just opened a store on the up-and-up and Vinkledoodle came to see me." Vinkledoodle, a.k.a. Philip Rothenberg, a yeoman working clown, according to court records, came into Gopnik's store looking to fabricate a contraption to train cats for feline juggling. Gopnik, as per Rothenberg's lawsuit, allegedly stole his plans, built the trainer himself and, over a nearly two-year period, trained the cats himself, too. "You've got to get them when they are really young," said Gopnik, "and keep them in cages. Very close quarters." The trainer [Editor's Note: Gopnik was awarded a patent on the trainer in 1942] imitates the juggling arc while keeping the cats in the prone position. "Since you start with cats that are three-weeks old," said Gopnik, "and resize the cages as they grow the kittens feel very safe and comfortable being juggled." Further, Gopnik described the "white collar" parts of the alleged crime: "I hired a secretary who came from an architecture firm and was proficient in copying blueprints by hand. There's no crime in that. I needed to have the plans."

"The SOB," stated Rothenberg in his deposition, a transcript of which was obtained by LIFE, "I was going in to his store each week to check on his progress on building my machine and the [LIFE CENSORED] was working with me day in and day out to refine the workings of it. All the while he was telling me it was for me, but all the time secretly training cats for his own use!" Gopnik counters, "Vinkledoodle brought me the idea in 1940. If he was going to perform the act why didn't he?" LIFE contacted Rothenberg to ask about this. Rothenberg refused to comment.

When Gopnik performed the act in his limited-run Broadway show it brought down the house. He was rewarded with a standing ovation each and every night. Rothenberg also attended each night and, at the end of each performance, registered his dissatisfaction with the theft. Gopnik maintains Rothenberg is "deluded" and "trying to profit from my success."

LIFE asked: if Gopnik is innocent, why has he taken up life in Cuba, which does not have an extradition treaty with the United States? Gopnik says, "I am a long-time bachelor and Don is a widower for 11 years. I am almost 50 years old. I wanted a place where I could enjoy the sunshine and avoid being recognized. Fame is a harsh mistress and Havana is a great place to heal from her."

✦

The LIFE Magazine article arrived at the Havana newsstand two weeks after it hit the stands in Hoboken.

Herbie and Don were on the cover frozen in time standing in the corner of the *Bar del Lobby* of the *Hotel Habana Primo*, arms around each other's shoulders, toasting with their cocktails in their free hands. The haze of smoke gave the black and white photo a noir-ish, cinematic feel.

Don grabbed ten copies at the newsstand, hastily stacked and paid for them, and brought them to Herbie in the *Bar Estrella del Rincon,* where he was drinking a local draft beer. They both grabbed magazines and opened them in unison, leafing to the centerfold where the cover story always began.

They read intently. When both had finished:

"Hmmm," said Herbie, "it's shorter than I thought it would be."

"And so many pictures," noticed Don. "Americans have the attention span of a cockroach. Can't deal with words."

HERBIE: I spoke to her for over two hours and this is what she paid attention to?

DON: Damn.

HERBIE: I spoke about our work in the Union. And about performing. I spoke about the fine art of clowning at length.

DON: You never know when you say it how it will come out in the actual article.

HERBIE: You know what burns me the most?

DON: What Herbie?

HERBIE: She calls you my valet.

DON: Yeah.

HERBIE: That's a laugh!

DON: Yeah...that's a laugh for sure.

ENTR'ACTE

The Barker

Brendan Hardy

NOW

I'm not the kind who'll sit around all day watching TV. I am not a golfer. Or a guy who will throw clay pots on a wheel in the basement of the YMCA. Or a guy who is going to go out in the invigorating pre-dawn air with an easel and a canvas to paint a sunrise. Nope. I am a talker. Agnés Sanchez, the Head of Nursing, says I have a way of talking that makes other people listen. Then talk themselves. That's not so surprising since all a barker does is talk. I could sure flap my jaw back in the day, barking for Maestro Morris's Traveling Curio Cabinet, then Wentworth's Side Show Caravan, then Carlos Sanchez's Carnaval de Rarezas and, finally. Barnum's Touring Company D.

   I wasn't the kind to let a live one get away. I'd stop you right in your tracks and bend my words like a snake charmer so they make you come in. I could wind out a line of talk so full of reasons to stop that you would turn into my tent before you even knew you did it. I could welcome you and that one next to you, peel you both off your intended route, and get you paid up and packed into my tent to see this or that incredible, one-of-a-kind, this-show-only, better-than-ever, more-than-you-think, worth-twice-the-price *thing. I was a talker, for certain. Born to the job. Right on the stage at the Belasco. As you know, ghost-light and everything. Like they say, a Broadway baby.*

I am the kind who visits people in their rooms to just sit and talk. And talk. It just comes to me naturally to sidle up by someone's bed or to take a sit on their loveseat, talk about me and ask about them. Which is how I got started writing down the stories of the people living here with me in The Home. Capital T. Capital H. I started out convinced I could—and would need to—make their stories interesting using my barker's talent for elaboration and embellishment. I thought I could take these people's dull lives and uninspiring existences and pump them up with my personal nitrous oxide to make them amusing, compelling, and interesting. However, in real life, my genius is hardly needed.

Let me elucidate. I started out by putting a flyer on the cork board over the coffee maker in the Day Room. Advertising always pays off. I posted this thing, laser-printed, that said: "Tell Me The Story of Your Life!" I went on to explain that I was aggregating the life-stories of people in The Home. Right off the bat, two noticed it—easy to notice because I know how to attract attention—and then I had my first victims. They told me, "Come into our room and we'll tell you our story."

I have to say I was disappointed. To be God's honest, I wasn't that interested in them. They were circus security people—Big Top Dicks—and to me that sounded like a snooze-and-a-half in big, bold, red-and-gold letters. I guess I imagined I'd be telling the glamorous stories. Stories of dancers and acrobats. I cast in my line and what fish bites on it first? Circus cops!

I'm not a mean guy and certainly not to my fellow residents. It's the last act for most of us, so why be mean? To be nice, I made a date to sit down with Larisa and Chance.

She is a little—I don't know—slow to get going with her story and he is kind of distracted by turning off the TV with the remote. He pounds the buttons and points it, first like a lightsaber, then a pistol, towards the TV. Nothing. All the time I am thinking, how did I get myself into this?

Larisa is very proper and sits, poised, on the edge of her bed in a sweater dress, leather boots, a big gold chain and bracelets like bangles which she shakes to emphasize her points. Chance is, what'll I call it, reticent? He had a stroke last year and he is all stumped on his right side and Larisa says he was always quiet but now he is like a fella who is turned inside-out with quiet.

Still, they started to tell their story and I started to listen. Kind of begrudgingly. Lazy-eared. But you know what? I perked right up. No dancer, nor any acrobat, has a better story of how he (or she) got into the business.

Meandering? Sure.

Odder than hell? Yes.

But also...well...you decide.

ACT THREE

The Security Agents

Larisa Yohantova Grayson and Chance Grayson

THEN

E vgeniya Preobazhenskya looked through the peep hole one last time. *He looks so old-fashioned in his four-button tweed and gold wire-rimmed spectacles,* she thought. *His boots are shiny yet I can see that is polish over scuffed leather. Clearly frugal. Shall I say he's, "practical"? Or must I admit, "poor?" Why are all of the easy marks limited in rubles?*

"Alright," she said to Martina, her maid and business assistant, who stood behind her looking over her shoulder and tweaking her collar. "Give me a final look-over for lint and then announce me!"

"Yes, Madame."

"Be sure you take his overcoat and brief bag while I entertain him. You will surely find his bank book in his bag. We cannot miss this opportunity to check what he is worth," said the Madame as she fluffed the midnight-blue lace around her collar and adjusted her cameo of St. John Baptiste de la Salle. "Oh! And bring the three-headed nutria stole. A touch of silver fur will perfectly complete my *mise-en-scene.*"

"Yes, Madame."

Martina brought the stole and placed it over the Madame's left shoulder, with its glass-eyed faces staring forward. Martina looked Madame over for lint, found a loose thread on her waistband, banished it, walked out of the anteroom into the parlor, and announced, "Madame Evgeniya Preobazhenskya, Head Mistress of Preobazhenskya School for Girls."

On cue, Madame Preobazhenskya swept in on a cloud of blue lace and sat immediately and stiffly in her throne-like desk chair, which was carved from a single trunk of oak and sized to hold both her and her ample petticoats. She offered her hand to her guest with what she deemed the perfect balance of warmth and disdain.

"Evgeniya Preobazhenskya. A pleasure."

Before he could respond, she addressed Martina with equal (though this time feigned) disdain:

"Girl, first tend to the samovar and then serve us each tea. And bring the fine Opex biscuits for our guest."

"Yes, Madame Preobazhenskya."

Martina fussed with the samovar, placed the hazelnut biscuits, served the tea, and departed with the visitor's bag and coat. The Madame sat silent, looking away from her guest, while the dead nutria on her shoulders stared at him on her behalf. She had made Piotr Mikhailovich Yohantov wait nearly three quarters of an hour for her arrival and now she made him wait again. She balanced her cup of black tea precariously on her unseen knee and reached forward to take a spoon. She leaned in, back straight, knees together, ankles united, and letting no light pass. She elegantly dipped her spoon into a pot of pomegranate jam and transferred it into her teacup. Her chin, as was proper, did not dip. Her eyes did not waver. Her body steady. Her soul serene. She began to spin her web.

"How kind of you to attend me. I am sure you are quite busy. I was indisposed. One of the young ladies here had a question of a most intimate nature having to do with a Count's...shall I say...startling? Or rather...fortuitous? I think it would be right at minimum to say unexpected, proposal of marriage. Oh dear, yet another Count. Her fourth Count this season. And her fourth such proposal. It is, well... you might say, a bidding war over her. How often does this happen here at Preobazhenskya School for Girls? Daily, I can assure you—"

"I see," said her visitor, feeling a bit shocked at her candor. They had only then been formally introduced.

"—once a girl finishes a term under me," the Madame continued, "she has men fluttering like moths around her flame!"

"My goodness," inserted Piotr Mikhailovich Yohantov.

"A girl must be prepared, Gospodin, for a well-born match if she schools here," she spoke in a tone that clearly said *everyone knows this but you.* "Before you can consider marriage for—is it your eldest daughter?— she must be finished. This everyone knows quite positively."

"She is my *only* daughter. If my wife were alive, I am sure Larisa would have been taught all she needs to know. Alas, her mother passed when Larisa was five years old."

"Oh, how sad! I am sorry," said the head mistress taking a sip of tea. "All the more reason for her to attend my next term."

"Regrettably," resumed the visitor, "my daughter has been raised by a man. By me. She knows nothing that a woman should know—save, perhaps, how to pour a glass of vodka or trim a cigar."

"Oh, dear me, no. This will not do. This is like owning a pistol with a finely carved handle and using it only to shoot bats! In the dark!" said the head mistress, putting her teacup on the oak desk between them. "That will hardly do. A well-finished girl knows all there is about life—cooking, cleaning, laundering, setting a fine table. Catering all of the Orthodox holy day meals. She knows how to roll a fine Kulebyaka of Salmon, which utensils are best to serve it with, how to take the bones from the flesh, and precisely which of Kiev's kitchen supply stores sells the fishbone-tweezers she needs to do it. There is nothing about home or hearth—I like to say about samovar or Samoyed—that one of my young ladies does not know when she departs my school."

"I do believe, Madame, that is what my Larisa needs. Yes, Samoyed. Samovar. Just so. I feel I have neglected her education in deference to her brother. I simply feel I cannot give her what she needs."

"Can she read?" asked Madame Preobazhensky. "Write? Play the fortepiano? Sew? Sing?"

"I know—well, should say I think—she can read. Wait! Of course she can. Of course. I have seen her write her name, too. Fortepiano? No. But she can sew. Yes. I am sure of that. Here is a bit of her sewing, right here on my cuff." He pulled up his jacket sleeve, leaned in and thrust his stitched cuff across the desk.

Madame Preobazhensky recoiled in horror. "That's quite enough!" she said, removing a handkerchief from her sleeve and dabbing her lips. She took a moment to recompose herself, smoothing her dress.

Piotr Mikhailovich Yohantov continued, "I have not heard her sing, although she must, mustn't she? Why singing? Is that important?"

"A wife must serenade her husband."

"I never knew...."

"Oh dear," said Madame Preobazhensky. "You present me not with a potential student, Gospodin, but an improvement project!"

Piotr Mikhailovich Yohantov sank in his chair. This was exactly what he feared: that he would be made to feel a bad father. "I'm sorry," he said, autonomically.

"Still," responded the Madame, seeing her opportunity, "this is precisely why I run this school. For needy girls like Lidiya."

"Larisa."

"I only do it as a service...perhaps I could say, a charity. Charitable in the outcome at least. You must take the opportunity presented by an opening in my coming term to correct your *petit faut*. You must place...um—"

"— Larisa."

"— Larisa for the next term, and by the time two years pass and she has turned 17, she, too, will be entertaining proposals from Counts!"

"I don't need that. A marriage of the heart is all I hope for her."

"Pishtosh! Would you rather she loves some dull bureaucrat or have a villa in Athens and crates of silver?"

"I'd like her to be happy."

"I guarantee you Gospodin, no woman is ever happier than when she knows she causes her husband to be the envy of his friends and colleagues—in the bar, at the gaming table, on his arm at the opera, in his beautifully laundered, perfumed sheets. Did I mention there is but one opening in the coming term?" She picked up a small crystal bell and rang it.

Martina appeared.

MADAME: [SNAPPING HER FINGERS IMPERIOUSLY TO SIGNAL TO MARTINA THAT THE GAME IS ON] Do we still, Martina, have an opening in the coming term?

MARTINA: [OBLIGING THE GAME] Unfortunately not, Madame. The daughter of Colonel Ukebov took that remaining place just this morning.

MADAME: That will not do. Our visitor has just spoken for the place for his daughter.

Piotr Mikhailovich Yohontov did not, he thought, speak for a place.

MARTINA: I regret to have accepted the Colonel's deposit paid today, as I said.

MADAME: And I said that simply will not do. I promised that last seat to our guest's daughter, Larisa.

Piotr Mikhailovich Yohontov did not, he thought, recall a promise.

MADAME: Larisa will have the last remaining seat.

MARTINA: That cannot be done, Madame.

MADAME: How can you say that to me? There is always something that can be done.

Gospodin Yohontov spoke for the place. He will pay today. Now. Not a deposit. He will pay in full.

Piotr Mikhailovich Yohantov did not, he thought, commit to pay— neither in full, nor a deposit.

MADAME: You must send word to Colonel Ukebov that you were mistaken and we are full for next term.
MARTINA: But Madame Preobazhensky, he is a Colonel in the Tsar's army. We cannot decline his daughter for just...anyone.
MADAME: We not only *can*, but we *will*. Larisa Yohontova is far— yes, I say far—more interesting to have in our next term class than the offspring of some high-born pretender.
MARTINA: Pretender? Madame, I simply do not agree. In fact, I will put my job in the gamble. If you take Larisa Yohontova into the place I promised to the Colonel, I shall have no choice other than to resign!

Piotr Mikhailovich Yohontov stood and looked around for his coat and briefcase.

YOHONTOV: I cannot cost this young woman's job! I shall find another place for Larisa at another school—.
MADAME: Gospodin, you shall do nothing of the sort! Martina has resigned. And so far as I am concerned, that is for the best. I desire girls of quality and potential in my school, not girls of mere social rank. Away with you, Martina! I need not have your supposed "assistance" when you choose our students wrongly!

Martina turned and walked out, slamming the door closed. A moment later she slammed the door open and walked back into the room, this time holding Piotr Mikhailovich Yohontov's coat and briefcase. With a look of scorn, she dropped them both on the floor next to the visitor's feet. Then, she turned to Madame Preobazhenskya:

MARTINA: Witch!
MADAME: [RAISING HER HANDS IN THE MENACING ATTACK
OF A CAT] Beggar!

As Piotr Mikhailovich Yohontov looked on in horror, Martina left, slamming the door once again.

"I am sorry," said the Madame, "to have shared with you such an embarrassing spectacle, Gospodin. Yet, if I have to lose a mediocre employee to ensure Larisa will be finished as a lady at this school, so be it."

Yohontov gathered up his belongings.

"Let us discuss the cost, requirements and starting date," he said. "You are very kind to have so forcefully made a space for Larisa."

"I did nothing of the sort," replied Madame Preobazhensky. "You have that space fair and square."

✦

Piotr Mikhailovich Yohontov stood beneath the stone lintel of the doorway to his heckling shop looking out over 300 hectares of flax and clover he had recently acquired. The purchase had taken his bank balance down to zero. Looking at this vast sea of green, he felt satisfied with his purchase, even though it had been dear. A rainy spring insured that the fields brimmed. Nature had done her work. Now he needed to match her effort with his—in the cultivating and in the harvest.

He knew nothing about flax. He had hired a foreman who knew what he didn't know, so he hardly felt a need to pay attention. The very idea of needing to learn about the crop brought bile into his throat. Yet on the other hand, he did like the idea of being seen as a gentleman farmer. Before deciding to spend his inheritance on linen, he had invested half-an-hour to read a pamphlet, "The Basics of Linen Production—From Seed to Loom," that told him (what he thought was) enough:

The plant needs to be pulled up with the roots in order to get the longest fibers. It must then be fluffed to dry, the seeds are removed, and the stalks retted (alternating rain and sun causing enzymes to degrade the pectin allowing the fibers to be pulled away from the straw). Men must turn over the straw to evenly ret the stalks. When the straw is retted and sufficiently dry, it must be rolled up and carried to the storage cribs to extract the fibers.

That was all Yohontov could recall from what he had read. He was armed with a few facts to spout over the bar or in the queue at the bank if someone asked about his *métier*. With that, he deemed his study done.

He had a plan, however. A plan by which he knew he would succeed. The plan was Jews. There was, he thought, a positive abundance of Jews in the towns around Kiev. It would be those Jews who would work his fields and make his investment pay. His foreman, a Jew himself, would set up a hiring table on the main road a month before the flax would be ready to harvest. Jews would line up to offer their hands—to commit to bend their backs in the Ukrainian sun—and bring in his harvest on time.

There was only one slight problem with his plan: Jews were getting scarcer lately as the Tsar called them into the army. They were conscientiously objecting and leaving for America or Britain or Argentina, bereaving the landed men of Kiev of their workforce. *Still*, Yohontov thought, *with a Jewish foreman recruiting, he'd skim the best workers off the top. The Jews would work hard like they always do.*

He need not worry. He would be fine.

So, Yohontov stood in the doorway of the milking-barn-turned-heckling-shop looking at his fields. Beech leaves shimmered in the flirty breeze. Mockingbirds elaborately sang their stolen songs. Bees made their tentative way to the fields, found the flax not-yet-blooming, and flew back with legs bare of pollen. In long, restless flight lanes they crossed in front of the shop, concluded that they could not do their work, and retreated to the hive. The day became warm and sun drenched. Morning glories shone like blue moons against their dark leaves. All the cogs of nature clicked into each other. It was spring.

Yohontov was waiting for Yeharon Keneivitch Kramerov, his Jewish foreman. Yeharon was coming to join him with two horses so, together, they could survey the condition of the acquired fields. Yohontov stared down the long beech tree-lined avenue patiently watching for Kramerov's approaching dust cloud.

Gradually, Yohontov became aware of the distant thud of trotting horse's hooves on the dirt road. A moment later he saw Kramerov astride his Postier Breton mare towing Trifen, Yohontov's favorite black stallion from his own stable. He waited and watched as the foreman made his way.

"*Zdarova,* Yeharon!" called Yohontov, once his foreman was within earshot.

"And to you! A fine morning it is, sir," the foreman called back as the two horses pulled up at the stone steps. "While it is a fine day, I do want to mention that I noticed some brown stalks just below the stream on the far side of the road. Probably a water issue, yet we should ride there first."

"What sort of water issue?"

"Too much? Or too little? Or a rusting pipe? Could be any of those," said Yeharon, bringing his horse around to face down the road. "I noticed it, although I was not close enough to see what the cause was, exactly."

Yohontov mounted his horse and followed the foreman down the path to the main road. They rode in affable silence surrounded by sunshine and bird calls.

"Follow the irrigation break just to the left," called Yeharon over his shoulder while pointing across his horse's neck.

They turned off the path, one, then the other.

"How do brown stalks signify both too much and too little water?" asked Yohontov. "That makes no sense."

"Over time, sir, you will get to know your crops and what they are telling you. Over the years you will see a bit of everything and learn from it."

"I do not wish to learn, either quickly or over time. That is precisely why I have you."

"Because I already know?"

"And because I do not want to know. Just bring in my crop, get it processed, and get cash in our pockets and I will be pleased."

Yeharon Keneivitch Kramerov thought, *what a hollow man!* Out loud he said, "You will learn from the crop, sir!"

They rode together down the narrow break, the horses stepped over stones left and right. Yeharon expected to see a broken pipe or a pooling of water. Instead, he saw all of the plants in that corner of the field were covered with orange-yellow dust. Kramerov dismounted and waded into the plants, grown to knee-height already. He took off his glove and ran his fingers down a leaf from tip to stem. Tiny puffs of golden powder rose as his finger traced its way.

Flax rust. *Melampsora lini.*

"Sir, how did you select the seeds used to plant these fields?" he asked.

"Select them? The fields were planted when I bought them! I didn't plant them. Why would I?"

Kramerov swallowed hard. "What you have here, sir, is flax rust—a fungus that brings these blisters and turns your crop first orange, then rots it to dust. By tomorrow, this whole field could be infected."

"Well," snapped Yohontov, "fix it!"

"It cannot be fixed. You can avoid it if you plant the right seed. This, obviously, was not the right seed. Within a few weeks, all your fields will be orange. Then they will die."

✦

Just as Yeharon Keneivitch predicted, the fields turned orange, the rust spread, and the fields died.

Piotr Mikhailovich Yohontov could do nothing to stop the blight, so he did the one thing he felt he could do: he took his small purse of remaining household money and invested it in eighteen cases of vodka. He employed this vodka to shift his energy and attention from an effort to grow flax to an effort to forget he had ever grown flax.

He drank all day and night, week after week, until he felt competent as a farmer, knowledgeable as an investor, and well-endowed as a lover. His thoughts of a love match for his daughter shifted from sober reality to the drunken hope that Larisa would marry well and that her husband might be kind enough to favor Yohontov in his old age with a pension, a modest estate, and a horse.

Thank Saints Cyril and Methodius, Yohontov repeatedly thought in his late afternoon stupor, *my daughter has high prospects. At least her future is assured thanks to the Preobazhenskya School for Girls!*

✦

Martina (still employed by Madame Preobazhenskya, her faked resignation a ruse to rush Yohontov into signing his daughter on as a student having worked) closed the shutters in the parlor office so only a tiny bit of daylight pierced through around the hinges. She moved the comfortable guest armchair into a dark corner and replaced it with an uncomfortable tall-backed armless chair with a prickly woven straw seat. She moved a silver salver holding a bottle of Samogon onto the desk, wiped a single cordial glass, and placed it next to the bottle. On the desk, in front of Madame's oak chair, she placed Larisa's student file and, on top of that, a gold and robin's egg blue enameled fountain pen. She looked it all over. Perfect. The stage was set for one of Madame Preobazhenskya's student conferences.

The Madame stopped in to check the room.

"Oh dear, no, Martina. This is not one of *those* meetings. Larisa is one we like. Give her the comfortable chair and bring a second cordial glass, immediately!"

Martina did precisely as she was told and, a few moments later, she led Larisa Yohontova into the darkened room.

"Sit." She pointed to the guest chair. "Madame Preobazhenskya will be with you straight away."

Of course "straight away" actually meant twenty minutes, carefully watched by Martina on the hallway clock, who then signaled to the Madame the precise moment for her entrance. Madame Preobazhenskya felt everything and everyone was improved by waiting. People become more circumspect, and therefore malleable, as they waited, held Madame, so causing people to wait was her preferred tool when she wanted to bend things her way. As a result, Larisa Yohontova sat in near darkness waiting and wondering why she had been called away from class to see the Madame.

Larisa realized she had fallen asleep in the dark room when the light from the opened door and the sound of rustling satin woke her.

Madame Preobazhenskya wore a Chinoise dress of robin's egg mirror satin, nearly metallic in its shine, with a sash of eggshell silk, embroidered with pink and burgundy roses, tied around her waist. An antique ivory netsuke dragon hid the knot. Her blue lambskin boots matched her dress, and she wore a gold locket around her neck, the chain of heavy gold links doubled to emphasize its opulence. An arc of silver-brown Emu feathers graced her hair on a comb. Her rose and cinnamon perfume matched her habiliments and soon filled the room.

She sat down and picked up her fountain pen (that matched her dress). Then, she opened Larisa's folder and called for Martina.

Martina entered, now adopting a bending, servile attitude. "Yes, Ma'am?"

"See, Martina, that Larisa and I are not disturbed. Cancel all meetings until I have dealt with..." She gestured with her open palm toward Larisa, who was still blinking awake, as if pushing an unappetizing plate of food away, "...this mess."

"Yes, Madame Preobazhenskya," said Martina as she left.

"Mess?" asked Larisa. "Is there a problem?"

"I am sure you were not aware, but while you have been sleeping in our dormitory, eating our veal blanquette, occupying a chair in our classes, and using our paper and pens, your father has not paid your tuition bill in nine months!" Larisa's eyes opened wide. "That is the mess of which I speak."

"This simply cannot be, " answered Larisa. "Why would he not pay?"

"At first I waited for him to visit. I was planning to inquire about his liquidity when he and I could have a private, personal conversation. But, as you know, he has not come. Desperate for further understanding of the situation, I sent my agent recently. I am sorry to say that, when my agent went around to collect from your father and, of course, to inquire as to his wellbeing, repeatedly, no one answered at his door."

"Oh dear. This is unlike father completely. Not visiting could be understood. He was busy with his new business venture. But not to pay, well..."

"My agent inquired of some of your father's workers who had installed themselves, as debtors, in your father's courtyard hoping to confront him. They, too, have not been paid. His foreman, Kramerov, said there was no harvest last Spring and cannot be another for two years. He has moved on from your father's employ as a result."

"This simply cannot be!" exclaimed Larisa.

Madame Preobazhenskya grandly leafed through the folder before her on the desk. She took out an envelope. She elaborately removed an onion-skin letter and showed it to Larisa. It was written in scrolly hand (by Martina) on her (fabricated) agent's stationery.

"This letter from my agent summarizes a conversation he had with your father when he waylaid him quite early one morning as your father tied his horse in the stables. In this letter, your father admits it would be impossible to pay for your education and offers to agree to—I say this delicately—an arrangement. To pay."

"An arrangement?"

"Yes. Your father has signed an agreement with me whereby I may take certain actions on his behalf. And yours. In return, I will retire his debt."

Larisa stared across the desk at the letter, silent.

"It was either agree to that," continued the Madame, "or I'd be forced to stand by while he went to debtor's prison. I could not countenance that. I saw no alternative. I simply had to agree."

"Prison? Oh dear." Larisa's eyes filled with tears. She took a small cotton handkerchief from her sleeve and wiped her eyes. "And what action does my father authorize you to take on his—or...my behalf?"

(There was, in fact no agreement. There was a forged document created by Martina against the possibility that Larisa should demand to see it.)

"The agreement, which has been signed by your father, allows me to find a likely man to engage with you in marriage. In exchange, I will initiate a full settlement of your father's liabilities. We will, together you and I, be saving his life. You know how life within the walls of a debtor's prison is, do you not, Larisa?"

(In fact, Piotr Mikhailovich Yohontov had told the agent that he could and would not pay and, as a result, abandoned any claim to his daughter. This fabricated arrangement would be pure profit for Preobazhenskya School for Girls, which was known to American men on the western frontier as the best source of Russian mail-order brides. Madame Preobazhenskya would bank 15,000 rubles.)

Larisa sat silent for a moment, deep in thought. Then, with resolve, she said:

"Madame Preobazhenskya, I came to your school to be prepared for marriage. You have provided me with an education. I accept such an arrangement if it compensates you for my education, saves my father's finances, and keeps him from the prison door."

"So it shall," said Madame Preobazhenskya. Having succeeded in hiding the truth about Larisa's father, she now felt she could move on. "I have decided on your best prospect, Larisa. He is a fine man," (she knew him only in letters), "Who will pension your father." (he would do nothing of the sort, not knowing of a father, since Larisa had been presented as an orphan).

"I am much relieved by this news," Larisa said quietly, setting her resolve to make this work.

Madame Preobazhenskya slid the silver tray holding the bright red Samogon into the center of the desk between them. She poured a glass for each of them.

"Let us toast your future marriage. Vzdrognem!" said Madame. "Let your table break from abundance and your bed break from love-making!"

The beetroot Samogon burned going down. Their eyes teared. They laughed at the strength of the liqueur together. After a moment:

"May I know about my future husband?" asked Larisa.

"His name is Leon Anderson and he lives in the town Wenatchee in the Washington state of America. He is rich. He owns a mill for grinding flour on many acres of land."

"Is he kind?" asked Larisa.

"Kind? Well...I do know he is...very enthusiastic...to have a bride!"

✦

Leon Anderson soaped the cracked leather seats in his wagon until they shined bright burgundy in the afternoon sunlight. Carrying a bucket and a cloth, he wiped every wooden surface until the grain was visible, open, and glowing. He planned to tie a pink ribbon to every fourth spoke on his wagon wheels, so he stowed a bobbin of ribbon under the wagon seat along with a brand new loden blanket in case the weather turned. Three-and-a-half days to Seattle and four days back to Wenatchee, since he would have to trot the horses to be sure the bride stayed comfortable. Starting with July 3rd—the day she would arrive, he booked two rooms in every hotel (one for him and one for her)—so she could maintain her privacy like a lady. He packed an oilcloth tarp to cover her things in the wagon. *She will surely bring things, won't she?* he thought. He picked a huge bouquet of wildflowers from a thicket upstream of the mill, counting three times to be sure he would present an even number of stems. He had heard that Russian women were superstitious in the extreme and odd numbers were inauspicious. He made a bouquet the best he could, placed it in a ceramic jar he had lashed to the wagon to keep the blossoms fresh.

For weeks before her arrival, he practiced ten phrases of Russian so he could say:

1. Welcome
2. My name is Leon
3. This will be your new home
4. I have this for you
5. Bathroom
6. Kitchen
7. Mill
8. Watch out!
9. Kiss me
10. Good morning/evening/night

Leon's mill property had a large house on it, although it would need considerable work to transform it from a rustic single-man's cabin to a refined manor that a lady could enjoy living in. It needed decorating. He had sent for printed wallpaper from Kenosha, Wisconsin, yet weeks after they arrived, the rolls still stood upended in a box in the corner of the room connected to the parlor, which he assumed would become their dining room. Leon used this room as his mud room. In fact, he used every room in the eight-room house as a mud room. Coming in from the mill, he would kick off his boots anywhere, creating a puddle of brown mud mixed with flour and grain that would dry into a mound of hard, crackled dirt with a pair of boots stuck to the floor in the center. That meant the place was desperate for a cleaning. It also needed to be painted. The kitchen walls seemed to have wallpaper of their own, since scores of mosquito carcasses ("the official bird of Washington State") were stuck to the wall by their guts where Leon swatted them and left them to dry.

A woman would want privacy. Window curtains, shipped from Liverpool, New York, sat folded in paper bags waiting to be hung on iron rods that leaned in a corner. Leon, knowing nothing about hanging curtains, even less about decorating and hardly anything about women (having been around his mother for only thirteen years before he moved out to be apprenticed to a millwright) convinced himself that his future wife would want to press the curtains and hang them (and the wallpaper) herself.

And so undecorated, dirty, and in need of curtains and paint is how Leon left the house on June 30th to go meet his bride at the dock in Seattle. In spite of his best intentions, the house that would greet the bride when she arrived at her new home nine days later would be a mix of hopeful gestures (buying wallpaper and curtains) and harsh reality (Leon). Lovely from the outside but a plague of projects on the inside.

At least, Leon thought, *she'll see the house from the outside first. She'll feel lucky to have a handsome log home. Then I can break the mess to her gradually. Besides, these projects will provide Larisa with ways to fill her time while I work. That's a boon!*

Leon was not tall. Only five-foot-seven in his moose-hide work-boots. His black hair was parted in the middle and Rowland's Macassar Oil kept it flat to his head and shiny like licorice. His eyes were small, which gave him an intense look—it often appeared like he was staring, even when he was simply glancing casually. His smile was winning, although his teeth were stained from tobacco, which he spat constantly, yet only while he worked. He had the body of a millwright—shoulders and chest expanded—a thin, long, almost delicate neck and muscular stomach, tight like a cat's. All in all, the impression he made was neat and vigorous. He was someone you could (correctly) place confidence in. Leon owned land, ran a successful business, and shunned drink. Any woman, let alone one who travelled 5,400 sea miles to meet him, would have found him to be a catch—even more so for having distinguished himself from the drunks, vagrants, and itinerants that constituted the largest part of the male population of Washington State in 1900.

That was precisely Larisa's reaction when she left the shipboard immigration desk and saw a man with a bouquet of flowers standing at the far end of the gangway. He had written in his last letter before her departure that he would have flowers. And he did!

She thought, *this man is worth my preparation.*

Leon became transfixed by her as she came closer. She looked stately, well-bred, yet completely approachable. She looked regal without looking haughty. She was elegant yet not over-done.

Leon thought, *this girl is worth my investment.*

Larisa had chosen her clothes for her arrival carefully: a brown bias-cut scotch-plaid skirt with a bishop-sleeved French flannel blouse. Around her neck hung a pink lapis lazuli cameo of Saints Piotr and Fevronia, Russian patrons of marriage and fidelity (their legs entwined in a slightly lustful pose), a gift from Madame Preobazhenskya on departure. She wore three rings on her right hand—a silver communion signet, a gold and onyx oval, and a plain gold band that had been her mother's wedding ring. Her hair, the best she could do given the small ship's cabin and the scratched metal mirror, was in a modified Pompadour—*au courant* in Kiev—curls piled high on her head, cascading down to her collar. It had been a while since she had fixed her own hair. There were servants for that at school. "One must learn how to live with servants as well as manage them," said Madame Preobazhenskya. "Being placid while a servant dresses your hair shows good breeding and fine birth." Larisa imagined there would be a similarly ample number of servants in the household of Leon Anderson.

With hope, Larisa Yohontova made her way down the gangplank toward her future husband holding five Russian rubles in her hand as her tip for the porter. As she got close to the man with the bouquet, she noticed more about him. He wore a deep blue denim work jacket over a collarless shirt. His tan oilcloth trousers fit tightly around his thighs and calves. His hair, in spite of the several days of journeying, was carefully combed (He had packed a hand mirror for the occasion and carefully made himself presentable using a gray horn comb while the ship maneuvered into its berth and Larisa waited to be cleared ashore). As she made eye contact, Leon bowed slightly at the waist and bent his knees slightly in what resolved itself to be an awkward curtsy. But he smiled at his awkwardness, so she smiled back.

She thought, *this man is worth my attention.*

Leon stuck out his bouquet hand in an over-enthusiastic thrust, gawkily destroying what he planned to be a perfect moment.

"*Dia menya?*" she asked, giving a slight curtsy of her own.

"These are for you," said Leon.

The smell of the flowers (or his hair oil) filled her nostrils.

"Thanks you," said Larisa. "I do not speak very well. English. Sorry...I.. do not speak English very well." Larisa had studied English conversation with Madame Schaeffer, the German and English language teacher, as part of the standard form at school, so she could speak and understand English conversation fairly well.

"That's fine English," said Leon.

"You are kind. It is school English. I have not had time much for speaking with someone for practice."

He took her hand.

"We'll practice together then," said Leon. Then to the porter: "My wagon is down the way, if you won't find it too far."

Leon thought, *this girl is worth my effort.*

They walked together to the wagon. Larisa laughed lightly when she saw the pink ribbons tied to the spokes. She could feel Leon waiting for her reaction. She touched two of the ribbons, feeling the fabric smooth between her fingers.

"How kind," she said. And thought, *this man is worth my trust.*

She squeezed his hand and they turned to look at each other. She stood on her tiptoes.

Leon filled with joy. *This girl,* he thought, *is worth my joy.*

The porter and Leon loaded the wagon and tucked Larisa's valises and boxes under the tarp. Larisa tipped him with her rubles and he set off back up the gangway.

"It is four days to Wenatchee," said Leon as he brought Larisa to the passenger side of the wagon. "We have a stop in Tacoma first to pick up a China set I ordered for our new home."

"China set?"

"Plates for eating off." He gestured a circle on his open palm, then pantomimed taking a bite.

"Oh, yes. *Blyuda.*"

"We will get to Tacoma by evening and stay at the Reynolds Hotel overnight." He helped her up on the running board and further up onto the bench. "We'll have supper there and get an early start in the morning. Am I speaking too fast?"

"You speak fast, although I understand. Hotel, supper. Early the morning we go."

They spoke energetically as they rode to Tacoma, asking each other questions and sharing details of the complicated circling that brought them to this place, this ride.

At the hotel, they both felt sad to part. Larisa paused before she climbed the stairs to her room and Leon looked up at her just before he left to get the horses watered, fed, and stabled. They made a plan to meet at eight for supper in the hotel restaurant.

Larisa ate that meal with gusto, having had only ship's food for ten days. During dessert—*baba au rhum* with vanilla ice cream—Leon took a small box from his jacket pocket and placed it in front of Larisa.

"*U menya yest' eto dlya tebya.*" he ventured in Russian. "I have this for you. Will you marry me, Larisa?"

"This is why I am here!" She opened the box and took out a modest diamond ring. She put it on and held her hand up to Leon. "Bright! Shining! Beautiful!"

"More ice cream?" asked Leon.

This man is worthy of my love, Larisa thought as she lifted a spoonful of ice cream to her mouth.

✦

The mid-summer sun was warming the morning air when Larisa came to the lobby to meet Leon. Before sun-up, Leon had the horses bridled and the wagon brought to the entrance of the Reynolds Hotel. Then, he sat in the lobby reading the Tacoma Times newspaper, which he rarely saw in Wenatchee. Leon got, perhaps, forty-five minutes of solitude before the hotel started to awaken. Although he was alone when he first sat down to read, guests began to filter in at about 6:45 a.m. A few moments later, when Larisa descended the stairs into the lobby, the benefit of a good night of sleep in a hotel bed, rather than a ship's berth, showed on her rested face. Her eyes seemed brighter and softer, her lips less stern. As soon as she came close, Leon put his hand out to take hers. Without rising from his chair, he dandled her hand, feeling her warm fingers resting in his palm. They were already at ease together.

Her peony-scented perfume was exhilarative.

"Good morning, fiancé," she said, smiling.

"Good morning, fiancée. May I take you to breakfast?"

"Yes, may," said Larisa.

They ate together, busily conversing about everything from the restaurant's folded napkins to the vagaries of running a profitable mill business. When Leon looked at his pocket-watch (bought especially for this occasion), he saw nearly an hour had passed.

They needed to leave before 8:00 a.m. or they would not make tonight's hotel before twilight.

The lobby was fully bustling by the time they finished their eggs (with sausage for Leon, kippers for Larisa), coffee (tea for Larisa), and warm, crusty sourdough bread. They left the restaurant and stepped into a lobby packed with milling tourists avid to watch the Independence Day parade. Several groups carrying red, white, and blue pom-poms assembled in the space close to the registration desk so that their leader could pass out streetcar tickets. A woman in suffragette white and wearing a tiered hat of white, blue, and pink silk roses admonished her group as she handed out tickets:

"...trollies stop directly opposite the hotel. It is a twenty-minute ride from the hotel to downtown. Only an early departure will insure you get the best standing place for viewing the parade! Take your ticket and board directly, please!"

Nearby, a group of men assembled—veterans of the recent Spanish-American War—in full dress uniform, ribbons, gold braids, cavalry hats, and parade swords. They practiced unfurling their banner, raising their swords and shouting, "Remember the Maine! Hip hip hooray!" This was followed by much confused clattering as they restored their swords to their scabbards.

Larisa and Leon made their way through this crowd hand-in-hand. As the porter finished loading their wagon and Larisa and Leon mounted the driver's bench, the crowd suddenly shifted. Trolley number 55 suddenly emptied, the crowd abandoned the streetcar and returned to the sidewalk. Leon overheard comments...

"We'll have to wait..."

"There will be room on the next one..."

"Out of commission..."

...as the destination signs rolled from "Downtown" to "Out of Service." The crowd engulfed Leon's wagon, so the horses were unable to move. Leon and Larisa had to wait.

Just a few moments later, a nearly-full streetcar (number 116) pulled up on a second track, next to streetcar 55. As if they were iron filings and the newly-arrived trolley was a magnet, the crowd that had occupied trolley 55 was drawn to fill every open space available on trolley 116. Leon overheard comments...

"Make way!"

"I was here first!"

"C'mon, make room!"

...as the passengers struggled to find a handhold on the packed car's railings.

With the sidewalk now abandoned and the way open, Leon carefully eased his horses forward, leaving the crowd on the streetcar behind to sort itself out.

Once safely away from the curb, he turned his attention to Larisa.

"We'll soon leave all this Independence Day hoopla behind and have a quiet day on the trail. I have to follow Delin Street this way. It'll lead us to the wagon trail. The trail runs below the C-Street trestle. Just shortly after we pass that, we'll be out of town. It will be a quiet ride from there."

"Please not worry. I am happy if I am with you."

Leon traced Delin Street for a few blocks and exited the paved road into the dusty wagon way. The morning did, indeed, quiet down and it was possible to hear birdsong between the beats of the horse's hooves.

Yet, as they crossed under the C-Street trestle, there was a deafening...

Buzz.

Grind.

Whir.

Thunder.

Metal. Wood. Glass breaking. Wheels falling.

A shower of hats. The white, blue, and pink silk rose hat bouncing, then rolling in the grass.

Large, bulky bags packed with ears of corn landing around them with a thud.

Not bags. Not corn.

People.

Dying as they thud onto the ground.

A falling sword, or a beam, or shard of glass, slicing through Leon's long, delicate neck, swiftly, like a guillotine.

His head landing on the wagon floor next to Larisa's feet, eyes fluttering closed, then open. Staring. His headless body slumping against her shoulder.

Blood flooding the wagon.

The smell of brake fluid. Engine oil. Shit.

The horses—spooked—galloped forward. The wagon jerked behind them.

Larisa, breathless, struggling to make sense of what is happening. Unable to put it together.

She knew one thing, beyond doubt:

Everything had changed.

✦

FORTY-THREE
KILLED IN TACOMA
Crowded Trolley Car Plunges
One Hundred Feet into Ravine

TACOMA, Washington, July 4.— Nearly a hundred passengers on a streetcar bound for Tacoma city were plunged into a gulch at Twenty-sixth and C-Streets shortly after 8 o'clock this morning. Those who were standing on the running boards of the car dropped off and tumbled into the ravine to be bruised, wounded, or killed by the heavy body of the car. Others inside were killed by the fall. The car jumped the track and broke to pieces in midair. What remained smashed to kindling wood in the bottom of the chasm over a hundred feet below. The dead number over three-score. Many of the injured are expected to die at any moment and others are now in the various hospitals and under the care of their own physicians.

The car that carried its human freight into the ravine was No. 116 of the United Traction Company's cars. It was on the Edison line. It left Edison via Delin Street at 8 o'clock under the charge of F. L. Boehm, motorman, and J. D. Calhoun, conductor. The car was crowded to the doors and beyond, due to the breakdown of a previously scheduled car, which released its passengers to board already-crowded replacement car, No. 116. Every inch of the standing platforms were occupied as people hung on to the railings. Everything went smoothly until the car reached the hill beyond Tacoma Avenue. It appears that the motorman, when starting down the hill, turned his current up instead of shutting it down. When the car had gained such momentum that it was getting away from him, he shut down the motor, yet by then it was too late. The car was moving at lightning speed and there was nothing to bring it to a standstill on the steep downward incline. Passengers on the front platform, who could see the sharp turn coming as the car left Delin Street, endeavored to jump. A few brave souls landed safely, but most fell nearly 100 feet to their death among debris, window glass and falling metal that included several swords carried by veterans of the recent Spanish war. One of the dead was the unidentified driver of a wagon unfortunately passing under the bridge trestle precisely when the car when it plunged off the tracks. The accident was one of the most hideous that has ever occurred in Tacoma city. The unfortunate victims were residents of nearby towns: Hillhurst, Lakeview, Parkland, Lake Park, and other places. They were bound for downtown Tacoma to attend the Tacoma Fourth of July parade.

✦

After the thunderous noise of the accident, the air, thick with the burnt smell of brake lining, stiffened and fell starkly silent. The only sound was the empty, overturned trolley sporadically creaking and cracking under its own weight, and the low, distant groan of people dying.

Without a driver, Leon's horses galloped 600 yards past where the mangled streetcar lay. When the horses pulled up, the wagon came to a stop on the far side of the trestle in a small grove of trees. Larisa realized she was out of danger. If she had known how to steer a wagon behind a team of horses (or was familiar with the route to Wenatchee) she would have driven on without hesitation. But she did not know how to drive, so she sat in the stationary wagon trying to will her heartbeat to return to normal. First, she imagined that she was in Kiev awaiting a rendezvous with an acquaintance for a picnic in Mariyinsky Park. That didn't work. Then, she daydreamed that she was moments from a tree-shaded tumble with a lover in a secret grove on Volodymyrska Hill. That helped a bit.

One of the horses whinnied and stamped, jolting her back to the reality of Tacoma, the blood-soaked wagon-bed and Leon's empty eyes. *This man,* she thought, *is worth my...* but she stopped mid-thought. She was shocked at the reality of what she felt as she looked at him: nothing. Leon was nice. He had been kind. Even pleasant to be with. During their day together, hope—maybe love?—had started to grow in her like a seedling. Had started. Useless, now, it withered. She felt forsaken. Alone. Yet she told herself that, in reality, she hardly knew Leon. She did not miss him, really. She could not mourn him. She looked back on her time with Leon and it felt like an interrupted dream. A dream that decays, slips away, ebbs from memory as moments of wakefulness erase it. Larisa thought she could either look back from the grove of trees and dwell on the time they had together or she could look forward and away, into the future.

She thought for a moment. *I am fine. Bestow wonder on St. Kristofer, there is not a mark on me. Aside from the mess on my shoes and the need to recast my thoughts of what life would be like for me from now on, I haven't a worry. There is a mill, a wagon. There are horses. And a house. A house with—who knows what?— inside. I need to be clever. I need to be resourceful. I need to have a plan. I must travel to Wenatchee. I must settle in my new home. Leon is yesterday. Gone. A song. A dream. A fairy tale. I must go forward!*

In a few moments of thought, Leon's death became a practical problem more than a personal loss. Larisa Yohontova used her foot to carefully roll Leon's head to the far side of the wagon and wiped his blood off her shoes using a blanket she found stashed under the driver's bench. She wiped the few blood spots from her blouse and quickly switched her mother's wedding band from her right to her left hand.

There. *From this moment,* she thought. *I am Leon's wife.*

She climbed down from the wagon and sat alone under a birch tree. It would just be a matter of waiting until she came to someone's attention. She wanted them to come to her.

✦

Nearly two hours passed. Larisa fell asleep in the July heat despite the buzzing cicadas, the distant shouting and the low, desperate moaning of the dying. When she was jolted awake by three men, talking as they approached, it felt as if it was tomorrow. As if she had slept a night.

MAN 1: ...no I'm quite sure. There—
MAN 2: Just under that tree?
MAN 1: Yes. By the wagon.
MAN 3: Careful of the horses—
MAN 2: —could be skittish.

The men came right to Larisa. She kept her eyes closed, pretending to sleep and hoping to suss out their intentions before committing to being awake.

MAN 1: Hey, lady! You okay?
MAN 2: Of course she's okay. Look at her, napping while hundreds breathe their last breath!
MAN 1: Not hundreds.
MAN 2: Nearly a hundred. Wanna bet it's that many? I bet it will be.

MAN 3: Gentlemen, stop.
MAN 2: Two dollars says it is!
MAN 1: Two dollars says it ain't!
MAN 3: Guys, quit it.
MAN 2: Quit what? I don't mean nothing by it. Just a good-natured bet—

Larisa opened her eyes. Police.

OFFICER 1: Lady, are you just gonna lie there? Can't you see there has been an accident?
LARISA: Yes. I know of accident. I, myself, was in this wagon, which, itself, was passing under the bridge when the train, itself, fell. My husband was killed by falling things. His body is there in the wagon.
OFFICER 2: Good God!
OFFICER 3: Our condolence, ma'am... We've come by to see about you. And offer help. LARISA: I need nothing.
OFFICER 3: Well, ma'am, I mean no disrespect but you've had some doings here. I'd say [GESTURING TOWARD THE WAGON] —just based on a quick look—you need help.
LARISA: Well...yes. [PAUSE.] Yes. Is so. [PAUSE.] What kind help can I have from you?
OFFICER 2: Why don't you say what you want—
OFFICER 1: —ma'am—
OFFICER 2: — and we will see if we can do it.
LARISA: [PAUSE] Emm...I will need to arrange the bury of my husband. That help I need. Here in Tacoma. He would want to rest here. I am sure. Where he is from. Is this kind of help you can do?
OFFICER 2: A funeral service attended by your family? We can see about that.
LARISA: He— we — have—no family. I am all of his family. No people to attending. Just to bury.
OFFICER 2: That'll take a few days to arrange, ma'am. Them horses will need to be put up for the few days it'll take to get your husband in the ground. We will take the body. Um... and the head, ma'am.

OFFICER 1: Ralph, you don't have to be so blunt.

OFFICER 3: Sorry for him, ma'am. Your husband's body—mister...?

LARISA: Anderson. Mr. Leon Anderson.

OFFICER 3:— will go with us to the morgue.

OFFICER 1: Do you need a doctor, ma'am? Anything hurt we ought'ta know about?

LARISA: No. I am fine. It is miracle. I am fine. Only I could use place to lie down.

RALPH: We will bring you to the Sheriff's operations desk up the top of the ravine. He will get you a place and keep an eye on your things and this here wagon.

LARISA: Kind.

It took several more hours of Larisa waiting alone for one of the officers to return. He came with a Sergeant Shinn, who addressed Larisa as Mrs. Anderson, which pleased her. Her plan was working.

SERGEANT SHINN: Mrs. Anderson, the city will provide you lodging space in the women's nursing rooms at the YMCA. You can stable your horses and store your wagon, which Ralph here tells me needs some cleaning, at Foster's Stables down the road from the Y. They will clean it for you.

LARISA: Mr. Shinn, I do not—cannot—drive. My husband was doing our driving to home to Wenatchee when this accident happens. I, sad, do not do driving.

SERGEANT SHINN: My officers will get your wagon and horses to Foster's. Then we will need to enlist someone to drive you and the wagon on to your home. We will get someone with his own horse to return on. I will discuss this with my superior officer so he knows about your situation, Ma'am.

Larisa passed three days mostly sleeping in a small, neat bed at the YMCA. When she wasn't sleeping, she was being questioned about all the details she could recall about the accident. She spoke to police, sheriff's officers, representatives of the trolley company, engineers. They questioned her about every sight, sound, smell of the accident, large facts, tiny details; hundreds of questions. The one thing no one questioned, however, was Larisa's marriage to Leon. From the moment she met the men in the grove after the accident, she was assumed to be Leon's wife.

On the fourth day there was a funeral for Leon in the yard of the Tacoma Lutheran Church. Elm seeds helicoptered down onto the mourners—the three police officers Larisa had met in the grove, Tom, Ralph, and Jeremiah—and Larisa (who subtly and repeatedly pinched herself in the soft skin under her arm to bring the tears she thought were appropriate to a grieving widow). Luckily, the minister, overwhelmed by the number of funerals suddenly demanded of him, relied heavily on the liturgy and didn't seek to customize much. This was good, as Larisa would not have been a fulgent source of personal information about Leon. The police officers plus the yard magistrate and the grave digger rounded out the crowd to make up five pall bearers. They sang "'Tis So Sweet to Trust in Jesus," recited the Apostle's Creed, and lowered the pine coffin into the hastily-finished grave. The funeral was over in twenty minutes. The men told Larisa how sorry they were.

Larisa thought, *I am one step closer to Wenatchee.*

✦

On the fifth day after the accident, a tall, serious-faced man holding a carefully-blocked brown straw cowboy hat inquired for a Mrs. Anderson at the YMCA. The day-clerk at the entrance desk walked to Larisa's door and knocked quietly. Larisa opened her door hesitantly.

"You have a visitor, Mrs. Anderson. Waiting for you in the lobby," said the clerk.

"It is not possible," said Larisa. "I know no one."

"He's a tall man with a watch chain and a cowboy hat."

Larisa was intrigued. "Just a moment. I come down to see."

She checked her face and hair in the mirror, applied some rouge to her chin and nose and walked down the stairs.

There was, indeed, a tall man with a cowboy hat standing in the center of the braided rag rug at the bottom of the stairs. Larisa stood one step from the bottom in order to make eye contact and put out her hand.

"I am Larisa Anderson," she noticed it was the first time she was using that name.

"William Grayson, Ma'am. People call me Chance."

"A pleasure, Mr. Grayson," said Larisa, noticing that his eyes were silver-gray. "What I can do for you?"

"I have been hired, Ma'am, to drive your wagon, your horses, and yourself to Wenatchee."

"Ahh. Now I understand who are you. Very good," said Larisa.

"I will be back in the morning and I'll be ready to depart at precisely 8:10," said Grayson, glancing at his pocket watch. "Please be ready for me then."

"Yes. I will be ready," said Larisa. "This is a work?"

Grayson put on his hat. He habitually felt to see if his watch was safely restored to his vest pocket, checked for his Derringer in his pants pocket, and turned on his heel.

"I will see you in the morning, ma'am."

He walked into the sunshine, leaving Larisa alone on the first stair looking into the empty air where his gray eyes had been.

✦

After "good morning," and the few bits of conversation needed to get Larisa and her things on the wagon, Grayson fell quiet. Larisa found speaking English tiring, so she retreated into silence, too, speaking to herself in Russian as they went along.

After about four-and-a-half hours of silence, as the wagon made its way under his guidance, Grayson's ventured:

GRAYSON: Yes.

LARISA: Yes? What is yes?

GRAYSON: Yes. It is.

LARISA: Is? What is?

GRAYSON: My work. You asked me if this was my work. It is.

LARISA: I ask you that all the way yesterday. And you answer now? Like no time passed?

GRAYSON: Yes. Did you want to know?

LARISA: Of course. I ask don't I?

GRAYSON: You did.

LARISA: So...I want to know.

GRAYSON: Yes. This is my work. I am a security agent with the Pinkerton National Detective Agency.

LARISA: What is National Detective Agency? Detective?

GRAYSON: A detective figures out crimes. Me? I am not a detective. I am a private security guard. Although, being a detective wouldn't be bad. It'd be a job with less risk.

LARISA: Risk?

GRAYSON: I am often on details—these sorts of jobs—that require me to guard someone.

LARISA: You guard me?

GRAYSON: Yes. That is my assignment. To ensure your travel from Tacoma to Wenatchee is safe.

LARISA: I am safe. I have travelled far already with no guarding.

GRAYSON: Sounds like you have.

LARISA: I come to America from Kiev. Russia. Ukraine. Lithuania.

GRAYSON: Those all one place?

LARISA: City is Kiev.

GRAYSON: Far? From here I mean?

LARISA: I travel for nearly one month from there to here. Well... to Seattle.

GRAYSON: That's a mighty while.

LARISA: I don't follow that English. Sorry.

GRAYSON: Mighty far. You traveled far to get here.

LARISA: Yes. Tired from traveling.

GRAYSON: I enjoy traveling. I'm not sure I could ever stay in one place. That becomes a foothold, I'm afraid.

LARISA: More words I do not understand.

GRAYSON: [MAKES A SWEEPING MOTION WITH HIS FINGERS] I'd like to move. Not stay. [POINTS DOWNWARD] In. One. Place.

LARISA: Yes. Understand. This from Kiev to Seattle was my first time to travel. All I know before is [POINTS DOWNWARD] stay in one place.

GRAYSON: Seeing this country is something.

LARISA: I would like to see. But rest first, then travel.

GRAYSON: Travel! I am grateful my job has given me an opportunity to travel. I've been from north to south and from sea to shining sea!

LARISA: Ahhh...America Beautiful song!

They laughed, quieted, and then drove the rest of the day in amiable silence. With a few polite words at the hotel they parted for the evening. Their plan was to meet at precisely 8:20 a.m. the next day to drive on.

In the morning, making brief, functional conversation, they left the hotel stables. It was cloudy, gray, muggy, and threatening rain. They both wore raincoats that were too warm for the day. Grayson pushed the team to a gallop when he could because speed meant a cooling breeze. At 2:12 p.m., Grayson checked his watch. He was itching to ask Larisa something but wanted to find just the right moment. He hoped to ask when she would be open to answer truthfully. It would take three more hours to get to the next hotel. He kept his eyes on the road and on a yellow stripe of sunlight beyond the clouds and just above the horizon. A threatening day, yet it hadn't rained. Now that he could see the sky clearing, he was sure it wouldn't rain. He felt relaxed and open. He hoped Larisa would, too. So, a few minutes later, he asked:

"You did not know the man you buried in Tacoma. Is that right?"

Larisa thought: *How does he know? How could he know? He cannot know.*

She cleared her throat as if she was about to speak yet said nothing. She thought further: *I have to tell him the truth sometime before arriving in Wenatchee because we will need to inquire how to find Leon's mill. I need to tell him. Yet, Madame Preobazhenskya would have counseled me to wait to answer. Everything, the Madame would say, is improved by waiting.*

So Larisa waited. A few hours later, when the sun was setting behind them, the air was cool, blue and had the smell of zinc, she felt ready.

LARISA: Have you been in love, Mr, Grayson?
GRAYSON: Well...that's personal. [PAUSE.] Why so formal? Why call me Mr. Grayson?

The ride had brought him closer to her. Her formality surprised and disappointed him a bit.

LARISA: Just to be polite.
GRAYSON: I'd be okay with you calling me William. Or Will. But not Mr. Grayson. When I hear that I think you are talking to my grandaddy!

She paused a moment. Then, smiling:

LARISA: Mr. Grayson, have you been in love?

He was beginning to like her grit. Her question signified she was not a woman who trifled.

GRAYSON: Ahh. Well, love is personal. I don't like to talk about personal things when I'm working.
LARISA: [LAUGHING] In other word, yes. You have.
He marked her playful tone. She was confident enough to doodle with him. That interested him.
GRAYSON: [PAUSE.] Yes. Indeed, I have. I loved the woman who became my wife.

LARISA: You have wife?

GRAYSON: No. No longer. She passed.

LARISA: What do you mean, passed?

GRAYSON: Died. Like your husband. Two years and seven months ago.

LARISA: Ah. I see.

She paused again. Then:

LARISA: I tell you now. Leon was, it is true, not my husband. But you say I did not know him. This is not true, quite, either.

GRAYSON: So...you did know him?

LARISA: I knew him. We are writing many letters back to forth. Many, many letters. With some public things we say and, later, many private ones. Knew him? I knew him well. Met him? Only I met him for a few days. Then he, like your wife, passed.

GRAYSON: Ah. That is sad.

LARISA: I came from Russia to be Leon's wife and he was killed by streetcar from sky. We were to be married, but his death is before we do. So, in Tacoma, I make funeral like wife. I bury this man who was my possible life. Possible life ends. So...then I go with you to my house. [PAUSE.] Well...would be my house. But...

GRAYSON: I see.

LARISA: You see?

GRAYSON: Yes. I do. You were...left...alone.

LARISA: Yes. Left alone. [PAUSE.] You see. What you see?

Grayson admired her indomitability. Different than any woman he had met before.

GRAYSON: Well...I can see what you're doing and I can see why you're doing it. Being a lady leaves you not much choice, really. If I was in your place, I might, by needs, do the same thing.

LARISA: Yes.

She has pluck, he thought.

GRAYSON: I will get you to your home sound and safe.

LARISA: Those words I do not understand.

GRAYSON: I will drive you to the mill and, once I am sure you are safe, I will leave and head back to Tacoma.

LARISA: Now I understand. [PAUSE] Thank you.

The conversation on the last two days of the drive to Wenatchee was a mirror image of the first two. Freed from her secret, Larisa became voluble. She effused about her life in Russia, her father, school, leaving for America to meet Leon. The long, solitary ship voyage. Her short time with Leon. Grayson, who had begun to regard Larisa, asked her to call him Chance. He returned her chattiness with information about his life: the wife of twelve years he had nursed but lost to the Spanish influenza, the many nights spent sleeping sitting up in train seats to guard Senator John Lockwood Wilson, keeping vigil on horseback to get a weekly strongbox delivered to San Francisco, and nights riding in a coach disguised as a dandy to protect a well-heeled gambler.

Floating on a river of talk, they arrived in Wenatchee late in the afternoon. They inquired at the post office how they might find Leon Anderson's mill. Chance followed the directions he was given to a clearing by a stream next to a brown-shingled building with a large waterwheel. The sluice was open and the wheel was not turning, A boy, about seventeen years old, sat on the mill porch with his hat pulled over his eyes. At the sound of the approaching wagon he raised his hat, rubbed his eyes and walked enthusiastically to greet it.

"How d'y'do?" said the boy as he walked up to the horses, scratching one between the ears. He spoke to it quietly: "Scarlet, you're a good girl." Then he looked harshly at Chance and Larisa. "I thought it was Leon. What are you doing driving Leon's horses and wagon? Where is Leon?"

CHANCE: Do you know where Leon was headed last week?

BOY: Went to Tacoma to meet his mail-order bride and drive her back here.

CHANCE: Well, this is his bride—his wife.

BOY: How d'y'do ma'am?

LARISA: I am well, thank you.

BOY: Where's Leon? Why do you have his wagon?

CHANCE: There was an accident in Tacoma and, sad to tell, Leon lost his life in it. Mrs. Anderson, here, cannot drive, so I was appointed to drive her home. I work for Pinkerton's, if you've heard of us?

BOY: [TO LARISA] You his bride?

LARISA: I am. Married in Tacoma.

BOY: I work here. In the mill. My name is Luther. Leon is my boss and I'm his apprentice. We work the mill while I'm learning the mill. He told me he would be back five days ago, so I've come everyday looking to see when he'd get back. I guess he won't actually be coming back now.

LARISA: He won't come. No...he won't.

LUTHER: Then should I go?

LARISA: [PAUSE] Let us say that for now only. Come back in three days. By then I will settle and be ready to learn mill. We work mill while I learn mill. I will be apprentice to you for mill.

Luther smiled faintly, thanked them, and walked off into the woods.

Chance liked Larisa's way with the boy, her honesty about Leon, and her saying she'd be his apprentice. She gave the boy confidence from the start.

After they looked around the house and the yard together, Chance unhitched, watered, and fed the horses, put the wagon up and then, keeping his promise, spurred his own horse for Tacoma.

Over the next week, Larisa cleaned the house, exploring as she went room by room. Luther came back as promised. Using Luther's knowledge and experience, they got the mill grinding. She noticed herself missing Chance, so she was pleased when, at the end of her second week alone at the mill, while carrying water from the cistern to the kitchen, she heard the sound of a horse coming up the mill road. As she hoped, but did not venture to expect, it was Chance, his saddle loaded with full bags and bedroll.

"Why you are here?" asked Larisa as she lifted her bucket to the house porch.

"Because you're here," answered Chance.

"Kind."

"I thought of you all the way back to Tacoma and then from Tacoma all the way back here."

Chance noticed that Larisa was wearing men's jeans and a work shirt. "You look like you work in a mill."

"That's for the reason that I do. I do work in mill," she answered. "I make use of Leon's old pant until buy some for me."

"Oh. Speaking of that, I brought you a catalog. Sears & Roebuck catalog. It's how you buy the things you need here. Just in case you need something—some things—for the house. Or for yourself. Like clothing. I have the book in my saddlebag."

"Come in. I about to boil tea. Please you join."

"Sure!" He unbuckled his saddlebag and grabbed the thick catalog to bring with him.

They spent the next few hours looking at items and laughing because they were extravagant or useless or odd, pointing at those they fantasized about having, debating which ones they could really use. Larisa had never seen anything like the catalog, and looking at it was the most indelible thing she had done with another person. When she finally tore herself from the table to refresh the water in the teapot, Larisa stood looking at the back of Chance's head. She felt her heart moving toward him. She asked him to stay for the weekend. He did, bunking on his bedroll in the mill's threshing room.

Two weeks later, he came back.

Then, back again two weeks after that.

Another two weeks passed. This time, Chance didn't come on Friday night, as she thought he might. She waited until 11:30p.m. and, in a wave of loneliness, climbed into her bed.

Saturday morning she was awakened by the scent of vanilla and clattering sounds coming from the kitchen. She pulled on one of the red union-suits she found in Leon's chifforobe and went to the kitchen. She opened the door carefully, not knowing what might be on the other side. When the door was opened wide enough, she saw Chance standing at the stove wearing a blue gingham apron, dusty with flour. He had a spatula in one hand and a long-handled fork in the other. He was bent over a black cast-iron contraption that, itself, was bent over one of the burners on the stove. He was surrounded by plates of various sizes piled high with stacks of flat pastries. Larisa had no idea what they were or what he was doing.

"Good morning!" said Chance sheepishly. "I thought you might want breakfast. I brought you this waffle maker. From Sears & Roebuck!" He tapped the black contraption with the fork and gestured to the plates and plates of waffles. "It works!"

"What is waffle maker? What is waffle?" asked Larisa.

"This," he pointed to a plate with the fork. "A waffle is like a pancake only square. And with divots? Pockets? Holes? To hold butter and syrup. Maple syrup."

"Maple syrup? More English I do not know," said Larisa.

"Here," said Chance picking up one of the plates of waffles and handing it to Larisa. "Put butter on these and then grab that tin. That's maple syrup. Pour some on and dig in! I made you tea. In the pot on the table."

Each of them sat in front of a pile of waffles, grinning as they ate.

"I like waffles," said Larisa with a laugh. "That is good since we have enough to feed all Wenatchee!"

"I got a little carried away," said Chance.

Larisa leaned across the table and kissed him on the lips.

That night, as usual, Chance retired to sleep in the mill. During the night he heard what he was certain were wolves, which concerned him.

CHANCE: Do you know how to shoot a gun?
LARISA: To shoot clay birds I do.

CHANCE: I see. I should teach you how to shoot a rifle. Leon kept one in the wagon. I'd feel better if I knew you could shoot that. When I left, I mean.

LARISA: When you left. [PAUSE.] Instead of teaching me to shoot, how about instead you do not leave?

Larisa did not need to ask twice. Chance made a final trip to Tacoma that Monday to gather his belongings. A week later he was back for good.

A busy year passed. Chance retired from Pinkerton's, and he and Larisa ran the mill, together with Luther. The business grew, expanding the number of customers as well as selling a line of Larance & Luther Genuine Wenatchee Pancake and Waffle Mix in a number of outlets, including the Sears & Roebuck catalogue.

One rainy and gray morning, with rain swelling the stream until it ran in streamlets and rivulets around the waterwheel, they were forced to shut down the mill for the day. Larisa and Chance sat in the room they designated as their office at their respective desks, Larisa pouring over the finance books and Chance applying a stag-horn letter opener to a stack of twenty or so envelopes of mail. Chance opened four envelopes, and all of them were orders for pancake and waffle mix. The fifth letter took him into deep concentration while he read it and even deeper thought afterwards:

The Barnum & Bailey Circus

```
Mister William Grayson
% Larance & Luther Mill
RFD-6491

Wenatchee, Washington

My dearest Chance,

Please overlook the affronting tardiness of
my writing to you. Don't you know Mary has
reminded me, at minimum once per fortnight,
```

to pen some sort of missive, however brief, to my friend in Tacoma? Well, here it is, finally.

I was recently made aware of the possibility that you have associated yourself with a business in Wenatchee. Wenatchee is a place where I and Mary have pillowed for the night more than once in the past few decades when the show found its winding way to the third-rate entertainment markets. I know the town and its unique longueurs. I also know it to have horrible weather almost year-round, save the sunny summer months conducive to making it the "Apple Capital of the World." As if that gives it an allure and doesn't make one think merely of the rotten smell at the bottom of the apple barrel.

Again, forgive my presumptuousness so I might ask: what the hell brought you to settle there?? Do I smell the intoxicating perfume of a dame?

I write, hoping I catch you at a moment of weakness regarding your faute de mieux, for I desire to lure you to take me up on the offer I made to you those several years ago. That of course being that I'd like you (and the dame, if there is one) to work security for my show. It would get you on the road, yet would be a so-much-easier gig compared to your body-guarding work.

Hopefully your domestic entanglement is not of the sort that has made you sensible and dull. Not so sensible that you won't jump at a chance to make some real dough, nor dull enough to miss the opportunity to run off with the circus!

Truly in honor,

Bailey

Front Office
   % Barnum & Bailey Circus
Cleveland, Ohio

A flash of lighting followed almost instantly by a clap of thunder
. The speed of the rain trebled, and it started to thrash the tin roof
and the windows. Chance and Larisa rose at the same time, walked
across the room and met at the wood-burning stove. They laughed
as they both reached for the same log of wood to feed the fire.

CHANCE: This is quite a storm.
LARISA: 'Rain like horses' we say in Russian.
CHANCE: Come away from your desk. Let's sit by the stove together
for a few minutes and warm.
LARISA: Of course. That would be nice.

They sat while the rain beat on the windows on either side of the
stove. The dripping raindrops rolled down the glass and made the
trees outside look like they were melting in the thin, gray light.

LARISA: Rain is good for the mill.
CHANCE: I'm not sure I can see any good in rain as heavy as this.
LARISA: Faster the water runs, faster we grind.
CHANCE: That's all we think about, though. Life could signify more
than how fast our stream flows and, thereby, how fast the millstone
turns. All we talk about is how many wagons are lined up in the
drive. Or how wet the wheat or how dry the rye is this year. We could
have fuller lives.
LARISA: When water runs fast, money comes fast. Wagons lined up
means customers waiting to grind. These are things we need.
CHANCE: Don't you get tired of it all day every day? Don't you want
more? I'll tell you, I do!
LARISA: I have you, Luther, my home, and the mill. How could I
want more?

CHANCE: I admire that in you. You are content with what life gives you. I guess I am a bit more restless. Maybe it's my nature. Or maybe it's this rain and being cooped inside.

LARISA: You are used to travel for work. It was exciting. No matter what I think about the mill, I am sure it is dull compared to your work with Pinkerton.

CHANCE: It—the mill— keeps us tied here. I think we have a good life, but it is bordered, truly, by this clearing, this mill, this stream, this house. In this small space, we fit our whole life. We could have more.

LARISA: I don't mind small, myself. [PAUSE. STARING AT THE RAIN. THEN:] I suppose you are right. Our life is not much more than weigh and grind and grind and weigh. How could we have more?

CHANCE: Well...I opened a letter just now from an old friend. Hachaliah Bailey. He runs a grand and popular traveling show. I was Bailey's bodyguard for three weeks when his Big Top Circus toured into Tacoma and Seattle. In the letter, he makes a proposal.

LARISA: Proposal?

CHANCE: He asks if I—and you—would work for him. He is asking us to run off and join the circus!

LARISA: Join the—just leave? Just run off and leave? No. We can't leave Luther. He needs you and me.

CHANCE: Luther doesn't need us to run the mill. We could easily keep most of our share, raise his share a bit and let him run it. He would be set up for a fine life and we would be free to do what we want.

LARISA: Yes. That's true...

CHANCE: Think of seeing the country—wouldn't you like to walk the hills of San Francisco? Sail on the ferries in New York? Ride the new train to Portland?

She thought for a moment. Then:

LARISA: I think I need to stay. You should go, though, if it is good for you.

CHANCE: I'd never leave here without you, Larisa. Never in a hundred years. A thousand. You are what goes beyond the mill for me. You make the mill work enjoyable. Besides, Bailey asked—in his letter—for both of us.

LARISA: I think I need to stay.

They sat in silence. After a few minutes:

LARISA: Being with you—seeing the country with you—tempts me. Yet, it would be hard to, as Americans say, "pull it off." I'm a woman. A foreign woman. Although my English is better than when I came, I am still foreign. You know how I came to possess the mill in the first place. There is no contract between you and me. Or between us and Luther. Everyone assumes it is you who owns the mill and has the money. I would not be able to safely leave—

CHANCE:—unless we marry?

LARISA: Yes. Indeed.

CHANCE: Let's take care of that right now, Larisa. When my wife, Benedicta, passed, I had many questions to ask of God. I asked why was she taken from me? Why must I sleep alone? If I would have loved her more deeply—somehow better—would she still be with me? None of my questions ever got answered.

LARISA: [DEEP IN THOUGHT] ...questions...

CHANCE: There was one question—my most enduring question— that stayed in my mind all these twelve years I was alone. I asked God...or myself...will I be able to open my heart to someone? To love anyone again?

LARISA: Love again?

CHANCE: Even if I can't love the way I loved Bennie...could I love at all? Or did my heart die when she died?

LARISA: Hard question...

CHANCE: Well...now I know the answer. Larisa, I know I can love again. My heart did not die when Benedicta died.

LARISA: A heart is never dead. It only sleeps. We say "zimovite." In English you say "hibernate," I think?

CHANCE: Yes.

LARISA: Your heart was just sleeping. Like a bear. In a cave.

The rain pounded like fingertips on a drum.

CHANCE: Yes, my heart was sleeping in a cave. But it is awake, now. I am awake. [PAUSE] My heart is awake to you. I love you!

LARISA: And I love you!

He took a deep breath and opened his gray eyes wide.

CHANCE: Larisa, will you marry me?

ENTR'ACTE

The Barker

Brendan Hardy

NOW

There's two kinds of people in the world. The ones who try to figure out how a magic trick works and the ones who don't want to know and who'd rather think of it as simply magic. You can study these different types by watching them watch a magician. The figure-it-out kinda guy will look around, under, behind, inside the magic, hunting for wires or mirrors or trap doors trying to scope out how a trick works. When asked to, "pick a card, any card," he will go out of his way to choose the most obscure card, hoping to trip up the magic and to prove it is fixed. Of course it's fixed! The other guy—the it's-pure-magic guy—just sits back and enjoys the illusion. In fact, he hopes to be fooled and complies to make happen.

I asked Wally about this. Wally has been around magic his whole life. So, one evening, when it was Texas Barbecue Dinner Buffet night set up on the patio out behind The Home, I got a plate, filled it with mac-and-cheese (plus a hot link and some pickles) and sat down next to Wally to ask him about these two types of magic watchers. Wally wears his pajamas all the time and big Terry-cloth house slippers with ducks on them. I think he has given up a bit, like some people in a retirement home do. But his pockets always bulge with puff balls or coins or cards. And he is ready in a second to do a magic trick, all I gotta do is ask. I talked to him about these two types. He said a magician wants to perform for the it's-pure-magic kind of guy. That guy's willful gullibility inspires and encourages the magician, Wally says. It makes a trick work even better and the magician work harder. It makes magic glow, says Wally, like a tent all lit up in the moonlight—an oasis glowing in the middle of a grassy field all golden—cricket sounds and moonbeams in the dark night. Poetic, Wally.

Colonectomy. Wally had his colon removed—most of it—six months ago. He is notable now for the amount of chewing he does. Wally chews each mouthful of food three, maybe four, minutes. He says he needs it the texture of baby food before he swallows. So, eating with him is a long haul and sometimes you wish he'd just swallow already. Swallow, Wally, I find myself thinking. But at the same time, he is a nice fellow so I want him to chew it until baby food so I don't see him suffer. One time he ate too much Pineapple Upside-Down Cake and the extra acid tore up his stomach. It was bad. Bad. Food should be a joy, and he sure enjoyed that cake while he was eating it. But after, he was a pile of moans and groans. He stayed in the hospital bed that got moved into his room after the surgery. Just all the time by himself. I visited him on my rounds, which I make every day visiting the ones I like and the ones who like me. Many of us here are completely healthy, but there are others that are older or sick or not strong. Wally is sort of in-between. He goes through weeks where he is engaged and other weeks when it takes all of his energy to just raise his electric bed high enough to see anything other than the ceiling.

On this barbecue night I mentioned, Wally is doing his usual prodigious chewing while I am discovering (with a cough) that the mac-and-cheese has chiles in it and we are talking about people who destroy magic tricks to prove they are tricks. These types of people are missing the point, says Wally. Magic tricks are tricks. *A good magician is not a master of illusion, Wally says, he is a master of distraction. A great magician, he says, always knows where he wants your eyes to look and makes you look there no matter what. Wally says these guys who try to see how the trick is done overlook the basic truth of magic: you see what you want to see. Or more accurately, you see what the magician wants you to see. Your choices about whether you buy into reality are cemented, says Wally, when you were a kid first watching magic. You decide then if you will let the magician win.*

When Wally had his surgery I sat for a long time in his bedroom and asked him to tell me memories. He'd talk a while, nod off, then wake up startled, but I'd still be there quiet and awake because people shouldn't recover alone. Wally has lived so long that he doesn't have family any more. He is alone in the world. I sort of try to fix that. While he was healthy that wasn't so hard. But now he has a stunted colon and has shrunk in his shoes. An old man.

ACT FOUR

The Magician

Walter Whalen, Jr.

THEN

At 1:26 a.m. clouds obscured the moon and rain began to fall, quickly creating brown, silty mud on Griswold Street.

Less than two hours before, the dry gutters in front of 1122 Griswold were filled with the accumulated dirt of a week of Detroit commerce: cigarette butts, candy wrappers, and the bluchered feet of Detroit's finest beat cops. Twelve members of the Municipal Force of Police had been dispatched to stand in front of the Garrick Theater, partly for effect and partly to actually contain the throng of ticket holders bustling to get through the two arched doorways all at once.

The show, billed as Houdini's Full Evening of Three Shows In One, started an hour earlier than most to allow for its full three-hour length. It ended with the wildly famous Chinese Water Torture Cell Escape: Houdini (handcuffs duly inspected and proven to be real) was cuffed, chained and padlocked. He was then sealed inside a water-filled cell. This was placed on a six-inch wooden riser and hidden behind a curtain of silvery deep blue (the same blue as Houdini's eyes). Before his concealment, The Maestro amiably invited members of the audience to hold their breath along with him, reminding them that, unlike them, for him, "Failure means a certain death by drowning!"

Tickets to the show had sold out in two hours, leaving the producers to turn away slightly over half of the people in line. The same producers started a whispering campaign that shows could not be added (although they, indeed, could) since the Maestro needed to be in Chicago in two days. Hastily, the producers announced an appearance at Navin Field (later Briggs Stadium, later than that, Tiger Stadium), "Open to the general public," where,

The Great Houdini
Would Perform His Astounding
Suspended Straitjacket Escape
Dangling from an 11-story crane
at noon today,
October 23, 1926!

This was easy to promise and difficult to deliver, which was no daunt to the producers, since they had no intention that Houdini would actually appear for, or even be cognizant, of the engagement.

A line began to form at the south gate of Navin Field as soon as word began to spread about the impromptu appearance. The promise of seeing Houdini perform one of his legendary feats as he had performed it in New York City—live and for free—sent an electric current through working-class Detroit. And since the show was planned for a Saturday, many in town would have the leisure time to attend. The line grew along with the audience's energy. The producers arranged for a crane to arrive at the field at 11 a.m., adding a required note of authenticity. This crane received an ovation from the crowd of many thousands when it parked just outside the fence enclosing the right field bleachers. It was Manny Emberger, the (unidentified) manager of publicity for Houdini, who started a whisper that Houdini was already in Corktown just a few blocks from the stadium having lunch with family friends (but not eating much, really, "in order to be fit for his fight with the jacket").

This rumor spread through the crowd like a brushfire, resulting in a spontaneous, rhythmic chant of "HOU-DI-NI! HOU-DI-NI! HOU-DI-NI!"

The next whisper started by the bebowlered Emberger was that the Maestro had escaped a similar (though less restrictive) straitjacket (which, in fact, was the precisely same one he was traveling with now) in two minutes and thirty-seven seconds, timing he would try to beat in Detroit. In moments the crowed— now many thousands and blocking side streets around the stadium for several blocks—soon frissoned with, "A more restrictive jacket this time!"

And, "How fast will he be able to escape?"

Nearly an hour passed after noon before Emberger started a whisper among the swelling crowd: the Great Man had been called to a reception in his honor hosted by Mayor John W. Smith at Dearborn House. A few minutes later, this same Emberger mounted the curb below the flagpole at the front gate of Navin Field, removed his hat and made the following announcement to complete his self-made illusion:

> The Great Harry Houdini, who was, indeed, to undertake for your delectation, to escape from a straitjacket of the strongest canvas and tightest leather straps, will not appear as announced due to an unexpected invitation that he could not refuse from Detroit's honorable Mayor Smith. He will appear tonight at the Garrick Theater, as previously advertised, and will forfeit $75 of his performing fee to anyone who can discern and prove the existence of false traps or exits in the execution of his feats of escape!

And so it happened that the disappointed crowd marched en masse to the Garrick Theater to demand restitution for their wasted time and energy. Of course, just as Emberger planned, they were met with shuttered wickets and

TONIGHT'S PERFORMANCE IS SOLD OUT

signs.

As designed, they banged on windows and doors demanding satisfaction, milled in frustration and generally made a scene that (to their dismay and the producer's delight) made—as reported by the Detroit afternoon papers—"not a single ticket available to be bought and every bought ticket more coveted."

✦

When dawn on the same day of October 23, 1926 brought gray, drizzly daylight to 53 Shakley Avenue in Detroit's Cokely district, Wally Whalen was just opening his eyes. The shadows from the streetlight still played on the wall across from his bed, painting a giant gray-black H across his bedroom wall. Wally blinked a few times and stretched, fists above his head, trying to force the transition from asleep to awake to complete itself. Then he caught the whiff of biscuits baking and bacon frying.

The rest took no effort. He could feel breakfast in his legs as he bunched up the covers and threw them aside. A little drizzle never hurt a guy.

Time to face Houdini Day!

Wally jumped out of bed and galloped to his dresser next to the door. He ran a comb through his hair (catching yesterday's Brylcreem like dragging a stick across a railroad track) and hopped around the corner to Ipana his teeth. Toothbrush. Water. A squeeze of paste. More water. Then brrrrrrussssh and done! Back to the bedroom for underpants, trousers, and an undershirt. The shirt itself would wait until after breakfast. Sock-shoe. Sock-shoe. (Not sock-sock, shoe-shoe). The freshly shined black ones with brand new woven laces.

It was Houdini Day, after all!

Today was the day he would find out if it was he who won the sweepstakes. The Healthy Grains Corn Puffules See Houdini Sweepstakes. He had done as he was told. Saved five box tops (which, when you think about it, might be thousands of Corn Puffules worth of box tops) and sent them in with the form cut from the side of the box (who could fit their entire actual address in the lines they gave? Impossible! Unless you live on one of the alphabet streets like Avenue L, which, who does anyway, or do they even have those in Detroit?). Now, today, the Corn Puffules Variety Show was going to announce One Lucky Winner of tickets to see the Great Harry Houdini in Houdini's Full Evening of Three Shows In One. Wally knew it had to be him. He would be the One Lucky Winner. Had to be. After all, he was highly deserving. Plus, he had folded his entry form in half *just right* so it would stand away from other entries in the giant bin they put entries in to pick the winner. A just right fold meant you hardly needed to be deserving, which Wally was anyway.

Wally shuffled the stairs two-at-a-time to arrive at the bottom lickety-split. He bounded into the kitchen fresh as a postman carrying the first letter of the day.

"Now, boy, don't you dare track those shoes on my new-washed floor," said his mom, turning over a slice of bacon with a fork. "It's raining. Rubbers!"

Wally tiptoed across the floor to the kitchen table, easing off his toes as he sat down in his chair. "Your floor is still span, Mom. No rubbers. I'll wear my rain boots 'cuz I don't want to spoil my shoeshine. It's Houdini Day!"

"Don't get your hopes up too high. You'll be sad if you don't prevail," said Mom, catching a bacon fat splatter on her cheek with a quick, "Darn!"

"Besides..." joined Dad, Walter Whalen, Sr., as he waltzed into the kitchen, tucking his tie behind the second button of his shirt.

"...they sold an awful lot of those Corn Puff sweepstakes things since Labor Day. You've got some real competition, Wally."

"But Dad, I've got to win. I'm deserving!"

"Deserving how?" Mom and Dad both said in unison.

Then Mom, alone: "There is nothing that makes you special to anyone but us, Wally."

"But, Mom...I studied Houdini's whole collection of card tricks and I do each one fine! Even the complicated ones and the ones marked 'For The Advanced Practitioner.' And I have read Card Conundrums and Handcuff Secrets three times! And Handcuff Secrets is hard reading when you don't own handcuffs. And I joined S.A.M. even though you have to be sixteen to be a member and I am thirteen-and-a-half but they let me anyway on a youth membership! Plus, every time he has been in Detroit Houdini has done the Chinese Water Torture trick—only this time they say he is going back to doing the Milk Can. I absolutely deserve to see that!"

With this last, Wally picked up his empty juice glass and held it above his head as if he were the Statue of Liberty. He looked at it, held it up higher and added one more, "I am deserving!" for emphasis.

✦

The dogstail grass turns from green to brown as the Milwaukee days grow gradually shorter. September gives way to October and the milkweed pods fill with white, silky fuzz. The fuzz jams the pods to bursting, and green seeds turn dark brown, then burst and dry along the Watertown Plank Road. Summer goes its way and steamy Wisconsin days cool into crisp autumn nights. The itinerants take over what local drayers call Century Park, a rugged, sandy lot—empty for nearly a century—bounded by the Oconomowoc trace just where it curves toward the lake.

The lot sits fallow and empty, except for the Buena Vista Tavern, for two-thirds of each year, and bursts into life to host traveling circuses and medicine shows during July, August, September, and

October. In this stretch of days—the shoulder between the deathly hot, humid Milwaukee summer and the Arctic cold Milwaukee winter—a fence is put up and an entrance gate erected. Then, a parade of wagons fills the half-moon of silty land. Tents are hoisted, a midway suggested by the lighting of lines of pitch torches (that burn greasy and smoky in the humid night) and this empty, useless land is transformed into a star-dusted milky way where bets are made, baseballs thrown, kewpie dolls won, romantic dreams born, and marriages tested.

Into this exact crucible (one day in 1888) drove the twenty-four wagons and carts of Maynard Diamond's Wayfaring Curiosity Show. Seventeen of the wagons were filled with the advertised curiosities— including a two-headed ox ("Nature's mistake!"), a tiger from the Bengal steppes ("Exoticsim Personified—She Can Eat A Grown Man Alive!"), a mermaid ("Procured by a Sailing Ship and Preserved for Your Edification!"), a pair of live Bats ("They Drink the Blood of the Unsuspecting!") and four African Chieftains ("These Africans Put Aside Their Differences Long Enough to Be Scrutinized by You!). Five of the wagons held scenery ("The Battle of Antietam Rematched Before Your Eyes! Including Five Thousand Gallons of Water Employed to Create a Lifelike Potomac River!"). The remaining two vehicles carry, "no fewer than 175 hand-sewn vestments the like of which you have never seen—including a replica of the Crown of Kohinoor containing over four-pound-weight in diamonds and gold and worn by Madame Constance Moltova, Medium of Spirits!!"

This exact Madame Constance Moltova—making her fourth and, this time, highly anticipated appearance in Milwaukee—has drawn most of the audience for the six-night residency announced by Maynard Diamond. The show begins with the Circus Parade, an act of horses being ridden by clowns and littles, Maestro Magnifico the Man of Steel ("Decorated this past summer with a Ribbon of Valor by President Chester A. Arthur!"), and a spot for a local pickup act—in this case, Milwaukee's own Erich Weiss, Prince of the Air Trapeze ("He Eludes Gravity at the Tender Age of Only Nine!")

Erich Weiss, born Erik Weisz and later to live as Harry Houdini, begins his act by entering Maynard Diamond's darkened tent so to remain unseen by the audience. The band plays a minuet by Mozart as a klieg light sweeps the walls of the big top. The same light zig-zags back and forth, cutting the air above the Prince's head, unable to find him initially due to his shortness of stature (he is, you recall, only nine years old!). The band pretends to stop, feigning to assume the Prince has not arrived, when Weiss jumps up and enters the ring of light.

(Audience laughs and applauds!)

The light operator makes an obvious and exaggerated realignment to begin following the Prince of the Air Trapeze as he climbs up a rope ladder (with silver rungs) to the trapeze platform. Silent and unseen, his partner, Satisha, climbs in darkness to a platform on the opposite side of the tent and stations herself to catch the Prince. But the spotlight illuminates Erich only, his eyes shiny and bright blue against his silver sateen suit. He grabs the trapeze and swings once, twice, three times then...launches himself into the dark, empty air. The original klieg spot stays stationary and for a long moment the air seems empty. The Prince has disappeared!

(Audience gasps!)

Then...suddenly...a second spotlight picks out Satisha who deftly catches him. The moment the Prince of the Air Trapeze is caught, the band starts to play the Glory of Youth March and the entire center ring shines with silver-pink light.

(Audience applauds wildly!)

The Prince of Air continues to entertain amid waves of approving applause. He swings, he leaps, he catches, he affects difficulty and bluffs, nearly falling only to catch himself. Finally, he does fall... into the waiting protection of his net, then bows, touches his heart in thanks for the applause, indicates Satisha (his catcher), grabs her hand, and bows with her and—with a somersault over the edge of the net and a hop—leaves the tent to its tumult.

Madame Moltova is next.

Introduced by Maynard Diamond, Madame Moltova, Medium of Spirits, dressed in deep ruby red and flounced like a Countess, parades in wearing the "Crown of Kohinoor." Wearing tin painted gold with paste gems, she parades around the center ring surrounded by "acolytes" who act as body guards now for the show, but during the day sweep behind the horses.

She begins her act by saying (in heavily Russian-accented English) that it is not an act:

> *I am gift with the abil'ty to converse with those who rrrreside as spirits in the grrrret beyond. Because I truly connect wit' spirits who come and go like shedows in daylight when der sun goes behind a clod. This is very difficult and rrrrequires the deepest concentrations, so I tanks you for the being of silence while Madame Constance enters her trance.*

The lights dim and Madame Moltova begins The Floating Orb. She presents a shining orb of glass on her open palm, showing it left and right. She then indicates there are no wires or levers by passing her hands left, right, up, and down. She indicates the weight of the orb in her hands and "carelessly" tips it off of her palm. Surprise! It floats!

(The audience is enthralled!)

It is at this moment that Erich Weiss, Prince of the Air Trapeze, positions himself behind the entrance curtain to watch. Even at the age of nine, having been in circus tents for several years and having seen orbs float before, he knows it is an illusion done with wires, although every audience seems to largely fall for it. He knows, even before he sees her foot tapping the seance table, that Madame Moltova is a charlatan, a fraud, and a dissembler. He knows, even at nine years old, that he will devote a part of his life to making sure people like her stop fooling the public.

This exact Erich Weiss, as Harry Houdini, crossed paths three more times with the same Madame Constance Moltova, Medium of Spirits—first as Constanza Manfredi, Messenger of Heaven, then as Madame M., Mistress of the Ether, and last as Madame C. M. Whitehead, Professional Medium. The first two times they met again, she refused to admit they had met before. The last, in 1924, was when Weisz had been Houdini for nearly thirty years, and he was booked on the Orpheum Circuit. They played together on the same bill in Toledo. By that time, he had spent several years focused on debunking psychic practitioners and mediums, proving them to be the kind of fakes Constance (Costanza?) had always been.

✦

On a windy Thursday evening in May, 1924, Houdini visited one of Madame C.M. Whitehead's Toledo seances. He was disguised as Thomas Throgmorten, Compounding Pharmacist, in a gray wig and beard, stick-on eyebrows, an out-of-season wool suit, carrying an ebony cane. The seance was attended by ten people: The aforementioned Mr. Throgmorten, Pharmacist, was the youngest. Also in the room (an oval shaped dining room wallpapered in dark navy ciré) was Sanford Eggermann, multi-millionaire and owner of Eggermann Mercantile Freight, and Robert T. Quist, President of Toledo Thrift Bank. Both men had become widowers in the past year. Seven widows also attended: Madames Debnerham, Falsgate, Smithton, Galloway, Shrimpshire, Gallentine, and Mrs. Joseph Zanter (of the Bancroft Street Zanters), the recently bereaved widow of the retired secretary of the World Bank. All hoped to sit in their assigned seat around the huge, ornate walnut dining table in Madame Whitehead's town house and commune with their deceased husbands and wives.

The group milled about the gaslit room until Madame Whitehead's assistant bid them take their seats. This request, followed by significant rustling of dresses, removal of gloves and banging of walking sticks, came precisely at 8:35pm.

"Madame Whitehead will join you presently. Please settle yourselves according to your name cards," said the assistant backing out of the servants' door into the butler's pantry.

Once seated, the participants remained quiet for a few minutes awaiting the arrival of Madame Whitehead. At once, the gaslights guttered, and a cool breeze blew over the table from left to right, gusting Mrs. Falsgate's silver gray bombazine neck bow onto her chin. As this gust came into the room, so did Madame Whitehead, who entered through a disappearing door in the wall of the room next to an ornate China cabinet. She wore a bone-colored silk chemise over an ankle-length chestnut silk skirt clinging close to her narrow frame and an oxblood Shantung duster with six large, pink, carved buttons in the shape of peonies.

MRS. FALSGATE: [AGITATED] Was I the only one who felt a gust just then?
MRS. GALLOWAY: [BREATHLESS] I did too! Quite otherworldly!
MADAME WHITEHEAD: We get gusts quite often. This house was built upon a colonial cemetery, which is precisely why Mr. Whithead and I bought it. I can commune with the spirits as I wish. That is the positive aspect. The not-so-positive aspects are the unexpected gusts, the spirit lights we see abroad so often in the night, and the constant sound of the treading of feet on our floorboards.

Here Madame Whitehead swept her arm in an arc indicating the floor and heaved a sigh.

MADAME WHITEHEAD: I sigh, but one must learn to live in harmony with [PAUSE] spirits! [PAUSE] For better and worse.

She pronounced, "worse" with a trailing hiss as if it had ten esses at the end.

She stopped to take her chair. She sat with her arms at her sides, hands buried in the pockets of her duster. As she settled in the chair, four loud knocks came from the center of the table. Or was it from the ceiling above the gas chandelier?

MADAME WHITEHEAD: The spirits call us! We must prepare to answer!

Hands in her pockets, she sat for several minutes with her eyes closed. Suddenly she began to nod. With each nod she spoke the word, "yes" with the same otherworldly hiss: "Yes, yesss, yessssss, yesssssssssssssssssss!" Then four more knocks from the middle of the room and the distinct sound of booted footfalls traced their way across the floor from the servants' door to the table-side.

MADAME WHITEHEAD: (EYES CLOSED AND HEAD NODDING) Yessss! Who is calling?..who?..who is it now? (EYES SUDDENLY OPEN WIDE AND STARING BLANKLY FORWARD) Mister... mister...speak to me, Mister...speak through me, Mister...Zanter!

A gasp emanates from Hilde, followed quickly by, "My Yossel! Is that my Yosseleh?"

MADAME WHITEHEAD: Is that Yossel Zanter? Come to us, Mr. Zanter!"

Then the gaslights round the room dimmed and another gust of wind was felt across the room. The table began inexplicably to rise off the floor (Inexplicable to the guests, at least)!

MADAME WHITEHEAD: Yossel Zanter, I speak for your wife, Hilde, when I ask you to make yourself known to us with three knocks if it is truly you.

Then came three knocks from the center of the levitating table.

MADAME WHITEHEAD: Are you at peace Yossel Zanter? Do you speak from the peaceful beyond or from...the other place? The place of trials and—

MRS ZANTER: Oh speak to me Yosseleh! Speak to me! Our children miss you and require your advice—should they choose Mendel to run the company? [TO THE OTHER GUESTS AT THE TABLE] Mendel is our first-born.

MADAME WHITEHEAD: [IN A BASSO REGISTER} I miss you... my dear Hilde...I reside in the peaceful beyond with God in heaven. Life here is a leisurely pastoral—

MRS ZANTER: Oh speak to me Yosseleh! Speak to me! Pastoral? How lovely!

The lights the room suddenly grew brighter.

MADAME WHITEHEAD:[IN BASSO] I miss you my dear Hilde... But I must go. My time with you is fleet—

MRS ZANTER: Don't go my dear...don't go!

MADAME WHITEHEAD: [IN YOSSEL'S VOICE] I can speak to you any time. Just come back to Madame Whitehead and I she will bring me forth...I must...I must...go...now... good...bye...goodbye... goodbye...goodbye...goo—

And with each goodbye, Madame W's voice faded a bit until the final goodbye was spoken in a bare whisper.

With slight variations, this routine was repeated for each participant, until—second to last—came Thomas Throgmorten, Compounding Pharmacist.

MADAME WHITEHEAD: Yes? Who is this? I hear a faint voice...it is but a sprite...a dimly energized spirit...who? Who? Throgmorten? Ahhh...Mr. Throgmorten, I speak now with your wife...your wife... who's name seems to be..?

It is at this juncture when the bereaved typically leans in and, desperate to commune, supplies the name of the deceased. But this Throgmorten didn't play.

MADAME WHITEHEAD: Mr. Throgmorten I speak now with your late wife...your wife...who's name seems to be..? Seems to be..? Ahh...Mrs. Throgmorten! [CHANGING TO A DOCILE, FEMININE VOICE] Thomas...Thomas...I am here. It is your beloved...your beloved...your—

The disguised Houdini stood up in his place and tapped his walking stick on the floor by his left shoe. "Madame Whitehead, if it indeed was the spirit of my late wife you brought forth, surely she would know her own name, would she not? She does not because you do not. I withheld her name, which prevented you from incorporating it into your charade. You cannot speak her name because you did not bring her forth, nor are you capable of bringing any spirit forth!

MADAME WHITEHEAD: Mr. Throgmorten I speak now with your late wife...your wife...this house is filled with spirits who cross the roadway of communion from the grave!
HOUDINI: You, Madame Whitehead, are a flimflam! A sharper! A passel of circus tricks! A vulture who preys on the bereaved! This room is fitted to make winds blow and knocks sound! Come with me, my friends and I shall show you! [REMOVING HIS WIG, BEARD, AND EYEBROWS]. I am Harry—
MADAME WHITEHEAD: —Houdini! YOU BASTARD!

✦

The "FOR RENT" sign had been in the window for seventeen months when Gershon Baitz smacked down his check for $79.00 (first, last, and security) and signed the lease. The empty walk-up storefront over the Fountain of Youth Bar and Grill would be his for at least two years. Baitz (known professionally as Enchantmo the

Thaumaturge) had been looking for the perfect location in which to open a shop. This place would, indeed, be perfect.

A grand foyer (well, almost grand: octagon tile in a geometric leaf pattern of white and green, oak wainscoting, an electrified gas chandelier and side-lights next to double entry doors) met visitors as they left the street. Two steps to the right led to the smoky Fountain of Youth. On the left, steep stairs ascended to a long, high-ceilinged room with a similarly long commerce counter backed by floor-to-ceiling glass-front cabinets. Baitz thought the former pharmacy would work exceedingly well for displaying trick paraphernalia: children's magic sets, balls, rings, coins, chains, and handcuffs. The counter would be perfect for demonstrations. The open areas were ample for displaying the large illusion kits like the Decapitated Doyenne that Baitz planned to have on offer to lure professional magicians.

It took a little less than three weeks to get the long-neglected space ready for opening day. Baitz painted the walls to cover the grease bubbles accumulated from months of Fountain of Youth nightly specials cooked on the flattop grill. He sanded then shellacked the floor. Then he assiduously swept the mouse dung from the corners of the cabinets, wiped them clean of roach droppings and mouse piss, and applied a fresh coat of shiny white enamel to the cabinets. Last, a meticulously drawn and painted ceiling mural of the rising moon and constellations in deep blue, moon yellow, and star silver brought the space into the mystical demesne that made it Enchantmo's Emporium ("Fully Stocked Supplier to the Discerning Magician").

Opening day included balloons, popcorn, knockwurst, and a day of close-hand magic performances by well-known Detroit magicians. The headliner was Magnificent Marty (Buford), who was driven in from a gig in Chicago in his 1924 Isotta-Fraschini Tipo 8A roadster with the windshield open. Marty went on at 8 p.m. to an elite audience of professionals and devotees. He wowed, as always, with coins and puffballs. 229 customers came through the store on opening day, spending on average $18.00, which gave Baitz a solid start. The energy of the custom remained high for weeks after opening day and settled into a better-than-expected fifteen to twenty customers per day for the first year. Things slowed down a bit the second year, and by the third, in spite of a highly-visible sponsorship on the title cards at the Fox Theatre, business had ebbed to seven to fourteen customers a week.

Gershon Baitz spent most of his days dusting the store's merchandise, petting Larry the Rag Doll mouser cat who kept the cabinets free from mouse dung, and practicing sleight of hand in front of a tabletop mirror. Each day he would mark the time: noon by the bong-bong-bong of the bar clock in the Fountain of Youth and 3 p.m. by the clamor of the school children passing as they made their way home from John Quincy Adams Secondary School down the street. He relished the distracted energy of the kids as they filled the sidewalks in the morning and dispersed in the afternoon. One day, the sound of children gave Baitz an idea: he'd offer an after-school magic class. The hope was that, if he could engage a few schoolboys, he would bring in several dollars per week in lessons. Doubtless they would end up buying equipment and supplies to support their magic shows. That income, added to the regular (although meager) customer revenue would, as his mother would say, "keep the wolf from the door."

Baitz posted a sandwich sign at the closest trolley stop and on the sidewalk to the left of the front door and directly in the path of the commuting students:

LEARN THE ART AND SCIENCE
OF MAGIC

from
ENCHANTMO the THAUMATURGE
in person

Starting with the Classic Magic of the Fingers and Hands

$00.30 PER CLASS
- CASH ONLY -

Then he listened for the distant sound of laughing to become the approaching sound of bustling children on the street. He waited for the squeak of the door hinge and the footfall of ascending children on his staircase. Monday...no one, Tuesday...no one again. Wednesday he heard a boy read the sign out loud, yet no sound on the stairs. Thursday the clamoring raft of gossiping girls and daring boys passed on schedule, yet neither Larry the cat or Enchantmo the magician were disturbed by a visitor. Another week passed, engaging no students (in spite of two inquiries by adults who were shopping for themselves about bringing their sons in for a lesson).

After three weeks of silence Baitz put a red slash through "$00.30 PER CLASS" and wrote "FIRST TWO CLASSES FREE." Then he waited again.

More weeks passed. Then one Wednesday when Gershon Baitz had forgotten temporarily about the sign and had stopped listening for children, the door of the shop abruptly opened. Before Enchantmo could turn around to welcome the customer he heard:

"What the heck ever is a thaumaturge?"

The question came from a boy of about eleven, his face saddled by a field of freckles. He wore a white dress-shirt striped with gray, summer wool trousers of similar gray, and a black belt with a silver buckle. On his feet were shiny black dress shoes (more shiny and dressy than you'd expect from a school child). He wore studious glasses rimmed in silver.

"What the heck ever is a thaumaturge and anyway why put it on a sign if no one knows what it means?"

"People know what it means!" said Baitz with a most un-Enchantmo tone of irritation.

"I'm people, yet I never heard of it."

"It means wizard. Or magician," said Baitz.

"Then why not just say wizard? Or say magician? Say what you mean."

"Thaumaturge sounds mysterious and magical," offered Baitz.

"Sounds stupid if you ask me," said the boy, dropping his book bag abruptly. "But anyway I am here for the two free lessons from the sign. I'm Wally. Walter Whalen, Jr., but Wally will do fine."

"I am Gershon," said Baitz with a slight bow and flourish of his cuffs (as if he was trying to make something appear from his sleeve). "Known in magic circles as Enchantmo."

"...the Thaumaturge. Don't forget that stupid part," added Wally. "So... um...let's get going with my lessons."

Wally took to magic like Larry the cat took to Wally, laying on his lap and double-purring while the boy practiced his sleight of hand. Wally's stays in the store started lasting about fifteen minutes—just enough time to eagerly chew and swallow the lessons Baitz had planned. It was not long, though, before Wally stayed to practice under the watchful eye of Enchantmo for and extra fifteen minutes, then half an hour, then an hour. After a few weeks, Wally stayed the afternoon, puttering around the store, chatting, dusting for Baitz, and leaving just before twilight with only enough time to run breathlessly home before full darkness fell. When Wally seemed in danger of walking home in the dark, Baitz closed the shop and bought them both a trolley ticket, accompanying Wally to his doorstep. After a week or so of evening trolley rides, Baitz paused before leaving Wally and knocked on the Whalen's door. He dropped Wally, introduced himself, and explained that he had been spending time with Wally after school teaching him magic.

"We've heard all about that," said Wally's mom in her flat Detroit accent. "Wally can't wait to learn more tricks from that Mr. Electro at your store."

"Enchantmo, Madame," said Baitz with his usual slight bow and shooting of his cuffs. "That is me. I'm Enchantmo. Gershon Baitz. Wally's teacher. I think Wally is uncommonly talented at sleight of hand and I am pleased to have him as my student!"

And from that moment, with the blessing of his parents, Wally's magic tutoring took off. Baitz taught him as much as he could, forgoing the thirty cents per lesson for just the satisfaction of cultivating the boy's talent. Besides, thought Baitz, Wally was curious, conversational, and astute—all of which made him good company to help the time pass in the mausoleum of a store. Occasionally, Baitz would introduce Wally to a regular customer as "my protégé." That made Wally feel proud.

Baitz felt proud too, and—with the permission of the elder Whelans—he gave Wally tickets to a few appearances by Enchantmo.

One day, about a year after Wally had first appeared in the store, Baitz came to work with a box of cereal.

"Healthy Grains Corn Puffules. Heard of them, Wally?" asked Baitz.

"Heard of 'em? I eat a bowl every morning! I like them." said Wally.

"There is a contest they are running, the Corn Puffules folks, to see Houdini. Harry Houdini. The greatest magician who ever lived," said Baitz holding up the box. "I want you to enter, win, and go see him."

"Let's enter together!" said Wally grabbing the box.

"I want you to go. With a friend, Wally. You go. They announce the winner three months from today on the radio and I want to be listening when you win. Gather enough box tops. Then enter. Come here to the store at..." Baitz grabbed the box back and peered at the spine, reading, "...noon...on October 23rd...and we'll listen to the prize drawing together. We will hear you win."

"Will do...," said Wally, "...Mr. Thaumaturge!"

✦

LIVE READ SCRIPT - Healthy Grains Corn Puffules Your Variety Show

Read Length: 5:59

Episode: #231-Houdini Contest Winner

0:01- 0:30- TRANSCRIPTION: Theme (Sky Schuyler and His Canadian Rocky Singers):

It's noon! It's noo-oon!
Healthy Grains are a boo-oon!
They make your body glow!
Settle back,
eat a pack
You'll feel better soo-oon!
We've got six minutes to go...
So just sit back and listen to—
The Healthy Grains
Corn Puffules
Va-ri-ety Show!

0:30-0:45- ANNOUNCER: It's noon and that means it's time for Your Variety Show, brought to you by Healthy Grains Corn Puffules—the only cereal that is healthy and fun! I am your host, Robert Venables, broadcasting from atop the Buhl Building in downtown Detroit, Michigan. Today's show features a favorite from the hits of today, a visit from Dr. Claypool with sound advice for staying fit and keeping up your vim. PLUS, we will announce the winner of the Healthy Grains Corn Puffules See Houdini contest as one hungry listener wins two tickets to this evening's show at the Garrick Theater in downtown Detroit! Before we break the mystery and reveal the winner, here is Art Landry and his orchestra featuring a bit of southern charm—the hit of the year—Sleepy Time Gal!

0:45- 4:25- TRANSCRIPTION: Art Landry& His Orchestra, Sleepy time Gal Fox Trot (Victor Record #19843-3:33)

4:18- 5:00- ANNOUNCER: That was the clarinet of Art Landry on Sleepy Time Gal with Art Landry and his Orchestra, and this is Your Variety Show heard daily at noon on this station and brought to you by Healthy Grains Corn Puffules, the puffed cereal made for healthy eating. They are healthy, yet tasty enough that your children will want them every morning! I am your host, Robert Venables. Today we are joined by our special guest Dr. Franklin Claypool, nutritional expert and lead dietician at the Healthy Grains company. Welcome Dr. Claypool!

DR. FRANKLIN CLAYPOOL: Thank you Bob. It is my pleasure to be here on behalf of Healthy Grains Corn Puffules and the entire family of Healthy Grains cereals!

ANNOUNCER: Dr. Claypool, what is it that sets Healthy Grains Corn Puffules apart from other choices for breakfast?

DR. FRANKLIN CLAYPOOL: Well, Bob, it is the healthy handful of unrefined grains that keep your body working well and add that nutty flavor your children will love!

ANNOUNCER: So…in other words, Dr. Claypool, doctors like you agree with the choice of Healthy Grains Corn Puffules and children do, too?

DR. FRANKLIN CLAYPOOL: That's right, Bob!

ANNOUNCER: My thanks to Dr. Claypool and Healthy Grains. He eats 'em too!

TRANSCRIPTION: STINGER (Sky Schuyler and His Canadian Rocky Singers):

Settle back,
eat a pack
You'll feel better soon!
We've got two minutes to go…
So just sit back and listen to—
The Healthy Grains
Corn Puffules
Variety Show!

4:25-5:45- ANNOUNCER: Esteemed listeners, we are now joined by Emanuel Emberger, professional assistant to the Great Harry Houdini. Mr. Emberger, hello!

EMMANUEL EMBERGER: Hello, Mr. Venables!

ANNOUNCER: Call me Robert!

EMMANUEL EMBERGER: Alright then. Robert!

ANNOUNCER: Thanks for joining us. We've got a big job to do today. One lucky listener to our program is going to take away two tickets to, "Houdini's Full Evening of Three Shows In One" playing this very evening at the Garrick Theater here in downtown Detroit!

EMMANUEL EMBERGER: That's true, Robert! Maestro Houdini set aside the two tickets from this sold-out show because he chooses Healthy Grains Corn Puffules for his breakfast and hopes you will, too!

ANNOUNCER: Would you be so kind as to choose the winner now from the giant drum at your side?

EMMANUEL EMBERGER: The lucky…winner…of the Healthy Grains Corn Puffules "Houdini's Full Evening of Three Shows In One" free show tickets is…

TRANSCRIPTION: Snare Drum Roll (sound effect #056)

EMMANUEL EMBERGER: Walter Whalen, Jr. of Shakley Avenue in downtown Detroit!

TRANSCRIPTION: Brass Fanfare (sound effect #434)

5:45-5:59- ANNOUNCER: Everyone here at Your Variety Show is delighted for our contest winner, Walter Whalen, Jr. Join us at noon tomorrow for another Your Variety Show broadcast brought to you in vibrant 500-watt sound by Healthy Grains Corn Puffules, the doctor-endorsed cereal that makes your body run fine and makes your breakfast run fun! This is your host, Robert Venables, speaking!

##END##

✦

In mid-1925, Houdini accepted an invitation to speak to a meeting of the Royal Order of Elks in Lexington, Kentucky, where he was visiting to promote a movie. After reciting a brief biographical sketch, he used a baffled candle lantern to project glass slide photos of various mediums. He described each of their acts, dissecting their technique and denouncing their supernatural abilities as a sham. Attendees knew of his columns explaining the techniques of mediums in the Lexington Post Gazeteer, where he would answer the questions of regular folks who thought they might have been taken advantage of by psychics or mediums. In this Lexington engagement, he focused on particularly on the "fraud" named Madame C.M. Whitehead. He did not know that the man in the fourth row, seated behind a pole, was J. Gordon Whitehead, husband of Madame C.M Whitehead, Professional Medium.

Nor did he know (how could he?) that the man who will come to visit his Montreal dressing room on October 22, 1926 was the same J. Gordon Whitehead.

On October 11th while performing his Chinese Water Torture Cell Escape during a performance in Albany, New York, a trapdoor closed prematurely on his leg. He hobbled through the rest of the show and later discovered a fractured left ankle. Against his doctor's order, Houdini continued his tour and traveled with a nurse to Montreal to give a lecture at the McGill University Union on the subject of Mediums: Fakes and Charlatans. A few days later (on October 22nd) he hosted some McGill students for a visit backstage to his dressing room at the Princess Theater. The Maestro's ankle was bothering him, so he laid on a dark green velvet dressing room divan and put his feet up to look through his mail.

"What brings you in, gents?" asked Houdini, looking up distractedly from his handful of letters to the group of three gathered around the coffee table. "Students of magic? Or interested in fakers?"

"I'm a student of your work," said the shortest. "I'm Sam. I have seen you in Brooklyn, Cleveland, Toronto, and now Montreal."

"Toronto in '23? That was...I'll be damned... that was Buried Alive? Or the Box and Chains?"

"Buried Alive. I have to say, seeing you has been nearly heart stopping each time. You really know how to play...or...um...inspire the audience."

Houdini turned to the other two—an overweight studious type in glasses and a tall one built like a casket who looked older than the other two. "And you two? What brings you gents in?"

"I am a longtime fanatical admirer, Mr. Houdini!" said the studious one. It was clear to Houdini that this one was to be ignored. The casket-shaped one, on the other hand, demanded attention.

"I..." he said deliberately, "...am fascinated by your work on psychics and mediums and fakers, as you said a minute ago. Your work's value is undeniable. Scholarly and incisive."

"Thanks, my boy. Your name?" said Houdini sitting up a bit and moving his good foot to the floor.

"I'm Gordy, Sir."

"Well, Gordy, thirty-five years of experience in examining psychic phenomena has taught me the frauds of spiritualists," said Houdini. "But mind, I don't attack spiritualism. By which I mean religion. That is entirely different from fakes who extort money from troubled people who long to speak with their loved ones."

"I admire that," said Gordy with a shrug.

"As you know, I am willing to forfeit $10,000 if I cannot expose any medium," Houdini said. "As a matter of fact, there are $825,000 of lawsuits directed against me by offenders. I mean mediums who are offended by my debunking work. $825,000 at the present time."

"As I said, I admire that, Mr. Houdini," Gordy said, looking at his shoes and rubbing his palms together.

"The fraudulent medium—and I have never met a genuine medium—," continued the Maestro, "is the most despicable creature on earth!"

Gordy lifted his chest and shoulders. "Sir, I have heard that you claim no blow to your stomach can harm you. Is that true?"

"Yes, my friend, it is. I have also proffered $10,000 to anyone who can harm me through blows to my abdomen."

J. Gordon Whitehead immediately strode to the couch and, without speaking another word, landed five punches on the Maestro's stomach.

One...

Two...

Three...

Four...

Five!

Houdini had no time to discern the man's intention, nor to react or prepare.

"Son of a bitch!" whispered J. Gordon Whitehead as he quickly slammed the dressing room door and sped down the hall to the stage and then to the exit.

✦

It was hard for Wally Whalen to choose who he would take with him to see Houdini that night at the Garrick. He first thought of his mom, who, after all, bought all of the cereal boxes that contributed the box tops. Mom was a solid choice if choosing from family. Then he thought of his Dad. That was a thought that lasted a millisecond. Dad was the sort of person who explained magic tricks and had to know how everything works. That just didn't go with a magic show of the magnitude of Houdini. Still staying within the family he thought of cousin Brian. Brian was Wally's same age and learned a couple of magic tricks along with Wally from a book. The reason that he most favored his cousin Brian to go was his ownership of a new pair of birding binoculars. Brian was a solid choice if the seats were located behind the fifth row.

Brian's binoculars were not necessary since the tickets turned out to be in the third row in the center. A nice man named Mr. Hamburger (or something) escorted Wally and his Mom to their seats and gave each of them a paper cone of popcorn and an H.B. Reese's peanut butter candy. The house curtain presented itself in front of them like a mountainside made golden by the rising sun. There were rosy-cheeked cherubs in lunettes on either side of the stage.

When the curtain rose, Wally heard a whoosh of air and suddenly the Amazing Houdini was in the center of the stage. He was as big as life, though shorter than Wally expected. The applause was deafening as Wally and his mom stood to welcome the great man. Houdini touched his heart with his right hand and made a strained bow. Without a word he launched into a series of sleight-of-hand tricks with handcuffs and cards. Wally was enthralled and so was his mother. Then Houdini did the East Indian Needle trick, in which he swallowed 100 needles, then a length of red silk thread. After gulping dramatically, he opened his mouth, reached in, and brought the thread out...with the 100 needles threaded on it!

By this time, Wally's mom was starry-eyed.

Houdini closed Act One with the Radio Illusion, producing a chorine from inside what appeared to be an oversized, yet-functioning radio, full of wires and tubes.

Act Two began with what Wally thought was a "boring" slide show about fake mediums and fortune tellers. Then came the finale: the Chinese Water Torture Cell Escape!

Houdini, dressed in a gold-embroidered red silk jacket and pantaloons, took about ten minutes to detail the description of the tank, stocks, grill, and steel chains, tackle, and locks that made up the exotic "Chinese Cell." After inviting a representative committee from the audience to inspect, Houdini stepped offstage to change while his assistants (similarly attired in red silk) rapidly filled the tank from a high-pressure hose and with heated water from Chinese-ornamented cauldrons at either side of the tank.

Returning in a tan canvas swimming costume, Houdini lay on his back in the center of the stage as members of the audience committee (oh, how Wally wished he wasn't a kid and could do these things!) adjusted the Maestro's feet within the stocks and applied the locks. A steel frame was next passed over the Maestro's body, which was chained and clamped securely. The frame was placed in the tank and pulleys hauled Houdini into the air, where he remained suspended by his feet ready for his plunge into the water, below. Suddenly—and with a satisfying "CHU-CLINK" of chains—he dropped, head first, into the tank. The stocks were fixed in place and the sides and top of the cell covered. The locks were locked, and a wall of draperies was pulled to cover the tank, leaving just enough space to allow the audience to view of Houdini's submerged head.

Two minutes of breathless suspense.

An axe was revealed by an assistant dressed in red and subsequently kept ready to break the glass in case of failure.

The orchestra begins to play, "Asleep in the Deep," presaging the Great Houdini's fate.

But no! A second later, Houdini burst open the cabinet and stood dripping wet—yet free—in the storm of applause from a bewildered audience. Wally stood up clapping and his mother did, too, the feathers on her hat bobbing with enthusiasm as she shook her head in astonished approval.

All of the lights go down except a single spotlight on the Great Houdini, who touched his heart once again, bowed, and completed his final performance.

Wally just remembers how blue his eyes were!

✦

A few days later, on Halloween Day in Detroit's Sinai-Grace Hospital, Houdini declared, "I am tired of fighting," and breathed his final breath.

Legend has it that the cause of death was a burst appendix brought on by repeated blows to the abdomen.

ENTR'ACTE

The Barker

Brendan Hardy

NOW

*I*n my whole life, I never fell in love. But I am close to being in love with Iris. She has a way of looking at me that makes me feel like I matter. Like I count. She also has blue veins that run over the backs of her hands and these serene eyes that could make anyone—even an elephant—sit up and listen to what she has to say. Iris worked with elephants. Those guys are hard to work with for several reasons, besides that they could trample you into the brown earth like you were a cockroach if they wanted to. Of course if they like you, though, they listen. They listened to Iris.

Iris is one of the people you see here walking in the hall and you think she is visiting someone rather than living here. She always dresses in a skirt and sweater with pearls around her neck and some nice high-heels that make her look taller than she is. She always looks well-dressed. And she always looks happy. Her room is always organized and her bed is always made with two needlepoint pillows on it (needlepointed by her daughter, Shelby). She has a steno pad where she writes her diary every day so when she is in the sunroom she is always busy. The thing you notice right away is, Iris just hasn't got the beaten-down senior-citizen look like the rest of us do.

She is what you call involved, too. She is on the Resident Board. Heads it up, actually. So she is always doing something to make our lives better, here at NJHRCCP, like when she got us all recycle bins in our rooms so we can do our part for the environment and also feel like we are doing some good in the world. Or when she proposed having more organic and vegetarian food in the Mess Hall. It's a good thing to be able to have our funnel cakes, morning oatmeal, and salad bar cherry tomatoes secure in the knowledge that we are not eating unhealthy chemicals. All because of Iris.

She fits me. She fits me just right. Perfect height for me. When we dance, we look like I am Danny Kaye and she is whoever that was danced with Danny Kaye in White Christmas. We look like Danny Kaye and Whoever-She-Was on the dance floor. Smooth and creamy with teeny hands and feet. Iris and I have been dancing pretty much since I first saw her and introduced myself on her move-in day about a year ago. We go out to have supper and dance every Saturday. We spruce up. Well, I do anyway. I'm usually in khakis, a polo shirt, and loafers. Iris seems maximally spruced, at any given time, with no further effort needed. On Saturdays, she wears a skirt that twirls out when I turn her and a blouse with a bow at the collar. She tops that with a jacket with piping trimming the pockets and plackets. And white gloves, even though those went out of style 50 years ago. She looks neat as a button and as pretty as anything.

The NJHRCCP courtesy van lets down its retractable boarding stairs and I take Iris's white-gloved hand to lead her up the stairs to one of the front two seats, where we always sit, her hand still in mine. Then, Lawanda, the van driver, drives us over to the Lancaster Farms Pay-One-Price Buffet on Route 27.

They serve the seven sweets and seven sours from the Pennsylvania Dutch, meatloaf, crispy fried chicken, and a bunch of other food. Iris starts with a bowl of red Jell-O (it could be raspberry, strawberry, or cherry—doesn't matter to her). They cut it in cubes and little red bits come off the spoon in the corners of her mouth. I enjoy this classy dame looking like a teenager loving her Jell-O. For an appetizer, I choose the liverwurst plate. It has liverwurst on lettuce surrounded by kidney beans, pitted black olives, topped by sliced scallions. Fancy. Or sometimes I am more in the mood for chicken croquettes, which come three-to-a-plate with white sauce that is flavored with herbs. Green flecks in gray-white gravy. I choose the smallest portions so Iris won't think I'm an eater. But at the same time, I want to get our $8.99's worth out of it. So I usually have both the liverwurst and the croquettes. Then, I joke with Iris will she still kiss me if I eat scallions? She laughs and so do I. Honest truth is, we don't kiss.

After dinner, they fire up the Conway Twitty, Loretta Lynn, Frank Sinatra, or Keely Smith and the dance floor fills up. The closest we get to kissing is looking into each other's eyes while we step lightly around the dance floor and I spin Iris and make her skirt go out. I don't want to sound show-off-y but I think we are the best on the floor. When we dance, something happens. I feel airy. Like I went to college. Like I am wearing a suit and tie. Of course, everyone is over 70, so there isn't much competition for best dancer, really. Most of us are happy just to be in public.

And me in public with her.

ACT FIVE

The Elephant Tamer

Iris Yancy

THEN

The sun, freshly risen and hot yellow, cuts across the kitchen at an angle dividing the room, like the heavens, dark from light. The smoke-gray walls on the dark side look stony and cold. The same-colored walls on the light side look silty brown like the dust behind a Packard on a Sunday morning drive. But this is a workaday Monday, just another day for grinding away at the earth, the crops, the dirt, the debt.

This kitchen (divided dark from light) hasn't been used since Thursday night, and it is already losing the cinnamon-clove smell of baked apples, the last thing to come out of its oven. Next to the sink, on the algid gray-white porcelain, there is a Mason jar. In this jar is a wilting Allium flower that turns its water brackish, producing a brume of mildew smell. This flower, the last vestige of a woman's touch in the kitchen, is falling apart, its white bracts dropping into the sink one at a time like chutes. A tiny version of the Mighty Parachute ride at the county fair.

The Monroe County Fair, Monroe County, Ohio, to be precise, where on Thursday night in a huff, or a tizzy, or—as he saw it—a cascading waterfall of deranged bad judgment, Sally left Rod.

Left abruptly. Abruptly left, in Rod's unbiased view. Abandoned. Abruptly left. And completely. Fucked.

On top of it all, she decided to break the news just as the midway calliope launched into "As Sweet As The Flowers in May Time," which would have, under other circumstances, been the perfect song to accompany a smoldering kiss under the midway lights. Those lights swung lightly in the summer breeze and twinkled like far-away headlights on a bumpy road. This comely effect, under the circumstances, was completely wasted on Sally and Rod. Wasted on Sally, because she had grown apathetic and cold like people do when they fall out of love. Wasted on Rod, because he was just now bringing into focus the feeling of being dropped. Abandoned. Abruptly left. Fucked.

Sally met Rod at a Future Farmers of America dance. The boys lined up against the wall and the girls lined up against the curtains. They stared at each other awkwardly and shifted their feet between songs. When the needle was dropped on the Victrola and the music started to play, boys shot across the room like pinballs and blindly grabbed whomever among the girls wasn't taken. Neither romance, interest, nor intention played in the coupling. Except for Sally and Rod. Rod was strongly intentional in picking Sally for each dance that close and cloaked June night, and they had been together ever since. Six years in June. Well...if they had made it to June. And in the midst of it came Iris, their daughter, born nine months and four days after the FFA dance where they met.

Sally repeatedly said Iris, "Signifies our true and everlasting love."

True. Everlasting. Until Sally met Mattis Dockern and true love became less true. And everlasting didn't last.

And so this kitchen, this morning, and the hot yellow sun dividing it, like the heavens, dark from light. On the light side: the window with its scalloped and lacy curtains blowing lightly in the morning breeze, the Allium slowly wilting in the heat, the floor gray with boot prints (not having been touched by Sally's usual morning mop). On the dark side: in shadow, the kitchen table with its cane-seat kitchen chairs jostled around as if a poker game had just broken up (instead of neatly placed like they would have been by Sally). At the foot of the table sits five-year-old Iris staring down at the tabletop. The water rings make the surface look like a lily pond (she thinks). Iris traces the water lilies with her fingertip and waits for her father (or mother) to appear as they usually would on a Monday.

Just at about the time that the sun began to shine on the tabletop and left Iris in danger of crossing (or being crossed) from darkness to light, Rod hustled from the yard into the kitchen holding a grease-stained bag of doughnuts to the chest pocket of his dusty indigo jean jacket.

"I got doughnuts," said Rod. "Apple cider ones."

"Oh," said Iris still staring down at the lily pads.

"They's still hot when I bought 'em. Fresh out the fryer."

"Where's my Mama?" asked Iris, not looking up.

"I told you. She's gone right now," said Rod rolling down the neck of the doughnut bag to expose the top layer of doughnuts.

"When she come back?"

"Now, Iris, don't get to hoping—" said Rod taking a doughnut bite, then: "—these are mighty crispy now but that won't last. Eat one. You won't do well with no breakfast, girl."

"When my Mama coming home?"

Overwhelmed with helplessness and unable to make sense of it himself, let alone explain it to his five-year-old daughter, Rod swallowed hard, took his jacket off, smashed the bag of doughnuts between his palms, and walked into the parlor, leaving Iris alone.

"When my Mama coming home?" called Iris, loud, at the swinging door.

He thought: NEVER! She's as gone as can be with that asshole Mattis Dockern to his daddy's goddam 470 acres in Madison, Illinois. And neither of us'll see her ass again!

But he stayed silent.

Instead of speaking, he looked around the parlor for some token of hope or potency—something to hold on to against the rising tide and howling wind of the truth he would have to tell Iris eventually. He grabbed the first thing he saw that qualified—Sally's abandoned King James Bible—and held it to his chest.

He mulled possible answers he could pick from:

Tender: I doubt she will be home any time soon, darlin'.
Or
Stark truth: She won't be coming home.
Or
Final: She ain't coming home—ever.
Or
Facts: She is already halfway to Illinois and neither of us will see her again.
Or
Truth: We are fucked, Iris. You might as well be an orphan!

Ultimately, he spoke this:

"Don't worry about your Mama, Iris. You and I are off outta here. To Salt Lake City!"

✦

In those days (just before the Great Depression), it was not difficult for a young hardscrabble Ohio farm boy with no more than a high school education to restyle himself as a preacher. All he needed to do was to wangle a gray linen suit, match it with a broad-brimmed hat, carry a poached King James Bible (well-worn by fingers and bursting with annotations), adopt the hauteur of a seminarian, and clean up his language a bit. Rod could do all of those things and did. It took only assertion to appropriate the required biography—childhood near Lexington, Kentucky, attended Kentucky Christian Normal Institute in Grayson, graduating in 1927. A self-assured change of name (becoming Rodrick O. Lusby) wasn't required, could only help, and certainly would do no harm since everyone knew Lusby was a name well-connected to the Christian community in Kentucky and Ohio.

A preacher was a fine thing for Rod to become. Traveling preachers required no explanation for being on the road and stood above question on details in general. Further, a Reverend asking for a bed, a handout, or discount was completely acceptable. Rod could conveniently become a recent widower, which would curtail people's concerns about a man traveling with a young girl across state lines.

And how hard could it be to establish a house of worship in Salt Lake City?

Iris and Rod (not quite yet Rev. Rodrick, which would wait until they had safely left Ohio) spent a hurried day throwing items into boxes and those boxes into the back of Rod's pickup. Rod figured the truck cab would stay cooler if they drove at night and slept during the day. So, at 7:43 p.m. on Tuesday night, Rod lit out on the Lincoln Highway toward Utah. He estimated a four-to six-day drive, even if they wasted time frivolously.

When they stopped for gas near the Indiana border, Rod grabbed the Bible, his hat, and Iris, and led her into the station shed where the gas jockey stood, smoking.

"Good evening, fine sir," said Rod touching his hat brim and trying hard to stand (and appear) upright. "My name is Reverend Rodrick Lusby and this is my daughter Iris. We's...that is we are... traveling west and would like to ask...er...inquire...if you would be so kind to provide us with a break...by which I mean a professional discount...for gas...by which I mean, gasoline."

Iris wondered at her father's new vocabulary. Who was this man, Lusby? The gas man wondered a bit at Rodrick Lusby's vocabulary, too, although not enough to think him illegitimate. He just struck him as a bit high-handed, although that kind of fit for a preacher. Rod himself, on the other hand, thought he did well for his first time speaking as a Reverend. Should he have included a Bible passage in his request? Rod wondered. He'd have to cultivate his religiosity and do it fast. He had four days to study the Bible (a book he had heard of, but never read) and get his story straight.

"Reverend? Um...sir?" said the gas man.

"Huh?" said Rod as if he was waking from a dream.

"I said I'd be right fine to take a penny off every two gallons as a discount."

"I am obliged, sir," said Rod bowing his head with a Reverend's reverence (he hoped). "As the book says 'he who feeds the pastor has done as good as to feed Jesus hisself. That's in...um...Falacians 2:24...you will find."

"Well, Reverend, I never heard of it," answered the gas man. "I am not up on my bible...sorry to say. You are providing me an education! Now...I will be right out to pump your gas." Then, to Iris, "Have a pleasant ride, little lady."

That night when they stopped at Salt 'n' Pepper Home Cooking along the route, Rod diligently spent his dinner time reading Genesis and copying out what he thought were the sprightlier bible quotes worth committing to memory. By the end of dinner (fried pollack with olive-drab peas and milky corn-on-the-cob for him and stodgy meatloaf with pasty cheese macaroni for her) Rod had copied out a page and a half of quotations. Tonight before bed he would commit them to memory. If he did the same every night before bed and every morning before breakfast, in a year—maybe two—he would get through the entire book. *More efficient than a Christian Normal Institute education, half as dull, faster, and free,* thought Rod. He was one day closer to leaving Rod Yancy behind and becoming Rodrick O. Lusby.

At the next morning's early gas stop 112 miles farther on, Rod inquired if there was a mechanic on the premises: "I got some trouble with my distributor cap, which is making my engine skip. Or I might need a new spark plug or plug wire."

"Ain't got no mechanic here now," said the gas jockey, locking his cash register on the suspicion that Rod was no good. "But he should be by here before too long. He's over to Claremore at the moment. Should be here by five, latest."

"We got time," said Rod, removing his hat and placing it on the counter. "In the meantime, we will have an RC Cola and a bag of Lay's, please. Do you mind if my daughter and I wait inside, sir?"

"Don't mind one bit," answered the gas man, pocketing the keys. "Not one bit."

There was a pause, during which both men shuffled. Then finally:

"My name is Reverend Rodrick O. Lusby. "Pointing to his truck. "That's my daughter. We are traveling out to Salt Lake and would like to inquire if you might be so kind to provide us with a professional discount on the gasoline. If you'd be so generous...to a recent widower."

"My gas is eighteen cents a gallon, which is mighty cheap. In Claremore the same elixir'd cost you twenty cents per gallon and you'd need to pump it yerself. I'm right happy you asked, and no. No discount. It's five cents for your soda. But...I'll throw the Lay's in for you, Reverend."

"I am much obliged, sir, for your generosity. As The Lord says in Genesis—"

"Now, friend, don't go quoting the Bible at me. Just enjoy the chips. I'll be grateful to pump you some gas." With that he checked the register lock once more and walked out of the office.

Rod waited a moment, then walked to his pickup and opened the door. "We's stopping here for about an hour, Iris. Come on. The man said we could wait inside."

Happy for an excuse to get out of the truck, Iris jumped down from the seat to the dusty pavement and ran into the office. Rod ran behind.

"Now, you be polite so we can stay inside," said Rod with a shake of his finger.

Iris looked around, found the only seat in the crowded space, and climbed into it. She put her elbow on the arm of the old leather swivel-chair, her chin in her hand, and watched through the dusty window as the man from the gas station filled the truck with gas.

When he was done, the gas man hustled back into the office, expertly navigating the narrow aisle from the door to the desk, where Iris was seated. "Hi, young lady," he said, tipping his dusty hat. "My name is Ephram. What's yers?"

Iris was silent and looked to Rod for permission. Rod made a gesture of assent, "Go ahead...what's your name?"

"My name is Iris-Jane-Yancy," said Iris, running all three parts of her name into a single three-car train.

"Lusby," Rod quickly inserted. "Iris Jane Lusby." Then, to Ephram, "She's only five."

"Well, Iris Jane Yancy...Lusby," said Ephram with an avuncular tone, "I have something I reckon you'd enjoy to see. Do you like puppies?"

Iris looked to Rod again to see if she could safely answer. Once again, Rod gestured permission.

"Yes," said Iris shyly. "Except not all-black ones!"

Both Ephram and Rod laughed.

"Well, you two come with me," said Ephram, "and I'll show you something."

He absently checked his pockets for his keys and led them out the front door. A quick right turn, then another right turn and they were at the back door of the office. There was an awning-like roof over the back door and on one side of the door was a fruit crate (labeled Dicky Moore Farms— Georgia's Best) covered seven-eighths of the way with a light-blue baby blanket. Ephram uncovered the crate and Iris saw puppies squirming inside. Two were brown spotted with black, three were black spotted with brown, and one was all black (except for an off-center white spot on his snout.

EPHRAM: They's just ten days old yesterday.
IRIS: Baby puppies!
EPHRAM: Yes!

ROD: You mean baby dogs!

EPHRAM: You can hold one if you'd like...

Ephram gently picked up one of the puppies (brown with black spots) and placed it in the dust in front of Iris. Its eyes still closed, it shook and instinctively raised its head to sniff for its mother.

"I been feeding them milk and water myself hoping they survive," said Ephram to Rod. "The mother walked off on the day before yesterday. Can't figure why."

Iris sat in the dust and took the puppy into her lap. As quickly as she took the puppy up, that's as quickly as it tried to crawl back toward the mews of its brothers and sisters.

"Try this one," said Ephram, offering the all-black puppy.

"I don't like black ones," said Iris, thrusting her hands to her sides. Ephram put the still birth-blind pup in her lap. It nodded twice in the direction of Iris's chin and curled up in her lap to sleep.

"Looks like the black one likes you!" Ephram said. "And it's not all black."

Iris gingerly reached down to pet the pup. The pup let out a long breath, yawned, and curled its tail between his back legs. It laid its head down and languidly started a snuffling snore.

"Can I have her?" Iris asked Rod.

"The pups belong to Mr. Ephram, darlin'," said Rod.

"He needs a good home," said Ephram. "So you sure could have him if you want him. Now...you'll have to feed him. That ain't too hard. I will wash out your RC Cola bottle and you can have one of my rubber gloves. You use the fingers to make a teat. That's what I've been doing. You'll need to nurse him for another two months or so. His eyes should open up in a few days."

"Can I have her?" Iris asked Rod again, insistently.

"Let me see..." said Ephram picking the pup up by the tail and looking squarely at its butt. "This one is a him. You mean to ask can I have HIM."

"Can I have him?" Iris asked her father.

"I suppose so!" answered Rod, feeling something fall into the space left by Sally.

"What should we name him?" asked Iris.

"Well...let's see," said Rod. "He should have a Godly name...um... how about...Paul? After Saint Paul of Assisi." Then, to Ephram, "He's the saint who cared for the animals on the Ark."

"Hi, Paul," said Iris balancing the puppy in her right palm. The puppy seemed to prick up his ears.

"Paul is a mighty fine name for him!" said Ephram, wondering who this preacher and this child truly were.

✦

Paul (in his box), Iris (low and wary in her seat), and Rod (hands at 10 and 2) chattered their way down the western side of the Wasatch Mountains, bumping out the last miles of the Lincoln Highway. Paul, the puppy, raised his head blindly and let out a yawn as the road flattened. It was just after 10 p.m. when Rod pulled over on Bridger Avenue at the Right Place bar to inquire about the best rooming house close by to stay overnight. He took his wallet from the dashboard, left his hat on the seat, grabbed the Bible, turned to leave the truck, thought better of the Bible, and placed it where the wallet had been.

"Don't touch anything, baby girl," he said to Iris. "I'll be back in a few." He shut the truck door, stepped from the curb, crossed the sidewalk, and opened the windowless door to the bar.

From the doorway, the Right Place looked like it hadn't been touched since the 1880's. The bar, long and ornate, filigreed with poles and lintels, looked frozen in time. Then Rod noticed everything had been painted black and he revised his assessment. It didn't look frozen in time—it looked dipped in tar, dredged out and left to drip dry. The walls were shiny black like the bar; the floor was red, rolled linoleum.

"I'll have an orange soda, please," Rod said to the aproned man behind the bar.

The barkeep rocked the bottle against the opener, popped the cap with a quick twist of his wrist, and set the bottle, bubbling, on the bar.

"You'll want to sit with him," the bar man said, pointing to the far end of the bar with his right thumb. A slim man with salt and pepper hair sat with half a bottle of orange soda warming in front of him.

Rod picked his way to the stool next to the man.

ROD: Another soda drinker I see!

ORANGE SODA MAN: Yes! Soda is as hard as it gets for me.

ROD: Same here. How do ya? I'm Rod.

ORANGE SODA MAN: Hello, Rod. I am Reverend Luke Hancock of the Simple Truth Gospel Ministries, next door down to the right.

ROD: Nice to meetcha, Rev.

REV. HANCOCK: Looks like I am too late to save your soul. You've ordered a soda after 10 o'clock in a bar. I know I'm too late. Someone got there before me!

ROD: Yes, Reverend, you are too late. I'm Reverend Rodrick O. Lusby, hailing from Grayson, Kentucky.

It was the second time Rod told all of these lies and the first time telling them all at once. He dropped them in the well of Rev. Hancock and waited to hear them hit the water.

REV. HANCOCK: I could have guessed, sir, by your drink of choice that you're a man of Spirit and by your clean fingernails that you weren't from the neighborhood. Welcome to Great Salt Lake City— Salt Lake City we call it now. What brings you to us, Sir?

ROD: The Lord... he...called me to leave...um...Kentucky and head west to minister to the copper miners here.

REV. HANCOCK: Now...seems to me—and it's my humble opinion only here, sir—Salt Lake City already has one too many churches. At least that's what those copper miners would tell us, Sir.

ROD: Well, the Lord called. I am just answering His call.

REV. HANCOCK: Just answering the Lord indeed, my friend. Did the Lord indicate the Salt Lake Valley in general? Salt Lake City in particular or Bridger Avenue in the specific? 'Cause I am quite certain [HIS EYES STEELING FROM BLUE TO SILVER] the Lord's work is being done adequately on Bridger Avenue. [LICKING HIS LIPS. PAUSE. THEN, WITH A SNEER] Friend.

ROD: The Lord? Well, He was not specific. But, like the prodigal, He led me here... [SPYING A WAY OUT] no doubt...so you...so you could...so you could guide me, Reverend. I'd be pleased if you'd take the Lord the rest of the way and suggest a—shall I say—more suitable location for my modest place of worship?

REV. HANCOCK: [MOLLIFIED] Indeed, friend. I am always ready to do the Lord's work, work on His behalf, or, as you said, take Him the rest of the way. Now...if you want work with copper miner's souls, it'll be Miner's Alley or Maiden's Lane where you'll meet your calling. Head there and you'll find 117 Miner's Alley is a recently abandoned house of worship. The Pastor got caught with his... what shall I? His...you-know-what...inside the wrong tradeswoman of Maiden's Lane. Good for you though, the rent is cheap and the population needy. Needy for the Word...Reverend Lusby.

ROD: Thank you!

REV. HANCOCK: As it happens...I own the property and I'd be pleased to make up a lease.

ROD: Well...I...

REV. HANCOCK: Go on by and see the place. Stained glass of the Via Doloroso. Simple yet bracing. See how it meets your needs... and...the needs of your...calling.

Rod swilled the rest of his NeHi in one gulp. He gave the Reverend a quick, "will do" and headed back to the truck, where he found his daughter asleep with her puppy—sleeping, too—on her shoulder. Realizing that he forgot to ask either the barman or the Reverend where they could sleep, he curled up behind the steering wheel, dropped his wallet on the seat and slid it under his right buttock, lowered his hat onto his eyes, and commenced his first night of rest in Salt Lake City.

✦

Ten seasons of snow fall paint the tips of the Wasatch hills feathery white each year. These ten years changed Rod from plain Rod to solidly Reverend Rodrick (now again Yancy), and his storefront church from a broom-cleaned empty space to the sometimes (partly, almost, could be) thriving Gethsemane Church of Hope. The church—white-washed inside and smelling of chlorine/rubber from disinfectant—attracted working men rinsing off the stink of bad luck, families with a hereditary quirk, gamblers reforming, and copper miners who sought something less corpulent than a Catholic service yet more lusty than a Mormon one.

Reverend Rodrick was now tall, lean, and an earnest speaker on a Sunday who—in over ten years of study and service to his community—had come to believe his own words are touched by God's Light, a delusion that might be required to unselfconsciously lead a spiritual community.

Paul, the dog, was in the middle age of a dog's years. He spent most sermons lying on the wooden floor of the dais. The floor, cool in the summer and warm in the winter, had a satisfying putty/ pine smell that reminded Paul of the wooden box he was born in. A spiritual connection if there ever was one. During sermons, Paul passed in and out of sleep, catching (what he thinks are) the salient points and filling the (all too common) lacunas between with dreams of grassy runs. His ability to openly drowse during the sermons made Paul much envied by Rodrick's parishioners. Paul's pantingly eager meeting of parishioners after services, his head amiably available for a scritch or a pat, made him more beloved by Reverend Rodrick's church than Reverend Rodrick himself.

Deacon Iris (which she is called by the members of the church, yet would never call herself) has also grown tall and lean with a modesty that beseems the daughter of the sort of Reverend that

Rodrick has become; shy and soft spoken, yet an ardent supporter of Her Father's Word. She was clear when anyone asks (though no one does!) that her father is Rodrick and Rodrick's Father (not hers) is Jesus. While she is present every Sunday fully supporting her father and his church, even at fourteen (about to turn fifteen), she knew true belief is applied willfully, not given recklessly. She was an ardent supporter, yet not an ardent believer.

✦

When it came to planning Iris's 15th birthday party, Rodrick was nearly without resources. He did fine at parenting functions he could compartmentalize as the domain of a father, yet had always felt ill-equipped to cross the line and provide a mother's touch. He taught Iris to fish. He taught her to throw a football. He dressed his daughter, although the results could best be called...practical. Witness when Iris started school. Rodrick dressed her in overalls, a plaid shirt, and neat round-toed brown leather work boots. He dressed her exactly the same when she went to her first school dance (although a flannel shirt, Rodrick felt, was more suitable for winter). It took a school conference with a sympathetic (female) teacher to get Iris into a knee-length gingham dress for school. When, at twelve years old, Iris had her first argument with a boy and came home crying, Rodrick took her to the bare, tiny yard behind the church and taught her what he knew about arguments: how to throw a punch. When at thirteen, Iris had her first menses, Rodrick cooly handed her a bar of soap and a box of Kleenex and called Mrs. Reid, who taught Gethsemane's Sunday school, begging her to handle it any way she would, so long as it was quick, brief, thorough, and out of his earshot. And, when it came to planning Iris's fifteenth birthday, Rodrick did what any self-respecting single father with a church would do: he handed the planning—lock, stock, and candles—to the Gethsemane Church of Hope Women's Auxiliary Celebrations Committee.

Miss Celia Garner, chairman of the committee, took the better part of fifteen seconds to come up with a party idea: a Cake Walk. These were the rage in 1884 and were now back in style, having been—in Miss Garner's words—"rescued from the Negroes for everyone's amusement."

"Why choose a Cake Walk?" Rodrick wanted to know.

Miss Garner ignored his question and steamed on at full paddle:

"—the first thing one needs for a complete Cake Walk is a chalk circle. We will draw one on the floor of the Assembly Hall. It's historical. A Cake Walk was originally called a 'chalk-line walk' don't you know? Of course, a chalk-line is needed. This could be accomplished, by the way, through making a large compass with a nail, some string, and a piece of chalk!"

Rodrick wanted to put an end to the idea right there but, with a toss of her Gibson Girl, Miss Garner continued breathlessly:

"Second, for a successful Cake Walk one needs...*cakes*! I, personally, will ask the Celebrations Committee, the six of us, each to bake a fancy cake. Those will be the prizes! Plus, I will make the plum cake—that's traditionally the grand prize at a Cake Walk—as Iris's birthday cake. Now... third—and I am not close to finishing—a Cake Walk needs walkers! These will be Iris's invited guests. They will do the walking. The cake walking. A promenade, really. Oh dear, that brings me to music! Music is required—a gavotte preferred. Actually, now that I think, I see that more than one recording will be needed. Oh! And a Victrola! So many details! But...you will agree, Reverend Yancy, that the magic, the enjoyment, the sub-lim-ity is in the details—large and small. It is by paying attention that we shall throw a triumphant Cake Walk birthday party for Iris!"

Celia Garner concluded, finally taking a breath.

Rodrick, not smitten with her party idea, was summarily smitten with the idea of the decision being made by someone else—and with that someone else doing the work. After a moment of feigned consideration, he agreed to the idea and funded the $30 budget simply to be free of further involvement.

Except the making of the guest list. Iris's school friends (maximum of ten to keep a lid on girly froth, thought Rodrick), and the entire church community: forty-two guests in total. Plus, family: Rodrick, Iris, and the Reverend Luke Hancock, Rodrick's longtime mentor, friend, and landlord. "Uncle" Luke brought the total to 45.

✦

The church assembly hall was a cold room (empty and dark, except during Sunday morning services and Tuesday game nights). 110 folding chairs stood stacked against the short walls and five folding tables were stacked against the long walls. For the evening of Iris's birthday, though, all the square, hard, unadorned surfaces were softened with cabbage-y bouquets and garlands of white and pink peonies, open blossoms alternating with closed ones to provide variety. One folding table had been wrapped in yellow crepe-paper and beribboned with green-dotted Swiss to hold the haul of presents. Two other tables, wrapped in light-green crepe paper (accented with yellow-dotted ribbons) were pushed together and set with seven cake stands, their bases ringed with violet and white jacaranda trusses. The blunt silver-gray fluorescent lights used every Sunday during services were turned off and replaced for the evening by tall beeswax candles (from honeycombs tended by church member Alsworth Kinderfreund). The candles stood on mismatched bread and butter plates. They made a homely gathering celebratory as they cast rings of light that took you to an earlier, simpler time. The combined fragrance of honey-tinged candles with flowers filled the room with mid-summer. The overall effect, "was magic and heliotrope, just as Shakespeare might have imagined the home of Titania," according to Miss Garner.

A plentiful table of food bulwarked the opposite wall. A huge platter of perfectly breaded and fried chicken came from Maisy Chillins, a punch bowl full of cabbage slaw (with bacon fat in the mayonnaise and mustard flowers as a garnish) was delivered by Christine and Darlene, the Shrash sisters. A platter of glazed, baked parsnips was contributed by the Thompson family. Guests brought three competing versions of the local favorite, Funeral Potatoes. One was made with shredded potatoes, cheddar cheese mixed with chicken soup, and topped with crushed cornflakes (brought by Sarah Whitcomb), a second made with potatoes, white cheddar, celery soup, and sausage (brought by the men of Coppermine No. 4), and a third made with Swiss cheese, potato soup, and topped with crumbled Ritz crackers (brought by Dina Whitely and her husband Donald). Two glass pitchers, one of lemonade and one of ginger beer, stood sweating in the front left and right corners.

At a fourth table in front of the altar—the cakes!

1. Sarah Whitcomb brought a Chocolate Bavarian Torte (her mother's recipe with Chantilly made from her cows' cream)
2. Clarice Reilly baked a sky-high Hummingbird Cake (four layers of banana and pineapple with vanilla buttercream. Her father's favorite!)
3. Linda Yeamans supplied a spiced Devil's Food Cake (with beetroot and cocoa to make the color bright red)
4. Carrie Bartlett made her grandmother's recipe of Lazy Daisy Cake (vanilla cake with coconut nougat frosting the top and sides)
5. Cleopatra Gosthke adapted the Lady Baltimore Cake for her church family by filling the buttermilk cake layers with dried figs and raisins soaked in cola, rather than brandy)
6. Lautrice Conrad brought her Gran Tabitha's Apple Cake (with cream cheese icing sprinkled with black walnuts from the Conrad family's own trees)
7. The Grand Prize was Celia Garner's Symphony of Plums Cake. Five layers of light sponge baked around the ripest black plums, filled, and frosted with lemon buttercream (with just a hint of vanilla to balance the lemon)

Upon seeing all the cakes in place, Miss Garner thought: *With each cake beaming on its cake stand and each cake stand trimmed charmingly with blossoms, surely no mortal on earth could resist a cake or the dance required to win it!*

Propelled by that thought, the party started.

✦

After arrivals and initial greetings, like many large parties do, Iris's birthday party devolved into small conversational groups. The matrons knitted themselves into a buzz about sewing, which meandered from mending, to newly available sewing patterns, to fitting adolescent daughters properly as they grew, to influenza, to husbands. The men took on the topic, "Which is the best combine to use in heavy rain?" leading to, "Why does it seem to rain so much more lately?" leading then to, "Can the newly widowed Lautrice Conrad hire a hand (who is just a hired hand)?" The daughters (who were Iris's schoolmates, but of scant interest to Iris) frittered in three small minims: those who thought the new Mathematics teacher graded harshly, those who thought he was too lenient, and those too overcome with thoughts of marrying him to notice. The sons: truck tires. There was a maverick group of late-teenaged young women and young men whose topic appeared to be kissing (including a clumsy practicum which caused individuals to sprint from the group into the center of the room, whooping, and then back followed by peals of laughter). Last, a small knot who assembled because of their common affiliation with Gethsemane Church of Hope started their conversation with, "What is the true nature of the Trinity?" and ended with each of the group members sitting alone staring at their hands.

In other words, the party chugged along like a neat small-gauge locomotive.

Iris, Rodrick, and Uncle Luke chose not to join any of the conversations. On Luke's arrival, the three started an obligatory conversation about the occasion, the flowers, and the cakes that finished when Uncle Luke exclaimed, "Isn't this an auspicious night?" Then they fell into the awkward silence that only occurs at the start of parties, before the mass of people arrive. Eventually, Luke and Rodrick walked together to embark on a conversation about the challenges of raising a fifteen-year-old daughter alone. That evolved to discussing a thorny issue each of them coincidentally faced with church expenses. When they finished those topics, they fell into unforced, fraternal silence. Eventually, Rodrick pretended to notice some party detail he had to tend to and he walked toward it, leaving Luke standing alone. Luke, who had not yet removed his coat, set a course for the platter of chicken on the buffet.

When Luke walked away, Iris felt she had finished her hosting duty. With almost everyone happily sewn up in conversation, she declined any further social obligation and walked off to quietly pet her dog. Once her arms were securely around his graying neck, she spoke reassurances (To him? To them? To herself?) that, although alone and seemingly friendless, they had each other.

After some languorous minutes of cuddling Paul the dog (Paul stoically bearing being over-loved, as he always did), Iris quietly excused herself to the practical solitude of the outhouse, twenty-five feet or so from the back door of the Assembly Hall. Absently and dutifully, Paul followed. After all, those twenty-five feet of dusty yard could be filled with perils. Perils only an old dog could sense. Perils only a loyal dog could mediate.

While Paul stood his droop-eyed vigil, Iris struggled in the confined darkness of the outhouse to raise her first long dress to her midriff and lower her underwear without it touching the mud-flecked floor. This accomplished, she finished what she had come to do.

Upon hearing the quiet squeak of the outhouse door, Paul the dog stood and waited for Iris so they could walk the remaining twenty feet back to the Assembly Hall door. Three feet from the door, Paul sensed something in the shadowy corner to the right of the door. It was Uncle Luke in his dark brown oil cloth raincoat, brown trousers, white shirt, and oiled bison leather hobnail boots. Paul saw nothing to worry about in Luke, so he raised his head for a pat.

"Happy birthday!" Luke said to Iris, the fingernail of his left hand parting his lips and picking at a shred of chicken between his teeth. "Yes. Happy, happy birthday. Seems to me it's time for you to be considered a woman. Thought of as one, I mean."

Iris instantly felt his intentions and fear began to rise in her neck.

Paul sensed (as only an alert dog could) a shift in the energy between Luke and Iris. The change caused Paul to plant his feet, lick his upper teeth, and lower his head for a better view in the harsh light of the clear bulb that hung over the door.

Iris stopped and touched her dog's haunch. "Yes, Uncle Luke, it is a milestone."

"Seems to me when you're thought of as a woman, y'oughta be treated like one too."

"I don't know what you mean, Uncle—"

"I mean that I intend to give you a taste of womanhood."

Iris, asserting normalcy, took a step to continue toward the door saying, "Uncle Luke...the party."

"That option is not available—"

Iris, summoning up as much spine as she could, stepped forward to grab the doorknob. Luke inserted himself between the door and Iris's hand, ending up with her hand planted in his midsection and his lips on hers. He grabbed the back of her head and held her in a spit-soaked kiss, his tongue forcing itself between her lips.

Iris immediately spun back toward the outhouse and bolted in that direction. Luke examined his suddenly empty hands. Paul lunged forward, targeting Luke's upper thigh with his open jaw. The dog bit only oil cloth and fell back barking hoarsely.

The dog lunged a second time. This time his head met the hobnail sole of Luke's boot. Luke kicked Paul's head again. And again. And again, until Paul finally fell to the dusty ground, stone still and bleeding from his right ear.

IRIS: [HALFWAY TO THE OUTHOUSE, IN A WHISPER] "Paul... Uncle Luke..."

Luke looked down at the bleeding dog. In that moment, he collided suddenly with the harm he had done. He took two confused steps back. Iris, her face smirched with tears and Luke's saliva, stepped over her dog and past the distracted man through the door and into the sanative candlelight of Assembly Hall. The Victrola was playing, "Bunch O'Blackberries" for the cakewalk and walkers circled, cake-obsessed and oblivious to Iris's arrival.

A moment later Luke walked through, leaving footprints of dust and dog blood.

Iris swallowed hard. In the warm light of the candles with the Victrola puling in the background, she felt bile burn its way to her throat. She coughed and wiped her lips of Luke's spit, which she now realized was mixed with tobacco chaw. Chewing tobacco all on her hand and forearm. A sin both Luke and her father preached against in sermons. As she looked at the greenish mess on her wrist, she turned away from the door she had just walked through. In that same moment, her heart turned away from Luke. All she felt toward him was bitter hatred. And turned away from her father, whose job it had always been to keep her safe. What she felt toward him was disenchantment.

Iris's heart turned toward Paul, her sweetly loved dog. She tried to imagine his still body outside the door, empty of the soul that had made him her special companion. She could not picture it. She repeatedly tried to imagine Paul's lifeless body, yet the image would not aggregate in her mind.

She was about to open the door to look one last time at Paul's body when she heard a voice. Somehow, she knew it was Paul's voice.

"See you tomorrow," he said.

✦

A shaft of dawning sunlight cast a hazy yellow square on the floor next to Iris's bed as she woke. On a typical day, Paul would be found basking in what early morning sunlight there was, his snuffling snore reassuring Iris that everything in the world outside her dreams was all right. Today, there was no snoring, no reassurance, and no Paul. Paul's body lay where he had dropped, now covered with a green wool blanket to keep the flies from burrowing in. Last night at a few minutes past ten o'clock, Iris had led Rodrick to the dead dog's resting place. In a weak lie (that somehow Rodrick had not questioned), Iris claimed that she found Paul lying in his blood when she went to the outhouse. There was no one to counter her story—the cakewalkers had been awarded their cakes and decamped. Iris had washed her face. And, nearly an hour before, Luke had stealthily left the party.

The plan was to bury the dog just before the 11 a.m. morning service. Mrs. Goodall from the Women's Auxiliary Bible Study Group hastily gathered together garlands of peonies left from the party and tied them together to fashion a grave blanket. Mrs. Freed, Women's Liturgical Committee, who had been engaged to distribute leftover food from Iris's party to the indigent, had been called into service to, instead, whip the leftovers into a post-burial/post-morning-service lunch. Mr. Freed, retired, had been asked to telephone as many congregants as possible to ease them the news of Paul's passing (Paul was, after all, the most popular church member) and to invite them to his funeral at 10:45 a.m.

Flowers, candles, fried chicken, Funeral Potatoes, and, this time, nineteen congregants—which was a hefty number for a weekday—gathered in the shade between the Assembly Hall door and the outhouse, where there was enough yard to dig a grave large enough for Paul's final rest. Never having officiated at a pet funeral before, Rodrick adapted the funeral service for canine use as he went.

RODRICK: Dear friends, Gethsemane family, we are here gathered to mark the life of Iris's and my dog, Paul, who was taken to heaven last night, here in the yard.

Rodrick nodded a signal and four bearers carried Paul in, covered in the peony blanket. They placed him on the ground in front of the congregation and just to the left of the grave.

Then:

RODRICK: [WHILE LIGHTING ONE OF THE BEESWAX CANDLES, IN A DELFT SAUCER, WHICH STOOD ON A WOODEN NIGHTSTAND TAKEN FROM HIS BEDROOM] During a time of loss, we light a candle of recollection to recall our loved one. May this flame remind us of the love we feel for our beloved... dog. May this light help guide... Paul...to a place in heaven—a place of peace and love. May the power of this flame bring us strength and set us on a healing journey so our sadness is replaced, over time, by warm memories of... Paul's...brief but...devoted...life. He was so devoted to Iris. [TEARS IN HIS EYES] So devoted. It is not easy to understand the deepness of the loss of a good dog. I am surprised myself how vacant I felt today when I walked here to the yard without Paul following behind me. I know many of you have loved Paul yourselves as Iris and I do. Did. Although we are saddened by the loss of...Paul...let us take this occasion to recall his life and appreciate the role he played in all of our lives and the lives of the people of Gethsemane Church. You are now invited to stand and share a memory of ...Paul. It might be a particular special moment or something that you learned from our loved one. I mean, Paul, as...um...well...a...dog.

Several congregants came forward to speak about Paul and to share a memory. Sniffles were heard. Rodrick read Ecclesiastes 3:1-8: "To every thing there is a season, and a time for every purpose under heaven..."

Then Iris came forward to read a poem she had torn out of McCall's magazine:

Friend, please don't mourn for me
I'm still here, though you don't see.
I'm right by your side each night and day
and within your heart I long to stay.

My body is gone but I'm always near.
I'm everything you feel, see or hear.
My spirit is free, but I'll never depart
as long as you keep me alive in your heart.

I'll never wander out of your sight—
I'm the brightest star on a summer night.
I'll never be beyond your reach—
I'm the warm moist sand when you're at the beach.

Here, as Iris paused slightly to reinforce the change of season, a strange thing happened: she heard Paul bark.

Or thought she did.

She pushed onward with the poem.

I'm the...colorful leaves...when fall comes around
and the pure white snow that blankets the ground.
I'm the beautiful flowers of which you're so fond...

Once again. Only, this time, clearer. A dog bark. Muffled by peonies.

...The clear cool water in a quiet pond.

Then she saw the peony blanket move.

I'm the first bright blossom you'll see in the spring,
The first warm raindrop that April—

Then, dead Paul stood and shook the blanket of peonies off his back. With a full-voiced bark, he raised his head as if he were surfacing from a pool to gather his first breath of air.

Iris burst into tears.

Gasps came from the first few rows of congregants as they struggled to make out exactly what was happening. Paul took a cautious step toward Iris. Then another. Then he licked her hand.

"Oh, Paul!" She said, encircling his dusty, bloody neck with her arms.

Rodrick invited the congregation to skip the morning service and go directly to lunch with Iris and Paul in the Assembly Hall.

✦

Most Sundays, the congregation numbered thirty to thirty-five. This number ballooned to fifty-five and sixty on Easter and Christmas and dwindled to eight to ten on the hottest summer Sundays, since the church was not air-conditioned.

The flyer Rodrick wrote and distributed brought 117 souls to the next Sunday service:

This Sunday!

July 12, 1942

PAUL
THE MIRACLE DOG

Returned from Heaven
And
Touched by Our Lord

11 a.m.

At
Gethsemane Church of Hope

Rodrick enjoyed preaching to a crowd. And, to Roderick, Paul seemed to enjoy the attention.

Rodrick made sure a new flyer was passed for each of the successive Sundays.

By August 9th, each folding chair in Gethsemane's Assembly Hall was occupied and a similar number to those sitting were standing. 230 attendees.

For August 16th there was a new flyer:

This Sunday at 8 a.m. and 11 a.m.!
August 16th, 1942
!Sunday Liturgy!

Featuring an Appearance by
The Christian Wonder

PAUL, THE MIRACLE DOG

RETURNED FROM HEAVEN
AND TOUCHED
BY OUR LORD!

Live and in Person!

Only at
Gethsemane Church of Hope!

This flyer packed the church with 383 congregants at a newly-added 8 a.m. service and 513 at 11 a.m. The tithe basket overflowed with quarters and dollar bills.

Then, word started to circulate that, after touching Paul's gold robe (sewn by congregant SaraBeth Eddins), seventy-three-year-old Madeline O'Bern was abruptly cured of the shingles. By Sunday, September 20th, Rodrick had rented a white tent and had it erected in the empty lot on the corner southwest of the church. A wooden sign now stood outside the church door:

Gethsemane Church of Hope
Home of
PAUL, THE HEALING DOG,
sent by The Angels DIRECT from Heaven!

Each Sunday service now had a line for entry, assembled an hour before the service began. Iris clicked her handheld counter 1,023 times, signifying the busiest non-Mormon Salt Lake City church service anyone could remember.

In early October, the Salt Lake City Post-Dispatch published testimony from three people who had touched Paul (or his robe) and each of whom declared themselves healed—one of recurrent impetigo, one of lymphadenopathy, and one of renal insufficiency.

On October 20th, the following quarter-page advertisement was placed in the Salt Lake Telegram:

Sunday at 11 a.m.!
October 25th, 1942
The Magic and Wonder
of
PAUL, THE MIRACLE DOG
TOUCHED BY HEAVEN
and
GIVEN THE GIFT OF HEALING!
Live and in Person!
Only at
Gethsemane Church of Hope

The crowds continued to wait in line and pack the tent with over 2,000 seated and standing worshippers at each service.

The Sunday before Christmas, too cold to use the tent, required the rental of the Uptown Theater and a full-page advertisement:

Sunday December 20th at 8 p.m.!

ONE SHOW ONLY
PAUL, THE MIRACLE DOG

Live! In Person!
HE WILL HEAL YOU!

Tickets $8 (second balcony) to $12 (inside the healing cordon)
Sponsored by Gethsemane Church of Hope

The seats sold out, less than a week before Christmas, bringing in just over $23,000 in ticket sales. 200 pot-holders imprinted with a drawing of Paul's head and the words, "Miracle Dog" sold out as well, bringing an additional $150. A box of 300 snow globes with a plastic dog inside (who bore only a slight resemblance to Paul) sold out at $0.25 each. Rodrick was convinced by this haul that Paul provided more satisfaction and better remuneration than his preaching. Although he never declared the change openly, Rodrick did not conduct services at the church for the next two years, splitting his time between the white tent and the Uptown Theater as Paul's manager. He hired a young seminarian to handle his preaching responsibility. Gradually, Rodrick's congregation got used to his absence, and the odd blend of church and show business that Gethsemane Church of Hope had become.

✦

In mid-April after Paul became the Miracle Dog, Iris was reading through yet another stack of letters addressed to Paul when she opened this one:

Dear Paul, the Miracle Dog,

I visited your exhibition and enjoyed both the spiritual and entertainment aspects very much. I have to admit

I wasn't healed, but some people seemed to be. I just enjoyed how quiet you stayed and how philosophical you seemed while doing all that healing. Having hundreds—maybe thousands—of people touching you must be a mixed blessing, but it is clear you are a good dog. I am sending this note to let you know I appreciate your generosity, which is palpable.

With all due respect,

Owen Silban

P.S. I noticed behind your berth there was a woman who took care of you. She displayed a sweetness I admire. Please inform her that she lit me up with her beauty—the beauty in her heart as well as on her cheek. I will be passing through Salt Lake City in early June and would be honored if a meeting with her might be possible. Paul, please ask her to respond by post. —O.S.

Once read, Iris created a ritual of rereading the note each afternoon when she took a break from the church bookkeeping to drink a grape soda. She sat on a window seat in the cool hallway just outside the church office, smoothed her dress on her lap, and laid the note there in the sunlight, being careful to reverently uncrease it before she read it. And reread it. And read it again.

She tried to construct a mental picture of Owen Silban from the facts she had. The name Owen translates as, "noble-born," so she imagined the narrow patrician nose and acute blue eyes of a man in a worsted suit, starched white shirt, and leather-soled shoes. Silban was undoubtedly a Spanish surname so, in her mind, she switched the worsted suit to a summer suit of tan seersucker and reimagined slicked black hair instead of the curls she originally thought Owen had. She examined his handwriting (clearly a public-school education) and his tone (secondary-school educated), so she mentally added a college ring. Passing through Salt Lake City could mean he does business with the Latter Day Saints, so she tried on the image of a salesman with a hefty sample case and ankle socks. These constructions of an imaginary Owen came and went as she read his letter each day with very little impact on her consideration of whether or not to write back. Iris could not imagine what to say.

Then one afternoon, after holding the note like an amulet for five weeks, she suddenly wrote a response:

Dear Mr. Silban,

I was very happy to get your note, which my mistress read to me. I have been quite stymied as to a response. I have watched her and kept her safe for over sixty-five years (those are my years). Then I received your kind and generous note. I asked myself, "Should I encourage a response?" After mulling it over, I am encouraging Iris (my mistress's name is Iris) to begin a correspondence of her own with you. She will write you soon under separate cover. I, Paul, will lie down and let you two carry on as you will, since I have my healing job to do.

with fond regards,

Paul

A few days later Iris wrote a brief note to Owen, formal and guarded. Owen responded with a note carefully written to be slightly more casual and open than hers. From this cornerstone, they built a correspondence of gradual disclosure and increasing openness, with a letter back and forth every three to four days. Iris noticed that each letter from Owen came from a different address. She responded to each address as it came, and her letters seemed always to find their way to him.

They made a plan to meet on June 12th at noon at the Dexter Diner, where a friend named Sarah, from Gethsemane Church, worked as a waitress. Having never seen each other, Owen and Iris agreed to meet just outside the diner on the busy corner of Temple and Dexter Streets. Iris would wear a daisy in her hair above her left ear.

At noon, Owen, in a jet-black suit, a crisp white shirt, a silver-blue striped tie, matching pocket kerchief, and black patent-leather shoes approached the only woman alone on the sidewalk and presented her with a dusty Ball jar of pickled green tomatoes. Iris took his gift with a laugh and an enthusiastic nod of her head.

"From my father's delicatessen," said Owen. "Silbanovitz is the family name."

They sat in the diner for hours and unreeled their stories as if they had been given a serum. Iris told about Ohio, her lost mother, her devoted father, and Paul, the Miracle Dog. She included Luke's stolen kiss, which she had never told anyone. She talked about her life in the church, her questions about Jesus and the (in her view, disappointing) stage show Gethsemane had become. Owen talked about growing up in Brooklyn, playing stoop ball, his love for animals and the Marx Brothers, and his current work as the elephant tamer for Maynard Diamond's Wayfaring Curiosity Show.

In this first meeting there were, as Iris would later describe it to Rodrick, "polka dots and moonbeams," for both her and Owen.

After four and a half hours, Owen mentioned his need to catch his train to Idaho Falls, where the show was starting a five night stand.

They parted with a touch of fingertips, a kick of Iris's left foot against the pavement and a plan to meet again when the Curiosity Show train passed town on the way from Lander, Wyoming to Flagstaff, Arizona.

As Maynard Diamond's Wayfaring Curiosity Show snaked its way around the West, Iris and Owen continued to write and meet, growing more open and unguarded with each meeting and letter.

By their 11th meeting, Owen had broached, "Do you love me, Iris Yancy?" And Iris had replied, "Yes!" with a stifled laugh. She had wondered about love but had never expected it in the form of this handsome little well-dressed Jew who smelled of Old Spice, bananas, and pachyderms.

At their 12th meeting, for which Iris had taken a train to Warm Springs, Nevada, Owen put forward a proposal:

"I have suffered a loss, Iris, and I could use your help."

"A loss?"

"Jeanie, my assistant, decided to stay on with a fella she met in Twin Falls, so I am without a beauty to adorn the shoulders of Kandula, my lead elephant. Jeanie was more than just beautiful. She handled all five elephants as commandingly as I. It is clear, knowing you and Paul, that animals like you. I can teach you the rest. Would you replace Jeanie and come on the train with me?"

[PAUSE]

In the space between his question and her answer, Iris did not think about whether going with Owen was the right thing to do. Instead, she thought about Rodrick, Gethsemane Church, and Paul.

Then, as naturally as exhaling:

"I'll come!"

And then she added:

"If I can bring Paul..."

ENTR'ACTE

The Barker

Brendan Hardy

NOW

You know those commercials for a Lexus? That woman's voice with a posh-y British accent? That voice that sounds to our ears like Lexus luxury is supposed to feel in our hearts? We're all at the point where, when we see a Lexus, we expect to hear that voice. We hear it and it says everything we need to know: class, luxury, leather, wood. Or it's the same with the Crazy Eddie guy— "His prices are INNNSSSANE!" As annoying as that commercial is, that guy Jerry Carroll has the perfect voice for it. You hear his voice and, in a snip, you think, "INSANE" just from the voice. Or, maybe, the other way around. You hear the word, "insane" and you think of that guy's voice. Funny how just a voice can do that. Trigger a whole set of stuff in us.

Bob Marcus's voice is just like that. Like, if you live in the New York Metropolitan Area, you—and everyone around you—know Bob's voice from when he says, "We overlook no reasonable offer at Metro New York Honda!" And if you live in Chicago, you can't turn on the radio without hearing Bob's voice say, "The happiest cows graze at Singing Cow Dairy!" Or, if you live anywhere in the whole United States, you hear that flute play that heeeewww-

hewwwww-dee-dum-doo-hayyyyy stinger and Bob's voice comes in with: "Five burgers. Ten-dollars. Is that a deal or what?" for Pappy's Burgers. Bob is the voice of the circus, too. The voice of the Big Top. Hundreds of thousands of people hear Bob's voice each afternoon and evening as the circus starts:

"Ladies and gentlemen, boys and girls, this is the Barnum and Bailey [or Shriners, or Pickle Family, or Moscow] Circus! Welllllcommmme to the Biiiig Top!"

While everyone who listens imagines Robert L. Marcus making this announcement from someplace in the same tent with them with Bob standing by a microphone and breathing the same air of hotdogs and caramel corn, in fact he recorded the announcements months, maybe even years ago in a tiny closet of a recording studio at Midtown Audio, 1271 Broadway, 21st floor, NYC. Bob recorded one announcement after another, changing only the company name, all in an hour. The circus plays it every night, giving you the illusion Bob is there with you. I know because he told me. We live together.

I am sure you, yourself, can hear Bob's voice your head if you think about it. Just imagine you are in the circus tent waiting. That delicious few moments before the show when people rush to their seats, glance through their souvenir programs, and wait eagerly.

The houselights go to half. I am no singer, but the band warms up with Daisy Bell:

> Daisy, Daisy
> Give me your answer, do.
> I'm half crazy
> All for the love of you...

I know you can hardly recognize the song when I sing it but, anyway, then: Once in Love with Amy:

> Once in love with Amy
> Always in love with Amy

Ever and ever fascinated by her
Sets your heart on fire to stay...

The music ends, creating a taut string of silence. A pin-spot cuts through the misty air. A shaft of silver brightens an empty space on the sawdust-covered floor. Into the silence, Bob's voice booms:

"Ladies and gentlemen, boys and girls! Welcome to the Barnum and Bailey Circus and the Big Top! Please welcome your ringmaster, Johnathan Lee Iverson!"

Or Daniel Pinter or Diana Seemasow or any of the other legendary bosses of the three-ring. The audience detonates into applause. The applause swallows up the voice. That voice that, all at once, says: "You're someplace special! Like no place else on earth! This is magical!" Robert L. Marcus's voice says all of that at once. It would be the same if he were reading entries from the phone book. Bob's voice just says, "CIRCUS!"

Bob started in radio. I've always thought people who work in radio are a tiny bit crazy. Radio people sit alone at 3 a.m. in Studio A in an empty building and talk about music or the news or their own life as if they are certain beyond a doubt that someone out there in the dark night is listening. Doesn't it take a certain kind of insanity to think people are listening? Especially at 3 a.m.?

When I talked to Bob about this, he said it's not just radio. It's true of all performers. We are a little crazy because we think people are listening. Or it could be we are hyper-sane because we know that no one is listening but we perform anyway. Whether we play to a full house or an empty one, we know that life is not as rich and full without the make-up, the lights, the music, the clowns. People out there need what we do. They need the respite that show people provide to get through life. Us performers know that you—the audience—needs what we do. Just like someone is called to become a doctor at a young age out of charity and caring for others, could a clown, an acrobat, or a contortionist hear the same voice calling them? Maybe show folk are called to entertain not out of personal weakness —as people say often—but because, for us, show business is a ministry. A ministry of distraction that helps people move from the callous world into the make-believe one just to survive.

Maybe radio people are the same. Maybe they sit alone in the dark because they know that, out there, alone in the same darkness, someone needs the sound of their voice, or to hear Build Me Up Buttercup on a Thursday morning at 2:12 a.m. Or because it is just plain comforting to hear a familiar voice talking about cars or cows or Pappy's Burgers? Or welcoming us to the Big Top?

ACT SIX

The Voice of the Big Top

Hiram Fitzgerald

THEN

"I tol' you Hiram. To them you is and you'll always be jus' anotha nigga," his mother said as she combed through his hair to wipe the blood away. "They is jus' as likely to lynch you, baby, as call yo' by yo' name."

Hiram winced as his mother's cloth skimmed over the edges of the wound sending white-hot, red-eye pain over his face. "Ow! Owww," he yelled. Then, quietly: "Mama, I don't know why white folks gets the fancy bathrooms anyway. Or why they get sinks while we gets a rag nailed to the wall to wipe our hands. Jus' ain't fair!"

✦

At 9:20 a.m. on April 8th, 1922, Hiram Fitzgerald, ten years old, of Raymond, Mississippi, left his home on 270 Dry Grove Road to pick up a loaf of bread at Bayer's Bakery on Railroad Street. He walked up Elm Street to Railroad, spotting four roving dogs, a three-legged cat digging in a milk carton, a drunk white man in ripped dungaree overalls passed out in a doorway breathing hard through his sawdust-flecked white beard, and a red rubber ball (which Hiram snatched up and placed, now an awkward bulge, in the righthand pocket of his black canvas pants). He walked up the boardwalk on Railroad past LJ's Bar, the HoneyBee Restaurant, and found Mr. Bayer amiably rocking in the whitewashed chair in front of his bakery window. The smell of baking raisin bread clouded Hiram's sense of time and place and transported him to a yeasty world of flour, salt, and cinnamon. Until Mr. Bayer broke the spell:

MR. BAYER: Hiram Fitz! Good day to you!
HIRAM: Hi, Mr. Bayer.

Hiram heel-to-toed in a shy rocking motion to the front case and bent to peer in. Yeasty yellow egg pastry, cherries, and sugar glaze peered back. His stomach opened like the petals of a tulip.

MR. BAYER: Your Mama need something, Hiram?
HIRAM: Uh huh. [TAKING IN A DEEP MOUTHFUL OF BAKERY SCENT] She need a loaf a' bread. Not sliced.
MR. BAYER: Your Mama usually gets bread from the day-old bin. All I got in there today is whole wheat.
HIRAM: I'll take it!

Having made the decision on behalf of his mother to buy whole wheat, Hiram leaned against the counter staring at the cinnamon buns while Mr. Bayer wrapped the bread tightly in waxed paper.

"May I offer you a butter cookie, Hi?" asked Mr. Bayer speaking as if the offer were a new proposal (instead of something that happened every time).

"Yes, thanks, Mr. Bayer," answered Hiram, accepting as if his acceptance were a new response (instead of something that happened every time).

"And will it be a green candied cherry or a red one, Hi?"

"Green one, today, please."

Mr. Bayer handed Hiram the loaf of bread, securely wrapped and twined. He then ducked his head into the window case and took a green-cherried butter cookie from its sheet pan, placed it firmly between his fingers (lined with a square of brown paper), and handed the paper and cookie to Hiram.

"Thanks again!" called Hiram over his shoulder as he walked out the door, bread under his arm, munching.

Mr. Bayer grabbed his pen and ledger, entered the bread purchase on Mrs. Fitzgerald's account, and contented himself once again in his rocker.

Hiram, for his part, walked down Railroad Street, counting the boardwalk boards absently to himself while he chewed his cookie. Suddenly, his cinnamon-scented bakery reverie was cut short by an intense call to pee. Since he was just in front of the Raymond rail passenger station when he felt the itch, he crossed Railroad Street to enter the station. He walked around to the right and stood squarely in front of the entrance to the bathrooms opposite the sign "Colored Only." There was a second sign hanging over the sign that said Colored, which said "Closed for Cleaning." Hiram paused a moment, looked around to see if anyone was by, saw no one, and walked speedily through the door marked "White Only."

✦

As cautious as Hiram had been walking in, he was doubly cautious walking out. He slowly opened the door so as to draw little attention, looked right, left and center and strode out onto Railroad Street looking around trying hard to give the impression he had been standing outside the whole time. Upon fully gaining the walkway, he headed straight for Dry Grove Road with his bread under his arm.

Suddenly a roar:

"Niggerrrrrrrrrrr!"

Hiram froze. In the seconds he needed to center himself (or summon his courage) another shout, raw and accusatory: "YOU CANNOT USE THE WHITE'S TOILET, NIGGER!" It was the white man with the messy white beard he had passed lying in the doorway in torn dungaree overalls. Now awake, perturbed and—still drunk—

reeling across the street yelling. "YOU DONE BROKE THE LAW, NIGGER! AND YOU GONNA PAY!

The man's yelling brought a few people to the street either looking for the source of the disruption of afternoon calm or in the hope of some distraction from the afternoon's boredom. Mr. Bayer stood in front of his rocker and shielded his eyes from the sun so he could see what was happening. He saw Hiram standing in the way of the yelling man. He took a step in Hiram's direction when...

Hiram suddenly took off running with the overalled man tumbling behind him. Hiram ran toward Dry Grove Road, increasing the distance between himself and the drunk man. He looked behind and saw the drunk coming after him. He noticed several other people standing still watching from doorways. Just as he was coming to the corner of Dry Grove Road, the red rubber ball tumbled out of Hiram's pocket and into his stride. The ball bounced under his left foot. His foot rolled on it. His leg went out from under him. The bread fell, the waxed paper tore, and the loaf tumbled into the sandy street. Hiram fell, his hands unsurely catching him, his forehead scraping the curb. He felt blood run into his right eye. Giving himself a few moments to gather up the ball and the bread was not an option. He could hear the drunk man shambling and cussing toward him. Hiram stood up, glanced at his sandy, bloody hands, and ran like hell until he realized the drunk man had fallen himself and was not able to get up again. Even though he was safe, Hiram kept running.

His mother called, "Hello," as she did routinely when she heard the screen door squeak open. Hiram started to cry as soon as he heard her voice. He entered the room crying. Tears, sand, blood all mixed on his face. He ran into his mother's arms.

"I tol' you Hiram. To them you is and you'll always be jus' anotha nigga. They is jus' as likely to lynch you, baby, as call yo' by yo' name."

Hiram winced as her cloth skimmed his wound sending pain over his face. "Owww. I don't know why white folks gets the fancy bathrooms... Jus' ain't fair!"

"Livin' roun' white people ain't never gonna be fair, Hiram. You know that. You jes' gotta stay small an' give them white folks they' way.

"Stay small? What does stayin' small mean, Mama?"

"It means fill the smallest space y'can in the white world, boy. Keep yo'self outta they' way. Plus...always try an' cool things when they gets hot. And don' rise. Don' act like you means much."

"But, Mama, what would I do if I do what you say? How I get something fo' myself if'n I'm thinkin' I don' mean much? If'n I am stayin' small?"

"Get sompin' fo' yesself? Baby, to white folks us niggas ain't got no self. Them white folks is like a big ol' mirror only when we stands in front a' that mirror what that mirror shows back to us is THEM. You don't need nothin' 'cept quiet and peace, Hiram Fitzgerald! Stay in the colored world, baby. That's where you'll find quiet. Steppin' into the white world— now that's a mistake. That is yo' mistake...if y' does it."

"But, Mama, the white world is where ev'thing happens. On our side of town they's nothing goin' on. Nothin' real, leastwise. To be sompin' you gotta be in the white world. On the white side of things."

"An' how is you—a nigga boy from down Dry Grove Road—gonna get onto and stay on the white side?"

"I don' know, Mama, but I is. I will. Not them, not ol' Jim Crow, not me—not even you Mama—not anyone gonna keep me down. I am gonna find a way somehow t' get in and stay in. I will! I will!"

✦

When he turned twelve, just such an opportunity presented itself to Hiram in the form of a job in Bayer's Bakery. Mr. Bayer (William to his wife and Will to his friends and Willie to his hunting buddies) asked Bliss Fitzgerald (Hiram's mom) if Hiram might be available after school for a few hours of baking pan cleaning and bakery floor sweeping at fifteen cents per hour.

Intrigued, Bliss put down her handbag and leaned over the counter.

"Fifteen cent? Why Missa' Bayer, let's talk!"

When he heard, "let's talk," Will Bayer assumed Bliss meant to negotiate.

"Now, Bliss, I pay my journeyman baker seventy-seven cent an hour so fifteen cent is right fair for the job. I tell you what, though, I can add toilet cleaning and up it to seventeen cent. That's as far as I can go!"

Bliss, who had, in reality, not intended to negotiate at all, smacked her white gloved hand on the counter with a hearty laugh. "HA! HA! Sold at seventeen cent!"

"HA! HA! Just like at the market in Natchez!" said Will Bayer, matching her laugh. "Jes' like at the old slave market in Natchez!"

Old slave market.

Slave market.

Slave.

When she heard the word, "slave," Bliss instantly felt her lightheartedness vanish. Suddenly, she felt the impact of what she had said, how quickly and improvidently Bayer had taken it up, and how they both sounded. She was shocked at what her swift, pay-no-mind comment had opened up in Bayer and closed up suddenly in her. And between them. She had known Will Bayer for the better of twenty years (since she and Hiram, Sr. had moved onto their street). When Hiram, Sr. passed, Will Bayer allowed her credit at a time when white-owned businesses simply didn't give credit to black folks. His store had always been open to her and over the years it felt like Will Bayer was almost family. Yet it took just one unguarded moment and a seemingly harmless joke to redraw the lines of privilege between them.

"...old slave market in Natchez!"

Bliss now faced a choice: she could take up Will's comment and take her stand as offended. Or she could step aside and leave things as they were with him unaware that he had moved a boulder into their path.

To them you is and you'll always be jus' anotha nigga, she thought.

Bliss made her choice just as reflexively as Will had made his comment. She swallowed the offense and moved forward the way she knew—as a negro woman in a white man's store.

"When you'd like Hiram to start, Mr. Bayer?" She asked politely.

Besides, she thought, *I know there is no hate in Will Bayer's heart.*

"Tomorrow at four o'clock is fine, Bliss."

And, so, Hiram entered the working world.

✦

Hiram's daily routine ossified during that first year at work at the bakery. At 7:30 a.m. he would stop in to sweep the bakery floor of overnight flour left by the bakers and then head for school. The bakery opened at 8 a.m., floors clean, just as Hiram's school bell rang for homeroom. Then, the morning rush for "donuts, Danish, and dough," as Mr. Bayer called it, in which Will Bayer served three-quarters of his daily customers and made over three quarters of his daily cash. From 9:30 a.m. onward (when the morning bread rush ended) Mr. Bayer would greet only three to five customers calling for coffee cake, fancy cookies, or a layer cake. In the meantime, Hiram would finish school. Then he would rush from the closing school bell to his locker, grab his apron, and run (as fast as a negro boy could run safely in a mostly-white town) to Bayer's Bakery. Once there, he would grab a blueberry Snagl (with sliced almonds and creamy sugar glaze), of which he would savor every bite standing by the brooms on the basement stairs. When the Snagl was gone, he'd sweep the store in time for the pre-dinner rush and Bayer's six o'clock closing. Hiram's time spent from the end of school to the closing of Bayer's wasn't long or particularly busy. He would sweep the store twice—once at the start and again at the end of his shift.

He spent 40 minutes elbow-deep in coconut oil soap suds cleaning the previous night's baking pans and he would scour the toilets (in the careless way a twelve-year-old scours toilets). His work summed to about an hour's actual labor in a three hour shift. The rest of the time he fetched for Mr. Bayer ("I need wax paper!" "Get me a new bobbin of string!"), helped with customers ("Wrap this rye for Mrs. Zimmermann!"), and stood, leaning on his broom-handle, watching.

During his fifteenth year of life and his third year of observing people from his lookout at Bayer's, Hiram wrote several lists: "What Makes Happy People Angry," "Things Girls Like (I Think)," "Favorite Foods of Hiram Fitzgerald That I Like and Don't Like," "Twelve, Yes Only Twelve, Things I Hate Most About Living in My Hometown of Raymond, Mississippi." And this one:

Things White People Do We Don't Do

1. Not Cuss: In general speaking, White People don't cuss or at least don't cuss where Colored Boys like me can hear them do it. Negroes cuss their brains out where every other word is sometime a cuss. And not just hell and damn, either. Negroes use the Big Ol' Cuss Words free like they are worthless. The words. Not the Negroes.

2. Eat the Outsides, Not The Insides: Give a White folk a pig or a chicken and they will—lickety split—eat all the meat on the outsides and throw away all the meat on the insides. Give that same animal to a Negro and they will eat the insides with relish and—while Coloreds don't throw any part away so they won't waste the outsides—it's the insides— the gizzards and gazzards—they have appetency for.

3. Carry an Umbrella: White people think hard about staying dry in the rain. When it is a rainy day, they all, every single one, will carry an umbrella. Colored People just never carry umbrellas as a general rule. Or maybe I should say don't carry one in the rain. I have seen old grandmammies carry

a white umbrella against the hard summer sun, but you just don't see Colored People carry one in the rain. Maybe it's 'cause we are just used to be wet when it rains or maybe it's 'cause it's too much trouble but you just won't see a Negro with an umbrella. In the rain. White Folks always got their umbrella. Sometimes it even matches their dress or suit or coat.

4. Bring Real Money With Them: White folks always have their money with them ready-like. If they might need $8 or $10 in a day, what do you know if they carry $20 on them. And they roll their money all organized by the way of how much it is—one, five, tens all tidy and neat together by type. A Negro will carry money, alright, but if they might need $8 to $10 dollars in a day, they carry five—a mix of dollar bills and coins—'cause they can always borrow if they need more.

5. Talk About Themselves: It is White to say "I" and Colored to say "we." A Negro thinks and talks about his people, his family. A White thinks and talks about himself. For example, when a White lady comes into a bakery she says, "I want a dozen biscuits!" all demanding. A Colored lady will say, "We'd like three of your best biscuits, if you please, Mr. Bayer," just like that.

6. Speaking of such, Don't Say "Please": White people as a rule only say please when they really, really want something. Coloreds say it when it isn't even needed. But it is always needed, really. And polite.

7. Call Things What They Are: Negroes call things by the name they have. For example: "pups," "sofa," "meat," "tornado" is what we call that stuff not "canines," "divan," "beefsteak," and "cyclone" like they call that same stuff. They communicate. We talk.

8. Not Wait: A White lady, when there is a line to wait for service will fidget and push and try to get recognized for the purpose of moving up in the line and not having to wait. A Negro lady

in the same line will wait. She might even get so involved in a conversation with another Negro lady that they will stay in the line talking and let two (maybe five) White ladies pass while they talk. If it is another Colored lady behind these talking Colored ladies, in just a few moments it's a gaggle of three Colored ladies letting white people pass. Colored people are just waiters and talkers, I've a mind.

9. Talk the Same For Everyone: White folks have just one talk for anyone—White or anyone— while Negroes have a talk just reserved for Colored folks they never use with White folks. Colored-to-Colored talk is familiar and equal while Colored-to-White talk is solemn-like and ceremonious. Like unequal.

Hiram kept this list, reviewing and revising it, for several years. When he was 20, he retitled a revised list:

Ways to Make It in the White World

1. Use Descriptive Language: Describe what you see, rather than using unsavory and poorly descriptive wording. People of class describe things.

2. Eat the Tenderest Food: Choose steak or the rib or breast or (if you really must) the thigh of any meat and leave the offal for others.

3. Carry an Umbrella: In the rain, or on days when it might rain, always carry an umbrella. Even better, own several, so it can match one's coat.

4. Always Carry Money: $20 minimum in a leather billfold.

5. Talk About Myself: Say "I" as often as possible. Center the world on "me."

6. Stop Saying "Please": White people, as a rule,/ only say please when they really, really want something. Do that.

7. Call Things By Their White Names: Make it a point to show you have been educated.

8. Cultivate Impatience: And entitlement.
9. Speak For Everyone: No Colored-to-Colored talk.

✦

As the years passed, Hiram matriculated from fetching inside Bayer's store to running errands outside. He went from being asked to bring small change for the cash register to counting out the day's cash while Mr. Bayer filled the day-old bread bin and packaged up what he could sell again the next day. By and by, Hiram became known in town as Bayer's Boy, a by-name which actually came with a good deal of respect attached. People knew that Will Bayer liked and respected Hiram and treated him more equally than some store owners did their negro help. Bayer would say, "I will send my man by with your order" and customers would be surprised when that man turned out to be Hiram, whom they knew only as, "the boy who swept the place." Now, seeing he was Will Bayer's Man caused some eyebrows to knit, some hackles to rise and some eyes to widen. Regardless, Hiram used his observations about white people to shape his presentation of himself. His determination to be accepted and equitably dealt with did, in fact, changed his behavior and caused him (for better or worse) to be more accepted by the white people he dealt with.

✦

"Th'ain't no reason on God's green earth y' should take that!" yelled Bliss Fitzgerald. "No earthly way y' should!"

Hiram stood in the center of the parlor of their three-room flat, his right hand illuminated by a shaft of sunlight coming through the front window. In that hand, he held a letter:

> Dear Mrs. Fitzgerald,
>
> As the Chairman of the Hinds County chapter of the National Congress of Parents and

Teachers, it is my pleasure to inform you that your son, Hiram Fitzgerald, has been elected to receive our annual award as "Most Improved Negro" for 1930. This award acknowledges his academic achievements and well as his excelled citizenship.

We are pleased to inform you as well that this award includes an annual stipend of fifty dollars for four years, which we hope Hiram will use to further his education, as he desires.

We invite Hiram to receive this honor at his high school commencement on June 16ᵗʰ of this year. He is invited to prepare and deliver a brief thank you address to the committee.

"No!" said Bliss emphatically slapping her open palm against her thigh. "Th'ain't no way!"

"But, Mama, I've earned this! I've worked hard and earned it!"

"Y'works hard as a student, Hiram. As a cit'zen, too. But, y'does it cuz it th' right thing t'do. That's why!"

"Yes, Mama. That's precisely why." Hiram walked to her and handed her the letter. "That's what the letter says."

"That's how me an' yo' Daddy raised you. T'work hard an' study up. That way y' can have all we's never had. Damn...mos' improved! Why they—"

"Mama, I did study up. You know how much effort I put in—"

"— t' be th' best you could be—"

"Yes, Mama...yes," said Hiram, calming.

"— th' best student y'could be. Not th' best Negro y'could be!"

"Yes, Mama. No! I mean yes! I tried to be the best student. Yet, also the best Negro. Best Negro student! I want to be something on my own, Mama. But there's never a moment I am not a Negro. To them, I can never just be something on my own. I am always being a Negro being something. That's how it is, Mama."

"Hiram, y'know I's proud as a mama c'be of you. But, baby, when th' says Mos' Improved Negro...what they means? I knows what they says—you improved to a fine student. But...they also sayin' something' else: what does they say you improved from..? Mos' Improved Negro. Improved from...what?"

Hiram looked at his mother sitting on the yellow hopsack sofa cushion in her cotton house dress and terry cloth mules. At the same time, he both thanked her and blamed her for who he was. Yet, the most honest thing he could say—to her and to himself—was, "Mama, you just don't understand."

✦

Hiram, at twenty-one years old, was present in the bakery when Mr. Bayer was unexpectedly visited by three men in striped business suits and gray overcoats inquiring about the current use and future availability of the unoccupied space above his store. Will Bayer was taken aback by their concerted interest. He had kept the space empty except for a few hogsheads of molasses and twenty bags of spelt flour that he used for Christmas baking, yet didn't want littering the store. He thought nothing of the second floor as useable space, yet here were three refined-looking business men making a legitimate inquiry about using it:

OVERCOAT MAN #1: This space, while seeming worthless to you, could be very helpful to us.
OVERCOAT MAN #2: It is in many ways a perfect location, you see. Close enough to the train to be convenient yet far enough so that the vibrations of passing trains will not be felt.
OVERCOAT MAN #3: This is important, sir...er...[NODDING TO HIRAM] sirs, because our work involves sensitive instruments that require a low-vibration environment.
WILL BAYER: What d' you'all wanna use th' place for exactly?
OVERCOAT MAN #2: I doubt you will have heard of what we do, sir.

WILL BAYER: But still...I'd need t'know what you'd be doing on my property. You understand?

OVERCOAT MAN #1: Of course, Mr. Bayer. We are not intending to be secretive. It's only that what we aim to do is not widely known. It is...well we aim...to build a commercial radio broadcasting station. Perhaps you have heard of station 1XG in Medford Hillside, Massachusetts? Or XG8 from Pittsburgh? 6XC from San Francisco?

WILL BAYER: I cain't say I have...

OVERCOAT MAN #3: There are, if I am being generous, about twenty such broadcasting stations in the United States. We intend to carry that number to thirty by opening ten to twelve stations in the next five years—.

OVERCOAT MAN #2: — in the service of the policy holders of Southern Indemnity Insurance Company. "We Cover the Country" is what we say—.

OVERCOAT MAN #3: —with both the most reliable insurance AND the most reliable radio signal. You'll be able to hear us from New York to New Orleans!

WILL BAYER: Hear you?

Will Bayer didn't understand a thing that any of them said. Yet, he did understand their offer of $328.00 per month to rent his second floor.

Over the next few weeks, Will Bayer and Hiram Fitzgerald learned that Overcoat Man #1 was named Victor Spanning, #2 was Robert Gottfriend, and #3 was Alberto Cinci. Vic Spanning was Director of Station Development for SII Radio Broadcasting, Bob Gottfriend was Regional Director of Operations, and Al Cinci was Chief Engineer. In a series of meetings with Will and Hiram, they shared their plans for the radio station and filling in the empty space above Bayer's Bakery with studios, offices, a small kitchen, and a bathroom. They (the four white men) came to an agreement that SII Radio Broadcasting would lease the entire floor above the bakery for $300.00 per month on a five-year lease.

Will Bayer acted agreeably in concluding and memorializing the deal and made only a few firm demands:

1. He could not agree to the large neon sign the SII folks envisioned to be placed on the roof ridge.
2. He stipulated that their sign be no larger than his bakery sign.
3. He would not agree to allow the transmitter tower to be placed on the visible street side of the roof gable.
4. And he required that SII carpet the entire floor along with the stairs used to access the station from the street, in order to limit the sound that could be heard by his bakery customers.

Bayer put each of these stipulations forward firmly, yet all were negotiable.

His last demand was the only one he would not negotiate on from start to finish: if Southern Indemnity Insurance Radio wanted the space above Bayer's Bakery they would have to employ his man, Hiram Fitzgerald, as Office Manager.

Overcoat Men #1, #2, and #3 agreed.

Station 7XG, which would soon after register with the call letters WSII, was born.

✦

The station signed on for the first time with a recording of Samuel Ward and Katherine Bates's, "America the Beautiful." This was directly followed by a live and dramatic reading by Thaddeus Smithsson, Mayor of Raymond (and eighth-grade English teacher at Raymond-Hinds Secondary School) of *A Message*, a Civil War poem by Elizabeth Stuart Phelps Ward:

Was there ever message sweeter
   Than that one from Malvern Hill,

From a grim old fellow, you remember?
   Dying in the dark at Malvern Hill.
With his rough face turned a little,
   On, a heap of scarlet sand,
They found him, just within the thicket,
   With a picture in his hand,

With a stained and crumpled picture
   Of a woman's aged face;
Yet there seemed to leap a wild entreaty,
   Young and living tender from the face
When they flashed the lantern on it,
   Gilding all the purple shade,
And stooped to raise him softly,
   That's my mother, sir," he said.

"Tell her"— but he wandered, slipping
   Into tangled words and cries,
Something about Mac and Hooker,
   Something dropping through the cries
About the kitten by the fire,
   And mother's cranberry-pies; and there
The words fell, and an utter
   Silence brooded in the air.

Just as he was drifting from them,
   Out into the dark, alone
(Poor old mother, waiting for your message,
   Waiting with the kitten, all alone!),
Through the hush his voice broke, "Tell her—
   Thank you, Doctor— when you can,
Tell her that I kissed her picture,
   And wished I'd been a better man."

Ah, I wonder if the red feet

Of departed battle hours
May not leave for us their searching
    Message from those distant hours.
Sisters, daughters, mothers, think you,
    Would your heroes now or then,
Dying, kiss your pictured faces,
    Wishing they'd been better men?

This was followed directly by the voice of Robert L. Marcus, a trained Shakespearean actor hired in New York City by Bob Gottfriend and relocated to Raymond as the anchor Voice of Southern Indemnity Insurance Radio. Marcus read, cleanly and clearly in his actor-trained basso, the upcoming daily schedule for the station:

> *Ladies and gentlemen, for your pleasure and enjoyment, this radio station will feature the following programs each and every Thursday:*
>
> *5:30 a.m.- The Consolidated Farm Report- Live from our downtown Raymond Studios*
>
> *6:00 a.m.- Our Men at War in Europe presented by the U.S. War Department*
>
> *7:00 a.m.- Keeping a Sound Home with members of the Raymond Women's Auxiliary*
>
> *8:00 a.m.- Sign Off*
>
> *12 Noon- Lunch and Learn with Letty Bingham, farm wife*
>
> *12:30 p.m.- The Music of the Mississippi Mudpuppies- Live from Studio A*
>
> *1 p.m.- Sign Off*

8 p.m.- The Evening Concert with the Raymond Good Shepherd Church Choir- Live from Studio A

8:40 p.m.- Sign Off

We hope you will join us as you can and make use of the information as you will.

This is station 7XG from Raymond, Mississippi. We are offered by the Southern Indemnity Insurance Company. "We Cover the Country!"

This is the voice of 7XG, Robert L. Marcus, speaking!

The voice of 7XG—Robert L. Marcus's voice—was, to Hiram Fitzgerald, like a glass of Rock and Rye: cool, smooth, and smoky. The voice was free of a regional accent so it sounded like a voice from anywhere. It was deep and sonorous, so when it said, "Raymond Good Shepherd Church," it sounded like God himself calling upon you to appear at 8 p.m. to fire up your radio receiver and listen. And Hiram noticed it was soulful. A negro, Hiram thought, might think Marcus also to be negro. Yet Marcus, balding with straight, chestnut hair pomaded and combed back over his ears, a massive 352-pound body mummified in a tight and wrinkled navy double-breasted suit, his alabaster skin blending into the collar and cuffs of his white cotton dress shirt, could not be more white. Still...when announcing, Marcus was, in a way that Hiram uniquely appreciated, faceless and race-less. Just a voice in the air, of any color.

Like Hiram dreamed of being.

There was a fallacy to all of this, which Hiram also noted: no one in town owned a device that could receive and play 7XG's signal. Marcus, Letty Bingham, and Ruth Chiles of the Women's Auxiliary each came to Studio B (the smaller, voice-only studio; Studio A was reserved for live music) every Thursday, stood behind the microphone, and spoke as if people were listening. Yet, in 1922, not a single soul in Raymond, Mississippi owned a radio!

✦

Two years later, in 1924, every household in Raymond, Mississippi (and all of Mississippi, for that matter) had a radio, and the programming on radio station WSII ran every day for 24-hours. By 1926, the twenty radio stations in the U.S. that Alberto Cenci had referred to when he met Hiram had grown to number 571. Radio listening was so widespread in the U.S. that radio stations were beginning to be thought of as a public convenience.

By 1932, WSII offered forty-two distinct program offerings, employed twelve on-air "personalities" and five support staff, and broadcast seven days per week. Hiram, using his natural abilities and keen sense for people, had worked his way from Office Manger to Station Manager. He now ran the day-to-day functions of the station, managed station technical operations, and grappled with the egos of the on-air (so-called) talent. Deep in his heart, though, he still wanted his own voice to be heard on the radio.

Hiram typically started his day at 5:10 a.m. when he arrived at the WSII studios to unlock the door for Bob Marcus and start the transmitter to warm its electric tubes so the station could sign on at 5:30 a.m. Marcus would start each day's broadcasting by reading the Hinds/Rankin County Consolidated Farm Report. This half-hour started with the previous day's livestock and commodity prices, as reported by the United Press Association. Earlier in the year, United Press had sold WSII a teletype machine that automatically tapped out anything the press organization thought newsworthy in pale blue print on a continuous roll of primitive, pithy paper. By buying the teletype, the station was awarded the right to say "from the wires of United Press..." when delivering the news.

The farm report was cobbled together from several parts of the 5:00 a.m. push from United Press. Marcus waited nearby as the teletype machine banged out the hourly news, Wall Street commodities report, and livestock auction results. He quickly read through the content as it came off the UP wire and edited it (which would interest local farmers most?) with a blue pencil tied with bakery twine to the teletype machine. Marcus then added local stories he picked up while waiting at the train depot, lingering at the post office, or drinking at Harvey's Tap (his favorite bar). These he organized into news stories following a simple journalistic outline. Last, to allow continuous reading without the sound of pages turning, these sundry stories were cellophane-taped together into a lengthy scroll, which Marcus read *en-basso* and credited (always better to look larger than you are!) as having been written by "the WSII Newsroom with the services of United Press."

Each weekday, once he had performed the farm news, Marcus launched *Our Men at War* (a prerecorded program, distributed by the U.S. War Department on a 16-inch shellac disc that played for thirty minutes in low-fidelity sound at 16-$^2/3$ rpm). Then he set off for the station bathroom—as he announced to Hiram each morning—to take his "daily constitutional shit."

Each day, Hiram heard the on-air transition from farm report to military through the speaker installed above his office door as Marcus signed off the Consolidated Farm Report and the theme song of *Our Men at War* began. This was followed, day in and day out, by the slam and latch of the bathroom door as Marcus began his daily intestinal cavalcade. Bob Marcus joked about how Hiram should stay away from the teletype room (adjacent to the bathroom) for the first ten to twelve minutes "until the thunderhead of fart, whiskey, piss, and sweat has time to dissipate." Marcus was the only human Hiram had ever met who drank a glass of whiskey at six o'clock in the morning. On the toilet. While he...well, you know.

So Hiram's early mornings were a cacophony of signal sounds: the "ching-ching-chingle" of the keys to the station door tapping against the brass mortise, the "shhhhhh-crackle-shh" of the station transmitter tubes powering on, the "tip-tip-tip—ding!" of the teletype machine, the soft "juj-crisssshhh" of Marcus tearing the teletype paper, the "slammm" of the bathroom door, the steady "poot-poot

poot" of Bob's morning farts, and the deep rasp of his overweight breathing while he sipped his whiskey. These pre-dawn sounds, when strung together, signified Hiram's daily progress toward another sunrise, the gradual re-population of the station with his co-workers, the predictable cycle of his daily routine. Through these sounds, Hiram's life fell neatly into place each day, propelling him excitedly forward and keeping him depressingly where he was.

✦

Until one Monday when Robert L. Marcus arrived at the station late and badly marred by the weekend.

Bob was, as he called himself, "A Morning Drinker." His early morning routine included enough bourbon to anesthetize a cow, yet it served Bob. An amount of alcohol that would have left anyone else face down on the office floor uniquely lubricated Bob's effectiveness, deepening his radio voice and lightening his personality. Somehow, from his first drink Bob functioned until noon. You see...Bob was also, as he called himself, "A Daily Luncher." Nothing got in the way of his roast beef special with gravy (baked cod on Fridays) with peas and mashed potatoes at Miss Millie's Meritory Cafe on Burchitt Street. Of course "Daily Lunch" included "Daily Lunch Bourbon." This particular glass of bourbon pushed the delicate balance of Bob's pickled brain from light and effective toward dark and nasty. Each day he would depart for Miss Millie's as amicable, effective Bob and come back ornery, serious Robert L. Marcus. He came back from lunch greasy with sweat, his collar unbuttoned and splotchy gray where the fabric touched his neck. His nose was spongey and red, his eyes angry and porcine. He often spent the afternoons sleeping, his feet up on the desk, his snoring paunch puddling around his midsection, his body greasy under his shirt, as he sat in his leather desk chair.

"I am a Napper," he would say when someone had the audacity to knock on his office lintel to wake him. "Now leave me the fuck alone!"

This particular Monday it was Afternoon Robert who showed up in the morning. It started when Marcus cantankerously pushed his way past Hiram as soon as Hiram had turned the key to the station door, knocking Hiram's umbrella out of his hand. Bob slammed his way into Studio B, lit a cigarette, and sat down heavily to inhale it. A few minutes later he slammed the studio door on the way out, too, as he headed for the teletype machine. Marcus did each usual step of the preparation for the farm report, yet—instead of his usual calm bourbon-lubricated professionalism—there was bourbon-agitated flailing.

Robert L. Marcus vituperatively delivered the farm report, festooning the foam microphone spit-guard with stringy saliva. Hiram ignored it as long as he could, yet when Marcus signed off the farm report "brought to you by Motherfucking WSII—1300 on Your Goddam Dial!" Hiram left his office for Studio B to see what, exactly, was bothering Bob.

He arrived just as Marcus slammed the bathroom door from the inside.

"You okay, Robert?"

"Yes. I just have to take a goddamned shit, Hiram."

This, followed by a long cochlear fart, led Hiram to believe all was well.

✦

On his side of the door, Marcus let out a long primordial fart. He felt slightly better, although his chest still felt tight. Like an anvil hung where his heart usually did. A furrow of acidic sweat fell into his eyes as he pulled his pants down to his knees. Underwear next. His man-stuff dangled loose, which helped him feel liberated and ready. He reached beneath the radiator and removed his flat pint bottle of bourbon. A dust bunny clung to his pinky, which he shook off. "Goddamn you motherfucker!" he whispered. Just as he did so he felt his belly fill with the precursor of another epic fart. He took a hastily rinsed low-ball glass from the cabinet under the sink and momentarily admired the gold R L M monogram on its side.

"No more goddammed corned beef hash...," he spoke to no one as he poured his bourbon into the glass balanced on his hairy pancake of a knee. "No more fucking..."

The rest of the sentence was swallowed by a deep crackling sigh, which Hiram heard ("Hsk...kkk...skkkkkk..kkk") as he made his way back to his office. He thought it was Bob's usual post-first-sip sigh of satisfaction. It wasn't. It was the rattle of Bob's last breath as his heart exploded in his drunken chest. Hiram failed to hear the glass fall and "crash-shatterrrrr" around Bob's right foot, the cement of Bob's final bowel movement "Shhhrushhhhhhh" into the toilet and quiet fleshy bounce "bu-u-u-brfff" of Bob's body as it heaved itself rightward and halfway off the toilet. Bob came to rest with one flabby buttock on the toilet seat and one against the wall, eyes awkwardly staring down.

✦

Hiram listened for the usual "Bob Marcus Emerges" sounds:

The slam of the bathroom door,

The steady "poot-poot poot" of Bob's morning farts,

The deep rasp of his breathing while he finished his whiskey.

All seemed to be present so, aside from Bob's unusually cantankerous entrance and aggressive sign off of the farm report, things seemed only slightly unusual. Hiram returned to his office, sipped his coffee, and went about his morning duties assuming Bob would return from his bathroom tarriance as he did every day.

Hiram listened for Bob's usual sigh upon standing, the metallic clang of the flush-lever before the gurgling water. Nothing.

And the usual mutterings Bob spoke while doing up his fly. None.

The fumbling of Bob's drunken fingers to open the lock clasp and bathroom door. Silence at five minutes to the hour.

Silence again on the hour when the broadcast of *Our Men at War* ended. Silence during the last bars of the *Our Men at War* theme. Silence when the theme ended and WSII began to broadcast empty, "dead air." No programming. No announcer. No Voice of WSII.

Hiram knocked on the bathroom door.

"Marcus! You're on!"

Hiram stood for a moment to listen. No response. He headed to Studio B.

Ruth Chiles, host of *Keeping a Sound Home with the Raymond Women's Auxiliary* was seated before the guest microphone, reviewing her script.

"I'm waiting for Bob," Ruth said. "He does a station identification. Then introduces me."

"Don't worry...I've got you!" Hiram stepped to the microphone desk, sat down stiffly and in a deep, smooth radio voice Ruth had never heard announced: "This is WSII. 1300 on the AM range. We now present *Keeping a Sound Home* with host Ruth Chiles of the Raymond town Women's Auxiliary. This is..." Hiram didn't miss a beat. "...Robert L. Marcus The Voice of WSII, speaking."

Ruth began her introduction while she held a shellac disk on the felt-covered record platter with her pinky. At the right moment she let go and an instrumental banjo version of *My Mississippi* began to play. She glanced up from her script and gave Hiram a thumb up. Over the music she mouthed "thank you" and continued to read her script.

✦

Hiram returned to the bathroom and again knocked on the door. "Bob? You okay? Bob...ARE YOU OKAY?"

He could tell by the deep silence that no one would answer.

Out of respect, he said "Okay. Robert, I'm coming in!"

Hiram pushed with all of his weight against the door. It flew open, sending him hip-first against the sink, crunching on broken glass. He gathered himself, looked at the toilet and saw Bob, one cheek off the toilet—dead—against the wall. He had never seen a person dead but Bob's expression was unmistakable; he had the rubbery lips and empty eyes of a dead man.

Through the fetor of bourbon, Hiram looked at Bob.

Through a cloud of sadness and regret for Bob's essential misery, Hiram looked at Bob...

...and saw...

...OPPORTUNITY!

Hiram knelt close to Bob's open legs, held his breath and gingerly reached into Bob's left pants pocket. He didn't know how many evenings after work at Harvey's Tap he had seen Marcus reach for his billfold, but Hiram knew exactly where Bob kept it. Hiram balanced on his haunches to quietly close the bathroom door and open the billfold. Sadly, all it contained was three cardboard I.D. cards—and twenty-eight dollars. Hiram took the cards and left the money. Just as he was standing upright to leave he knelt back down and grabbed the wallet once again. He opened it and quickly replaced Bob's I.D. cards with his own Hinds Community College Student I.D. card, Raymond-Hinds Public Library card, and his WSII employee card. He glanced at the cards he took: a Veterans of Foreign Wars I.D., WSII employee I.D., and Actor's Equity membership card all in the name of Robert L. Marcus. Just enough.

Hiram Fitzgerald calmly returned to his office, called the Operator, asked to be connected to the sheriff's office, and reported the coronary death of Hiram Fitzgerald at the studios of WSII above Bayer's Bakery. Then Hiram walked calmly to the train station and bought a ticket on the next train. The train happened to be headed for Chicago, where he would subsequently live for thirty-seven years.

Occasionally, someone who heard Robert L. Marcus's voice on the radio wondered if he was a Negro or a white man.

Through the wizardry of radio, no one knew for sure.

ENTR'ACTE

The Barker

Brendan Hardy

NOW

*T*he daughter and son-in-law come to visit too often if you ask me. Not that I don't want to see them. I do. But there's a limit to how much you can love other people when you live with show folks. All the love you have inside you sort of gets sucked up by this huge vortex of needy. I mean, think about it. A home. For performers. First, home. Most of us never even had a home. Or a mailing address. For us, this is the first time we are rooted to a place, so the social skills we need to live together aren't genetically programmed, or socially learned, even. Second, performers. Black hole of needy. Thrown together by fate. Suddenly, people with no social skills have to live with a bunch of folks they hardly know, and the only reason they're together is their voracious desire for applause or lust for limelight. The grandson says it's like high school Drama Club. I think it's worse. The Home is until death do us part.

So what if I worked the carnival midway and someone else did, too? Does that really make us compatible for living together?

Add 'em up, Bobby. Add 'em up.

Okay, so maybe...just maybe...we do belong together.

We share a common diet. We will eat any crap you give us—deep-fried, corn-breaded, on-a-stick. A hamburger topped with spicy marshmallow fluff. Cheese curd Poutine. A turkey leg, smoked. Then baked. Then deep fried. Pickles soaked in strawberry Kool-Aid. To us residents, this is wholesome eating. Chef Angie runs the Mess Hall here at The Home. She doesn't like when I call her labor of love the Mess Hall. She likes me to call it the Cafeteria, but this son-of-a-bitch is no cafeteria. It's way too short on skinless chicken, boiled peas, or mashed potatoes and way too long on Chocolate Dipped Donut Ice Cream Sandwiches. While other homes for the aged employ nutritionists to limit residents to the healthiest food, here at the NJHRCCP, we employ Chef Angie, who—like an intrepid explorer flying the flag of an off-kilter monarch—forays, on our behalf, to far flung fairs and carnivals to bring back bounty like Chocolate-Bacon Macaroni 'n' Cheese.

An ability to appreciate or ignore smells. The scent of horse hoof glue on stage flats. I bet you never smelled that. I'll warn you, you don't want to. Like sniffing lint, freshly dug out of your navel. The stink of costumes we sweat in and the costume department never launders. Of course, animals. The smell of endless pails of dung—small, medium, and large poops—grassy to hummus-y. That cheesy smell of imitation butter on stale popcorn. Or the sweet vanilla bouquet of fresh-spun cotton candy. The whiff of tar-touched underarms that follows the roustabouts from town to town as they set up and knock down and never rinse. The cheap amber worn by the dancers to cover up their own musk since there is no shower between shows—and they've got people to meet!

An itinerant life. To most of us The Home is our first home. We are used to sleeping at hotels, in wagons, or on trains. Or under wagons, or on benches in train stations. You know Randall Rhodes, the tightrope walker, in room 317? He is so used to not having a bed, he sleeps upright in a chair even though the beds here are a major part of the—whattaya call it? —decor. Or Shelley Shondell, the stripper Miss Raspberry, in number 142 who spends the better part of her day napping in a rattan basket because it feels like home. Or Harry Goldblatt, the horse trainer in room 136, who rubs himself with mud and grass torn up from the field out back because he is used to being caked with it. Trying to make it feel like home in a home that doesn't feel like home.

At all.

Acceptance. In our world, you learn to step around people's differences. Our differences can be the pretty usual ones, ones like you'd find in any group of people you threw together. Or they can be downright strange. Like the Siamese twins—who aren't Siamese at all—and have different sized feet. Not different from each other, but different left and right. And exactly the same for both. One foot size 8 D and one foot size 10½ EE. And oddly—but also perfectly—one has the big foot on the left and one has it on the right. They fit together like book ends, with Martin on the left and Jackson on the right. As a fellow resident you just avoid the topic. Unless they bring up feet, you just accept.

You also do that with personal details. Like who never got married but has lived together for forty-five years, which is pretty common among the show business crowd. "Living in sin," I guess would be how non-show folk call it. But we in the theater are surprised when a couple actually is married. Marriage isn't something people have time for on the road, or a value for in the carny yard. Plus, you get married, you just need to get unmarried when it all goes wrong, you know? But just live together in a wooden wagon and you've got the best of all worlds: physical relations, plus company while you're on tour, plus shelter when you're old. The ability to dump Miss Peoria when you get to Davenport, then take up with Miss Davenport, be an item until you drop her for Miss Lincoln as the tour ends in Nebraska. Sin. Convenient and portable. In The Home, one man's Miss Peoria might room right next to the same man's Miss Davenport. I speak hypothetically, here, of course. These two girls might hate each other like scorpions in a bag. Or love each other like sisters, bonded by their shared knowledge of the presence of a hairy mole on his right ball. We avoid noticing that the same way we ignore body odor on roustabouts. Endemic, expected, and always politely overlooked.

We are predisposed to care for each other. In the old days, if you worked a traveling show, you showed up every year on July, say, 15th, like clockwork. This was a good thing, since most people back then only knew it was July at all because the show-flyers got posted up on the telephone poles. Once they were up, people knew it was two weeks until the show opened, three weeks until it closed and, after that, two weeks left in summer. When we'd arrive in town, people would whisper and point. We were always visitors, never friends. Always show folk, never just people. We've spent our entire lives being out-of-towners. Sometimes feared, sometimes envied. Always strangers. That makes it unlikely that, if we need something, we'd ask a local. Instead, we stick with our band. Look after our own.

The stories. Everyone has got a story. Some longed to be in the spotlight and worked to climb the ladder. Some got recruited. Some, like me, got born into it. Others got kidnapped by it when they least expected it. Some thought they were doing one thing, but ended up doing something else.

Some just happened to be right for the job: small or exotic looking.

Or fat.

Or tall.

Or thin.

ACT SEVEN

The Thinnest Man

Norman Rockwell

THEN

The smudge man walks down the Midway lighting black globe-shaped pots that are sitting in red-brown dirt. The flame on his lighting stick sputters bright orange as it touches the wick on the pots. The wick ignites, half-fire and half-smoke—sooty black smoke—releasing a licorice-kerosene smell into the lowering dusk.

The Midway. Late July. Eight o'clock. Neon marks the destination—tubes glowing pink, blue, green, yellow. The smudge pots light the way.

After each big "TADA!!" of brass blown by a red-coated trio of trumpet players, a rowdy Barker names sideshow acts fast, his milky-white teeth make the sound of shuffling playing cards: "Step this way, sir! You, sir! You, sir! Step in here! See the sights of the side shows!"

The distant clang of the, "YOU CAN DO IT!" bell rung by a high school sledge-hammerer, showing off.

A brass-keyed Miner Calliophone plays the hit song of 1928, "I Wanna Be Loved By You," above the rush and whoop of the crowd as it makes its way down the Midway towards the 8:15 show.

The steady putt-putt-putt of a traction engine adds an off-beat to the song. It also supplies the steam for the calliope, and the electric power to the whole fair.

The Douglas County and Omaha City Fair.

Now, friend, you can approach a county fair in any one of several ways: you can approach in a meandering way and let the neon, the sensational names, the French perfume, the shouts, and the music lure you, siren-like, to the Den of the Devil. There, you will find strippers, freaks, dancers—the exotic, the foreign, the strange. These offerings are better happened upon, rather than sought out. Or at least it, is better to pretend you just happened on them by chance. To seek out these sorts of acts is risky if you happen to go to church, or have children, or a reputation to keep up. That's one approach—meandering. You can also approach a county fair in a strictly mechanical way. For example, you might look forward to the ("High! Fast! Unforgiving!") Giant Wizard rollercoaster that you rode every day the fair was open last summer. You might recall, nostalgically, that climb number three on the Giant Wizard brings the bile into your throat and that the drop after climb number five loosens the imaginary string on your bladder enough to leave a dark spot on your trousers. As a direct result, not only this summer, but every summer, you enter the fair's main gate and make a bee's line directly to the Giant Wizard entrance. There, you stand in line to have the distinction to be one of the first fans to ride the coaster this year. That's the mechanical approach. If you don't choose either the meandering or mechanical approach, you can take the scientific approach to a fair. Using that method, you give your attention only to the biggest, oldest, longest, rarest, most exotic, or most what-have-you (just so long as the word "most" or the suffix "-est" lures you there). Ah, the scientific approach. Yet, if you're not an extremist, you can take the gustatory approach. To approach gustatorily, you are led by your nose or by your lips—or when it is most satisfying, both!—deep into the carnival, from Latin *carno + levare, "to give up meat"*. Early Carnivals took place only during meatless Lent (as

Mardi Gras does). Carnivals were meant to distract from the ascetic core of Lent to make the time of deprivation pass more quickly.

Lenten origins aside, you can expect a bounty of meat (and other foods) at a carnival or county fair. You'll find beef barbecue fixed according to the local recipe: dry-rubbed or vinegary or brown sugared or smoked, and chicken grilled with green garlic or fried in cornflake batter, served with hushpuppies, or fried potatoes, or tomato pie. At the Omaha fair, you'd taste the work of Reubin Kulakofsky, known locally as Reubin Kay (Reubin with an I, not an E, before the N) at the booth occupied by the kitchen staff of Omaha's Blackstone Hotel and featuring the newly-introduced and highly-lauded (though not Kosher) First-Eaten-in-Omaha Reubin Sandwich. Plus, lots of non-meat food: sugar floss, fried dough, candy on a stick, pancakes with rhubarb jam, roasted peanuts or boiled peanuts or peanuts with caramel popcorn.

I've mentioned the gustatory approach to a fair. That's fine for some. Yet, if your approach is not only gustatory, but that rare, delectable approach-sandwich of the gustatory approach stacked on the scientific approach, topped with the mechanical approach, you deliberately (and with some peculiar pride) march, head held high, past the smarmy smells, the tawdry tastes, the lights, the acts, the music, the dancers, the exotics, the games, and past the tents, booths, rollercoasters, and tilty-whirls to the starkly lit, canvas-tented back corner occupied by 4-H (head, heart, hands, health). Here, fairs exhibit the best what-have-you that rural people, their god, and nature can create: most beautiful piglet, richest tasting pork, most perfectly shaped apple, county's best apple-raspberry pie, largest cucumber (seven pounds, two ounces!), tastiest spicy piccalilli. On Saturday morning, the place is taken over by animals and their owners as they apply science to nature in competition for "best of breed." By Sunday morning, all that is cleaned up and replaced by the "best of bread" competition (as insiders call it): first the bread competition, then the pickles competition, then pies, then jams, then jellies, then candy, then one-pot dishes, then cookies, and then bars.

All to be tasted and judged, "Best at the Fair."

Every Sunday, Norman Rockwell—all seven-feet-and-eleven-inches of him—follows the hidden, employees-only passage past the booths, the back stages, tent poles, guy-wires, pulleys, and work-lights to make his bee's line to the 4-H area (About his name? Coincidences happen. So, two babies born to Rockwell families happened to get named Norman. What's it to you?). Every Sunday, proud as punch, Norman makes his way, the back way, to 4-H.

Odd place for a man to spend his day off? It is no coincidence. To this particular Norman Rockwell, it is the only place he *can* be in his spare time. He carries a mop in his left hand, which is both his reason to be there and his excuse not to leave. Ask him and he will tell you he stands by in case of breakage or spillage.

He is really there for the food.

Bread. He thinks of a rich knot of eggy dough, kneaded until the strands stand like a horsetail from the farmwife's fist. Quickly braided, the plaits laid on parchment in greased aluminum, butter melting to oil in the summer heat. Proofed until twice its size, then baked until the parchment curls and turns brown, the loaf a mass of yellow horsetail strands, tawny, salty-sweet and buttered like a golden pillow, steam rising to biff Norman's eager nose.

Then pickles. Crisp lilypads of cucumber with firework-explosions of dill, spearheads of okra with ribbons of red pepper, ova of white radishes in beet juice and vinegar, sweet bread-and-butters yellow with mustard flowers and fillips of peppercorn. Garlic and sunflower root, onion, and sweet corn with soused red cubes of capsicum studding a bright, deep relish. Norman drools from the corner of his mouth and catches it, self-conscious, with his pinky.

Then pies. Pies that just that morning were piles of fresh fruit, flour, water, and lard. Transformed into dough, veined with shortening, baked blind or just baked, latticed, woven, cut, and vented so a Vesuvius of berries or apples or custard, or cream erupts through. Norman thinks of the white pie shelf his mother had a neighborly handyman add to the kitchen window where she'd cool her apple-blackberry pies, redolent with cloves and fragrant with cinnamon. His cheeks pink when he thinks of it.

Then jams. The judge's briefing booklet clearly states: "Jams are made from pulp and juice of a single fruit, rather than a variety of several fruits. Berries or other small fruits are most frequently used, though larger fruits such as apricots, peaches, or plums cut into small (one-quarter inch to one-half inch) pieces or crushed may be used for jams. Award-winning jam has a soft, even consistency with small, yet distinctive pieces of fruit, a bright color, a strong and satisfying fruit flavor, and a semi-jellied texture that is easy to spread but has no free liquid." Of course, the briefing booklet kills the mystery and magic that comes with just the right balance of fruit, sugar, and pectin, which, thinks Norman, can cause jam-related euphoria when it is done right.

Then jellies. Crystalline fruit juice. Jelled, jarred, and arranged like a rainbow in neat long rows. "The trick here," says Norman's Aunt Beatrice, "is to capture the true flavor of the fruit while keeping the pectin in balance. Too much and it's tough, too little and it is juice. Just right, and the fruit speaks, no, sings, nay, *harmonizes* in a barbershop quartet of flavor, texture, color, and sweetness." The one thing he remembers about his Aunt Beatrice's Des Moines home was the stained cotton jelly bag that hung from her kitchen ceiling and the steady drip-click drip-click of blackberry juice falling into the enameled bowl beneath it.

Then candy. Secretly, Norman's least favorite. He'd readily tell you anyone can clobber you with sugar to get your attention. Any no-talent cook can artlessly combine peanuts, egg whites, and sugar, doll it up like a whore on a Monday night with cherry lipstick, and top it with a smoky chocolate eye, put it on a platter, and call it a Jubilee Bar. During the right summer, when there is a dearth of competition, said Jubilee Bar could win a ribbon. Maybe even pull down, "Best at the Fair," the sneaky floozy. "But," Norman will remind you, "that don't make it good to eat and it certainly isn't gonna make it good for you!"

Then one-pot dishes. Norman maintains (and testily argues with any dissenter) that, just as the Wright brothers are undoubtedly the fathers of modern flight, so the 4-H is undoubtedly the mother of the modern casserole. "Only a single pot," Norman fervidly explains, "yet it contains all of the ingredients of a nutritionally complete modern meal—meat, fish or poultry, vegetables of any kind, starch (potatoes, noodles, biscuits), broth (or gravy or cheese) in one pot— or, pan." How to make these oven-baked extravaganzas is taught in 4-H-sponsored after-school *Keeping the Better Farm Kitchen* classes that, Norman avers, "Solidifies 4-H's indisputable mother-of-the-casserole standing and ensures a steady supply of 4-H graduates who vie yearly to bake and deliver the best King Ranch Chicken Bake or Summer Squash Hot Dish or Baked Macaroni or Turkey, Chicken, canned Sardine, or Tuna Pot Pie."

Then cookies and bars. In summer of 1927, the following cookies were entered in the 4-H competition: Apple Oatmeal, Boston Shortbread, Snickerdoodles, Maple Spritz, Lemon Cornmeal, Oatmeal Rollout, Honey Nut Swirls, Stem Ginger Almond, Chocolate Pinwheels, Cardamom Sugar, Virginia Reels, Lemon Snow Drops, Pecan Butter Horns, Martha Washington's Tea Bites, Laura Kimball's Prairie Gingersnaps, Frosted Spice Drops, Mulling Spice Drops, Exotic Spice Drops, Cinnamon Sandies, Date Swirls, Omaha's Forgotten Spice Nuts, Chocolate Crinkles, Walnut Tasties, Black Walnut Sugar, Walnut Shepherd's Purse, Walnut Blackies, Walnut Tea, Walnut Roll-out, Pennsylvania Dutch Walnut, Weak Man's Maple Pies, Poor Man's Plum Tasties, Single Man's One-Bowl Oatmeal, Married Man's Tuxedo, Grandma Krause's Coconut Drop, Grandma Sue's Bing Cherry Chews, Grandma Sadie's Walnut Rugelach, Grandma Agatha's Peppernuts, Aunt Betty's Crisp Sugar, Aunt Hermione's Plum Chunk Oatmeal, Aunt Claire's Gingerbread Sandies, Mr. Macomber's Rum Balls, Mabel Osborne's Fruit Balls,

Scotch Shortbread, French Elephant Ears, Greek Date Pies, Turkish Date Thumbprints, Italian Lemon, French Iced Orange Mounds, Montana Fruit & Spice, Labadie's Whoopie Pie, Washington Cherry Snowballs, Peanut Butter, Anise Horns and Molasses Mix-er-Ups.

Norman Rockwell compiled this list, studied it, and committed it to memory. Then he went to the Omaha Public Library on 18th and Harney to research each recipe, assiduously copying each one in neat pencil script onto a file card. This was hard work for anyone, obsessive work for someone who was gainfully employed, unique work for a man—especially if that man appeared each night of summer at the Douglas County/Omaha City Fair, standing under the banner "Meet Norman! The World's Thinnest Man!"

✦

Norman was born to Samuel and Ruth Rockwell at 11:54 p.m. on December 31st, 1899, making him a frustrating near-miss for their town's first baby of 1900.

"Damn it," said Sam, upright in a strict wooden guest chair in his wife's hospital room. "I was hoping my son would amount to something!"

From there, the mood in the room established itself as funereal. Sam sulked silently as young Norman suckled his first teat and Ruth adored her handiwork.

Fate stepped in when, seeing as he was born in Beatrice, Nebraska (population recently fallen to 491) no other contender for First Baby of the Bright New Century presented itself within 24 hours. Norman Rockwell was duly re-determined to have been born at 12:01 on January 1, 1900. The hospital notified Sam and Ruth of the change and arranged a brief interview with the Daily Drover's Journal family columnist, who by-lined two inches in which Sam was quoted as "being proud as a peacock" of his revised son.

On his third day of life, Norman, Beatrice First Baby of the Bright New Century, had his well-baby check from the pediatrician. Along with being, "rosy where he should be rosy, creamy where creamy is desired, with a slight, though healing, cradle cap," Norman was noted to weigh a remarkable 12 pounds at a length of 27 inches.

"In other words," Dr. Rosenkraut explained, "this boy is mighty tall and singularly lanky. He is not only the first born of the new century, but the tallest newborn boy I've ever seen!"

Hearing this, Sam jumped up from his chair and bawled, "My son is gonna be somebody!"

Ruth took her son back from the nurse into his receiving blanket and held him close, his long, pearly toenails shining in the light.

✦

In spite of Sam's hard work and every effort, by the time he reached the age of 11, Norman still was nobody. Mostly, Sam pursued his Norman Improvement Project alone. Like the time he brought two carrier pigeons home for Norman to raise and train. Norman was indifferent. He didn't train them. They died. Sometimes, Sam could enlist Ruth's apathetic help (like when Ruth used her purloined Amish Bread recipe to help Norman come in second at the Gage County Fair bread competition, losing to Andrea Stone Bumstead's Sonnenblumenbrot). Yet Sam's efforts, singular or with Ruth, were unable to produce anything like a somebody out of Norman. Norman concentrated instead, with single-minded effort, on growing the tastiest stalk of celery.

Looking at the row of seven different celery hybrids lined up against the clapboard house and reflected in his son's proud, eager face, Sam insisted: "Celery is worthless. It tastes terrible and what's more, it never fills a body up—no matter how much of it you eat! Worthless. Like you, son!"

Surprisingly, this pronouncement provided Norman with the incentive to pursue something his father would see as more worthy. To support her son's burgeoning interest, Ruth suggested Norman make use of the entire rocky patch of land outside her kitchen window and suggested he plant a garden in earnest. Norman sanguinely planted a couple of rows of seeds. Within a few days he was fanatically protecting each tiny green shoot that rose tentatively into the Nebraska sky with a red and white,

KEEP OUT:
GARDEN

sign. When those tiny shoots became vines and those vines produced a curly jumble of yellow crookneck squash and those squash became food for his family and a proud smile on his mother's face, Norman was hooked. Each year, to Sam's dismay, Norman's garden expanded. In his teen years it grew from a dabbler's four-by-eight patch to a knowledgeable gardener's half-acre. Norman believed he learned more in his solitary hours using a spade than he did in school using a pencil. Yet, from his eleventh birthday (the quest for the coolest, crispiest celery) to his seventeenth birthday (the pursuit of the earthiest, creamiest potato), his annual summer vegetable garden produced, in his father's view, nothing but "stupid, stupid shit."

Ruth (and Norman), on the other hand, was tickled when Norman was successful with a fussy crossbreed or when he auditioned a new flavor at supper (Celery Root! Salsify! Dandelion Greens!).

To Sam, all of this failed to stack up to the one thing he wanted: a son with a prosperous future.

Sam peddled doorknobs. Wholesale. He believed "a man must provide for his family so they feel safe and secure—always. Doorknobs do that. Doorknobs are the difference between privacy—a man's home is his castle—and a lawless, ruleless society where thoughtless people barge freely into another's private room." His job, in what he called, "the privacy assurance industry," also had the advantage of being highly-secure in another sense. "There will," according to Sam, "never come a day when a man won't slap down his forty cents to buy a well-made doorknob!" As Sam would tell anyone who asked (and a sizable agglomeration who didn't ask): "I know what makes a man something, and I know who is and who isn't something. And Norman isn't."

Yet...right under Sam's nose...without Sam noticing...Norman was growing.

5'11" at nine years old...
6' 2" at 11 years old...
6' 6" at 12 years old...
6'8" at 13, 6'10" at 14, 7'2" at 15, 7'5" at 16...
7'7" at 17.

"One day," said Sam, "I woke up and said to myself—fuck, that boy is tall. And skinny. Now isn't that something?"

To Norman, on that same day, he said, "Dang boy...you're a tall, thin one. That's for sure. Why if I were you—and this is the best advice I can give you as your father—if I was you, I'd run away and join the circus. In a circus you could be the World's Tallest or World's Thinnest Man, which I am pretty sure you are. At last, you'd be somebody!"

It happened that this "one day" was the same day the United States entered World War I.

✦

The circus Norman ran away to was the United States Army. Or at least he tried.

Bunny Rattigan.

A month later, Norman Rockwell found himself standing, alphabetically, next to Bunny Rattigan in the Army Induction Office registration line:

BUNNY: I am Bunny. Bunny Rattigan. The Hanscome Park Rattigans. How do you do?
NORMAN: How do you do? I'm Norman. Norman Rockwell. [PAUSE] The Sheelytown Rockwells.
BUNNY: Sheelytown is it?
NORMAN: Yes...it is.

BUNNY: Well...I know that exists but I've never been there.
NORMAN: Oh it exists alright. Sheelytown exists in the same way that a fever exists.
BUNNY: Common?
NORMAN: And no one wants one!
[BOTH LAUGH]

They got called, together, to take the literacy test. They got called, together, to take the assessment for following technical procedures. They got called, together, to see if they could learn to assemble a rifle. At noon, they both sat on a bench and ate a neatly wax-paper-wrapped Kraft American Cheese sandwich provided by the government while balancing a Chero-Cola on their knees. At 1 p.m., they got called, together, to be weighed, measured, and inspected for hernia and venereal disease. At 4:15 p.m., their induction day ended when a grizzled veteran of the Spanish-American War thanked them for hearing the call and doing their duty. "And, gentlemen, I wish you...good luck."

Norman had never heard a wish of "good luck" sound so dreadful.

Bunny and Norman walked to the doorway of the induction center together, then paused.

BUNNY: Well, Norman, I suppose it was nice to meet you.
NORMAN: Suppose? Uh...well, I suppose it was nice to meet you, too. I never met anyone named Bunny before.
BUNNY: My name is actually Alexander. So is my father's. His friends, joking about our family name, call him "Rabbit" Rattigan. And since he is Rabbit, it made sense—if anything about this makes sense—that I'd be Bunny.
NORMAN: Well...I am happy to know you, Bunny.
BUNNY: And I you.
NORMAN: I suppose the next time we'll see each other will be in Germany. Or on the train to New Jersey before we ship out.

BUNNY: You're so tall that it will be easy to spot you on a battlefield or in crowded train station, even from afar, Norm. May I call you Norm?

NORMAN: Oh Lord! No one calls me that. [PAUSE] And yes. I'd like it fine if you would call me Norm. It'd be like we're friends...so I'd like that.

BUNNY: I'd like it if we *were* friends. What do they say? War makes for strange bedfellows?

NORMAN: Well, we are certainly from opposite sides of the tracks.

BUNNY: Germany won't know anything about Omaha. And any Germans we meet won't care about Hanscome Park.

NORMAN: It's good—at least to me—to know someone. Over there I mean. It will be nice... good...to know someone. And not be alone. That man's eerie 'good luck'—

BUNNY: (TURNING HIS JACKET LAPEL UP AGAINST THE APPROACHING SPRING EVENING) Norm, I will see you over in Germany.

NORMAN: Yep. I'll see you there, Bunny.

Two weeks later (to the day) this letter arrived, incorrectly addressed to Mr. Norman Rickwell:

> May 28, 1917
>
> Mr. Norman Rickwell
> 245 Snowhill Road
> Omaha, Nebraska
>
> Dear Mr. Rickwell,
>
> You appeared at the U.S. Army Ernest R. Laramie Selective Service Office on May 17, 1917 to render yourself for volunteer duty. We regret to inform you that, for the reason(s) listed below, the Army will not avail itself of your service.

*Reason not eligible: Height in excess of
specification*

*I trust you will seek and find other ways
to be supportive of our country's efforts
in this endeavor.*

*This letter is proof that your future draft
obligation, should there be one, has been
met.*

Status: 4-F

Sincerely yours,

*Maximillian Tagerent
Pvt. Class 1
U.S. Selective Service*

"Height! In excess of specification!" sneered Sam after reading Norman's letter. "You want to know who gets classified 4-F? Country hicks, that's who! 4-F started during the War Between the States to disqualify recruits who didn't have four front teeth in their mouths! That—four teeth—was all you needed to qualify. Four front teeth required to tear open gunpowder packets! 4-F for 4-Front teeth!"

Norman reached between his father's arms to take his letter back into his hands.

"My son!" continued Sam with a guffaw. He evaded Norman's reach. "4-F for tallness. Worse than no teeth!"

"But Dad...I can't help I'm this tall. I just am!"

"You oughta do what I say and join the circus!"

Norman reached in again. This time he grabbed the letter back and ran up the stairs to his bedroom.

The next day, Ruth took Norman aside when they were alone. "Your father can be just rude, NaNa." She used his childhood nickname. "He might get it wrong most of the time, but he loves you."

Norman kneeled and then sat on the floor. He rested his knee against his mother's knee. "I'm not sure how true that is, Mama. I think he loves his idea of me, but not me. Me being him—or like him—that's what he loves more than he loves me. But I am me, Mom. And he is right. The me I am is too tall to serve this country."

"Maybe so, NaNa. And maybe not," she ran her hand through Norman's thick brown hair. "I read something in the paper this morning that seems like it might work for you."

"Work for me? Work how?"

"The government has started a United States War Garden Commission—headed up by this man named Charles Lathrop Pack. He's from Michigan, NaNa. A Midwesterner and a very rich man. George Washington Carver came up with the idea of asking us normal citizens to grow a garden to support the war effort, because they're going to start rationing food soon. Gardens can replace food we usually get from far away by growing it closer to home."

"So, I can grow my garden to give it to the war? How will that satisfy Dad?"

"Oh…well, I had bigger ideas in mind for you than just satisfying Dad," Ruth replied. "I think we should write a letter to this Mr. Pack explaining your garden experience, garden knowledge, who you are."

"Who am I?" asked Norman flatly.

"Why, you're someone with six solid years of planting and growing experience. You know how things work on the ends of a hoe and a shovel. You could help Mr. Pack and his War Garden Commission. Think about it, NaNa. I am sure they'd take you. Tall or not!"

Norman thought.

Two days later, he and Ruth had composed a letter. In it, they explained that Norman had sought to volunteer for the Army and been rejected for being too tall. He was, the letter admitted, indeed tall. Yet, Norman and Ruth asserted, that should not keep Norman from serving his country. They went on to detail Norman's intense devotion to fruits, vegetables, and herbs, and significant practical knowledge of how they grow. The letter proposed that Norman volunteer, just as he had for the Army, but instead of fighting in Europe, he would devote the war's duration to serving the nation's domestic War Garden effort. The letter closed reminding Mr. Pack of Norman's Midwestern origin and avouching President Woodrow Wilson's mightily-correct assertion that "Food Will Win the War!"

A month later (to the day) Norman received this letter:

The Offices of Charles Lathrop Pack

Tuesday, June 5, 1917 15:17H

Mr. Norman Rockwell
245 Snowhill Road
Omaha, Nebraska

Dear Mr. Rockwell,

I write on behalf of Charles L. Pack, who sends you his personal greetings from Washington in the District of Columbia.

Mr. Pack is very appreciative of your generosity in contacting him in re: the War Garden Commission. He is also appreciative of your kind offer to volunteer your services to the Commission and to your country.

In order to support the home garden effort, the United States School Garden Army has been established under the auspices of the Bureau of Education, funded by the War Department at Pres. Wilson's direction. Since the Garden Army is in much need of help the sort of which you propose providing, Mr. Pack has asked me to accept your offer with his many thanks and to proffer you the post of Coordinator of Gardening Education, United States School Garden Army, which he assumes you will accept forthwith and occupy without delay.

Relying on this assumption, Mr. Pack has accredited you to work in his offices in Dupont Circle here in Washington, D.C. I have begun the process of your U.S. Army enrollment through the Office of Selective Service.

Two letters shall follow this one:

1. A letter from the Office of Selective Service officially accepting your volunteer enlistment into the U.S. Army, and
2. A letter detailing the post of Coordinator of Gardening Education, United States School Garden Army, along with outlining how you shall transport yourself under Army sponsorship to Washington by train to appear for duty on Monday, July 16, 1917.

Your service shall be deemed completed three years from your date of arrival in the capital or at the conclusion of United States efforts in the War, whichsoever comes first.

We at the War Garden Commission are grateful for your kind offer to serve your country and are looking forward to meeting you.

Very truly yours,

Miss Kelly-Anne Smith
Personal Assistant #4 to Charles L. Pack
U.S. War Garden Commission
CLP:kas

As Norman read the letter out loud, Sam erupted with laughter.

"Who in hell is Charles L. Pack?" Sam mocked, grabbing the letter from Norman. He held it daintily between his thumb and forefinger. "Charlie, Charlie L., Charlie L. Pack! Oooohh! A fancy letter from Charlie L. Pack!"

"Hey, gimme that!" yelled Norman, reaching down to recover the letter and return it to its engraved cream vellum envelope.

"Charles Lathrop Pack," inserted Ruth. "Timber money...rich... he's a Michigander. He—"

"And how does this rich man know my son?" Then, to Norman, with one hand flat as a saucer and one holding an imaginary cup with his pinky up. "You been sneaking out to the Omaha Club for tea with the upper crusters, Norman?"

Sam reached up, in one quick movement grabbed Norman's now-enveloped letter again, folded it in half and shoved it into his back pocket.

"Sam—," Ruth said.

"Dad!" pleaded Norman. "Come on! Give it back!"

Sam sat on his hands. "I've got your fancy letter now!"

"Sam, give him back his letter and then I'll explain," said Ruth.

Sam rolled onto the back pocket containing Norman's letter. They could all hear the paper crease and crinkle.

"It's mine!" yelled Norman.

Ruth stood between them, her hand out and palm open. "Samuel. Come now. It's Norman's. Give it to me and let me explain."

"Explain first!" said Sam with a derisive laugh. He rubbed his eyes with his fists and in a baby voice, "Then I'll give your baby back his 'wittle wetter!'"

"Okay. Okay. But you return it this time," said Ruth.

"I will!" said Sam, putting his elbows on his knees and his chin in his open hands in a caricature of an attentive child.

Ignoring Sam, Ruth persevered. "Norman and I wrote a letter to this Charles Lathrop Pack, a rich timber man from Michigan, now serving President Wilson in Washington. A letter, which—truth be told—I never thought he would receive, never mind read."

Sam continued mocking, "Why would a 'great man' in Washington pay any attention at all to a lowly housewife and her kid from Omaha?"

"I have no idea. Simply no idea. But...we told Norman's story—just briefly—and proposed Norman enlist to use his gardening knowledge to help the War Garden effort—."

"He does have knowledge..." Sam said begrudgingly, looking up at his son.

"And Mr. Pack, Charles Lathrop Pack," continued Ruth, "much to my—our—surprise, has asked Norman to come to the Capital to join the Army."

"Well...the 'School Army.'" This time, Sam was more serious, less derisive.

"The *United States* Army, Sam. President Wilson said, 'working in a war garden is just as real and patriotic an effort as the building of ships or the firing of cannon.' Norman will make a real contribution to the war. And you and I should be pleased he will be safe while doing that, in Washington, out of the way of harms."

"4-F one day," said Sam reaching into his pocket, removing and unfolding the envelope, "and saved by some fancy-pants railroad man the next. Who could think it? My son. A rich man's flunky."

"Timber. And he is hardly that, Sam," said Ruth, patting Norman lightly on the back. "He is just serving his country, that's all. Serving like any boy—should I say, young man—would want to do."

"Yes." Sam was almost won over (or simply out of energy).

"And," added Ruth, "can do with pride."

Sam stood up, rocked onto his toes and handed Norman back the letter. "Just serving his country like any young man would want to." He smiled. "I suppose so..."

✦

The next morning, Sam arrived at the breakfast table fully dressed in a gray summer suit with his toquilla hat in his hand.

TO RUTH AND NORMAN: "Good morning!"
TO RUTH (WITH A HASTY KISS ON THE CHEEK): "Sleep good, Ruthie?"

TO NORMAN (SNAPPING HIS FINGERS): "You, boy! You're going to school late today. You and I are going to J. L. Brandeis to get you a traveling trunk and clothes for the train!"

"Wait...what about school?" asked Norman, hoping to avoid time with his father.

"It's the last week of the year. What are you doing, anyway—cleaning out your locker? It's not every day you take a train across the frigging country to polish the knob of a millionaire. I want my boy outfitted!"

"Mom?" pleaded Norman, looking for an ally.

"Go with your father, NaNa. You need a trunk. And dress clothes for a Washington, D.C. summer. I don't have time to sew. You'll need to buy big and I will take it in. Dad will help you shop and you and I will have two weeks to make everything fit."

"Like she says, Norman, I'll help you." Then, mockingly, he added, "you'll look swell for your trip east and for meeting your Mr. Pack!"

Reluctantly, Norman got up and gathered his school bag. "Okay," he said, reconciled.

Norman and Sam trundled to downtown Omaha in Sam's Nash Light Six, the rear seat full of crates full of doorknobs. The loud rattle of the knobs made it easy for both Sam and his son to avoid initiating or continuing conversation. Each time Sam did venture a question, Norman gestured with his thumb toward the clattering knobs and shrugged as if to say, "I would if I could." The knobs saved Norman from needing to speak for the entire two hours it took to drive from Beatrice to Omaha.

As soon as they entered downtown, Sam veered off the route to J. L. Brandeis's department store and headed onto Douglas Street instead. He steered for Doolittle's Drug Store. He pulled up right in front, set the brake and turned to Norman with an expectant smile.

"Doolittle's!" No reaction from Norman. "Doolittle's, Norman!"

"What?" asked Norman, straining his neck to look out the windscreen and up under the awning of the ornate storefront. "What's Doolittle's?"

"Doolittle's Drugstore's soda fountain is home to—you have got to taste it, Norman— Goody's Yellow Pop! Bright yellow as your morning pee, but sweet as cotton candy and only sold here!"

"But Dad—."

"No whining, Norman. Live just a little bit of life before you go to war!"

"I'm not going to war!" Norman protested.

"To Washington...to war...who cares about the details? To your mom and me, it's as good as you were gone to Europe to the front. We won't see you. Or know about you. Maybe except from letters?" Sam developed a tear in his voice and in the corner of his eye yet, as soon as he felt it, he wiped it away and set his jaw toward the door. He was sure Norman didn't see. "Aw...c'mon. Let's go in. I come here all the time when I am on the road. They know me. Get a Goody's. Or maybe you'd like a root beer float better? Let your dad give you a treat."

Norman unraveled himself warily from the car seat and stood stooped under the black-and-brown striped awning. He ducked into the door and lumbered along the neat, tiled walkway past the compounding counter and into the soda fountain. As he did, he passed from functional cherrywood paneling to hand-carved mahogany panels artfully depicting cavorting dolphins and mermaids surrounded by scallop shells. Norman (although the wished he had not left the car) had to admit the transition was a little bit magical.

Once in the fountain, Norman took in the room. Twelve raised chair-backed stools at the marble bar were upholstered in shiny cream-colored leather. The bar's marble was the same cream color, run through with veins of silver, black, and brown. On the customer's side, the bar was equipped with seahorse-shaped hooks on which several gentlemen had hung their hats and women had hung their pocketbooks. On the attending waiter's side, similar hooks hung towels, spaced about every two feet. In just the same towel location on the countertop stood giant glass jars, bulbous and gleaming like great ocean bubbles, each filled with a different sort of candy in huge, play-land quantities: one of red-and-white-striped peppermint chalkies, one of pink, purple, and gold sugar pastilles, one of pineapple-shaped exotics mixed with lime and lemon hard candy wedges, and one of red and black licorice. The licorice chunks (hand cut with shears) were displayed in the jar in stripes of red and black topped with a tousle of red and black licorice strings. Each of the bubble-jars contained thousands of pieces—tempting in both appearance and quantity. The fountain featured five soda spigots, also about two feet apart, the plumbing set into cast metal dolphin heads styled so that when the waiter lifted their dorsal fin, soda shot from the fish's mouth. All of this—panels, sunlight, marble, candy jars, towels, dolphins—was reflected in a silver and glass mirror extending the length of the bar and engraved about the edges with mermen jousting with tridents. Doubling all of this in the mirror's reflection caused everything to shine and twinkle in a way that caused Norman to feel it was enchanted.

Norman's spell was broken when one of the waiters called to his father "Mr. Rockwell! Welcome, sir!"

"Thanks, Roger!" answered Sam. "Meet my son, Norman!" Then, stunning Norman, "I am so proud of him! He leaves in two weeks to Washington for the War!"

"Say, Mr. Rockwell, he's a tall one, ain't he?" replied the waiter. "Anyone who is going to war gets a cookie added to his sundae or float on the house today. Pull up here," he indicated two stools and dropped a round cardboard coaster in front of each. "What'll you have there, Norman?"

NORMAN: [to his father] But I'm not going to war, I'm—
SAM: SHHHH!
NORMAN: It's not fair to take the cookie if I'm not—

Just then, another seventeen-year-old walked in with his father.

"Mr. Schear! And Tommy!" said Roger the waiter, dropping another two coasters in front of two adjacent stools. "Here for your weekly Tin Roof?"

TOMMY: I'm off to war, Roger. Next weekend I head east.

MR. SCHEAR: So he'll have that Tin Roof sundae with double scoops, and extra fudge and triple peanuts!

ROGER: And a free cookie! Say Mr. Schear...do you know Mr. Rockwell?

MR. SCHEAR: No...I don't think I do. [EXTENDS HIS HAND] Martin Schear. [POINTS TO HIS SON] And my son, Tommy.

ROGER: Mr. Rockwell's son, Norman, here, is off to join the fight, too.

SAM: [EAGERLY OFFERS HIS HAND] I'm Sam Rockwell. This is my son, Norman.

NORMAN: How do you do? I'm not—.

SAM: Norman is off east next week too.

NORMAN: But I—.

SAM: Say that Tin Roof...let it be on me. [TO ROGER] Roger, add Tommy's Tin Roof to my bill, please. Along with whatever his dad wants, too.

MR. SCHEAR: We are thankful, Sam. [TO ROGER] I'll have butter pecan in a sundae with hot cara—.

Just then, another seventeen-year-old walked in with his father.

ROGER: Mr. Matthews! Randy! You'll have to wait. We are full up of seats at the moment.

A man and woman at the far end of the bar stood, gathered their belongings, dropped some coins on the fountain bar, and sidled between the stools and the windows past the Matthewses toward the door. As soon as the couple passed, the Matthewses grabbed their seats.

ROGER: Good to have you. You know Mr. Schear? Tommy?

MR. MATTHEWS: We do. How do you do, gents?

MR. SCHEAR and TOMMY in unison: Good. Good to see you!

MR. MATTHEWS: Randall is off in two weeks to fight in Germany, I am happy to say.

RANDY: Yessir! I am gonna put it to them krauts!

Sam abruptly stood, walked over to the Matthewses and shook their hands.

SAM: That's the spirit! [THEN, TO ROGER] On me! Whatever they want— it's on me!

ROGER: Yes, sir!

MR. MATTHEWS: That's awfully kind of you, Sir.

SAM: I'm Sam. All of our sons are off to fight—.

NORMAN: I'm not off to—.

SAM: Pie! I want pie! Pie for everyone! On me!

ROGER: Yes, sir! Apple, peach, or blueberry?

SAM: A slice of each for everyone! These boys are going to war! They need goodbye pie!

NORMAN: I am not going—.

As new groups of fathers and sons came in, Sam greeted each pair with an eager handshake and entreaty to order anything Doolittle's served on his tab. After the round of pie, he ordered rounds of:

1. Goody's Yellow Pop
2. David Harum Sundaes
3. Butterscotch Aggie Sundaes
4. Goody's Yellow Pop (a second time)
5. Raspberry Lime Floats
6. Brownie Sundaes
7. Split Banana Boats
8. Goody's Yellow Pop (a third time)
9. Hot Fudge Sundaes

Since Sam and Norman arrived and the feast began, twelve groups of fathers and sons had entered Doolittle's fountain and none had left. Boys sat three-to-a-stool, balancing sundaes or Pop bottles on their knees as fathers stood smiling close by. Empty plates, bowls, bottles, and glasses were piled in milky, melty pools on the bar with spoon-handles sticking out like sea-urchin spines.

Over this, as if he were Caesar, presided Sam, regal, yet benevolent—as sociable and generous as anyone could be. Using his salesman's skills, Sam spoke briefly to each father and son, earnestly inquired about them, open-heartedly commented on their story, profusely complimented their relationship. Norman— watching Sam greet, host, gloat, coax, welcome, and cajole—barely knew the spirit emanating from his father's body. *This* man, *this* father, was all generosity and fun. All host and co-conspirator. All intimate, new best friend. While an astounded Norman looked on, Sam turned the afternoon into a party. Duly, Sam's guests indulged with him, converting humble ice cream, soda, and pie into a splurge. An intended brief stop at a soda fountain into a blowout. A private goodbye into a spontaneous party—a binge, a bender, a bacchanal.

"It was just as it should have been," replied Sam afterwards when Norman asked him, "Why?" as he folded himself back into the car. "See, Norman...I am quite sure you'll come back from Washington in good health and high spirits. At least I know for damned sure you'll come back *alive*. Those fathers don't think of it now, but half of them—or more—will wait for their son...yet their son *won't come home*. You and I, for a few dollars, we gave them something to relish. To remember. Someday...today might be...when those fathers look back... all they have."

Sam and Norman had arrived at Doolittle's just before noon. They left Doolittle's, in a crowd of laughing fathers and sons, after 6 p.m. Since J. L. Brandeis routinely closed each day at 4:15 p.m., they would have to return the next day to shop for clothes.

✦

Much taking in and letting out filled Ruth's and Norman's afternoons and evenings as they struggled to make the off-the-rack clothes from J. L. Brandeis fit Norman's decidedly not off-the-rack body. The suit pants came without a hem, so there was fabric enough to make a cuff break just above Norman's shoe. Shirts had to be bought in the largest size and taken in throughout the body and neck and let out (with muslin inserts) to extend the length of the arms. Only so much could be done to the suit jacket and overcoat arms, which were fixed with bombazine sleeve extensions. The results were, "Not bad, if you don't look too hard or too long," according to Sam, as he and Ruth looked on while Norman modeled his new wardrobe.

Ruth—with three days left until Norman would present his ticket to the conductor of the "Union to Union Express" train in Omaha's Union Station—wistfully packed his trunk in the late-afternoon sunlight. She sat on a low stool with his clothes and gardening tools in small, neat piles around her. She thought how lucky she was to have a boy who was going to a safe place when so many parents were saying goodbye to sons leaving enthusiastically to fight the Germans—completely oblivious to, unconscious of, or just plain contemptuous toward the newspaper stories that told of the grim conditions in the trenches. She sighed and, looking up to God, gathered up another small bit of Norman to fold neatly and put in the trunk.

Just then, she heard footfalls on the stairs. *Norman, home from school*, she thought. As she listened, though, she realized it was Sam's size 8-½ wingtips, not Normans size 14 work boots, coming up the stairs.

"Ruth?" called Sam when he was a few steps below the landing. "Ruthie? You here?"

"In Norman's room," answered Ruth.

Sam, walking in, hat still in his hand and seeming preoccupied: "Ruthie, I have something I want to hide in Norman's trunk." Ruth looked skeptical. "Not hide. Put in so he won't find it until he unpacks in Washington."

Ruth pursed her lips. "Now, Sam Rockwell, what are you up to? Trying to make a wreck of your son's unpacking. This is not the time for your pranks and jokes!"

"No prank, Ruthie. No joke. It's something I want to give him but haven't got the heart to stand up to it in person. It's a gift, sort of. He will like it. Don't worry."

"Sam, did you get him a tie pin? A billfold? No...a Brownie camera so he can take pictures?"

"No. Well, yes. I did get him a Brownie. We'll give him that day after tomorrow. The evening before he goes. This is more...well, personal. Private. Let me just slip it in between his clothes in there. Just secret-like."

"Go ahead, Sam. You do what you want," said Ruth standing and walking away to give him room.

Sam kneeled next to the trunk, reached into his righthand jacket pocket, and pulled out a well-worn spoon with the name "Doolittle's" stamped on the handle. He quickly slid it between the layers of clothing and smoothed them so it could not be seen.

"Okay, Ruthie," he said, "I'm done."

Ruth quietly returned to her packing. Halfway out the door, Sam stopped, turned around and came back to her. He grabbed her hand and held it. A moment later he let it go.

"To Washington, D.C.!" he said.

"Yes," said Ruth, wiping a tear. "Yes."

✦

Three days later, Ruth stood on the platform on Track Six in Union Station, wiping her tears again. At the same time, Sam was lackadaisically picking lint off of Norman's overcoat sleeve and looking past Norman's arm into the crowd of boys in khaki. The "Union to Union Express" had been commandeered as a troop train, and hundreds of Omaha boys milled around waiting for the conductor's whistle to blow, signaling them to board. While Norman waited patiently and Ruth dabbed her blueberry-flowered handkerchief in the corners of her eyes, Sam looked at the milling crowd and tried to spy the color of piping each boy wore on his khaki to identify his branch of service.

"Is this something or what?" Sam said, buoyed by the parade atmosphere on the platform as boys shook hands with their friends. Cigarettes were nervously lit, filling the station with thin silver smoke. Occasional whistles blew as porters pushed their way through the eddying families and jockeyed for an open place in which to stand.

"I heard of this in newsreels!" shouted Sam over the rising roar on the platform.

Sam had never been on a train. Ruth kept quiet about her two trips to Chicago before she met Sam. No use showing him up. For her, today was about Norman.

"I never saw so much...what? Enthusiasm!" gushed Sam, smiling from ear to ear.

Norman looked at his mother, hoping she'd help. "Samuel...it's Norman's last few—."

As the clock-hand locked in on seven minutes before departure time, the conductor crisply called "ALL ABOARD!" at the steps of Norman's train car. The same shout echoed up and down the train. The milling crowd became purposeful as fathers tipped porters and fumblingly embraced their sons and sons gave mothers awkward goodbye kisses.

Sam suddenly looked up and pointed.

"Hey, Norman—there's the Morrisons! Randy must be on your train...and look...Tommy Shear, too!" Sam charged into the crowd shaking his hat over his head as he called out "Randy! Randy! Hello Morrisons! You! Randy! Tommy! Tommy Schear!"

It took him a nearly a minute to drive through the crowd. Once he arrived, he gave Randy and his father each a breathless handshake and overly eager hug. "Leaving on the same train as my boy, Norman. You met Norman at Doolittle's. Remember Norman?"

"Awww," said Mr. Morrison. "I'd like to say a proper goodbye to Norman, but they just called all-aboard so we've got to...well...get Randy aboard."

"And this must be Mrs. Morrison?" said Sam, seeming not to hear. "Nice to meet you. I'm Sam Rockwell. My son is traveling today, too. He's the tall thin one over there." Sam gestured back across the platform to where Norman stood just as the conductor's whistle blew. Sam looked around quickly for his tall son, easily picked out, even in a crowd. Norman was no longer on the platform.

"Gotta go," said Sam. "Sorry, Ma'am. Pleasure to meet you."

As he turned to go, he noticed that Tommy Schear stood almost next to him hugging his father goodbye while his mother looked on. He fought his way briefly to where Tommy stood.

"Tommy Schear! Well I'll be darned! Sam...Sam Rockwell...you recall? From Doolittle's—"

"Hi, Mr, Rockwell!" said Tommy as he turned away from hugging his mother. He then waved to both his parents and gestured to Sam pointing towards the train.

Tommy's father turned to leave the platform and almost stepped squarely on Sam's foot. He tipped his hat and said, "Rockwell, good to see you."

"And you, Milton. I was just over there when I saw you and the Morrisons. Over there...did you see them?" Then he remembered Norman. "I've got to go. Got to go...sorry. Hey Tommy, you go safely, now. Me? I've gotta go!"

Sam turned into a crowd that was no longer milling. Now families were leaving the platform. Porters tipped their trollies. Conductors raised the boarding stairs. Sam swam upstream as he made his way through the departing crowd.

"ALL ABOARD for the Union to Union departing for the Nation's Capital!" cried the train conductor, waving to the brakeman. The train's departure whistle blew.

Fighting his way through the crowd, struggling to find a clear path Sam suddenly realized he was yelling, "Norman! Norman!"

When he got back to where Norman had been standing, there was only Ruth.

"Norman!" yelled Sam.

"He said to tell you goodbye, Sam," said Ruth, matter-of-factly folding her handkerchief over the belt of her dress. "He waited as long as he could. The train man said he'd leave without him."

Sam looked down at his hands. "The Morrisons. The Schears. They had ice cream with us, Ruthie."

Ruth had no idea who, or what, he meant.

✦

For Norman, the trip aboard the Union to Union Express, as a troop train, was half heavenly adventure and half hellish obligation.

The heavenly adventure: Norman had never seen anything outside of Beatrice or Omaha and now every mile of American soil between him and Washington, D.C. was visible on both sides of the train, moving past his fascinated eyes at an average speed of twenty-five-miles-per-hour. All he needed to do was watch out the windows, the biggest pieces of glass he'd ever looked through. Norman drank in the passing picture of country life, train life, American life presented to him in varying levels of detail depending on the speed of the train. It sped by in wide-angle view at high speed, then crept by at slow speed as if it was under a microscope. Norman felt as if the most captivating museum was moving past his worn leather throne, curated just for his majesty. First, acres of farmland—tilled, fallow—stretched to the horizon in a roiling wave of windswept golden green. Then forests. Then rivers. Then empty grassland, occasionally tenanted by a rusting water windmill or contemned scarecrow. There was a chunking noise as the train wind buffeted past stations (the Union to Union made only five stops) leaving a hail of blowing newspaper pages and perplexed pigeons. Gray towns stoutly presented themselves, bowed briefly, then receded, replaced by weedy green backyards with whitewashed storm basement doors peaking. Then, again, uncounted acres of farmland until the next town came forward. This repetitive parade was allayed by short stretches of rusty brown at railroad crossings and switching-yards. Sometimes the train would tear through a crossing, horn blowing, steam puffing, bolting past full wagons driven by alert farmers, hands on their hats against the train draft or hats in their hands, waving them at the train. Or unloaded wagons drowsily dragged by nodding horses, slack-reined in the hands of dozing farmers (hat over their eyes in the feverous air) as the train crept past, engine hissing and safety bells clanging. During the day in the switching yards, Norman watched long stretches of track disappear into itself and heard a satisfying KER-CHUNK as the train switched tracks. He saw blue-and-white-stripe-coated yardmen stepping (recklessly or daintily) over the tracks, clipboards in hands, checking boxcar loads and initialing manifests. At night, he watched black-canvas coated yardmen holding dim lanterns chase men with the stubble of hard travel on their cheeks away from warming their hands at sparky barrels of orange cinders. The cinders flew up in cyclones as trains speed by. In early morning, while the yardmen drank their coffee in shacks, with their backs turned to the yard, these same travelers hid and waited for the best moment to creep out from trackside bushes and jump into red or yellow boxcars, lay out their bedrolls and slide the giant wooden doors closed behind them. In these boxcars—train engines idling—they made their roving home. Norman knew as soon as he settled into his worn red leather seat that he could do a version of the same: his luggage safely stowed on the rack above his head, his size 14 boots carefully moored by their laces to the legs of his seat. There was a coziness he created on the crowded train: his seat, his new socks, his camera, his overcoat (it gave privacy even if it was too warm against the summery breeze that blew through the aisle), his window, and the landscape, feeling like his, fading now from shadowy to black, tapering away.

The hellish obligation: the heavenly was largely outside the train; the hellish was inside. Atmosphere: the train was crowded with boys spitting, burping, farting, sweating, sock-footing, as boys freshly released from parental supervision do. It only took two hours after departure from Omaha for the air in the train to ripen like a pungent sour-milky wheel of Liederkranz. Add to that a cloud of cigarette smoke that filled the Men's room (where smoking was allowed) and billowed into each car (where smoking was not allowed) each time the door was opened. A zinc-tobacco haze swirled in the aisle and blew out to the windows each time someone walked the length of the car. Food: breakfast each day was the same, catered by the War Department and delivered from a four-wheeled cart by a gray-haired Negro Pullman porter: three Uneeda biscuits and one hardboiled egg per passenger. By barter you could create three variations—all Uneeda biscuits (which Norman, to himself, called "Morning in the Desert"), all egg (known to Norman as "Sunrise Over The Henhouse") or half-biscuits-and-half- egg ("Bountiful Breakfast Buffet"). Lunch was similarly un-extravagant—a metallic-tasting tuna salad sandwich on Holsum bread with a single string of pimento added, served in a neat waxed-paper bag. Norman thought of three variations for this meal, too—eat the sandwich only, eat the wax bag only or eat both sandwich and bag ("Lavish Lunch Buffet"). Dinner, it turned out, was a positive feast, comparatively—the first night: chicken soup with an undercooked dumpling; the second night, leftover chicken soup without a dumpling (these, Norman called "Dinner Denial" and "Supper Subtraction," respectively).

The hardest of the hellish? The transition from day to night. The dazzling parade of day—his quick-moving extravagant view of America—was exchanged for the dull, dark vacuum of night—a static ghostly view of the inside of the train car reflected in the train window. With no view, all there was to do was sleep. Yet, four things conspired toward difficult sleep even though the gentle rocking of the train should have made it easy:

1. The harsh gray lights in the passenger cars stayed on all night,

2. The metal-against-metal screech the train wheels made on turns in the track, or anytime the train came to a signal,

3. The banging jolt the train (and its passengers) absorbed every two hours in the early morning when the train moved to a siding and added cars, and

4. The general buzz that emerged from a trainload of eighteen to twenty-year-olds who couldn't sleep.

This buzz hushed slowly as boys put their playing cards down and one-by-one (or in small groups) retired with an amiable and hopeful, "I'll try and sleep now." With these partings, the train gradually grew quiet as boys let conversation ebb. Yet, those who tried sleep soon discovered sleep was not possible (for the four reasons mentioned), so they said to themselves or their seatmates, "maybe I'll sleep in an hour or so." And the train gradually got noisy again. By midnight, the train buzzed at medium volume. The renewed conversations multiplied as more and more boys gave up their attempts to sleep with a mournful, "aww...fuck sleep." By 1:30 a.m. the train was lively again with conversations, as restless as during the day.

On the second evening most of the boys gave up the idea of sleeping even before trying and socialized all night. Norman, unable to sleep, frustrated by the noise yet unwilling to socialize, slumped in his seat (as much as he could slump) and stared with spiritless eyes at his own face reflected in the now-black mirror of the train window, moving through the night towards the District of Columbia.

✦

Norman's destination was Washington, D.C., although that was not true for the mass of boys on the train. In D.C., they transferred to the Empire Express for a four-hour trip to New York City's

Pennsylvania Station. From there, they would further disperse to either Manhattan or Weehawken harbor, then board re-fitted cruise ships to sail for Saint-Nazaire, France.

As soon as the Union-to-Union train engine stopped, the conductor cleared the doors and lowered the steps. The rest of the boys hurriedly grabbed their luggage and, *en masse*, headed to their New York-bound train, a few tracks over. Norman didn't exit the train; the train exited him. He didn't mind that, abruptly, he sat alone in the car, abandoned. For a few moments he relished the silence. Then he gathered his trunk, his hat, and his overcoat, and stooped down the gloriously empty aisle, to the gloriously empty steps, and down onto the nearly-empty platform. A few straggling boys clasped hands or lit cigarettes, then quickly made their way. Norman stretched to his full height for the first time in almost three days. He savored the open air and relative quiet.

Then:

"Norrrrrmmmmmmmannn!" a woman's voice called from a distance, "Hey you! Norman Rockwell!!"

He looked in the direction of the voice and saw a pert young woman in a dark gray poplin skirt and short-sleeved, pearl-gray-and-burgundy-striped silk taffeta shirt-waist with a deep-burgundy man-style collar, open at the neck. She waved her hands as she wobbled toward him on neatly-buttoned black calf ankle boots. Deep-red-tinted sunglasses perched precariously on her pink powdered nose. She arrived in front of Norman out of breath and planted her feet firmly.

"So sorry! I'm late!" she began. "I walked. Walking on a summer day in Columbia is a chore or I'll be no account! My goodness, but the walkways are crowded this morning! Quite the chore coming over, as I said. Not that I mind..!" She took a breath and looked up at Norman. "My goodness, you *are* tall aren't you? I've seen tall people before—I mean six-feet-three...maybe four...could have even been five? Midgets compared. You? You're a tall one or I'll be no account!

And skinny! It looks like you haven't eaten in days. But tall! You are, aren't you? I am surprised you haven't joined a circus!"

She glanced around, took in the filagree complication of the train platform roof, and seemed to recover her focus.

"Oh my goodness, I am sorry. You must wonder who I am. I'm Kelly-Anne Smith. Personal Secretary Number Four to Mr. Charles Pack. I wrote to you. Mr. Pack couldn't make it in person. Well...to be honest...he doesn't do things like this. That's what I'm for. The reason he has five secretaries. I'm the youngest. Least tenured, I mean. So I get the train pickups. Er...meetings. Um...*wel-com-ings.* Welcoming."

With this word she curtsied jauntily, raised her arms to exaggerate the dip of her hips, flicked the bangs of her Polaire-bobbed haircut out of her eyes, and said:

"So. You are welcome!"

Norman raised his right hand to tip his hat and realized his hat was balanced on the corner of his trunk, which he held in his left hand. He awkwardly put the trunk down, placed his hat on his head quickly and touched the brim.

"Hello."

He absentmindedly took his hat off again, put it back on the corner of his trunk, which was standing next to him. Kelly-Anne laughed at this odd on-then-off ritual.

Norman realized he was once again hatless. Remembering his mother's admonition to always wear his hat, he quickly replaced it firmly on his head.

"Hello, again," he said, with some anguish, realizing he had made a mockery of his hat duties on his very first introduction. "Sorry. I don't know what to do with a hat."

"I'd wear it," said Kelly-Anne tartly. "If I were you."

"Yes. I got to that. Although, I grant, it did take a while."

"Well-done in the end, though," said Kelly-Anne with a smile.

They both paused. Kelly-Anne because she had said what she wanted to say. Norman because he didn't know what to say next.

Kelly-Anne broke the silence.

KELLY-ANNE: So you're—.
NORMAN: Oh my name...sorry...I am Norman Jathan Rockwell.
KELLY-ANNE: Formal.
NORMAN: My mother's maiden name. My middle name. I included that in case there might have been two Norman Rockwells on the train. Just to be sure. [PAUSE]
KELLY-ANNE: To be sure of what?
NORMAN: That you got the right Norman.
KELLY-ANNE: You're over seven feet tall. I don't think I'd get you wrong!

They laughed. Norman heaved his trunk up from the platform and started to walk. Kelly-Anne walked next to him, standing as tall as his right wrist.

"Oh, don't carry that! See that man standing down there at the end of the platform waiting by the gate? He is our porter. Let me get him." She placed her forefinger and pinky finger on her lower lip and made a loud wolf-whistle. The porter immediately turned, grabbed his dray, and began to walk their way.

NORMAN: That's impressive.
KELLY-ANNE: How else could I get him from so far?
NORMAN: But still...for girl number four—
KELLY-ANNE: I may be Secretary Number Four to Mr. Pack, but I am not *actually* fourth to anyone. And I am no girl!

They laughed again, stopped abruptly, and stood awkwardly silent as the porter covered the remaining ten yards. When the porter arrived and had heaved Norman's trunk onto his dray, they all started down the track for the station.

Norman continued:

"If not a girl—what then? What are you?" asked Norman, too late to get an answer.

Kelly-Anne continued:

"This is Mr. Remington, Mr. Pack's porter," said Kelly-Anne in an instructive tone. "He will take your trunk to Dupont Circle. You may want to entrust him with your overcoat as well, since you will be warm carrying it. Oh...and your hat—."

"No!" inserted Norman, checking to see if his hat was on his head.

"—since you are obviously new to hats."

Norman, to Kelly-Anne: "I will keep it."

Norman, to Mr. Remington: "Thank you very kindly, Mr. Remington."

"Soon," added Kelly-Anne, "you'll call him Mr. R., like the rest of us."

"You are welcome, Mr. Rockwell," said Mr. R. Then, he walked ahead into the terminal.

✦

A wall of humid air and bright sunlight met Kelly-Anne and Norman as they exited the cool darkness of Union Station onto Massachusetts Avenue. As Mr. R. wove himself into the crowd, the two fell comfortably into a column of pedestrians to make their diagonal way toward the Potomac River and DuPont Circle. Norman immediately noticed the powerful effect of walking diagonally as the street cut through square blocks, leaving small triangles of open ground planted with lilies, roses and hydrangea.

"A diagonal street creates vistas—grand open views—befitting of a capital," said Kelly-Anne as she pointed left, then right, providing a tour as they went.

For Kelly-Anne, the street was a feat of design ingenuity; for Norman, the street was a brouhaha of sights and smells. He had never seen so many stone buildings, statues, Negroes, or women. Vendors of apples, boiled and roasted peanuts, oysters, shaved ice (advertised as "Snow Cones") created bursts of aroma in succession, luring Norman (sweet sugary vanilla egg custard) and repelling him (peppered fishy Chesapeake blue crabs). Kelly-Anne seemed to ignore all of it as she kept up her architectural commentary, regularly punctuated by, "Or I'll be no account!" this and, "Or I'll be no account!" that and helpfully pointing out low-hanging Oak tree branches that might come in Norman's way.

After successfully dodging vendors, bicycles, carts of various sorts, souvenir sellers, and low-hanging branches, and struggling to keep pace with Kelly-Anne's comments while controlling his hat on his head for two-and-a-half miles, they arrived at number 4 DuPont Circle.

Just as expected, Mr. Remington stood in the carriage way with Norman's trunk.

"Miss Smith," said Mr R., "and Mr. Rockwell, welcome home."

Another member of the household staff bowed slightly and opened the Edwardian home's heavy, white door.

Kelly-Anne stepped in first and Norman followed. He was instantly bowled over by the sweet smell of lilac flowers coming from a huge arrangement displayed on a marble table in the vestibule. It looked as if the entire population of lilac bushes living in all of Columbia had lent each and every cluster of its blossoms to this Salute to *Syringa*, which cascaded, purple and white, over no fewer than ten levels of green porcelain plates, stands. and vases. Norman was captivated. Kelly-Anne pulled on his sleeve to focus his attention as they passed through the vestibule and into the reception hall. There, under a marble rotunda, stood a similar floral salute, this time to paper white garden roses, which Norman knew as *Rosa Alba Maxima*. Huge clusters of dozens of white-pink blossoms in no fewer than twenty-five cut crystal vases were arrayed to look as if they had grown naturally on a marquetry side-table. These two flower arrangements together held more cut flowers than Norman had ever seen in his life.

His dreamy consideration of flowers was interrupted by a whispered hiss and a single word.

"Psssssst! Hat!" whispered Kelly-Anne urgently.

Norman touched his hat, which was right where he expected it to be: on his head.

"I have it!" he said.

"Off!" hissed Kelly-Anne, "you want to have it—off!"

"I do?" Norman was flummoxed.

Kelly-Anne kept her hands by her side and gestured with her chin towards the top of the rotunda and the upper landing of a massive circular staircase. "Him!" she whispered.

A nattily-suited, kind-eyed, red-haired man with a neatly-combed beard and waxed mustache stood at the top of the stairs considering a sheet of 1847 Ben Franklin postage stamps that was framed on the wall.

Norman grabbed his hat from his head, clapped it over his heart and stood upright.

KELLY-ANNE: Mr. Charles Lathrop Pack, may I introduce Norman Rockwell.

NORMAN: Norman Jathan Rockwell, from Nebraska, Sir.

MR. PACK: [COMING DOWN THE STAIRS WITH HIS MANICURED HAND EXTENDED] Norman. I am pleased to have y'here. Thanks, Miss Smith, for your introduction. Norman, y'be welcome. This'll be your home for the duration of the War. In return, I will make you a gardener. Wait. You already are a gardener. I will make you *the* gardener. That is, America's gardener. I believe that, in war, a garden will get us just as far, is just as important an asset in this war, as a gun or a cannon. Or a whole battery of cannon! Yes, Norman, what y'do back in Nebraska is needed here. The war garden effort, modest now, needs to be, will be, amplified, emboldened, magnified. It will win us this war. You, my boy, will lead us to victory! Willing to do that?

NORMAN: Yes sir! I am!

MR. PACK: For now, get settled. See your room. Miss Smith, show him his room.

KELLY-ANNE: I will, Mr. Pack.

MR. PACK: You're free until tomorrow, Norman. Tomorrow morning at 10:30 I want y' t' meet me and Mr. Wilson on the South Lawn. We are going to plant a war garden there. The nation's war garden.

Norman thought for a moment. "Yes, sir. Certainly, sir. Sir... would you mind if I say something here?" He looked to Kelly-Anne for support. None came. She shook her head to advise him not to go forward. Norman did not see or did not accept the advice.

Mr. Pack nodded, "Mind? No...young man, you steam right ahead and tell me what is on your mind."

"I think that garden might mean more to people if we call it a Victory Garden. Not a War Garden. Like you said, sir, victory is what we are after."

Mr. Pack thought for a moment. "Norman...I am seventy-years-old and I made millions of dollars planting trees and then coming back twenty years later and cutting down the very same trees for a profit. The timber business isn't, as y'might say, eye surgery. My success in timber required a simple idea, some patience, and a fine ability to execute. I had the simple idea. I've got eons of patience. And I search for and then engage people who have an ability to execute..."

Kelly-Anne smiled at Norman.

"...Y'been here ten minutes," Mr. Pack continued, "and you're already having fine ideas. Norman, you meet me and President Wilson at 10:30 on the South Lawn of the White House. Tomorrow, we are going to begin to plant the nation's *Victory* Garden!"

✦

Special to the Beatrice, Nebraska Daily Sun

FAVORITE SON ROCKWELL RETURNS FROM THE NATION'S CAPITAL

Will Get Keys to City

December 11, 1918 - Beatrice resident Norman Rockwell will return to town on Saturday, December 14, to be greeted by a delegation from City Hall after a 15-month stint in Washington D.C. as what President T. Woodrow Wilson called, "the nation's gardener." Rockwell, a graduate of Beatrice High School, left Beatrice nearly 16 months ago to assist timber man Charles Lathrop Pack in the work of the U.S. National War Garden Commission. While under the aegis of that Commission, Rockwell is credited with having coined the term, "Victory Garden." He also employed his extensive knowledge of food combined with his expert knowledge of gardening to publish the 4-H Victory Garden Cookbook.

Rockwell, 18 years old, son of Samuel and the late Ruth Rockwell of Beatrice, will be greeted at the Beatrice train depot by the Hon. Burt "Slim" Ferkin and William Sow, members of the Beatrice City Council, City Council President Grant "Whoopty" Dowty, and Mayor Teddy G. Greene, who will award a golden key to the city to Rockwell in recognition of his service to the nation, "and his fine representing of Beatrice to our nation's capital," said Mayor Greene.

Rockwell's wartime efforts, it is estimated, yielded 3 million new garden plots planted in 1917 and more than 5.2 million cultivated so far in 1918. These gardens are estimated to have generated 1.45 million quarts of canned fruits and vegetables. Rockwell worked through the National War Garden Commission to encourage Americans to plant, fertilize, harvest, and store fruits and vegetables so that incremental food could be exported to U.S. allies during the war. Citizens were urged to garden on all arable land that was not already engaged in agricultural production, including school and company grounds, civic parks, house yards, or vacant lots. Rockwell authored several citizen instruction pamphlets on how, when, and where to sow, a manual on the best crops to plant, along with tips on disease control and insect infestation prevention. His work was so well-received that the government turned its attention to canning and dehydrating to help preserve surplus crops. As a result, Rockwell authored the 4-H Victory Garden Cookbook, currently the largest-selling cookbook in the nation.

Rockwell will arrive at Beatrice Depot at 1:38 p.m. on Saturday. Well-wishers are instructed to arrive in advance of the train so as not to block the tracks and to wave the Stars and Stripes if they have them. — Reported by: Lemuel Hanson

✦

Norman stepped off the train and into the glare and blare of the Arthur Babich's Beatrice City Boy's Band playing *Pal O' My Heart*. Just over fifty citizens of Beatrice, many with flags in their hands, waved him on, cheering. The mayor had written in a letter that he would meet him at the depot. Norman expected the Mayor alone. This was a crowd!

Just to Norman's right as he departed the train, a platform had been erected. The Mayor stood on it, along with three other men who looked official but who Norman did not recognize. A podium stood in the center of the platform, on which sat a gold box tied with blue ribbon. Next to that stood a walnut chair that Norman recognized as having been borrowed from the reading room in the Beatrice Public Library. The chair had a foolscap sign masking-taped to the back which said, "Reserved for Mr. Samuel Rockwell." Norman could read the sign because the chair was empty.

"Welcome to you, Norman...," said the Mayor. There was a round of applause and a cheer of hip-hip-hooray. Norman thanked the crowd and bowed low to shake the mayor's hand.

Norman looked around for his late-arriving father. He recalled that Sam had written that, since Norman's mother had died, from time to time he had trouble getting himself dressed and out of the house on time when he needed to. Norman hoped this was not one of those times.

"...Welcome also to the members of our City Council and Council President Dowty. Today, I have the honor to confer upon you, Norman Rockwell, the key to our city of Beatrice. This honor is a rare one. It is reserved for..."

✦

Norman arrived at the front door of his home.

He realized the error he had made nearly eighteen months ago when he declined to take the house key his mother proffered as they left for the train. He thought there was no need. He would be back soon—returning unchanged to a home that was unchanged. He hoped for his home to be the same when he got there as when he left. Instead, his mother developed heart failure and her lungs collapsed, drowning her in her bed and taking her from him. So, instead of the quiet murmur of her voice, which he had hoped to hear, there was silence as he stood on the porch.

With no key, he was obliged to knock. The sound in response on the other side of the door was "Shit!" followed by a repetitive hollow tap of wood against wood coming toward the door. Then the sound of the door being unlatched.

His father opened the door slowly. Sam squinted at Norman. A few months into Norman's stay at Dupont Circle, he got a letter from his mother telling him that his father had a stroke. That did not prepare him for the reality of what his father looked like: he had clearly gone several days without shaving and was wearing food-stained pajamas. His face slumped unresponsive on the left side. His left arm hung lifeless and left leg dragged behind him as he banged his wooden cane on the floor to angle into the doorway.

"So," said Sam, suffusing that single syllable with all the cantankerousness he could. "You came back."

"Of course I did," said Norman, standing tentatively on the uneven wooden porch with his trunk in one hand and his hat in the other. "This is my home."

"It isn't your home anymore," Sam turned his back to Norman and gestured to the empty hallway and the parlor beyond. "It was." He turned back. "Now you're all fancy-Georgetown-meet-the-mayor proper. You have no place in Nebraska. You have no place *here*."

NORMAN: Sure I do, Dad. I worked in Columbia, made friends, met the President. Yet all that time what I thought of and pined for was to come home to Mom. And you.

Norman's eyes filled with tears.

SAM: That's stupid. You shoulda stayed there. You had a chance of becoming something there.

A pause. Norman put down his trunk and placed his hat on his head.

NORMAN: Well, Mr. Pack and Mr. Wilson would say—they'd say I *did* become something.
SAM: Nahhhh. Fancy men don't know.
NORMAN: They really would say that.
SAM: Your father knows you better than anyone. You did some gardening. That's all.
NORMAN: I did more than gardening. I led a gardening movement. Millions of gardens. The president said—.
SAM: Bahhhh. Women's work.
NORMAN: President Wilson said those gardens were central to—.
SAM: —central to nothing!
NORMAN: No—.
SAM: You had a chance of becoming something.

Norman looked at this bitter, grizzled, dirty, half-of-a-man and saw him like a pathetic stranger.

Hopelessness clicked into place inside Norman like a tumbler in a lock.

Norman turned away and crossed the porch to the steps. In a glance, he noticed a hash of sun-bleached seed packets and dusty wooden stakes, the rubble of his childhood garden, tossed in a windblown pile. He thought of his mother bending next to him as they seeded the rows. Norman reached into the deep pocket of his overcoat. He felt the gold box containing the Key to The City of Beatrice and ran his fingers over the ribbed blue grosgrain ribbon. He pushed hopelessness away.

"Well, Dad, I think I became something fine."

Norman looked at his father for the last time. He picked up his trunk, turned, and walked down the dusty porch steps into the dappled, late-afternoon sun.

He reached into the inside pocket of his overcoat where he carried a spoon from Doolittle's he had found when he unpacked his trunk in Washington. With a flash of silver, he pitched it into the pile of seed packets.

"Now," he called over his shoulder to his father, still standing in doorway, "I am off to join the circus!"

ENTR'ACTE

The Barker

Brendan Hardy

NOW

*L*ike I said, everyone has stories. In The Home, I just needed patience to hear them. After I put my coffee-room poster up and yakked with a couple of people, word got out that talking to me wasn't half-bad. Soon I got more people coming to me and telling their stories. It wasn't very long until I had a whole big pile of—as we say in the biz—material.

It's funny. No...not funny. Odd. It's odd what people chose to share about themselves over coffee. What people say first about themselves tells you a bunch about them. It's almost like what we say first is our marquee—One show only! So-And-So in "Life Story." Don't get me wrong, when people told me about their lives, they told me interesting stuff, but I had to work for it. At the beginning, people told their best story—this incredible incident or that amazing coincidence and a whole bunch of stuff that doesn't matter. Bullshit. The Barker version: only what gets 'em into the tent. I guess you could call it the actual story, plus some added molasses to make the story go down easy, smooth, without getting stuck in your craw. The story you tell strictly for PR purposes. I'd always ask for more, and they'd tell me more and the more was *more interesting than the molasses-y version that makes it sound like life sails on smoothly and everything happens like you plan. Some happied-up, bullshitted version of the truth. Where things seem solid and tight. Planned and positive. Wrapped up neatly with a pink satin bow.*

Life just isn't that way. Not real life, anyway. We all go along just fine heading due north until we want to make a sharp left while Life offers no other option but a gradual right. We consider the offer, realize there is no reasonable alternative, and go the way Life requires. We say we made, "the practical decision." I am not sure we decide at all. The progress of our growth, our career, our family life, or whatever, is a negotiation between us, with our ambitious plans and big ideas, and Life, which has the power to stymie our plans and crush our big ideas. Or, indeed, light a fire under them. There is no winning at life unless the universe buys into our plan. If the universe doesn't want us to have something, it will do what it needs to—the uphill downhill of lymphoma, or an over-the-speed-limit wipeout on a wet turn for a quick adios, or the long, slow seeping away of Oldtimer's disease—to keep us from realizing our hopes.

Like they say, Life eats plans for breakfast.

It's funny. No...not funny. Interesting. Sometimes, the person I talked to turned out to be a Third Shepherd—a bit player—in the nativity pageant of their own life. People we cross paths with sometimes have greater impact on our life than people we are related to, or even us, ourselves. And as much as we want the spotlight on us, decisions made around us—not by us— change the direction our lives head in. Sometimes we notice and other times we don't. We always think we are running things. But look how a puppy in a box changed things for Iris in Suite 406. Look at how a cereal contest entry to see Harry Houdini entirely changed life for Wally Whalen in room 222. The guy started out telling me about magic lessons and mentioned nothing about Houdini.

I asked what other stories he had four times. On the fourth ask, damned if he didn't tell me how he really got into show business.

If you listen close when people talk about their lives, you hear secrets. And lies. Everyone I talked to in The Home had at least one. Some had five. Or twenty-five. We want to stop the future from having its way with us. The universe doesn't just fuck with our idea of our life. It laughs at it right in the face. We are weaklings endowed with a few rudimentary tools to use to eke out the life we want. But there is a strong opposing force working against us: fate. Sometimes all we have that we can leverage against fate is a secret. Or a lie. We try to bend the universe to our will. We fabricate. We leave out details or change them. We tell one person one thing and another something else. All in the hope that our made-up, manipulated version of things will be believed and vanquish fate. That rarely works. In the gamble of life, the odds favor the house. It is a stacked deck between us—who thinks we have power—on one side, and fate—which actually has the power—on the other. We only win if the grand Ringmaster In The Sky turns aside for a moment or stops paying attention altogether.

We all lie. Is it wrong? Or is it a necessary way to even the odds?

If we depend on the blindness created in others by a secret or a lie in order make our life better, is that wrong?

Who cares if we aren't exactly who we say? Or haven't done what we say we did? Or never got that high school diploma like everyone thinks? If we take an alternate route in life and going that way is predicated on a lie, or leaving something out, or adding a not-so-factual fact—why not?

That's why they call it show business. Right?

ACT EIGHT

The Siamese Twins

Jackson and Martin Armstrong

THEN

E mpty, as it often was, the alley dripped mist from its wooden walls and eves, leaving its steep cobbles slick and shiny. The wind roiled a tide of fog against a battered wooden door. The door's bottom edge was cut at an angle to match the steepness of the hill. Almost invisible in darkness, this door had—at eye-level and centered—a small round peeping window. This window let weak golden light out through half of its grimy lens, causing the peephole to look, from outside, like a half moon and the door to look like the door to a privy. To make it through, the dim light was required to penetrate a dense rind of soot, cooking grease, and dried spittle to reach the outdoors. If you were unfortunate enough to be standing outdoors in the cold, dripping alleyway looking back into this peephole, you would see—about every four minutes—a shadow cast itself over the opening. This shadow would quickly be supervened by a threadbare tweed elbow—blackened by elbow-leaning of all sorts and on many unsavory surfaces—like a hungry tongue licking the rime on the inside of the half-moon hole. The elbow wiping would promptly be followed by the appearance of an eye, murky-black and bloodshot, looking out, up the alley, then down, finally drawing back as its owner limped away on a left-foot bunion with a quick, "Not yet!" spat loudly and emphatically at no one.

The bar was always empty at this hour. Yet, also always, Amos Daughtry limped back and forth from behind the long oak bar to the tiny window in the door to look for incoming patrons. In half an hour, by half-past ten o'clock, the constable would make his last round about the docks knocking up vagrants. Those same vagrants, roused from their doorways and benches, would hobble up the Pacific Street hill into Randolph Alley (often called Randy Alley for reasons you can imagine, yet will soon be made explicit) and to this, the battered wooden door of the Final Spike: alehouse, whorehouse, and opium den.

At capacity, which took twelve people at the bar and seven more divided between the stiff-backed table seating in the two remaining corners, the Final Spike reeked. First, there was the yeasty aroma of ale brewing in the cabinets behind the bar. This mixed with the dog-piss aroma of yesterday's ale still lying in spills around Amos Daughtry's jackbooted feet. The third aroma in the Ale Layer of the Aroma of the Spike was hops—resiny and medicinal. Hops deepened the aroma as it met smoke at hip-height. The Smoke Layer of the Aroma of the Spike whistled high with the sweet smell of opium being smoked behind the arras under the stairs. The low note of the smoke layer was provided by tobacco—sweet-spicy pipes and sour-earthy cigars—that filled and clouded the air above the waist when the bar was occupied and hung like a stale ghost over the entire room when it was empty. Maple-scented whisky—at bar height—had a layer of its own. As did shit. Shit was everywhere in turn-of-the-century San Francisco—contributed by chickens, pigs, cats, dogs, and horses all sharing Pacific Street as their wanton toilet. What lay on the street ended up on boots and boots ended up on the sawdust-covered floor of the Spike. The Shit Aroma Layer was a concoction of the stuff itself combined with the pumpkin-earwax smell of sawn Redwood dust that covered the floor. The People Layer of the Aroma of the Spike bloomed when it was crowded as nineteen to twenty-five (most often) men breathed, farted, sweated, spit, drank, and spilled on the floor of the place. Their stink hung in their clothing, mixing the cheesy-egg of uncombed hair with the ripe-dark souvenir of last night's quiff—woven like hair in a locket of underwear they changed once a week. If then.

The people who came to the Final Spike would tell you they came for the ale or whisky, maybe a few for the fire (which Amos kept stoked in the functional cast-iron firebox year-round). They did not come to the Spike for the company. Yet, several customers had established themselves as regulars over the years and arrived daily, taking refuge from the foggy alley by 11 p.m. to assume their established places on five stools at the bar. These regular customers were: one-eyed/one-eared Dick McCallum, veteran of the Spanish war; Monty of Varrick Street, a knife fighter relocated from New York to bring his brand of violence to the western docks; Smitty "Slender Fingers" McKey who taught the art of pickpocketing to Chinese immigrants who couldn't (or chose not to) make an honest living; and Denis (pronounced in the French way "Den-ee") LaFleur who delicately worked the bar (in a stained, chartreuse, floor-length satin robe) offering men oral pleasure under the stairs (when it was not occupied by opium smokers). The fifth stool was taken by a regular visitor who was not a customer. She was Amos's boss, Señora Carmen, who owned the building which was occupied on the first floor by the Final Spike. On the second floor she ran her own business employing six girls and two male transvestites, each one marketed as a medically-certified virgin and available by the hour or the act, whichever might suit the patron.

So, on any day, by 11 p.m., you will find Señora Carmen, Dick McCallum, Monty of Varrick, Denis LaFleur, and Slender Fingers McKey on their habitual stools in the Spike with Amos pacing and compulsively elbow-wiping the tiny peephole to check for new arrivals. As the vagrants dislodge from their benches or doorways, climb the hill, and join the crew by 11:30 p.m., The Final Spike hits its peak of occupancy and its valley of conviviality. It is a mean place, a dirty place, a smelly place, and a smoky place. Yet...as a place to drum up, beat down, or put a bloody knife edge into any one of a number of outlawed activities...the Final Spike cannot be beat.

✦

Kanten Armstrong was a shard of a man. Sharp and angled. On foot, in his grey canvas hunting coat, he was all planes and corners. On horseback, in his rabbit-lined Cavalry jacket, he was all angles and elbows. Seldom on horseback now. There was a time when he was (literally) leashed to a horse all day and all night. That was when he was Stable Master for P.T. Barnum and trained, fed, shod, and cleaned the horses and other animals for Barnum's Grand Traveling Museum, Menagerie, Caravan & Hippodrome. It was no small feat to do the job with nearly 100 animals to husband. It was an even greater act of legerdemain (and a tribute to Armstrong's Scottish gift for gab) to get the job in the first place. In this job seeking effort, Armstrong (who grew up on a corn farm in Missouri) passed himself off as a Wyoming cattle rancher's son. He measured five-foot-and-eight-inches in his stocking'd feet and five-ten in boots. For his job interview, he used particular mathematics (plus a hat) to become fully six-feet tall. He also advertised that he was a boxer ("1893 Tri-State Bare-Knuckle Champ with twelve knockouts and two kills") and a marksman ("1894 Wagoner Helmsley Shot of the Year Medal - six shots and six bullseyes plus the target set afire by sparks from the original and each subsequent bullet shattering!"). In reality, he had never hit another man and he had only fired a gun once. In the air. And that was a blank casing fired to start a controlled stampede during an audience preview of Act Two of Barnum's Great Roman Hippodrome. The bulls quickly got out of control, trampled three scenery flats, and spilled a couple of hundred-gallon barrels of water meant to constrain their movements. The stampede was responsibly cut from the show after the incident and was completely forgotten, although Kanten Armstrong's sole gunshot, which lives eternally on his curriculum vitae, begat hundreds of imagined gunshots and bolstered the reputation of Armstrong as a tough man to beat.

That was in his youth, comparatively. He left Barnum when he was twenty-seven to open Armstrong Acts, a booking company specializing in finding and presenting, "the unique, unimagined, exotic, and iconoclastic in circus and carnival acts." Although unknown itself (except to show-business insiders), Armstrong Acts represented some of the most notorious, curious, beloved, and feared sideshow entertainments of the time.

Armstrong started with what he could scratch up from the hard clay of the carnival soil:

Bridie, the Devil's Six Footed Hog: Bridie, a Tamworth pig, was born with two extra legs—both on her left side. These legs dangled rather than functioned as support, yet they were clearly intended by God (or nature) to be legs. Featured prominently one Tuesday in the "County Curiosities" column of Delavan, Wisconsin *Plain Dealer* newspaper, Bridie caught the eye of Kanten Armstrong. Posing as a Tamworth Pig expert and breeder, Armstrong represented that he would use the sow for breeding and would pay the up-to-the-minute per pound price for a breeding sow. $37 was all she cost. The creation and donning of two "devilish" pointed wax ears plus some rouge brushed under her eyes, on her jowls, and on the dangling extra feet cost a few cents more. This investment was easily made back in ticket sales during the first two days she was on sideshow display as the Devil's Hog.

Pip-squeak, the Gambling Chicken: Traveling in Arkansas and stopping at a smalltown cattle auction, Armstrong got wind of an Orpington hen with a remarkable winning record at Blackjack. The chicken pecked twice to draw and once to stand pat. It could even turn cards with its beak. Sure that this talent would make hundreds at the box office, Armstrong paid $28 for the hen, and had a chicken-sized brocade vest and tiny rhinestone tiara crafted for an additional $12. Pip-squeak lasted five years and three months as an attraction with four carnivals at a flat fee of $26 per week and five-percent of the gate. She averaged $80-$110 per week in earnings. Plus, she was a steady layer, keeping Kanten Armstrong in eggs as well as talent fees.

After about three years of building a reputation as a booker of solid acts, Armstrong Acts made a step up in sophistication of its acts:

Jeffralia, African Leopard Woman: Hilda Jefferson was a freed slave who suffered from Vitiligo, a disease that caused her skin to lose color in blotches. Armstrong met her on a railroad platform in New Orleans, where she slept in poverty. Seeing an opportunity to both profit from her condition and alleviate her suffering, Armstrong offered Jefferson $18 per week plus room and board to be displayed as the African Leopard Woman. For eight years, she traveled with sideshows until edema limited her mobility. At that time, she asked Armstrong Acts to represent her to Dr. Fabulous's Carnival of Curiosities, a non-touring show based in Cincinnati. Armstrong negotiated a weekly fee of $37, of which Jeffries took $20. She died in Cincinnati with every dollar she had ever made (save $13.43 spent on a tuffet onto which she hoisted her ankles to defeat the swelling from the edema) stowed in a carpet bag under her bed.

Dr. Raven Bull, the World's Tiniest Doctor: Kanten Armstrong met Bob Schmidt, born dwarfed and fully grown at 27-inches tall, when Bob was age twenty-six. At age twenty-five, he had graduated from the University of Rochester Medical School. Due to chronic digestive issues that resulted from shorter intestines than usual, Schmidt was only able to work hospital hours for his first week when it became clear that he could not be more than a few yards from a bathroom. Rather than start and maintain a medical practice, he took up residence at the bar of Mount Hope Tavern and drank himself into a stupor each day. Armstrong "rescued" Schmidt, taught him "the art of sideshow presentation," changed his name to

Raven Bull and put him up against Tom Thumb as an attraction: "The Same Size as Tom Thumb Yet Educated as a Physician!"

In his latest bookings, Armstrong sought the truly exotic:

Real Ethiopian Monster Hippos, Pygmy Hippopotamuses: Armstrong found himself in London in 1883 with pockets full from a profitable night playing Ruff (two grand slams in one night!). Across the table was an ex-Barnum gent, who was, at the moment, high in African livestock but low in luck and gambling cash. To pay his debt, this ex-Barnum man proffered four pygmy hippos he owned in Addis Abeba. Armstrong, knowing he could sell or show them, agreed to take them in lieu of his winnings. He arranged transport aboard a merchant ship (a month from Ethiopia to England and another month from London to Boston) in two custom-made tanks. The ship had to be loaded with 1200 pounds of hay per passage (a pygmy hippo eats about forty pounds of grass each day). Three of the animals survived the trip to London where Armstrong sold one to the London Zoo (sadly, winter weather killed it the following January). Both remaining cows made it to Boston, barely survived the over-road transport to Miami where, for $12,000, they joined *Captain Neverland's Acroamatic Zoo and Gardens*.

Established as a purveyor of high-quality exotic attractions, Armstrong Acts was a beast that needed constant feeding. Kanten Armstrong was routinely required to seek and sign new, more interesting acts. He soon adjudged that he needed to go to the Orient to obtain the next level of quality, and he set out from Santa Fe (where he had been obligated to see Manfred, the World's Largest Heifer—"disappointing.") for San Francisco, the first of six legs of travel taking him, ultimately, to Bangkok.

✦

From Brooklyn to Manhattan was now an easy passage! The New York and Brooklyn Bridge had opened four years ago, yet Rose had not been across it until today. The Broad Way wound through New

York, bold and barging, then it abruptly narrowed its threaded way out of the city north of 14th Street. Cobbles gradually gave way to paving stones, paving stones to gravel, gravel to mud and finally mud to grass. Only four hours from home in Brooklyn, yet here she was, bouncing along in a hay wagon through waving slivers of frog-green sawgrass entwined with pale-purple hollyhock.

She noticed the sky during the trip through the Allegheny Valley as if it was new—as if she had opened her eyes for the first time. The sky over Brooklyn was dull with coal smoke, smudged familiar gray—a pale, neutral backdrop to a pale, neutral, and repetitive life. Yet here, lying on her back in the wagon, the sky was open—blue as a duck egg—deep, ovular, and welcoming. In Brooklyn, life was lived at middle distance, always having to watch where you were going. Here, life seemed to stretch in front of you, yet also above your head and below your feet. Everywhere! Rose noticed the clouds were wispy and quick-changing in the morning, they mounded like cotton bolls in the afternoon, and they simmered, lightning-filled and bullying, just before she climbed down from the wagon to help water the horses. Usually, she noted, it started raining plump, cold drops just as, with a crack of thunder, she and her fellow travelers took shelter from the green-black sky. *How lovely*, Rose thought for the first time, *RAIN!* Day by day, as harsh Brooklyn slipped farther away, she noticed the moon had its own light, the earth churned with worms, trees rioted with birds, fields hummed with bees. Smells, aside from rotting Brooklyn garbage, presented themselves for the first time. Rose became intimately educated in the sweet, rich perfume of honeysuckle, the crisp sweetness of wild lavender, the cheesy, buffeting musk of Black-Eyed Susans. In four days, Brooklyn seemed a distant tintype—frozen in the past—and this new world of smells, storms, earthworms, and bees, seemed so much more present, rich, full.

Rose felt herself shedding her old life as Pittsburgh loomed on the horizon.

The con. Rose Kleyn had been skimming cash from the register for two weeks before Mr. Pawshorten (Pawshorten Dry Goods and Mercantile) became suspicious. She entered the cash-in amount as whatever was the sale amount minus ten dollars. If a purchase was $17.00 she entered $7 and pocketed $10. If it was $43 she took $10 and rang up $33. If it was $6 she took nothing. In two weeks she had not caught the eye of Mr. Pawshorten and amassed just under $380. More than enough to make her trip. She conspired to calmly resign at the close of business Friday before Pawshorten reckoned the bi-weekly receipts.

The plan. Her plan was to meet Frances Mulhetter, pay him a $20 fee, and climb into his wagon for the bumpy ride from Brooklyn, N.Y. to Pittsburgh, Pennsylvania. In Pittsburgh, Rose would pay Mulhetter a further $200 to make the four-month wagon train passage to San Francisco. The objective was to leave before April 10th to arrive in late August, traveling all the time with what Mr. Mulhetter called "the fortunate weather." By this, he meant they would arrive before it snowed. He noted that summer rainstorms were impossible to avoid and imagining they would do so was beyond pollyanna—it was completely unlikely.

The lie. Her con and plan were derailed early when Rose heard through a co-worker that Mr. Pawshorten suspected that someone was skimming the till. Although she desperately wanted a third week of proceeds from her gambit and needed the extra week's take to fully finance her trip, Rose put an unwelcome end to the skim. Instead, she concocted the story of a cousin, Filena, with a club foot, who lived in Pittsburgh and had been hit by a runaway pushcart while limping her way up the Canton Avenue hill. In Rose's fabrication of the accident, Filena broke her pelvis, "in seven places and could not depart her bed!" Cousin Filena was in desperate need of care and money and Rose, being her sole kin, was, "all she had as a resource!" Rose explained that, as a result, she needed to borrow $100 from Pawshorten and take two weeks away from work to provide Filena respite from the Catholic nursing care which had been procured for her by the pushcart owner. Mr. Pawshorten, woven of trusting strands of Dutch frankness and Irish kinship, swallowed this story all the way to the pole. Rose walked away with two weeks off (with pay) plus a loan of $100 against her April wages. Of course, she would be approaching the Mississippi River in a wagon and would be too far to pay him back (had that ever remotely been her intention) by the time he realized she was gone.

The fact. Since she often ran into Mr. Pawshorten as he came and went from the cigar store, steam room, or liquor store in the streets around the building where she lived, Rose knew it would not do to stay at home while she was purportedly in Pittsburgh. She decided to leave for Pittsburgh on March 28th, one westward trip earlier for Frances Muhetter. She planned to make the trip, then stay with her actual cousin, Gertrude Schwetterling, who ran a washing and blueing service out of the basement of her home on Coal Hill. She bolstered her conscience by telling herself she would be doing almost exactly what she had told Mr. Pawshorten she would be doing— minus the cousin, the accident, the injury, and the need.

When it came down to a conclusion, she didn't care. It was *her* needs she was worried about at the moment. She needed to feel fulfilled.

Rose had briefly lived the high-life—kept for two years by a New Jersey magnifico who never hesitated to buy her what she coveted and to show her off in the best restaurants. He did, on the other hand, hesitate to mention he was married and had three children. When that had crashed and burned around her like the Chicago fire (that fire happened ten years earlier to the day) she took a solid job of work in Pawshorten Dry Goods and Mercantile. For any other woman, it wouldn't have been easy to go from silk gowns and silver furs to a gray gabardine uniform jacket over a linen shirt and twill skirt and make that transition without a word of regret. Yet Rose was not any other woman. She did what was needed to protect her reputation and a modicum of status in a city where those precious assets still mattered. She lived the Brooklyn working-girl life, scraping to get by in the helter-skelter of the world's most populous city. She worked hard under the searing gaze of Mr. Pawshorten and flourished, lasting months longer than her tenderfoot coworkers. Those girls smiled demurely at Pawshorten and giggled a bit when he barked his instructions to add merchandise to bulk up their orders. Rose showed him her steel by driving hard bargains and bulking up orders before presenting them to the boss. Over time, she matriculated from clerk to senior clerk to head cashier. And during this rise, Rose realized what truly motivated her: she wanted *her* name on the store. *She* wanted to count and deposit the bi-weekly receipts. *She* wanted to hire the wide-eyed rookies (like she had been when she first arrived) and to stingily fire them a few months later for being inadequately shrewd in business. *She* wanted to be the boss. She thought:

> *I am close to the bottom of the beehive in Brooklyn— an honest woman doing an honest job.* (In actuality, a dishonest woman using an honest job as a pretense, although she was right about the beehive). *I need to go where an upright woman* (if not an honest one) *could end up near the top of the beehive! A place where a woman was needed, admired for her grit, and respected for her abilities.*

That place, she knew beyond any doubt, was Fairbanks, Alaska!

✦

If hell froze over it would be because Hagpenny Thistlewaite finally gave a gratuity.

Proof? Thistlewaite boarded the steamer LA PAZ in New York; a month later, he off-loaded his double trunk in Montevideo to survey a two-headed mountain goat; he reloaded his luggage there, then he off-loaded it in Callao, Peru, to size up a herd of vicuna; he reloaded his bags there, then off-loaded them yet again in Acapulco, where there was a particularly-competitive horse auction; he reloaded after procuring a dozen pure white stallions (to be shipped % Barnum to Indiana). He sailed past La Bufadora to the port city of Ensenada and then off-loaded his trunks there long enough to drive a few miles out of town to procure a family of five dusty brown desert tortoises. Yet, through all of that loading and off-loading, all of that carrying and hoisting, up all of those gangways and down, Hagpenny Thistlewaite did not peel a single dollar or peso off the fat cash roll in his pocket. He consistently ignored the eager, outstretched palms of the porters. Thistelwaite did, however, expect every porter to provide white glove service for his valises in every port.

Word of the existence of a fat, red-faced, reprobate spread through the crew quarters, where he quickly became known sarcastically as *El Valedor*, the Big Man. The name fit. He was rotund of body, tight and pinched of spirit. He was dismissive of anyone he perceived to be stationed below him in class—which was, in his view, practically everyone. Within a few days of boarding the LA PAZ, Thistelwaite drove away from him almost every soul aboard the ship, save the captain (in whose cabin he played Whist) and the Maitre d'hotel (whom he lubricated with the gift of five dozen fat tourist-trade cigars—which Thistelwaite pronounced, "see-gars"). Becoming so derided in such a brief time was an impressive feat of alienation given how, on a packet ship, passengers are typically desperate for companionship. Thistlewaite became known among some passengers as "that greasy S.O.B." A number of others referred to him as "Thistle-weight." Others called him "El Señor Cabbage" because he had an appetite for brassicas as a side-dish to his pork loin that bordered on a mania. Among the small group of passengers aboard the LA PAZ, he was seen as miserly, greasy, overbearing, and farty. Suffice to say not a single one of his fellow travelers was even slightly disappointed when, after several months, he debarked in San Francisco.

Upon arriving in the Golden City, Thistlewaite checked into the Bright Morning guest house in Chinatown. It was a place habituated by Chinese merchants and officers. He hoped a few days in the atmosphere of the place would help him acclimatize for his upcoming sail to Bangkok (with stops in Hong Kong, Canton, and Singapore). The Bright Morning was crisp and clean. It was flanked on the right by Peking Duck House and on the left by Moon Luck Laundry; their aromas met in the middle and blended so that the Bright Morning was steeped in what amounted to the fragrance of barbecued bed sheets.

An hour after arriving in his hotel room, Thistlewaite sat by his open window facing Joice Street and puffed on his best Cuban cigar, which he had earmarked for the occasion. The sliding, argumentative sound of Chinese wafted up from the street and, hearing it, he felt a bit at home. He had spent a good deal of time in the far east scouting for Barnum. What sounded like contention when he first heard the Cantonese language turned out (according to his translator) to be precision and exactness. He was proud to have concluded many (in his opinion) solid deals (to him, "solid" meant "to his advantage," of course) across a red-clothed table with a Chinese seller (to him, "Chinese" meant "easily duped," of course). One only need recall his negotiations over the Ching Wing Stallion, or the Maximum Goose, or the Ti'An Snow Tiger, or the Haw Wah Brothers, to cite four masterful examples. He had got close but could not close the deal with the Handsome Mufti and the bearded lady, Sunny Tang. And, of course, he was still in earnest pursuit of a pair of genuine Siamese twins. Still, he felt, to some extent, more at home among Asians than with his own people. He sat, puffing green-gray cigar smoke, thinking over his deals, listening to Chinatown life swirl and eddy around him until his shadow moved from the floor to the wall and the light changed from clear blue to pink-orange to gray-black as the fog came in off the ocean. Then, he watched the day, floating on still water, dock in the shadowy harbor of evening. The gas lamps were lit outside, the streets emptied, and it turned dinner time.

Thistlewaite bathed and dressed. Renewed and ready for the street, he made his way down the Bright Morning's narrow main staircase to the Hall Porter's service desk in the lobby.

"Good evening, Mist' This'waite," said the porter. "How may I assist?"

"Good evening, Mr. Wing..." said Thistlewaite, although this man's family name was Kong. To Hagpenny Thistlewaite, every Chinese had the name Wing. He neither desired nor cared to get their name right, nor to distinguish any Chinese from every Chinese.

"Keep it simple, I say!" he'd say.

For his part and in his mind, Mr. Kong immediately relegated Thistlewaite to the classification, "Ghost Eyes" and, filled with indignant hate for the man, he made a silent vow to obstruct his every step.

Thistlewaite continued: "Mr. Wing...it is supper time for me and I need your recommendation for a comely and flavory place to eat."

"Flavory, sir? What sort of flavors you desire?"

"Chinese!"

"There are many of those nearby, sir. And among them, there are many flavors. Could you please specify?"

"Chinese, you fool! Chinese! I have said what I want thrice!"

"Yes, sir. As you wish, sir," Here, Mr. Kong, having had about enough of this worst sort of tourist, made broad show of consulting a list in front of him, entirely in Chinese. "Let me see, sir..." running his finger from the top of the list to the bottom.

"I have wasted enough time with you, Wing. Understand? Takeee toooooo mucheee time," barked Thistlewaite, turning red.

"Ahhh, yes. This place will suit you well," said Kong pantomiming selecting a name from the list (which was actually a list of nearby imported furniture purveyors) but, in fact, naming a place he knew very well. "I'd recommend Hin Hi Noodles on Stockton Street, just around the corner to the right out the door. Just say I sent you and you will get rare service!"

"Sounds like just the place!" said Thistlewaite, turning to go. No goodbye, no nod, no thanks to Mr. Kong.

Hin Hi Noodles will suit you fine! thought Mr, Kong. *You round-eyed bastard!*

Hin Hi Noodles was widely known to the Chinese community as, without competition, the worst restaurant in Chinatown. Not Chinatown—all of San Francisco. Not even all of San Francisco—all of California. Wider than all of California? Quite possibly! Chef Hin had elevated cooking badly, using the cheapest ingredients, and gouging caucasian tourists to the level of cultural art. For example, where a traditional recipe might call for Chinese mustard greens, Hin used Miner's Lettuce harvested from cracks in the Filbert Street wall. In place of Sea Cucumber, he used banana slugs plucked from under rotting redwood boards in Santa Cruz. It was widely reputed that he marinated corrugated boxboard in lamb fat, then sautéed it with onions and served it as "Lamb in the Mongol Style." He added carpet lint to his noodle dough, "to give it body." And he mixed locally-collected dog sperm with sugar, water, and lime to place on offer as "Juice of the Mangosteen."

Thistlewaite walked the hundred yards from the Bright Morning to Hin Hi Noodles as if he owned the pavement, full of himself for having got a personalized recommendation for a fine restaurant. He stopped in the doorway to note the metallic gold-painted exterior trimmed in red. Weathered paper lanterns hung above the front door. This door had been lacquered black year-after-year until the Foo dogs on its surface could have easily been confused for Foo pigs. Above the door hung a sign that read "-hinese Cui-ine," the C and S missing. Two steps tiled with broken dinner plates led into the establishment. Thistlewaite hiked his sturdy thigh and hoisted himself to door level. Then he pushed the door open.

"The Great Thistlewaite has arrrrrived!" He announced into the dimly lit dining room with a sonorous Welsh rolling rrrrrr. "Sent by the Bright Morning Hall Porter!"

"Good evening, sir," said this establishment's Mr. Wing (although, in fact this was the restaurant's eponymous Mr. Hin, himself, serving as chef, waiter, and Maitre d'hotel all in one). With a sweep of his compact open hand: "This way, sir, to our very best table reserved for you, sir, especially by the hall porter at the Bright Morning guest home."

"Yes, Mr. Wing, you come highly recommended for your fine food!" said Thistlewaite, tucking a slightly stained (cursorily laundered) napkin into his shirt collar. "What do you recommend?"

After some negotiating over which meat to choose (although each—excepting lamb—was, in fact, horse) and which preparation to choose (although Mr. Hin did whatever he needed to do to make horsemeat taste like pork, regardless of the preparation the customer chose), Thistlewaite's order was placed:

Spicy and Sour Porridge with Ground Pork (horse)
and Wood Ear (actually roach wing)
Ti'an style Chicken (in fact, park-caught pigeon) Dumplings
Lamb (the aforementioned marinated boxboard)
in the Mongol Style (sautéed with actual onions)
Sea Scallops (sliced King mushroom stems) with Ginger
White and Black Rice (the white being rice and the black being
Rice Weevils, *Sitophilus Oryzae,* the weevils being removed only
as well as Mr. Hin could do without his spectacles)

The food arrived on spotted enameled metal plates and Thistlewaite dispatched each accompanied by several spoons full of rice (and weevils). After the fourth course, he stretched out his hammy legs, put his hands behind his head arched his back, took a deep breath, and farted.

"Ahhhhh. So tasty. Now...Mr. Wing, I'd like to cap this lovely meal off with a whisky!" said Thistlewaite. "Would you bring me some straight away?"

"Sorry, mister. No whiskey. We don't serve whiskey. Very sorry!"

"No trouble. Perhaps you might suggest a superlative refuge in the night where one could imbibe a glass?"

"Oh yes, mister. I know of a place perfect for you needs. The Final Spike—just up the hill on Pacific Street, then into Randolph Alley, Mister."

✦

Two hours later, Hagpenny Thistlewaite trudged up the steep Pacific Street hill powered by lungs that had been tanned to leather by cigar smoking. His breathing was labored and his arches stretched flat by the steep incline. He puffed and huffed and hacked like he hadn't since climbing to Machu Picchu three years prior in search of Señor Montoya's herd of alpacas, which he promptly bought on speculation and sent—all dusty fur, alert eyes, and chewing cheeks— to the Cincinnati Zoo, where they were the year's sensation. As he walked up the hill, he left the food and laundry smells of Chinatown behind and met the smell of the Pacific Street horse stables carried aloft by the swirling eddies of fog.

The gaslight and fog brought him back to his school days in London, where he had escaped from an ordinary working-class upbringing in Wales, due to the generosity of his father's brother Uncle Fryd. He stood an apprenticeship under A.B. Whitehead, who was four levels under Darwin at the Geological Society of London. He lasted until his career was (as he told it), "interrupted by an unfortunate accident with chloroform," or (as the newspapers told it), "ended for drugging and raping one underaged Clara Paige, age fourteen." By the time Clara un-obligingly registered her indignant perception of Thistlewaite's "accident" with London's City police, Thistlewaite had packed, boarded, and sailed a ship for New York, where he relaunched his career and himself as, "Procurer of the

Exotic." He procured first for the Zoo of the City of Brooklyn for nearly five years, doubling the number of beasts on display and placing the first white rhinoceros on show in North America. After Brooklyn, he began a self-financed business, first procuring animals for zoos and circuses and later procuring circus acts along with animals. After five years (Clara Paige now safely silenced by an early death from the clap), Thistlewaite became free to travel the world and use his freedom to become famous in the circus and carnival worlds for having placed more successful acts than any other procurer. Thistlewaite held himself up as a self-made rich man whose life began (honestly enough) in the slums of Swansea, was transformed in the highly-educated halls of the Geological Society, and whose riches came exclusively from hard work. No one knew that he owed his success partly to an underage girl, between whose already-varicose legs lay his crucible. He, himself, would never let the truth slip.

He was, after all, "the Great Thistlewaite!"

Great or not, he was about to enter The Final Spike, where who you are—no matter who you might actually be—matters less than if the bills you present to pay your bar tab are genuine. No one rises above anyone else at the Spike. Everyone might as well be a rapist from the slums of Swansea. On any given night, you might find more than one of those at the bar. In fact, on this particular night, there were three rapists in residence *before* Thistlewaite arrived; two of them claiming a higher level of crime, having accompanied their carnal threat with the point of a knife. One claiming a lesser crime, having forced the capitulation of only a Negress.

It was into this typical crowd of Spike miscreants that Hagpenny Thistlewaite announced himself:

"The Great Thistlewaite has arrrrrrived!"

SILENCE.

No one looked up from their drink, depressed stare, opium stupor, or general lethargic disinterest.

"Thistlewaite! I say..!" Waiting for an answer, he surveyed the bar looking for a bartender.

NOTHING.

Then, a loud, long, almond-scented exhale from the opium den. Thistlewaite's glance, pulled to the sound, fell upon a slight, tall man with bloodshot eyes, unsteadily balancing four glasses in this left hand and wiping a corner table with a rag in his right hand. He wore what could be presumed to be a bar-keep's apron (although torn and stained). This was, indeed, Amos Daughtry.

"Whiskey, my man!" Barked Thistlewaite thumping the bar with his downturned hand, as if to say, *and deliver it here!*

Of course, Amos Daughtry was as likely to deliver a harsh blow to the temple with a stick as to deliver a whiskey in response to a request as arrogant as that. "Go fuck yourself, fat man!" he replied.

Thistlewaite, stood still, stupefied by this response, mouth agape.

"There is a three-dollar charge for a table..." asserted Daughtry, making this up as he went. "... usually reserved for women...but I'll make an exception for a refined gent like you. Sit and you can order what you want...[then, under his breath]...*you stupid fuck.*"

"I shall take a corner table!" said Thistlewaite, sidling into his chair with a flourish of his hips. "Your three-dollar levee is no daunt to me! I will have a bottle of Three Coins Whiskey at my table, Sir!

"We serve Red Rooster Bourbon. That's the best you'll get here. Think of it as the equivalent of one of your three coins...One Coin Whiskey!" Daughtry laughed at his riposte, coughed, and slapped his knee. "Now...sit the fuck down, pay your three dollars—plus 70 cents for the Red Rooster— and I'll bring it."

Thistlewaite adjusted his pudgy ass in the bentwood chair and fastidiously dusted some crumbs off the table onto the floor. He took a cigar from his breast pocket and laid it on the table in front of him as if he was going to slice it with a knife and eat it like a sausage. He absently picked it back up, sniffing at it deeply. He sat, staring proudly at his cigar dangling between his fingers, waiting for his bottle and surveying his fellow occupants:

1. A one-eyed tough; seeming to be hard of hearing.
2. A pale man with thinning hair; a spring-loaded jackknife, ineffectively hidden, peeking from his pocket.

The two sat together at the table in the opposite corner, absently rolling dice.

3. A man who had the lean, dexterous, abalone hands of a magician or a jeweler in a gray suit jacket dealing himself Solitaire.
4. A poofter with a fever blister on his lower lip wearing a pink satin robe.

This feminized one periodically visited the curtained-off space under the stairs, where the smoke of opium puffed out like a following ghost as he quickly came and went.

5. A dark-skinned woman wearing a mantilla and threadbare silk bedroom slippers.
6. An Oriental man in a sharply tailored suit.

These two shared a bottle of gin that sat between them along with a couple of limes. She held a small knife, with which she pointed at numbers in a ledger book.

7. Two nondescript men at the far end of the bar, testily playing cards and smoking cigarettes in the corners of their mouths.

And, also at the bar, another man...whom, oddly, Thistlewaite thought he recognized.

✦

Rose Kleyn leaned awkwardly against a silvered wood-rail fence watching a hatted, booted Chinese teen bridle the horses. These horses, with their narrow hooves, looked so different from the draft horses she knew on the streets of Brooklyn. Frances Mulhetter stood by, also leaning, fretting with the buckle on his hat band while he explained, "these here horses were bred to pull a wagon, yes, but in our case that wagon needs to get from here to the Mississippi and then thread its way on the Mormon Trail to the far side of the Rockies and on to Frisco. These horses is hard workers, who goes for distance and over many terrains, but we will leave them in Nauvoo," he said, pointing with the front dip of his hat brim to the four still unbridled horses remaining in the paddock.

"Is that so?" said Rose, mildly surprised and hardly paying attention. She was absently trying to fill in each silence in Mulhetter's near constant commentary with pretend interest. *Does he assume me to be keen on horses?* she wondered. *Does he think I care which were bred for what?*

"I will pick these up next Spring on the way back. For the Rockies, they's replaced in bridle by single-footed Rocky Mountain horses. Them horses is called single-footed 'cause they amble. They got an ambling gait. That's something 'tween a walk and a canter—what you might call a gallop. Ambling gaits have four-beats—BA-BA-ba-ba—whereas these here regular wagon pullers got a two-beat gait, BA-ba, BA-ba, BA-ba. Them extra footfalls provide more smoothness to our wagon because the Rocky Mountain horse always has at least one foot on the ground."

"I see," said Rose, distracted by the sun glinting off the Chinese boy's belt and boots simultaneously. *How old might that boy be?* she wondered.

"Always having one foot on the ground," said Mulhetter, placing his hat back on absently. "Y'see that cuts down the movement of the horse's top line and takes away the bounce you get with a two-beat gait, caused by the quiet just before the jolt of them opposed two feet hitting the ground as the horse shifts from one pair o' legs to the other."

"Ahhh." Unsatisfactory.

"I see." Not quite.

"Fascinating!" That's it!

Rose cycled through responses until she found one she thought best fit the moment. At first her goal was to *appear* interested. Yet, when she heard her first response ("Ahhh") she felt she seemed too bored to be polite. She quickly replaced it with "I see." She felt that was not quite right; it sounded schooled but not genuinely interested. She wanted to sound interested. So "fascinating" fit and was apt.

"Ahhh. I see. Fascinating, Mr. Mulhetter." She was fascinated, although not by Mulhetter. She could not keep her eyes off the boy, his longish hair slate-colored under his brown felt hat.

"Well, if we's gonna spend a while of time together in that there wagon, there, you oughta know something 'bout the whole enterprise," said Mulhetter.

"I should!" She noted the considerable lines around Mulhetter's eyes that implied a life in the sun.

At that moment of increased attention to Mulhetter by Rose, the sound of gravel being crushed underfoot came from the road and broke the flow of the moment. Both Mulhetter and Rose turned to see where the sound came from.

A round-faced woman in a dowdy dress printed with tiny pink flowers walked up to the fence. She carried an overfilled travel pack and a tattered pebbled-leather valise. She squinted. She looked like she had been sired by a loaf of country bread or like a doll whose face was carved from an apple—her face all white flesh with sudden ruddy cheeks.

"Why, you must be Miss Smith," said Mulhetter, with an affable touch of his hat brim. Rose noticed he didn't take his hat off like he had done when he met her. "I am Frances Mulhetter...and this here is Miss Kleyn. Miss Kleyn is taking the long road with us all the way to San Francisco."

"Howdy do," all around.

"Miss Kleyn," Mulhetter continued, "Miss Smith'll be on board until Nauvoo, Illinois (he pronounced the final "s" making it sound like "Illy-Noise"). She'll be your company for nearly half of your trip. Miss Smith, you'll have Miss Kleyn 'til Nauvoo along with me. Oh... and Chin. Chin's that Chinese shaver bridling the horses. He's our cook, launderer, horse-wrangler, and," pointing to a passel of guns and knives piled on a square of oil cloth, "our protector. Sixteen years old but the best damn teamster I could find and hire. Oh... and...there's a Miss Clagsterhorn. She will be joining us in Nauvoo for the part of the Mormon Trail we'll be taking with the wagon train. Miss Clagsterhorn is going to Frisco, too. So...Miss Kleyn, between her and Miss Smith, you'll have lady-fied company your whole way."

Chin. Sixteen years old. Oh lord, thought Rose.

Mulhetter touched his hat-brim again. "Now that you've met, I better get working." And, with a slight nod of his head, he set out across the paddock toward Chin and the horses.

Rose looked this Miss Smith up and down to qualify her as company. "I am Rosamund Kleyn," she said, extending a hand gloved in gray kid. Miss Smith extended a dimpled hand limp as a doe's udder.

Her Christian name, thought Rose. *Will it be Clementine? Hermione? Phoebe? If not, I'll be damned. I am sure it will be something equally simpering.*

"I'm Michael. Michael Smith. It means 'from God.' That's why my parents chose it. People of faith."

Rose and her train of thought pulled up fast, "Oh...Michael is it? Yes. Michael," said Rose. "I am sure we will get along fine!"

And they did. Michael Smith turned out to be a teacher of French language, traveling to Salt Lake to take a teaching post at a Mormon school. Unlike the first impression made by her traveling clothes, she was both worldly and urbane. She had lived in Paris twice— once for secondary school to learn the French language and again at seventeen years old, to study French inheritance law. "An outgrowth of my fascination with genealogy," Michael said.

After that first day, she put aside dresses (and pink flowers). Once on the trail, she wore trousers—brown twill—with brown roping boots, pearl buttons on her work-shirt, and a wide brim Mexican caballero's hat. She turned out to be an adept horsewoman—skillful both astride and sidesaddle.

Michael was striking company. During the lengthening spring days on the trail, she easily out-talked, out-argued, out-concluded Rose on any subject. Rose had always seen herself as well-educated, yet she had no formal education past secondary school. Her father had insisted she go to school and (once she completed the first eight grades) secretly passed her books he thought she should read on history, economics, and spiritual exploration. Her reading had to be done in secret, though, due to her mother's disapproval. Still, finding herself more educated than most women she encountered, Rose routinely lauded her intelligence and book learning over others with gratification. Thanks to her father's unstinting attention, she rarely met or had to contend with a woman more educated or articulate than herself. Rose was the first to assert she was "no Seneca Falls type," yet, thanks to the insistence of her father, she could unhesitatingly assert herself as a smart, capable working woman.

Michael was also intimidating company. Her education, yes—but also her confidence and independence. Rose had never met a woman so comfortably inattentive to what society expected of her. While seeming to be equally conversant as Rose with what polite woman were expected to do, Michael chose mostly *not* to do it. No fuss. Just not the conventional road. Michael did not speak of her divergence, she simply did it. An example: the second morning in the wagon when she came to breakfast essentially dressed like a man. Simply did it and left those around her to throttle, swallow hard, and accept her as she was. This, as a way of acting publicly, had not once occurred to Rose as a possibility. As a result, Rose found Michael's company by turns strange, then daunting, then thrilling, then invigorating.

And, there would be weeks living in a wagon with this woman.

The wagon was light and strong, a hay wagon remodeled to serve as a traveling wagon. It was, in essence, a wooden box—ten feet long and five feet wide—on four-and-a-half-foot-high wooden wheels. The box walls went up two feet, where they met undyed canvas, which ran up and over the pinewood bed and hung from six hickory switches, bent in bows. There was some privacy from the outside world; flaps hung at the front and a "puckering string" in the back allowed for either ventilation or complete closing. Mulhetter had built a false floor 14 inches from the bottom of the bed; this created a space below to hold supplies, providing passengers with more floor space, but also less headroom. In the space between each bed, he had hung a panel of twill, making a "bedroom" (about five-feet square) for each of the women inside the wagon. Both women could stand upright along the center line if the wagon wasn't moving too fast. This was fortunate, since the "bedroom" was the only place where a tiny bit of privacy could be had to dress. Sleep would be, "rough" on a straw mattress. Days, between packing to move in the morning and unpacking to sleep in the evening, were long and empty. Baths were a weekly luxury (providing they had time to stop in a town between Pittsburg and Nauvoo where a barber or hotel with a tub could be engaged). Between baths, it was the job of eau de toilette to make the air inside the wagon bearable. Rose used toilet water that smelled of heliotrope, rose, and neroli. Michael wore Carmelite water, made with lemon balm, angelica, and orange blossom. It took just two days before Michael stopped wearing any scent at all and three days before she took Rose aside and told her:

"I think we can give up the formality of eau de toilette, my dear. Let's only start up again should we really, truly need to. In the meantime, we can travel with the flaps open." Although her bias was toward naturalness in all things, the truth was she could not stand the banging cymbal clap of neroli that greeted her each morning as Rose did her toilette.

"Oh, Lord," said Rose, looking away. "I don't know if I am prepared for the frankness of that. The realities of 'Life on the Trail' and all. Can we be so free?"

Michael looked her straight in the eye and gently touched the back of her hand. "This trip will be packed with opportunities to choose formal or free. I prefer free at any turn. Yet, you must feel right, my dear. You choose. I think life in this wagon will be immeasurably richer if we are less formal and more familial. Mais, c'est à toi. You choose."

Rose thought for a moment. *NO!* She was not prepared to drop years of social conditioning and carefully cultivated grooming. It was just not possible!

Instead...

It took two days.

Two mornings later, at seven o'clock, (not her usual nine-o'clock) Rose got up from her straw-filled mattress and declared abruptly to herself no need for her toilette. She chose a dress in a minute (unlike her typical fifteen to twenty-five minute decision process) threw on a petticoat, the dress and a pair of half-calf-high buttoned boots, and climbed down the back wheel of the wagon at 7:12 a.m. Chin, sitting on a crate with a glass of tea, could not believe his eyes. Michael (who by that hour had fed the team, helped Chin cook, eat, and clean up breakfast, boiled a second pot of coffee for the trip, and read a chapter of the popular French novel of the moment, *Noblesse Oblige*) sat bolt upright on her crate and stared as if she was St. Joan seeing the archangel. Then she noticed—no neroli!

Rose made no fuss from that day onward. She wore her dresses because they were all she had. The towns they passed through had dress ordinances, so a woman could not buy trousers, although Rose declared herself ready to wear them when they were passing through eastern Ohio. She wore her dresses, but with a new reckless abandon. She cut the side seams of several skirts to allow her greater movement. This was helpful since she began, along with Michael and Chin, to work the horses each morning. Chin, in rudimentary but serviceable English, taught her the correct mix of grains to feed the horses and how to measure and bag them. He taught her how to water the horses in the morning and groom and brush them in the evening. After a few days, Rose paid little attention to the condition of her dresses, stirring them like bedsheets in the laundry pot. As the trip went on they faded, trim fell off, buttons broke. The new Rose seemed not to notice.

Mulhetter didn't travel on Sundays, declaring a camp day on his sabbath. Rose and Michael slept late (because they could) while Chin tended the horses and his boss puttered around the wagon, looking for small projects of repair that would pass his time. At about eleven o'clock, Chin focused his attention on biscuits, rolling them out on a board balanced between his flour-covered knees. The biscuits were baked flaky and hot by noon when he put bacon on the fire and scrambled a dozen eggs and served them atop hashed potatoes. This meal, the heat, and the buzzing of the locusts led every Sunday to each of the participants retiring for a nap—Rose and Michael tumbling into a potato-induced slumber in their sides of the wagon, Mulhetter reclaiming his shady under-wagon berth, and Chin climbing to his usual place on the driving bench. Rose, who generally kept her eye on Chin, noticed he fell to sleep as quickly and soundly on the driving bench of the wagon as she had on her four-poster bed in Brooklyn.

This particular Sunday, though, Chin did not retire to his usual place. Rose was curious to see why, so—rather than nap—she kept her seat on an overturned bucket. Chin walked past her, smiling, to the wagon and opened a door in the wagon undercarriage. He strained a bit at the weight and, with some effort, set a wooden chest on the ground. He brought a key out of his pocket and quickly unhooked a small iron lock. He opened the box, rummaged for a moment, found what he was looking for, closed the lid, relocked the box all in one deft movement. In a few moments he was walking back toward Rose. He pulled up in front of her holding a roll of fabric in his hands and looking at his boots.

"Miss Rose," said Chin in his heavy accent. "I have for you." He held out the parcel of cloth to Rose.

"What is that, Chin?"

"This belong my mother. Now I make to you. Chow-sa."

"Chow-sa?"

"Yes. Lady chow-sa for you, Miss Rose." She took the parcel and unrolled it. It was a pair of drawstring pants, clearly sewn by hand, and made of cotton hand-dyed robin's egg blue.

"Oh...trousers! For me?"

Chin was suddenly overcome by shyness. He looked away. "Yes, for you. They belong my Mother, who dead in China before I come America. This only memory her. Now I make to you."

Rose clutched the trousers to her chest and put out her hand. "How kind of you, Chin." He hesitated a moment, then took her hand awkwardly in his. Their fingers intertwined briefly before he dropped them and glanced under the wagon to assure himself Mulhetter was still asleep. He turned, climbed the wagon, and made it to his perch on the wagon bench. He looked quickly back at Rose, but she was looking at the trousers in her hands.

✦

One evening, five days travel and about 148 miles east of Pittsburgh (near the town of Alexandria where they had put up and made a fire for the night), Michael produced a banjo—with faint white elderflowers painted on the skin—from her travel pack. At first, she picked the strings abstractly as if reminding herself how to play, just jumble of notes. After twenty minutes or so, jumbled notes became snippets of songs. Before long, she was playing and singing "Beautiful Dreamer," along with several other Stephen Foster songs, in French. Her voice, low and lovely, grabbed Rose's attention immediately. Within the half-hour, Mulhetter had joined Rose by the fire and, a few minutes later, finished with his chores, so did Chin—captivated by Michael's surprisingly-delicate playing and singing.

"How do you come to know those songs in French?" Rose asked.

"Actually, my dear...I came to know they could not be sung in French, although I wanted to sing them. So...I translated twenty-five of them myself. I published them in Paris last year as *Partie 1: Oeuvres Complètes de Stephen Foster*. I laugh at the title. *Complete Works!* Now I have an obligation—178 songs still to translate!"

"Oh my Lord, Michael!" Rose banged on the wagon wall. "How do you do such things? You decide on something and you put your whole soul and being into it!"

Michael laughed so hard the muscles in her neck stiffened.

"I am a serious woman, Miss Rose Kleyn! A serious woman!"

Then, six days later, as if to prove she was not, in fact, a serious woman, an incident occurred on the road between Peoria and Nauvoo, Illinois. It had been pouring the wrath of heaven with rain for two days. The mud ran red on the road, no longer silty but slick and slippery. Mulhetter said, "hazardous as the dickens." Everything not under oilcloth was wet to the core. By the afternoon of the first day, everything was so wet and so completely outside the possibility of ever drying again that Rose and Michael passed the time under the soggy, dripping canvas listing words for impossibly wet:

ROSE: The obvious... soaked, soggy, sodden...
MICHAEL: The obscure... muggy, saturated, aqueous...
ROSE: Less obscure... raining! [LAUGHS]
MICHAEL: [LAUGHING] How obvious! Ok...Ok...Descriptive... dank, soused...
ROSE: [LAUGHING] Soused is drunk! In-tox-ee-cated
MICHAEL: [LAUGHING] ...filled with liquid, dearie.
ROSE: No!
MICAEL: I stand by my choice of soused!
ROSE: Then I stand by the descriptive *and* obvious: rainy!
MICHAEL Stormy! drizzling! Certainly...moist! moistened!
ROSE: Moist-lested— that's what we have been...moistlested!
MICHAEL: Clammy!

ROSE: Dewy!
MICHAEL: Soppy, teary...wringing-wet...slippery
MULHETTER [FROM UP FRONT AS HE STEERED]: Slimy!
ROSE: Yes! A voice among the horses says slimy...misty! Soaking!
Sopping!
MICHAEL: Teeming!

They all laughed. The rain was so heavy, Mulhetter's mouth filled with water as he laughed. He gulped the mouthful down and thought...*serious women, ha!*

Two days later and still drenching rain. The way was so muddy, Mulhetter could safely work the team at about quarter-speed. They were supposed to be in Nauvoo already, yet it remained four days away. Four days of tracing country roads through muddy woods and fields made for slow, ponderous going. At about 4 p.m. the sky was dark as a dutch oven, yet the air was warm. Mulhetter, drowsy from the vigilance required to make their way, was just about to hand the reins to Chin when he heard the sound of wet canvas billowing behind him.

He turned in the dim light to catch a glimpse of Michael, entirely naked, untying the last set of ties on the canvas wagon roof and heaving the canvas into a corner of the wagon-bed. A minute or two later, the sound of more unlashed canvas. On his second glance: Rose, also naked, trying to catch her balance in the wagon. She held onto the wagon wall, her breasts swaying as she gripped hard against the wagon-roll and—falling the last few inches—sat down, whooping and laughing. Michael, on her haunches, finished piling the canvas then laid back, face up in the rain. Her hair pooled under her head and neck, her white skin and ruddy cheeks nearly glowed in the half-light.

"Come, Rose, lie down!" called Michael.

Best as Mulhetter could make out, he had two naked women in his wagon, laying in the rain, face up.

From their new point of view lying in the wagon bed they could see the silver-gray drops falling towards them. The muddy reality of the road now tilted away, their whole world became the majestic, agitated sky. Their faces, pelted at first, got used to the unguarded feeling as they surrendered to the rain and its stony smell. They grabbed hands and laughed, feeling part of the storm for a few moments, ceding to it, giving in.

A few moments passed...

...then the sound of their voices:

> *Beautiful dreamer, out on the sea*
> *Mermaids are chanting the wild Lorelei;*
> *Over the streamlet vapors are borne,*
> *Waiting to fade at the bright coming morn.*
> *Beautiful dreamer, beam on my heart,*
> *E'en as the morn on the streamlet and sea;*
> *Then will all clouds of sorrow depart,*
> *Beautiful dreamer, awake unto me!*
> *Beautiful dreamer, awake unto me!*

Serious women... thought Mulhetter. *I'll be damned!*

Then he noticed Chin in the withers balanced on the wagon tongue taking off his shirt, his skin tanned and hairless. A moment later he, too was naked, bounding toward the wagon bed, climbing over and lying on his back in the wagon.

A muffled protest of "Chin!" from Rose. He shimmied himself between them—all smooth tan flesh with a shock of black hair between his legs—and took their hands.

The three—and eventually Mulhetter—peeled with laughter as the rain came down.

✦

Hagpenny Thistlewaite knew he knew the man at the bar, yet in exchange for his life he could not figure from where. He sorted through a mental cache of calling cards:

Shanghai? No.
London? Likely London. Yet no bells ring.
Morocco? Last year? This man is tanned like someone who spent
time in Africa, yet when?
New York? Could he be associated with Barnum? Mennard Cicely!
That's it! No...he heard Cicely now resided in Australia. Shan't be
Cicely. Snowball's chance...
Wait. No. Yes. London. Coming back to me now. Charing Cross.
Cards. Frightfully drunk. What IS his NAME?

At the same time, Kanten Armstrong's eyes fell on Thistlewaite. He knew him immediately.

Hagpenny Thistlewaite! Armstrong thought, *you horse's ass!*

The last time he saw Thistlewaite was London in 1883. The two sat across the table playing French Ruff. Thistlewaite was highly intoxicated and over-leveraged on his bets. Despite the years and miles, Armstrong knew the man as soon as he saw the fastidious way he attended to his cigar. No one but Thistlewaite could be so persnickety about a cigar.

Yet...thought Armstrong...should I ignore him? Pretend I don't see him? Pay no attention so as kindly not to recall the unfortunate circumstances under which I left him in London (newly deprived of his forty-thousand-dollar hippos!)?

The room was suddenly filled with an orbicular roar:

"Hagpennnnnnny Thhhhhhhhhhhhistlewaite is here!"

The pronouncement followed immediately by the arrival of the orbicular man himself at the bar.

"Helloooo! Hail fellow and all!" enounced Thistlewaite, "I bow, sir, to the King of the Clubs Card Room, Cockspur Street, London City, and a superior player of the French Ruff!"

"I was hoping," said Armstrong, "you would not recall."

"I *do* recall, Sir! I shall not say I do not. You won square and I could not pay you. You did me a kindness and took the four most useless creatures on God's green earth off my hands. Kind of you. Quite useless. HA! Hippopotami stink to heaven, do they not?"

Armstrong took a swallow of hot rum from his cup. "When hippopotami are well cared for and carefully fed, they do not, sir. They smell like clean earth when they are well kept. The conditions in which you kept yours were dire, if I venture to say."

"I cared not," sniffed Thistlewaite. "Not a whit. I might say, to pun, not a Ruff! HA! I was sure those animals would become as great an albatross around your neck as they were around mine."

Armstrong laughed, "If an albatross can feed you for four years as you travel the world, then yes, they did!"

"Fed you? You butchered and ate them, then?" laughed Thistlewaite.

"No. I sold them for about $40,000. Enough to feed me lavishly for four years and allow me to tour the world while I ate. So, thank you, sir!"

"Truthfully, I had heard about those deals and I have no hard feelings," said Thistlewaite, leaning against a close-by stool. "Well done, I say! Please, sir, I must inquire your name, for it has slipped my now-aged mind, although your preeminence as a deal maker has not."

"I am Kanten Armstrong."

"Ah, yes! I recall now that I hear it. Armstrong it is!" Thistlewaite extended his open hand and Armstrong ignored it. "Oh dear...I hope there is no grudge kept over our game of French Ruff?"

"None by me...," began Armstrong.

"I am delighted to hear that!"

Armstrong continued: "...notwithstanding that you knowingly bet high that night with no money in your britches, nor that you obtained four hippopotami—amongst the most majestic and seldom-seen of God's creations—and kept them in life-threatening squalor until you pawned them off to me. Nor that you have a reputation for being—by far—the least-scrupulous man in a profession rife with unscrupulous men, so much so that you are both admired and reviled for it. Those notwithstanding, I keep no grudges."

"The least scrupulous man in a profession of unscrupulous men?" asked Thistlewaite. "You count yourself among those unscrupulous men, I assume?"

"If I am honest with myself, then yes. I do."

Thistlewaite paused as, across the room, Amos Daughtry delivered his bottle of whiskey to his empty corner table.

"Why, Armstrong, since we are met so far from Cockspur Street—and so unexpectedly—and you hold me—shall I say, hold us both—in such high esteem...why not join me for a drink? I have a bottle and a table!"

Armstrong's first thought: *Now...what good could come from taking a drink from this buffoon? Free whiskey, I suppose!*

Then, his second thought: *Well...if I could take a drink and turn that into an opportunity to best this antic nitwit, it would be satisfying. Further, if I can best him in his business dealings, it would be superlative!*

Armstrong gathered up his mug of buttered rum and followed Thistlewaite to his table.

At the table, there was a bottle of exceptionally-cheap whiskey (the edge of the bottle poised upon a half-smashed, half-dead cockroach, its feelers still waving) and one glass.

"Thistlewaite needs the barkeep! Keep! Keep! Barrrrrrrrrrrr-keep!" Thistlewaite bellowed in several directions.

Amos looked up from behind the bar yet did not move. Humorlessly, "What is it you want, old man?"

"There is an insect of some exotic Pacific type here that needs your attention and Mr. Armstrong is in need of a clean glass."

"I barely attend to people," Amos monotoned, "I won't attend to an insect. Attend to it yourself. And fuck your Mr. Armstrong—he can use the mug he has already or march his prissy ass to the bar where I'll pay off his trouble with a glass. With luck, it might be a clean one!"

Kanten Armstrong picked up his mug, gulped down his last mouthful of tepid buttered rum, and smashed the copper butt of the mug down on the exposed portion of the cockroach. He then picked up the whiskey bottle and brought down the mug a second time, this time squishing cockroach guts to the bottom of the mug. Then, he walked to the bar and set the mug (and the mangled insect) on it.

"Glass, please."

Amos Daughtry handed him a glass and Armstrong turned to make his way back to his seat.

Once seated, Thistlewaite poured a finger and a half for each of them. He toasted Armstrong by silently raising his glass and winking. Armstrong nodded, and they both took a burning swallow. They sat in silence for a minute or so, each feeling the warmth of bad Scotch spread across their chests like a potent dyspepsia. Then, Armstrong, setting his first trap, asked Thistlewaite:

"What brings you to San Francisco?"

"Sir, I am a procurer of the exotic. This city is the gateway to the exotic, is it not?" answered Thistlewaite. "And what brings you to the Barbary Coast, Mr. Armstrong?"

"I sail for Bangkok in three days' time, doing the same as you. I seek the exotic, the strange, the oddly endowed or situated."

Thistlewaite poured them each a quarter-glass more of whiskey. They drank and then sat in silence for a few minutes. Then, feeling the whiskey loosening his tongue, Thistlewaite added:

"Bangkok. I will eventually alight in Bangkok, myself. Meantime, I have appointments in Hong Kong, Canton, Shanghai, and Singapore."

Armstrong, noting Thistlewaite gradually succumbing to his questions, unwound a second trap:

"I make the same stops. Will you see Master Li in Canton? I hear he has some complicated and difficult escape tricks for sale at the moment."

"Trifles! Trivia! Minutiae!" said Thistlewaite with a drunken and over-delicate wave of his hands. "You waste your time, sir. Patrons today want more. Excitement, imperilment—that is what sells tickets, my friend. Not predicament boxes!"

"Now you are the arbiter of audience taste? I doubt that!" said Armstrong, setting a third trap.

"I beg the opportunity to change your mind, sir. I do have my finger on the very aorta of public taste. I plainly do."

"Again, sir, I doubt that," said Armstrong disdainfully. "I have placed the top acts in circuses worldwide—El Señor Hormiga, Sheena, the Hirsute Maiden, Gagedorn the Mysterious!"

"Gagedorn? Mysterious? I could have found Gagedorn! Anyone could have!" shouted Thistlewaite, stepping into the center of Armstrong's trap.

"Anyone could have, perhaps..."

"Wait...no. I beg your pardon. No!" gulped Thistlewaite.

"...but only I did!" Armstrong sprang the jaws of his trap and saw his quarry gasping for breath.

"I...I...I, Hagpenny Thistlewaite can...nay *will*...out-find, out-procure, out-deal, and out-sell you—you wet-eared moppet!" This was shouted while standing, his fist in the air, spitting. Outraged.

Armstrong sat, requited.

All of the other patrons in the bar stopped and stared.

ARMSTRONG: However would you do that? How would you out-find, out-procure, out-deal, and out-sell *me*? You, who foolishly fed me for four years?

THISTLEWAITE: [STILL HAVING HIS DECLAMATORY MOMENT, LOSING HIS BREATH AS HIS PASSION RISES]: Why, I shall climb the peak of procurement to that vertex we all quest for, sir! I shall climb to the very tip of the mountaintop! I—Hagpenny Ifan Thistlewaite—will become the first—unlike you, Armstrong, and the other procurer bastards like you—I...will become...the very first...to procure...genuine...unassailable...captivating...SIAMESE TWINS!

Got you, you fool! thought Kanten Armstrong. *Now, knowing what you are after, I will beat you again!*

✦

The sun emerged from a silver curtain of clouds, warming the sky to the deepest azure Rose had ever seen.

"Nothing like a midwest sky after it's rained awhile," noted Francis Mulhetter. "Nothing so welcome or so blue."

"Why, as long as I live, Mr. Mulhetter," said Rose with a laugh, "that sky is as pink as it is blue! I see pink if I am a day old!"

The four of them, Mulhetter, Chin, Rose, and Michael, now friends, sat together in the bench seat of the wagon as they crossed from dirt to cobbles to enter the town of Nauvoo. Rivulets of rainwater, remnants of the storm, still ran downhill, snaking their brown, milky way toward the Mississippi. The trees still dripped leftover rain as the wagon made its way to the river, too. There, Mulhetter would trade horses, switch passengers, and take his place in the wagon train for the long trip to San Francisco. Rose and Michael let the sway of the wagon toss them together, forcing welcomed intimacy, since they both knew that they would soon have to say goodbye to each other as their paths divided.

Michael had her thirty-day trip to Salt Lake before her. She originally had planned a few days of transition in orderly, German Nauvoo, but the rain slowed Mulhetter and his horses down so much she would need to depart in the late afternoon tomorrow. Chin would transfer her belongings to her wagon on the Salt Lake train as soon as they set down on the riverbank. Michael would follow Chin on foot after saying her proper goodbyes to Mulhetter and Rose.

They wound their way through a thicket of wagons, tired snuffling horses, families in various stages of pack or unpack, piles of crates, and stands of hogsheads, tierces, and rundlets filled with provisions waiting to be loaded. Women (mostly) standing by their cook-fires with wooden spoons preparing what would be one of their family's last meals made with fresh ingredients before trail cooking took over as a requirement. Men and older boys checked leather bridle straps, buckles, and iron wheel hubs. Families met their neighbors, men sizing each other up for what they might contribute on the way, women silently assessing others to establish who might be reliable, who would come through in a pinch, might know home remedies or be stalwart in the face of death. Children, oblivious to the moment, carried on with their play as if life goes on forever and nothing ever changes—allowing grandparents something trivial to focus on ("be careful or someone will put an eye out!") instead of the impending departure. All of this was overseen on the work side by routine-toughened teamsters, veterans of this twice-yearly leave-taking, who knew from experience that these nonce friendships would last about three and a half months—tested by boredom, bad weather, mountains, illness, even mourning—and dissolve at the other end as people took up new lives.

The general atmosphere of industry in the wagon train encampment quieted the four travelers in Mulhetter's wagon and put them in a mood of anticipation and preparedness. They turned, in this final leg of their final ride, from the end of one trip to the start of the next. Suddenly, Michael grew curious about the Grant family, her wagon-mates for her next leg. Rose began to speculate about Miss Clagsterhorn (her wagon-mate to San Francisco), whom she began to imagine. She saw a tall and gawky woman with hair like a bird's nest atop a long, horsey face. Rose imagined hen-like movements, pecking here and there with her chin. She imagined an unpleasant woman, strict, bossy, irritable, and phlegmy with lacy handkerchiefs tucked in her dress sleeves. She knew beyond doubt that she would not compare in any way with Michael. How could she?

"Well, my dear Rose," Michael said. "We must deal with goodbye."

"I will not say goodbye, Michael, only—as you would say—'au revoir'. I am quite sure we will meet again soon."

"I am afraid not," said Michael.

"Oh! Don't say that!"

"This country is vast and there will be many miles between us with you in Alaska and me in Salt Lake. I wish you the best in Fairbanks—

all the success you can have. Yet I am quite sure you will accomplish all you will accomplish without seeing me again."

"Oh no! I will write you letters with details of Alaska and you will send me replies full of details of your life in Utah with your students. Surely you will take the time..."

"I will certainly. And your life in Fairbanks will soon eclipse our little adventure here. I promise!"

"And I promise it won't!" said Rose. But she could feel the shift already—the new beginning overtaking this ending. Rose could feel San Francisco tugging at the bridle and taking her heart out of saying goodbye. She leaned forward and kissed Michael on the cheek. "Be strong on the way. And get there. And when you're there, make a mark on each child you teach. I will think of you often, along with all you have taught me."

"And I you..." smiled Michael, her hands confidently on her hips, "I wish you all the same!" She reached out her hand. "Mr. Mulhetter, thank you and safe travels."

With that she stepped intrepidly into the lane between wagons. In just a few steps she blended into the busy travel preparations and was gone.

Rose stood for a moment in the ebbing space left by Michael's departure.

Then: *I have reading to do*, she thought, and hoisted herself up on the wagon wheel and into the privacy of the canvas walls.

A long early-summer sunset turned to a warm evening. Mulhetter, expecting Miss Clagsterhorn, had Chin cook for four, although by nine o'clock the camp had settled for the night (save the solitary sound of an occasional banjo or harmonica), and Miss Clagsterhorn did not appear. Chin served a late meal of river catfish on a plank, pattypan squash with young garlic, and four knotty local potatoes, split three ways. Without the arrival of the fourth journeyer, Mulhetter, Chin, and Rose sat around the fire (about eight feet apart), balanced enameled dishes on their knees, and ate tentatively. They thought Miss Clagsterhorn might arrive at any minute, so the conversation stayed brief and tenuous to make room for her arrival. Still, she did not come. Finished, they cleaned up quickly and stowed the dishes ready for tomorrow's breakfast. After, Rose got her book and sat by the fire. Chin turned over a bucket and took a seat. Mulhetter sat on a stool whittling a stick of alder into a pile of shavings. When he finished, around 11 o'clock, he walked the now-quiet lane to the registrar's office to inquire after Miss Clagsterhorn. During dinner, a wire had come to the registrar to say the lady was delayed in Chicago and would not travel after all.

Mulhetter walked back to his wagon. He got paid either way, so he saw the occurrence as an opportunity to save energy. The long, hard trip would be easier and more relaxed with just one passenger— especially with one he knew already.

"That lady...Clagsterhorn...she ain't coming," he told Chin with vague attention, also, to Rose. He paused awkwardly, took off his hat, nodded again to both. "I'll turn in now. Goodnight." He climbed onto his blanket bed under the wagon. He fell quiet, then snored.

Chin sat, shirtless, on his overturned bucket, staring into the fire. Rose had noticed Chin had his own way of relaxing toward sleep. He would sit, absently swat at midges, stare into the fire, and breathe. He did this every night for about fifteen minutes before climbing up to the wagon bench, tipping his hat over his eyes and falling into a sound sleep.

Tonight, he did his usual midge-swatting and fire-staring, but it was broken by long deep stares at Rose as she sat with her book, straining to read in the firelight. She didn't notice at first, yet she eventually felt his stare and looked up. Caught looking, she glanced away as she had been taught to do in Brooklyn when a stranger locked eyes. Yet, this was not Brooklyn, which lay weeks away in her past. And this was no stranger. This was Chin—who cooked with her, taught her to care for horses, laughed with her in the rain. Considering options, she asked herself what Michael would do in a similar situation of being stared at. She decided that Michael, disregarding what women were taught, would stare back.

Rose closed her book, leaned her elbows on her knees and looked fixedly back at Chin. The stares began as just stares, but quickly they became something else. She began to *feel* them. More than looking *at* her, Chin looked *into* her. Past her eyes. Down her throat. These looks, the crackle of the fire, the rush of Chin's breathing, the long days and nights together somehow mathematized, unspoken, into a question...then, an invitation...and, finally, an agreement.

Rose took her book and climbed the wheel to the wagon bed. She lay on her straw mattress and waited to see if Chin would keep his end of the bargain...waited...to hear Chin's boot sole fall on the wheel-spoke. She knew eventually he would come into the wagon and he did. Brown boots, dusty from driving...jeans dirty on the knees with catfish entrails...brown leather belt dull with sweat...the sixteen-year-old was small enough to stand upright, close to her in the wagon. He took off his hat and dropped it beside him. He unselfconsciously stripped off his boots and trousers while Rose watched.

"Come. Join me...," said Rose eager for a new beginning.

Chin dropped to his knees next to her. She took him into her arms, feeling his heartbeat in his hairless chest as he lay against her. They held each other just long enough for him to get hard. Rose wanted it to last, to smell him near her, to kiss him. There was none of that. Two or three sixteen-year-old's thrusts and it was over.

A whiff of catfish and he was dressed and gone.

Rose felt full...and empty.

And somehow she knew she would conceive.

✦

The ache in her breasts was the first sign. Second, she found herself hoping the weather would stay warm; she could not imagine linen against her nipples. The third sign was that she could no longer stand the smell of Chin's food or cooking fire, when, for most of the trip, she had relished it. Each time she returned her plate (almost as full as when he handed it to her) Chin reacted as if her very existence offended him—he looked down, or away, or over her shoulder.

Rose had to admit she longed for some reaction from him and was grateful, even for this one. Since they had made—well not made love, but...did what they did—she had hoped for some continuing... something. Chin, however, acted as if he deposited some of himself into every woman he drove to the West. Perhaps he did? Yet she still hoped he would acknowledge the incident. Or her standing in front of him. Or anything. Now that Rose had a suspicion that she was expecting, a new layer was added to her hope: she hoped Chin would notice her again. Yet she now also hoped he wouldn't notice (or sense) she was pregnant.

Thinking beyond Chin toward the future, which was easy in her cooler moments, she was sure she would be safely on her way to Fairbanks by the time anyone would see that she was with child. She would easily make it to San Francisco before any outward signs. She could hide modest weight gain, headaches, morning sickness. And she did. What she didn't anticipate was the blood. At first just spots. Then, one morning about five weeks after Chin, clotted blood stained her coverlet.

She addressed the wagon train medical man, Dr. Greene:

ROSE: ...and the bleeding has come daily. And what I would say is that there is quite a good deal.

DOCTOR GREENE: That is not unusual in itself for pregnancy.

ROSE: [SIGHING] I am relieved to hear so. So I needn't worry?

DOCTOR GREENE: There is always room for worry. With child on a wagon train is not a preferred state. Still, if you are careful, move your mattress to the center of the wagon to cut down the sway, rest as you can and get fresh air—walk a few miles a week—your worry ought to be less.

ROSE: So worry is still warranted?

DOCTOR GREENE: Have you met Marjorie Armstrong in Wagon nine? What wagon are you?

ROSE: Number twenty-two.

DOCTOR GREENE: Miss Armstrong is a midwife. She might be helpful to you. Make acquaintance with her. Tonight when we camp, take the walk to Wagon nine and say hello. Both the walk and the acquaintance will be salutary for you, I think.

That evening (after eating the lone potato picked out from the ample dinner Chin cooked for her and Mulhetter in his dutch oven) Rose walked the train camp to Wagon nine. Like hers, it was a farm wagon converted for the trip. Unlike hers, Wagon nine was filled with household goods. Chairs of several sorts were wired to each other, then wired to a felt-topped card table, itself sitting wired atop an oak hope chest, this whole was then wired to some provisioning barrels. A similar sort of wired tower existed in each corner of the wagon, filling it three-quarters of the way (and to a height of ten feet!) and leaving a small living area for a passenger. Any space open in these piles was stuffed with books, framed art, table linens, cook pots, or leather travel bags, themselves filled (best Rose could make out) with miscellany of every kind. From a wagon's length away, it looked as if a bric-a-brac store picked itself up, made the perfunctory effort to organize itself into stacks, and lit out on wheels. This lavish assembly was presided over by a no-nonsense woman in denim, a fringed deerskin shirt, and a pair of men's Beckman boots. When Rose approached, this woman was sitting on a barrel looking into a stereopticon viewer.

ROSE: Evening, Miss.
THE WOMAN: [CONTINUING TO LOOK THROUGH THE STEREOPTICON] Good evening to yourself...Miss.
ROSE: I'm Rose Kleyn from Brooklyn. No...Wagon twenty-two. I'm from Wagon twenty-two.
THE WOMAN: [STILL LOOKING AT HER SLIDE] I've been to Brooklyn. I've crossed the magnificent bridge into New York.
ROSE: [NOW AWKWARDLY VYES FOR A LOOK FROM THE WOMAN OR INTO THE STEREOPTICON] The bridge is a prodigious work, is it not?

THE WOMAN: I could say it looks like one from where I saw it. [POINTS TO THE DEVICE] I saw it here. One of the slides in "The Complete Stereopticon Baedeker of New York." At this moment I am looking at our final destiny, San Francisco. Oh! The hills! Would you like to see?

ROSE: [TAKING A TENTATIVE STEP FORWARD] Very much. I would. [BEING HANDED THE VIEWER] What do I do?

THE WOMAN: Hold the handle steady and look through here and you will see. Slide it this way or that to sharpen the view.

ROSE: Oh! My goodness! That is where we shall end our trip? The hills! I see what you say!

THE WOMAN: Here, give it back a moment and I will show you more. [LOADING A NEW SLIDE]

ROSE: [LOOKING AGAIN] Goodness, how elegant! A town square!

THE WOMAN: Union Square, also in San Francisco, where Thomas Starr King held his rallies to support the Union during the war. Quite near to the Tang People Town where the Orientals live. That's near to where my brother lives, too. I am moving my home to be nearby his. That's why I am making this trip with all of my duds. I will be keeping his house while he travels. Oh! I nearly forgot the formalities...I am Marjorie. Marjorie Armstrong.

ROSE: Just so. I am Rose Kleyn. Formerly of Brooklyn, latterly of Wagon twenty-two. Nice to meet you. Do you travel alone?

MARJORIE: I do. With all my earthly goods piled on, I have only room for a tiny mattress in my wagon. I do the driving.

ROSE: My goodness! You do? On the first leg of my journey which, as I said, was from Brooklyn...I travelled with a woman, Michael, who was also a fine horse woman. I never met so many women doing men's work.

MARJORIE: I do what I must. I was raised on a ranch—the ninth of twelve children—in the Montana Territory. Horses come natural to me as people. It could be I enjoy horses more! [BOTH LAUGHING]

ROSE: I have been so impressed by Michael, now you. But... perhaps I stopped at the wrong wagon. I heard there was a midwife in Wagon nine.

MARJORIE: And you heard right. I have birthed many a foal, but many more babies. You hardly look in need of a midwife.

ROSE: Then I deceive. I am sure I am carrying a child...

Marjorie got Rose through her daily bleeding with a mixture of common sense advice and natural curiosity. She asked so many questions about Rose, her changing body and her thoughts, ideas and fears. Using what she learned, Marjorie became a fountain of advice about surviving pregnancy on the plains.

"So many women hear things that are simply wrong," she told Rose. "I want you to tell me everything you think is right so we can sort the truth."

Through this sharing, along with many meals partaken (while helpfully avoiding Chin's indifference), Marjorie and Rose became friends. One Sunday, a little more than eight weeks after they met, the wagon train was at rest. Rose was finishing lunch when Marjorie suddenly produced a stethoscope.

ROSE: What is that?

MARJORIE: This tool will allow us to hear your child's heartbeat!

ROSE: How is that possible?

MARJORIE: The baby should have a heartbeat by now, I am quite sure. Let's listen!

[POSITIONING THE SCOPE AND LISTENING PAST THE SOUND OF CICADAS] It is quite strong *here* [HOLDING THE BELL JUST SO WHILE PASSING THE SCOPE FROM HER EARS TO ROSE'S]. Can you hear it?

ROSE: Oh yes! I can!

Rose listened intently to the baby until she knew she had listened long enough to remember the sound.

MARJORIE: Don't be a hog! Let me hear!

ROSE: I am sad to let you and leave him—I am sure it is a boy!

MARJORIE: Not so fast, chickadee. No way to know.

ROSE: I know my own body and baby. It's a boy. And shhhhhh! If I can't listen at least you should. [MARJORIE LISTENS]

MARJORIE: Oh, you know your body, do you?

ROSE: I do, Miss Armstrong, I do!

MARJORIE: [LISTENS AGAIN, THIS TIME MOVING THE SCOPE] I don't think so—. [MOVES THE SCOPE TO A FEW PLACES, LISTENING.]

ROSE: Don't be a boor!

MARJORIE: —because if you did...you would know you are...not with child...but with...children. You are carrying twins!

ROSE: WHAT?

MARJORIE: I just heard it. A second heart beating...[MOVING THE SCOPE, LISTENS AGAIN AND THEN HANDING THE EARPIECES TO ROSE.] ...here.

Silence while Rose listened. In the silence, Marjorie was suddenly met with an uncomfortable feeling of envy. She had examined many new mothers, yet this time she unexpectedly found herself wishing that she was the one who was expecting twins.

ROSE: Two! [LISTENS AGAIN, MORE INTENTLY] Oh my Lord!

As evening fell, Rose walked, alone, back to Wagon twenty-two.

✦

One night at nearly midnight, when the train camp was encircled and sleeping in Nevada, four days from trip's end, Rose and Marjorie sat, up late, talking about their hopes for San Francisco:

ROSE: You know...my destination has never truly been San Francisco.

MARJORIE: Oh?

ROSE: No. It is merely a stop for me. My dream is to go on to Fairbanks. To own a store in Fairbanks.

MARJORIE: Fairbanks? In Alaska?

ROSE: Yes. Such a place is Fairbanks!

MARJORIE: You have been there?

ROSE: Of course I haven't! Not even by looking at photographs. Yet I've seen the advertisements in the Brooklyn papers. They want people, Marge. People are moving to Fairbanks in throngs. And those people need goods. People need dry goods. My hope—dare I say my dream?—is to open a store. It's what I did in Brooklyn...sold dry goods. I will open a dry goods store on a good street in Fairbanks and be a store owner!

MARJORIE: Oh dear...I don't know how things would be in Brooklyn, but in the places I know—Montana and Iowa leastwise—a woman with two children and no husband will be roundly looked down upon... seen as either a camp follower or a shamed woman... but not a store owner.

ROSE: It would be the self-same in Brooklyn. I'd be a "fallen woman." But truth be told, Marge, if we were to set aside this particular situation and I am still no...let me say...paragon of incorruptibility. Yet, from everything I have read in the papers, I can start over in Fairbanks. That is what I hope for.

MARJORIE: For a single woman I think a new start in Fairbanks would be possible. Or should I say...not *im*possible. Alaska is a harsh place—a hard, harsh place. Yet I think a girl of your temper and steel could do it. If you had a stake of money to start you—,

ROSE: —You think I can do it?

MARJORIE: As a single woman, yes.

ROSE: I do, too!

MARJORIE: Yet with children and no man, you're choosing a river that is mighty swift. And deep to ford.

ROSE: Too deep? Too swift?

MARJORIE: Perhaps not. Perhaps I can see a way—.

ROSE: A way? No, Marge...you're not saying—.

MARJORIE: Heavens NO! Not that. I am suggesting you stay in San Francisco and have these babies—.

ROSE: Oh...thank God you suggest that Marge...I could never do... the other—.

MARJORIE: —then find a good home for the babies in San Francisco and leave them there— .

ROSE: Leave them?

MARJORIE: —in a good home.

ROSE: Good home?

MARJORIE: And...that will allow you make your way to Fairbanks unattached...with a brighter prospect.

ROSE: A good home?

MARJORIE: San Francisco is a booming town. It ought not to be difficult to find a good home for your children. Perhaps a family that cannot conceive? That will allow you make your way to Fairbanks unattached. Affording you a much brighter prospect. I wish it weren't so, yet you know how the world is, Rose. I wish it weren't so...but... it is.

That night Rose climbed into the wagon with the words, "good home" thrumming in her head.

This progression of thoughts assembled itself:

...a good home. Leave them. In a good home. I left a good home in Brooklyn for Fairbanks. I left it expressly to settle in Fairbanks. I risked my job, my reputation, even my freedom, if I had been caught. To settle in Fairbanks. I did not plan to have children. Children were never my plan... Leave them. In a good home...there are stories I could tell. I could say I am a widow. Or my husband is in Europe. Or working on the railroad. Stories could make my life bearable. Bearable. Is that what I want? A bearable life? Never. I want a full life, to thrive, not bear or survive... Leave them. In a good home. I left Brooklyn for Fairbanks to thrive. In Fairbanks. I risked my job, my reputation, my freedom had I been caught. I did not plan to have children. No. Children were never my plan...

And, so, repeated over and over, all night. From this repeated chain of thoughts emerged a strategy, which she set in motion the night before they arrived in San Francisco. That night, she quietly asked Chin to come inside the wagon. Before he could climb in, she climbed halfway down onto the wheel blocking his way. She held up her hand in a stop motion and said: "Chin, I have something to say. I have discovered and known now for many weeks now that I am carrying your child. Children. Two, it is suspected. Twins."

Chin looked away and stepped off the wheel.

Rose continued, "If you intend to go, let me say before you do that I mean to find a home for the twins in San Francisco unless you wish to take them yourself."

Chin, no longer looking to leave, took off his hat.

"If your aim is to take your children, I will expect your answer by morning." She wiped her eye. " It is not easy for me, this."

Chin looked at the dirt around his feet.

"I wish it weren't so," continued Rose, "but it is."

Nearly a full minute passed in silence with Chin looking down and Rose looking at him. Then, without looking up, Chin began to walk away.

"You take them," he said over his shoulder. "Do how you want."

Rose climbed down from the wagon and, at first following Chin as he walked away, swiftly turned to make her way in the moonless dark to Wagon nine. Once there, she knocked on the tailgate:

ROSE: [In a whisper] Marge? PSST...Marge? I wish I didn't have to wake you.
MARJORIE: Rose? Is everything alright—are you alright?
ROSE: I am.
MARJORIE: Why wake me if everything is alright?
ROSE: I have thought of what you said. What to do. I thought about it over and over—not stopping—over and over without end. I have agonized over it and litigated it in my mind. MARJORIE: Yes?
ROSE: I will do as you say.
MARJORIE: Yes?

ROSE: I will.

MARJORIE: And I will help. When we arrive in San Francisco tomorrow, I will introduce you to my brother, Kanten. He is meeting me. He is resourceful and well-connected. He will know how to find your babies a home.

ROSE: I will do as you say.

MARJORIE: You will stay with us.

ROSE: I wouldn't impose?

MARJORIE: It is no imposition. You will stay with us until the children can be housed and you leave for Alaska.

The next morning in the crowded arrival yard, Rose wished Frances Mulhetter a safe trip back east. Chin made himself busy with the leathers. Their eyes met briefly, although neither had a word for the other. Once the porter's cart was loaded, Rose and the porter made their way to Wagon nine. There, amidst the bustle of unloading Marjorie Armstrong's wagon on to no fewer than fifteen carts, Rose met Marjorie's brother Kanten with a polite handshake.

"Rose will be staying with us," was all Marjorie needed to say and Kanten immediately turned from formal to friendly.

"And you are welcome!" he said as he turned to a pile of Marjorie's belongings that needed sorting.

From that moment Rose was like family. She stayed a total of eleven months, until the twin (boys) were six months old. Living with Marge and Kanten was an amiable and a functional arrangement. Marge was, after all, Rose's only friend. And, by staying with the Armstrongs, Rose need not struggle to find lodging or, indeed, explain her situation. What is more, in staying with Marge, she gained a sound birth plus a close-by and ready source of advice for a new mother.

Kanten took to Rose kindly as if she were another of Marjorie's many sisters. He seemed especially pleased when the babies came and particularly delighted, for some reason, that they were half-Chinese—thrilled with their single eyelids.

It seemed to Rose weeks after she gave birth that surprisingly little was undertaken in pursuit of a home for her still unnamed children. Yet each time she asked, Marjorie replied, "we will find a home."

A few weeks before she planned to depart for Alaska she inquired seriously again:

ROSE: I must inquire again—what of your efforts to find a home?
MARJORIE: We have been contacted by a couple from the town of Jenner who will take your boys and, with that, make a gift to you of five thousand dollars!
ROSE: Tell me of them?
MARJORIE: Simple to tell. A newly married couple—married a year. He is a pastor and she a pastor's wife.
ROSE: Well...I shall need to know more. In order to decide.
MARJORIE: That's not possible, Rose. Because of his position in the town they ask for discretion in the matter. He is a pastor. They are recently married. Unable to conceive. This is all I can say—.
ROSE: But—.
MARJORIE: We are lucky to have found them at all. And for them to pay you five thousand dollars! I would take that if I were you.

Rose did, thinking she desperately wanted to be free again—to have her agency back, as she had only a year ago, in Brooklyn.

✦

The very same day as Marjorie told Rose about the Jenner couple, Kanten Armstrong walked into Pelican Alley. Pelican Alley wound its way off of Grant Street meandering eastward to the Bay. On its way it tumbled from respectable homes (nearest Grant Street) to acceptable ones (on Jackson Square) and finally, just a block or two from the Embarcadero seawall, into slums. Pelican Alley was infested by pelicans and covered by their offal. It was not unlikely at all for a pedestrian here to be pelted by a broken clam or oyster shell, or to be roped around their nose or mouth with the half-eaten and regurgitated flesh of former inhabitant of a shell, dropped by a careless pelican. Pelican Alley was named for its chief avian inhabitant. If it were to be known, instead, by the chief occupation of its human inhabitants, it would be known as Undertaker's Alley, or Mortician's Way, or Gravediggers Crescent, for Pelican Alley was predominantly populated by those who traded in the storage of the dead, conductors of inhumation, and sellers of funereal accouterments.

Three blocks from the water, though, Pelican Alley housed a standout among the funereal: Anders Schuylkill's "MedMart of Appliances, Mechanisms, Appurtenances, and Apparati." The first floor of Schuylkill's store was devoted to mechanical substitutes for faulty body parts and samples of body parts in various states of disease and deformation: a gangrened liver, a hydrocephalic baby, examples of several types of deformation of the foot (cavus foot, tarsal coalition, club foot), hand (polydactyly, flexion deformity), and skull (craniosynostosis, plagiocephaly), among hundreds of similar samples lined up in jars, filtering the limited and hazy sunlight.

Kanten Armstrong tried the door, found it open, and walked into a forest of jars and components.

"Ahoy, my good fellow!" called Anders Schuylkill from a tiny oasis in the jars where he occupied a desk piled high with dusty glass eyes, rubber fingers, and noses. "What bring's y'my way?"

"I am looking for Mr. Schuylkill, whose name is on this building," said Armstrong, straining on his toes to see where the voice came from.

"I am here!"

"Where?"

"Here." Armstrong looked around to no avail. "Here, sir! In the northwest corner!"

Armstrong adjusted his direction accordingly and found a path through the jars past two jars (half his height) with severed elephantiasic human legs floating in them.

"And so you are!" Kanten said coming to rest in front of a birdlike man in gold spectacles with a tuft of yellow hair not, Kanten thought, unlike the tassel feathers on a Crested Kinglet. "You are Schuylkill?"

"I am. Anders Schuylkill." He reached out his hand, gnarled and calloused like a craftsman's hands would be. Armstrong ignored it. "I haven't seen a man in here in six weeks. Nor a woman. No one comes to see Anders Schuylkill. Not one dime has crossed my desk in months. And you? Curiosity? Is that what brings you in?"

"Curiosity of a sort, yes. And your reputation for fine work."

Schuylkill gestured toward the jars. "I have things here most have never seen. Likely most won't see in life. Likely some wish they never saw. If you came to look, have your see. Nothing in jars is for sale. Of course, the appurtenances *are* for sale. And I make 'em custom. But you ain't in need of them, unless you need something I can't see? A peg for between your legs, perhaps? Ha!"

"I am in search of an appurtenance. That is what brings me in. Yet, it is not anything you have in your stock. I am looking to have a custom appliance built."

With a bird-like flutter of his elbows, Schuylkill stood. "Custom? Quite so, Sir. I build to match the owner. I am a specialist in that. It is for someone you know, then, this custom device? To mediate a club foot perhaps? Or equalize a distended arm? Tell me what you are looking for...."

"In fact, Schuylkill, what I seek is both custom designed and secretive. Here are the terms: if you agree to make it, I will buy it from you at a pre-agreed price twice per year for twenty years, for it will need size adjustments. From that time on, I will buy one once per year in perpetuity. No one can ever know you manufactured it for me. Or that you know me, nor the intended use of the device you build."

"Sir, you must know that I will not pursue any felonious or unlawful activity that would besmirch the name of my business," said Schuylkill. "If that would be so, sir, so I must decline your custom early in this discussion."

Armstrong replied, "What I ask is neither unlawful nor felonious. Only secretive. For reasons I will fully explain, should you be willing to undertake my charge, you must keep my secret. The device and its secret will harm no one. It will merely be worn by my twin sons."

Schuylkill thought for a moment. Then:

"You have chosen well. No one does better work than Schuylkill's. And this is a good place for a secret, sir, since no one comes by more than once in a Sailor's Moon. Still...why so hush-hush?"

"I shall explain...." Kanten Armstrong told the story of his career in side-show procurement and the race to display Siamese twins. He explained his need for a device that would unite two healthy, independent boys in such way as they would appear to be conjoined bodily through the rib cage. "It should be built in such a way so as to look completely real and utterly plausible," said Armstrong. "Will you do it?"

"I will, sir. I will make the jig and keep your secret."

✦

With Rose's departure only a day away, there was no sign that the twins would be leaving. Rose pulled Marjorie aside during dinner-making in the late afternoon:

ROSE: And what has become of the Jenner couple?
MARJORIE: Why? Do you worry?
ROSE: Frankly yes, I worry about burdening you any longer than I must.
MARJORIE: You're no burden, never have been.
ROSE: That's kind. [PAUSE] And the Jenner couple?
MARJORIE: I told you they desire to be discreet. They wish not to know you, nor for you to know them. So...they have agreed to come

to get your boys the day after tomorrow. That way, they won't stand a chance of meeting you here, which they would prefer not to do. You'll be safely on your train for the north—all the way to Seattle, I estimate—when they pick up the boys.

ROSE: I see. [PAUSE] I suppose I might want the same arrangement if I were them. I understand.

Marjorie stayed with the twins, and Kanten sat in a hired carriage waiting to take Rose to the train. Rose avoided a goodbye to the twins, swiftly stepping past their cradles to enter the parlor where Marjorie stood in a grey skirt and a starched white blouse.

"You look as if domestic life suits you," said Rose as she entered the room.

"And so it does," replied Marjorie.

"How odd that is," asked Rose. "You, the horsewoman, now keeping house in bustling San Francisco."

"Like always, I do what I need to do," said Marjorie. "I came to run Kanten's household while he spends a year in the far east and that is what I shall do."

"Yes," said Rose, "and I wish you both the best outcome. I cannot thank you in any way adequately. You gave me my life back, Marge. I do not have words to thank you."

"You, Rose," said Marjorie, "eased my travel here and helped me settle. I am—"

At this point Kanten burst in with his knife-like elbows sticking out as if he were a rooster about to crow. "Come! Enough blubbering you two. Or she will miss her train!"

Marjorie kissed Rose just below her ear. Rose turned and walked through the house's engraved-glass double doors and down the stairs to the curb. Kanten leaned out of the carriage door, took Rose's hand, and helped her into the carriage. As Rose turned to sit, Kanten closed the carriage door. The horses started with a loud jangle of leather and chains as the carriage pulled away.

Marjorie whispered to the empty room:

"Don't worry, Rose. Kanten and I will provide a good life for your boys!"

CODA

The Barker

Brendan Hardy

NOW

I think it was Murray the Clown, the bastard, who brought in the virus, along with the balloons. Maybe in the balloons. "You seniors love balloons!" he said. Balloons of death. I call it a virus but I am not sure what it was. All I know is it went through this place like a meat slicer. A hot knife through motherfucking butter. Eleven days and you're left with me. The star of the show. Your one and only.

Me. The Broadway Baby.

I did what I could once the thing hit. Watered plants, administered pills. Sopped up vomit and wiped up snot. Rubber gloves and a surgical mask. And like a veritable man of steel—tall buildings and bullet trains—here I stand. Not stand. Lie. Assisted living. No assistance here, though. If I need toilet paper, I have to get up (it helps to lean the walker against the empty lunch cart) and go to the "Room 563-Supplies" supply closet and get it for myself. This self-service situation (not appreciated at all, by the way) comes since Beanie—last Negro standing—wait, is Negro okay? Socially acceptable, I mean. What do the kids say now? Politically acceptable? Socially correct. Ehhh...who the fuck *knows? Anyway, Beanie the Negro doesn't call, doesn't stop by in person. Nothing. Just disappeared. Like every god-dammed resident. Assisted living. Ha! If you call being taken out in a body bag disappearing. I mean, I didn't get to say good-bye to them. Not one. If you don't count what I said to them after I piled them up and before I walked away, numb and panting.*

Twenty-two of us here. The Home. Retired. Circus. Was it a circus? Hell-fucking-yes it was! A lion-tamer lived in Suite 335! He lived with me in my retirement, dammit. Stories from the Big Top. Until what?

And an elephant tamer. She was...let me look at my notes...she went last Tuesday. Tuesday a week ago. Number nineteen. Fine at 10:40 in the morning watching Let's Make a Deal and chuckling. Two hours later a fever and spitting up blood. An hour after that— butter treated to the hot knife. Gone by the time Beanie brought me my egg salad club. That left me ("good times and bum times, I've seen them all and my dear...") and the twins. They went day before yesterday. Not true! Wait! Two days before yesterday. That's Monday.

Leaving me, the barker for Hell's Carnival.

Your host for a little race in Pamplona.

Who knew? Ten of us remained. My daughter, Sylvia, and Ralph, her stupid husband with braces on his teeth at fifty-two. What is with the vanity so much? Anyway, Ralph says to me a year, eighteen, twenty months ago, "Dad," he says, "you got the gift of gab; why don't you...maybe you interview your friends?" Only he says "fellow residents." But they weren't fellow residents. They were friends, even before I sat down with each of them. "Your story," says I. Tell your story. So I can tell about The Home. Story of The Home. The Jersey Home.

Where is that fucking Negro—can I call him that?—when I need a Kleenex? So much goddam snot. Like a faucet. Yet they go, one by one, except the twins who go together. Beanie and I (okay, mostly Beanie) toss them in body bags and out to a pile next to the Ambulance Entrance in the back.

The result of assisted living? Assisted dying.

Aw hell. Dr. Pantages (just like the theaters!) stopped coming to work on Monday, too. But me— Man of Steel—I still water the plants in the office. Check the mail.

Air conditioner. I think maybe that's what carried the virus. The A/C like a Nile of germs. The fucking A/C.

The elephant lady—now there was an independent woman, Iris. So engaged in life. Closest I ever came to love. Wednesday a week ago Dr. Pantages trying hard I am sure...hard as he could to stem the flow of the Nile—spores? Germs? A/C? Who knows? Just that it spared no one. One by one (except five on Wednesday). The doctor like a sideshow tap dancer trying to save...but no nurses. Took three days for those motherfuckers to stop showing up. Sick? Dead? Cowards?

No nurses. Just the doctor, and Beanie. And me. Your reporter.

Everyone got sick but me. Why spare me? The Barker. Born on the stage. Of the Belasco. The Last Man Standing—Man of—why me? So I sat with them, each and all, and had them tell their story and—hardly embellishing—wrote them down. Well, maybe a bit here and there.

For your delectation!

"In short, there's simply not a more congenial spot for happy-ever-aftering than here in Camelot."

Then Beanie bit it. Or gave up? Compassion burn-out? I read about that in the Philly Enquirer. Compassion fucking Burnout. Must have been what got Pantages. Beanie. Leaving me here to slap together my own turkey club and down to one last bag of Lay's.

But you know, Beanie, I like my sandwich with two bags of chips.

Watch my weight? Eventually it will get down to zero. Everything gets down to zero. Maybe I will zip up my own body bag and toss myself out.

But before that...living like one of those survivors with a safe room on TV.

Sylvia, why do you call the day before you visit? Just to be, you say, sure I still want you to come by. How about now. Where are you? Why no call?

I can't get an outside line from my room so I can't call her. Do I know how to use the telephone system? Never occurred to me I'd be assisting my last fucking self and survival would come down to how to dial an outside line.

Supposed to know? Supposed to be able to fix it? Nope.

Never.

There was always someone here for that.

A NOTE FROM THE AUTHOR

I hope you enjoyed Circus Home!
   If you liked this novel, you can help get it into the hands of more readers by writing a review on the Amazon website. Leaving a review is quick and easy, yet it has a powerful impact on how visible this book is to other readers. You can also help by posting about your experience with Circus Home on social media. Tag Circus Home and recommend it to your friends and family.

Visit jokstoryteller.com for more information about my writing, where you can meet me and hear me read a portion of the book and get important information about my next novel, which will be out in 2025.

ABOUT THE AUTHOR

J ason Ollander-Krane grew up in a theatrical home. His father conducted the pit orchestra for musicals and his mother was a theatrical costume designer. He was starstruck at the age of five when his parents took him backstage to meet John Raitt after a performance of Carousel. By age eight he was lip-syncing The Music Man in his grandparents' living room. At the age of ten he got his first professional theater job building sets at the Tenthouse Theater in Highland Park, Illinois. He studied English Literature at Rutgers College and worked as an actor in New York City. After college, Jason became an HR executive in Silicon Valley. He worked as an executive at Polycom, Informatica Corporation and Sony Playstation. He retired as Vice President of Organization Effectiveness and began to write fiction full time. Jason enjoys travel and avidly attends theater, cabaret and music performances all over the world.

Made in the USA
Middletown, DE
26 September 2023

38984713R00191